Bloodline

Series:
Louisiana Secrets Book One

Patti Corbello Archer

Copyright

Bloodline   Romantic Suspense   Series: Louisiana Secrets: Book 1

This book is a work of fiction that includes a real historical French pirate and privateer, Jean Lafitte (1780-1823), that frequented Lake Charles and other coastal areas in the Gulf of Mexico. For purposes of my book, he became a make-believe ancestor driving the story line for the main character. All other characters and the story itself are fictitious. Any similarity to real persons (other than Jean Lafitte) living or dead, is coincidental and not intended by the author.

--Cover design created by the author through Canva.com.
--Swamp photograph on the cover: Permission for publication and reproduction was received from photographer Gary Meyers, 209 Arnould Blvd, Lafayette, LA 70506 http://www.flickr.com/photos/imagehunter1
--Published through Kindle Direct Publishing with Amazon.

This is for you, Zeb.
The greatest son ever.

Introduction

Bloodline – Book One in my Louisiana Secrets series, embraces an intriguing storyline about dangerous secrets deep in Southwest Louisiana on the Calcasieu River. You will find extraordinary characters and incredible relationships. You will find attraction. Passion. Mystery and suspense. Great interaction. Actions and thrills. But most importantly, you will enjoy a wild love that changes everything – one steamy moment at a time.

As for me, Louisiana is also my home. I was raised here. A place full of legends, tales, and stories. "What if" stories. Like this one. So now, sit back. Relax. And follow me down the river…

Patti Corbello Archer

Louisiana Pronunciations:

Calcasieu	(Kal-Kuh-Shoo)
Atchafalaya	(Uh-Cha-Fuh-Lai-Uh)
Pirogue	(Pe-Rogue)

Bloodline

Chapter 1
Lake Charles, Louisiana

It was dark as the river lapped against its banks in the humid, pre-dawn air of southwest Louisiana. Mysterious to all. Dangerous to many. Life-giving to others. The long winding Calcasieu River knew everything about the beautiful land it traveled through. The secrets especially. And there were many. Buried and alive.

Hiding secrets was easy. Much of the land along the river was uninhabitable by humans. Marsh. Swamp. Canals. Bayous. Bays. Tiny cuts trailing through the Cajun jungle. And even islands in the river. All of which were unnavigable terrain that traveled far inland filled with reptiles, mammals, birds, and insects. Everything was controlled by the ebb and flow of the tide. A special haven for predators of all kinds.

The habitable land along the river was coveted, priceless, and gorgeous. Some became river neighborhoods. Some were private homes far from everyone on purpose. Like this area of the river…

A sudden screech and flutter of wings disturbed the stillness as a hawk swooped low and snatched a small rabbit off a sandbar. With breakfast in its powerful claws, the hawk flew up the hill toward an Acadian home on piers and settled in a nearby tree to feast.

***

Deep in the woods, a woman hung from a tree. Terrified. Hair chopped to her scalp. Hot. It was blistering hot by the fire, but she was too afraid to sweat. The man. She watched him. His eyes were demon-red above the branding iron he carried. Closer. No. No. Fear surged through her. Smothering her. Out of her mind with panic, she yanked against the ropes that held her, slinging tears as she struggled.

He grabbed her shorts, and leaned close, memorizing the terror in her beautiful young face. His foul soul inhaled her fear for a few delicious moments, then inch, by inch, he turned her around. Anticipation built for him. Terror for her. He licked his bottom lip, and in one savage yank, he ripped her shirt - leaving her bare back completely exposed. She arched away from the red-hot metal and her scream echoed through the dark.

***

In reflex, Gabrielle rolled and hit the floor on all fours, ready to run - but lights blinded her. Covering her eyes, she blinked, and recognized her bedroom just as her one hundred twenty-pound, German shepherd reached her.

With a deep breath she wrapped her arms around his neck, and whispered, "It was just the nightmare. Thank you, God. It was just the nightmare."

For a few seconds, she knelt there as her pulse calmed. Then a loud screech from outside interrupted the quiet. She called, "I'm coming!" And in a few moments, she entered the security code and walked outside on the second-floor deck.

In the peeking dawn, Gabrielle watched the large, red-tailed hawk she had raised from a fledgling, circle above, obviously upset by her scream. She pulled on the falconer's glove and held out her arm. He glided down to land perfectly on her forearm.

Noticing a bit of blood on him, she figured her scream had interrupted his meal. Soothing him, she said, "Hey, Hunter. I'm ok, big guy." And she gave him a quick chest rub and off he flew.

Her shepherd nudged her, and with a brisk neck and chest rub she assured him that he was still her favorite. Then wiping his appreciative lick off her check, she turned and smiled at the landscape around her.

It was beautiful as the morning sun began to filter through the trees. She loved her home on the Calcasieu River, north of Lake Charles. It was far enough away from the commotion of city living, that her quiet peacefulness was rarely interrupted. And quiet peacefulness meant everything to her.

She leaned her elbows on the deck rail and allowed herself a few controlled minutes of reflection. It had taken her four years to physically, mentally, and emotionally, get to the point she was at today. The kidnapping had permanently changed her life – and her. But now she was well trained in survival, self-defense, and lived alone with her dog and hawk.

And she was good with that. She still didn't trust or let strangers into her life easily - much less let them into her personal space. The people closest to her understood and loved her just the way she was. But as for a date, forget that. She hadn't dated since the kidnapping. Maybe one day. But in all honesty, she couldn't fathom it.

Her alarm went off, and glad to quit thinking about men, she headed back inside.

Her days always began early. She put a quick braid in her long dark hair, then limbered up with a yoga routine.

Afterwards, she opened the vintage leather trunk at the foot of her bed. Her weapons were organized inside. Her favorites were the throwing knives, drug dart gun, and pistol. They stayed in her weapon's belt so that she was always prepared. Her formal fencing uniform was stacked to one side in the trunk and the razor-sharp swords were strapped to the underside of the lid. Two more pistols lay loose, loaded, and ready.

Gabrielle grabbed her weapon's belt and shut the trunk. Dressing quickly in camo leggings, a tank top, and tall moccasin boots, she buckled the belt around her hips. Reaching under her pillow, she grabbed her ten-inch hunting knife. She strapped on the ankle sheath and inserted the knife.

As she headed down from her loft, her dog danced around the kitchen ready for their daily run. She laughed and glanced at the clock – time was good.

She figured her workout would take about an hour and a half and that would work. She just needed to stay on schedule. Today was going to be a busy day.

Once they reached the yard, the hawk screeched and flew above them like an arial bodyguard. Her shepherd, Zeus, matched her stride as she jogged down the hill behind her house toward the river sandbar. Her workout always began at the trail on the left side of the sandbar, then looped back around her five-acre property, to end on the other side of the sandbar.

Before entering the woods, she looked around. It was quiet. No voices. No people. And in a flash, she darted into the woods without a sound. She ran amongst the trees, crossed gullies, and zipped through ravines near the river. Small hills rose and fell along the way. Her goal on this run were the fifteen live oaks spaced throughout her land. They were not just the arms of the forest; they were the safe places she had made for herself.

As she neared the first oak, she slowed, then leapt. She climbed up a series of nooks in the trunk of the tree, then grabbed a nearly invisible rope and pulled herself up. She hid amongst the tree canopy as she walked across a large branch, then stepped into a bungee cord loop, and lowered herself to the ground. And off she went again.

Over an hour later, she rounded the last bend in the trail before reaching the river and stopped. Alligators sunned close to the riverbank. Baby ones rode on their momma's back to snap their needle teeth at dragonflies flying way too close. A fish leapt out of the water nearby and landed with a splash, and one of the momma alligators darted to make it a quick meal.

Making a few mental notes for a drawing idea, Gabrielle wiped sweat off her face. She glanced toward the end of the trail where her dog waded out from the sandbar to drink. As she joined him, she glanced back at her house to make sure no one was around. Her dog growled.

She spun to see what alarmed him. Across the river, a tall man with long dark hair leaned against a tree and watched them. Smiling, he gave a salute wave. She gave a small wave in return, then looked at the black pickup with a horse trailer parked in his driveway. The shepherd neared her, hackles up.

Then the man's phone rang – echoing across the water. He answered and spoke as he headed back to the truck. Wondering who he was, Gabrielle headed uphill.

She climbed the long flight of steps leading to the main floor of her two-story, double-decked Acadian house. White with unpainted cedar storm shutters, it sat atop massive wooden piers for protection against flood waters or unwelcome visitors. This was her safe house.

She pulled an ice-cold Coke from the refrigerator and stood on the first-floor deck overlooking her yard, and the river. She loved the light green cypress trees, with all the rooted knees along the bank. Random sandbars. Branches of all sorts reached over the bank providing shade, great fishing spots, and perfect areas for snakes and alligators to fade into the background.

She rubbed the cold can on her forehead. She was not a fan of the heat. But raised in southwestern Louisiana, everyone knew the Gulf of Mexico was the boss. Only thirty miles away, it blew heat and humidity across the land. She knew southerners had to be addicted to air conditioners, fans, porches, and ice. She sure was.

Across the river, activity caught her attention as more vehicles pulled up. Curious, but concerned, she watched. She had lived in her house two years, and surprisingly, the log cabin hadn't been occupied in all that time. It was beautiful with gentle hills. Pastureland. Forests. Bluffs. Perhaps the man had bought it. Maybe he had a family.

But she didn't want neighbors – even on the other side of the river. She liked being the only one on this lone stretch. Not because she was reclusive by nature – but because of fear. She needed to control her environment and people were not controllable.

She had been alone for a while now. Only memories of family remained. She thought back to her parents and her childhood. Her parents had been wonderful. She had been three years old when they had adopted her. Kind and loving, they raised her with God-focus and a mix of Cajun and Texan cultures.

After graduating from Sam Houston High School, she had moved to Baton Rouge to attend Louisiana State University (LSU). It had been a great life. Terrific roommates had turned into forever friends and her future as an artist had filled her dreams. At age twenty-three she had graduated with a degree in art and a minor in history. She would have labeled her life as perfect at that time. Until the kidnapping.

But how could she have known?

It wasn't long after college graduation that her roommates moved off to begin their new lives. In a shockingly short time, life outside of school became lonely. Empty. So, to fill that void, she carefully researched, then joined an online Christian coffee shop. That's when the bottom fell out of her world. Painfully.

Once she had been released from the hospital, she had been invited to enroll at a relatively secret academy in northern Louisiana. It was specifically for victims that were able to learn survival skills and self-defense. They trained her in knives. Guns. Physical endurance. And they taught her how to live again – even helped her train her PTSD guard dog. When she left there, she was ready to step into her life as who she was now. As an artist. And a warrior.

Then on her twenty-fifth birthday, her parents gave her this house just before they left for vacation. But they never returned. They were killed in a freak boating accident. Now she was alone.

***

Startled by her phone, she saw who it was, and answered, "Hey girls!"

Her college friends, screamed, "Happy Birthday, Gabrielle!" as she laughed.

Jade said, "You're not old by-the-way."

Gabrielle said, "Yeah, right."

Zoe said, "Twenty-seven is the prime - ripe - luscious age for the love of your life."

Samantha said, "That's what I say!"

Gabrielle said, "Are men all you think of?"

Jade said, "What a silly question. Of course, it is!"

***

Gabrielle laughed as they hung up. They were coming to celebrate her birthday today, Friday, May 20 – all weekend. Tonight, they would dine in Lake Charles at Loggerhead's on the river. It was a local bar and grill with amazing food and scenery. They would arrive around four o'clock this afternoon, so she needed to hurry and get her work done before they arrived.

After a shower, she pulled on a sundress and headed to her art studio, which was a corner nook of windows on the main floor. Sun poured in. She knelt to check her recent paintings to see if they were dry. Almost. Most of her work was wrapped up and set aside for an art show one day. She picked up one of her newest paintings and smiled. The girls would love it.

Once she was settled, she glanced to see where her dog was. Sound asleep on the rug. Her hunting knife was on the kitchen table. The door was locked. Everything appeared peaceful and safe. She began to sketch the alligators and dragonflies she had seen this morning.

***

Several hours later, Gabrielle was startled when her alarm went off. She stretched her lean five-foot-eight frame, stiff from leaning over as she sketched. The shepherd stirred too and yawned. She went to the kitchen and opened the refrigerator for iced tea, and he joined her. She laughed as he snatched a raw steak off his personal dish, then let him outside to enjoy it.

It was time to prepare for her guests. She turned on her Cajun chandelier – a cedar pirogue (Cajun canoe) covered in fairy lights mounted on the ceiling. The lighting softened the room beautifully. Her boho styled kitchen included a terrific snack bar, a large gas grill stove with an oven, and a great red refrigerator. Open shelves filled with mismatched vintage bowls, plates, and glasses. Fabulous old teacups hung from the bottom of one of the shelves.

The table and stools were carved out of local cypress and positioned directly under the chandelier. A red floral pillowed sofa and a couple of easy chairs were arranged near the television - that she never turned on. The rest of the room was art studio with a bunkroom and bathroom in the back.

She lived simply and loved it. In a nutshell, she was a Christian, believed in self-defense, loved her friends, and wanted to help others overcome trauma. Her dog and hawk were her angels on earth. And her art…well, it constantly reminded her that there really was beauty in the world – beyond her experiences.

But she used to have other dreams too. Love. Passion. Children. But her reality now didn't allow for that. She was too afraid to let a man get close enough. While it was true that forgiveness set her free, trust had to be earned. That meant physical and emotional intimacy and she couldn't imagine how that would ever happen.

Shaking off those thoughts, she headed up to her loft to get ready for the girls. She pulled out frayed jeans, flip flops, and a peasant top. She dressed and looked in the mirror. She looked like a 70's hippy chick and laughed. She turned on *Michael Buble'* and sat at the dressing table. She gave her amber eyes an upper coat of green shadow, black liner, and mascara. She sprayed perfume and added big loop earrings. She left her hair braided.

***

Zeus barked before Gabrielle heard the car fly up the driveway. She ran downstairs and met them as the red SUV stopped. She laughed as all three climbed out singing *Happy Birthday* to her. They met for one big group-hug, then individual hugs, as they inspected each other's clothes, accessories, and makeup.

Samantha said, "You look beautiful, birthday girl!"
Gabrielle said, "You do too! Your long blonde hair is killer."
Samantha was an assistant prosecutor at the Baton Rouge District Attorney's Office. She was a gorgeous, type A personality. Bold and assertive, she liked being in charge. She looked casual this afternoon with her blonde hair in a ponytail, jeans, and a pink poet shirt. She was petite but easily became larger than life. Her blue eyes didn't miss a thing.

Jade said, "I love your shirt. You look like a hot hippy."
Gabrielle said, "You get a reward for that!"
Jade was an independent investigative reporter in New Orleans. She was always a seeker for the truth. She was curvy with black braids and dark almond-shaped eyes. Her sincerity drew people to her in many ways and she never met a stranger. Dressed today in blue jean shorts and a floral boho top, her playful personality was revealed.

Zoe said, "Move – it's my turn to hug the birthday girl – and you're always beautiful!"
Gabrielle gave a model pose, and said, "Who me?" as they laughed.
Zoe was a veterinarian from Lafayette. She was the tallest and quietest. But her auburn hair and green eyes revealed that feisty could arise at any time. Never one to encourage a conflict, she was still able to meet any threat head on. And no one hugged like she did.

In a short time, the women were relaxed on the deck of the main floor. Catch-up time was always the best.

After the flurry of conversation slowed to a steady stream, Gabrielle said, "Okay girls, we need to set up our next armor teaching. I know we usually only schedule one exhibit every three months or so because of our work schedules, but I just received a request. It's in two weeks - can you manage that?"

They checked calendars and agreed.

She said, "Great! I'll let them know. And… I still have something new to tell you."

Samantha drawled, "You met a man."

"No," Gabrielle said, rolling her eyes, then said, "Oh wait! I did actually. A tall, dark, and handsome guy waved at me from across the river today." She glanced at the log cabin, and exclaimed, "Look! There he is," and she pointed.

A man, shirtless, with long dark hair, raced a black horse across the pasture. It was striking and sexy. They turned and looked at her - shocked.

Jade said, "You're kidding, right? That man is your new neighbor?"

Gabrielle said, "I guess. Isn't that horse gorgeous?"

Zoe burst out laughing, then said, "Yeah, it's all about the horse," and they laughed till they cried.

Trying to stop laughing, Gabrielle said, "Stop! Please. My sides hurt. I really do have other news."

They settled back down, interested, and she said, "I thought my adoptive parents bought me this house when they gave it to me a couple of years ago. But while going through some of their old paperwork recently, I found out a woman named Serena – no last name - gave it to them after they adopted me. I also found a small key with the document and a note. I think maybe the key is for a safety deposit box."

She paused, then said, "So…after that, I decided to run my DNA to see if I could locate any relatives. And I still can't figure out why my parents didn't tell me about Serena."

Seeing their silent shock, she shrugged and continued, "Which…yes, I know is my first attempt to expose myself online again since the kidnapping, but I didn't see any harm in looking for distant relatives."

Jade said, "Well…what did you find out?"

"Several weeks ago, I received my results. My DNA shows that I am mostly French, Spanish, and Irish. How is that for a combination? But what surprised me is the large list of distant relatives. Lots of them have connected by email and are working on their family trees. But what blew my mind were the email stories that indicated my most famous ancestor is presumed to be the pirate, Jean Lafitte!"

Samantha sat up, astounded, and said, "You're kidding!"

Gabrielle said, "Right! And it appears that people are still looking for his hidden treasures. Can you believe that? I just assumed buried treasure was ancient history."

Chapter 2

On the east coast, a very powerful man sat at his desk contemplating a problem many states away. It had gotten complicated. And although his line of work was always complicated, this scenario was…different.

He walked to the window, not really noticing the lake, or tourists. His mind still sifted through all the details. He was used to tough decisions. Painful decisions. Decisions that no one else wanted to make. Especially bloody ones. But he had learned a long time ago to do what had to be done.

And…his decision had been made weeks ago. The ball started rolling today. Which meant, it wouldn't be long before the bodies began to fall.

Chapter 3

FBI Special Agent Dakota Nash gazed out the window of his log cabin toward Gabrielle's house. He liked her place. It had decks around the first floor and around the loft floor. His research indicated she had great security too. And he loved her yard and beautiful sandbar.

And researching her wasn't uncommon because he knew her. Had known she was here. Though he doubted she would remember him with all the trauma that night. It still twisted his gut to remember. His rage. Her pain. Her clutching him. Her weeping amber eyes even as he laid her on the stretcher. But the EMTs had quickly taken over, and in a moment, she had been gone with sirens screaming. Four years ago. He had never forgotten her.

His thoughts were interrupted by a loud engine, and he glanced back. The moving van had arrived. Getting busy, he directed as they unloaded his furniture. Upstairs, his brother helped as a security team installed all the technical equipment that would be needed. And his youngest brother was in the barn with the horses.

***

A few hours later, Dakota received a call from his boss.

"Nash, give me an update."

"Sir, we are in place. I made casual contact with Gabrielle across the river this morning. I plan to make face-to-face contact at some point today. Her college friends arrived. So, I may get a chance to do it socially if they go out to celebrate her birthday."

"Just protect her. I chose you and Sean personally. She's the perfect survivor as far as I'm concerned. I don't want her to have a setback with what's coming her way."

"We'll protect her. Keep us updated and we'll alter the plan as needed. Nothing will get by us to get to her. I stake my life on it."

***

Ending the call, Dakota walked into the equipment room upstairs to talk to his brother, FBI Special Agent, Sean Nash.

Bent over hooking up wires, Sean said, "Hey Dakota, we'll have surveillance set up after dark. If anyone comes on her property, or ours, we will know."

"Perfect. Can we track intruders?"

"Yes. But there is one other thing we need."

"What's that?"

Sean picked up a box and said, "We need to get these GPS trackers on her and her vehicle in case she is taken."

"I'll do it tonight." Dakota said. "I plan to run into her later and it should be easy enough to tag her car and purse. But based on current intel, we have a few weeks before we see any immediate danger to her. At least I hope so."

***

Once the movers left, he headed outside to give his stallion a run after being couped up in a horse trailer for hours. Midnight saw him coming and pranced back and forth along the fence line, ready to run.

Before long they moved as one racing across the fields. It was at times like this Dakota thought of his Sioux ancestors. He figured they had felt the same way – a natural affinity for nature and horses. And although he hadn't been raised in a Sioux household, he was taught the story, the truth, of that part of him.

His great grandmother, Lillie, had traveled to Minnesota to visit a horse ranch with her family when she was a teenager. She had fallen in love with the man who trained the horses. He had been educated, and of Sioux descent. After a couple of months, the family noticed the relationship and ripped them apart. She was taken back to Virginia – unaware she was pregnant.

But Lillie bore the shame and gave birth to a baby girl with black hair and blue eyes - Jasmine – who was raised on the east coast. When she came of age, she was told the story of her lineage and swore that all her firstborn descendants would be named in honor of her birth father's Sioux ancestors.

He was her firstborn grandson and knew that he would follow the same tradition with his firstborn.

***

After the ride, Dakota showered, and while dressing, watched the women across the river on the deck. He figured they would head into Lake Charles soon for dinner and it was already six p.m. He slipped on jeans, boots, and a black fitted shirt. He was clean shaven and smelling good. He chuckled. That's what his dad always said.

He grabbed his keys and went to get the trackers from Sean, then headed to his truck. Undercover. Which was necessary for most agents at some point in their career. His experience had found him active in many roles through the years, until he had settled with a team that specialized in tracking serial killers. Where he connected with Gabrielle.

After her kidnapping case, he transferred to the FBI training academy. With his profile skills, experience, and black belt in Karate, he had been able to provide powerful insight, as well as battle techniques for up-and-coming agents.

And with a new mission in mind for his life, a year ago, he semi-retired to write FBI thrillers. He loved the strategy and thrill of the books, but the royalties went straight to help victims and survivors. He didn't need the money. His part-time FBI income, and family inheritance, would provide for any need he would ever have. He stayed semi-active with the FBI in the event his skills were needed on a case. This case for Gabrielle was one of them.

He glanced at the time again and looked across the river. Gabrielle and her friends headed downstairs to the cars. He started his truck.

Chapter 4

Gabrielle loved to drive through the curvy woodsy roads sprinkled with late evening sunlight as they left the river and headed toward Lake Charles. Louisiana was home for all of them and they thought nothing of crossing a large swamp and big bridge to go out for dinner.

Before long, she turned down Old Town Road in between the English Bayou and the Calcasieu River – right outside of the Lake Charles city limits. Just before the second big curve, they pulled into the long driveway to where Loggerheads Bar & Grill bordered the river with live music, waterfront cabins to rent, event centers, and a few pet alligators the guests fed.

The parking lot was full. Friday night was already hopping. The scenery and local cuisine were great. Guests even came by boats and Jet Skis to join the fun since many people lived along the river.

The girls headed to small tables overlooking the water to get away from the large, loud parties. Once they were seated, they ordered Cokes and appetizers of crawfish pies and duck tenders.

After finishing a tender, Samantha glanced at Gabrielle, and said, "How do you feel about being in the bloodline of Jean Lafitte?"

With a tiny shrug, Gabrielle said, "Well, I was excited to get my DNA results of course. Being adopted leaves you with a hole in your life – a question mark. But I have to say, I didn't expect what I found." She frowned slightly. "I know he's been romanticized through the years, but history shares a truth that was not always pretty. It is even kind of scary being connected to someone so notorious."

Zoe said, "I didn't realize people still searched for his treasure."

Gabrielle said, "Yeah, crazy huh. It makes me wonder what that bank key is all about. I didn't say anything about my history to anyone online. Social web was a nightmare for me with Liam and the kidnapping. You never know who or what is lurking on the web."

Jade said, "Why don't you let me do some research and check into the key. I won't say anything. Just keep your knowledge private and we will try to find some answers. Just promise that I get the story if you find a bunch of treasure," and they all laughed.

***

Dakota pulled into Loggerheads parking lot as Gabrielle and her friends exited the Jeep and walked into the restaurant. He waited awhile to give them time to get settled inside and order. He walked by her Jeep. As he reached the rear wheel well, he dropped his keys on the ground. A casual glance showed no one around and he leaned down to pick them up – and stuck a tiny tracking device where it couldn't be seen above her tire.

He headed inside. He would just kick back and keep an eye on them until he could find a way to put the other tracking device on her. He sat at the end of the bar, so he was closest to the ladies' restroom. She would pass this way at some point.

At his angle he could see their table outside. He ordered a tea and fried crawfish and enjoyed the food as he watched her. Gabrielle was gorgeous. He looked forward to a personal connection more than his boss knew. He had long been ready for this meeting. But not for this reason.

Thank God, anything to do with Jean Lafitte or his treasure was red flagged on the DNA website she had used. Otherwise, he might not have known she was in danger until too late. Her connection on the site had caused a flurry of activity on the dark web and the FBI received notification. Because of his previous connection to her, he was personally assigned to head her case. So, here he sat, watching her, and waiting.

***

On the deck outside, Samantha said, "Back to the fine man on the horse across the river – you know he might be looking for a wife, Gabrielle."

"Who said I was in a hurry to marry?"

Jade said, "Well, we aren't getting any younger and how many available men are in your circle these days?"

Samantha said, "I hear that. What do y'all think about long engagements at our age?"

Zoe said, "Really Samantha? We're only in our twenties."

After a sip of her drink, Gabrielle said, "You know, a pastor told me one time that after high school or college, Christian couples that save themselves for marriage, rarely have long engagements."

Samantha said, "Well that is no surprise. Living on your own as an adult is different. You would have to be careful not to cross the line into the NO ZONE without parental supervision," and they howled in laughter.

Jade responded, "So, who defines long engagement?"

Samantha said, "Forget long engagements, I want to know who defines the NO ZONE," and they laughed again.

Gabrielle said, "I would think the couples define long engagement on how long they are willing to wait."

Zoe asked, "What's the shortest engagement you've heard of?"

Samantha said, "I had an aunt that married after four days of meeting the guy."

Gabrielle said, "No way! I can't imagine that. Now, hold the NO ZONE conversation till I return," and she left them laughing as she headed to the bathroom.

Dakota saw Gabrielle coming. Wow. She was something else. But without looking at anyone in the bar, she walked right past him. He waited for her to come back out.

Then there she was. He fumbled his drink and jumped up to avoid getting wet, running right into her. She was about to lose her balance when he caught her around the waist. She gasped, grabbing his arm, and raised surprised amber eyes to his.

For a shocked second, Gabrielle looked at the gorgeous man holding her against him. Dark eyes. Golden skin. Long black hair. Then balanced again, she hurriedly stepped back, disbelieving she had experienced an intimate moment like that with a perfect stranger. Even one that looked like him.

Using her distraction, Dakota dropped the tracker in her purse, and said, "Forgive me! I'm not usually clumsy with my drink. Did I hurt you?"

Deciding to laugh off the sudden encounter, she said, "No, I'm fine. At least we didn't get drenched in your drink."

He smiled, flirting now, and said, "Ah, but the night is young," and she laughed.

How long had it been since she had done this? Then something about him seemed familiar and she cocked her head, looking thoughtfully at him.

She said, "This isn't a pickup line – but, somehow, you seem familiar to me."

"A beautiful woman like you would never need a pickup line. But yes, I'm pretty sure you are the woman I saw across the river today with a very formidable German shepherd."

Surprised, she said, "That was you?"

"Guilty," he said with a grin. "I bought the log cabin. It's amazing. And so is your place." He held out his hand, and said, "I'm Dakota. Seems like we're neighbors."

Amazed to realize who he was, she shook his hand, and said, "I'm Gabrielle. My German shepherd is Zeus. Welcome to the river." Then deciding to be cautious, she cut the conversation short, and said, "But I do need to run, I have guests in from out of town. I'm sure we'll run into each other again. Have fun tonight," and with a smile, she walked away.

Her heart still fluttered as she returned to the girls.

They took one look at her flushed cheeks, and Samantha said, "What happened?"

"What do you mean?"

Zoe said, "Come on – give it. All of it."

Gabrielle leaned forward for privacy. They leaned forward too, ready for the news, the secret, or whatever had put that look on her face. She said, "He's here."

Dumbfounded, they looked at each other, and Samantha said, "He who?"

"The guy riding the horse at the cabin."

All their heads swiveled toward the door she had come out of…and stared.

Dakota smiled as he strolled leisurely their way. He reached them and leaned against the deck rail, closest to Gabrielle.

He said, "I thought I wouldn't be much of a gentleman if I headed home without meeting your friends." And with a sexy grin, he said, "Ladies, I'm Dakota. It's a pleasure to meet you."

Gabrielle's friends were thrilled at this turn of events. They introduced themselves – and the embarrassing questions began. Gabrielle wanted to melt away. She knew what was coming.

Zoe said, "That was one fine stallion you rode today. And I must say, both of you are fit. Do you work out a lot?"

He grinned, and said, "That's Midnight. Yeah, he's a beauty. And yes, you could say I work out a bit."

Samantha jumped in for her turn at him, and drawled, "Tell us something unique about you – that will surprise us."

"That's easy. I have a gorgeous Bengal cat named King. He looks like a tiger leopard mix with green eyes. He stole my heart because," and he glanced at Gabrielle and winked, "it seems I have a thing for beautiful eyes."

Cheeks pink now, Gabrielle wanted to kill her friends.

Ignoring Gabrielle's embarrassment, Jade said, "How about the big question. Are you married?"

Gabrielle interrupted, "Stop it. Now. All of you." Exasperated, she looked at Dakota, and said, "Please disregard this ridiculous interrogation. They do know better."

Reaching out, he gently touched her cheek, and said, "I'm single, Beautiful. But that answer is just for you."

Then saying goodnight, he smiled and headed out.

Once Gabrielle caught her breath, she glared at them and said, "There are no words for your behavior," and they laughed uncontrollably.

***

Driving back to the log cabin, Dakota called his boss, and said, "I made contact with Gabrielle."

Abruptly, he asked, "Did you place the trackers on her and her car?"

"Yes. But unless we get an escalation in intel, I will let her get comfortable with me before dumping the danger on her."

"I get your point, Nash. But she's in your hands. You need to find out what she knows – that's why she's in danger. Let her know we have her back. We don't want any repeats of the Treasure Posse's previous kills. You know they don't mess around."

***

After the call, Dakota thought about the connection with Gabrielle tonight – holding her against him. Touching her. Looking into her eyes. Feeling the sizzle. He always figured their attraction…the impact…would kick off a blazing fire. This case would entangle personal and professional no doubt, but he was ready for it. For four years he had thought about her. Checked on her. Prayed for her. She hadn't been a stranger to him for a long, long, time.

As a profiler, he knew her. He read her confidence, intelligence, strength, and wit, but he was aware of the hidden side of her. Her craving for safety – and knew that her fear would play a big part in all of this. He had to get her ready for what was coming. He had to keep her alive. And they would be thrown into an intimate relationship to do it.

***

The girls were still laughing as they drove up to the house. Motion lights popped on. In seconds they headed upstairs as Zeus barked for them to hurry. They went in and loved on him – all aware that Gabrielle depended on him. It would have been impossible for her to be alone on the river without his protection. Or anywhere for that matter.

Gabrielle said, "Hey, do y'all want to play a game?"

Samantha groaned, and said, "I play games all week in court, let's talk about your hot neighbor again," and they laughed.

Zoe walked out of the bedroom carrying a gift, and said, "Put men on time out. Come see, Gabrielle."

They smiled and gathered around, as Zoe handed her the beautifully wrapped box.

Gabrielle said, "I didn't need a gift! All of you being here with me this weekend is a huge gift."

Zoe said, "Just open it."

She untied the bow, then opened the paper. Inside was a tiny black box. Smiling at them she lifted the lid and a sparkling silver bracelet lay on a bed of black velvet. Hanging from the chain were four miniature diamond swords. She gasped and picked it up.

Zoe took it and clasped it around her wrist. She said, "One sword for each of us."

After the tears, they celebrated with red velvet cake balls and lots of laughter.

***

It was late when Gabrielle climbed the stairs to her loft. Lights across the river caught her attention through the window. She looked at the log cabin, now occupied, and thought of meeting Dakota tonight.

She had let him hold her against him. Gazed into his eyes. Looked at his lips. Flirted for heaven's sake. And were men supposed to be that beautiful? Why hadn't she been afraid of him? And where had that burning in her belly came from?

Then the questions faded away and she smiled. How unexpected. How intriguing.

She whispered, "Happy birthday to me."

Chapter 5

Dakota pulled on jeans the next morning and walked to the window. He could make out Gabrielle on her top deck with what was probably a cup of coffee. No lights were on downstairs at her house so her friends must still be asleep.

Then the aroma of fresh brewed coffee caught his attention. Aunt Jaz was up. Grateful, he headed for the kitchen.

Aunt Jaz smiled and popped a pan of biscuits in the oven, then pointed to the coffee pot.

He gave her a quick hug and said, "You know that I am happy to see you in this kitchen."

She smiled and said, "My pleasure, Dakota. I love it when I get to feed my handsome nephews. You're the first one up. Sean and Adam will be smelling coffee any minute."

A few minutes later, he walked on the back porch with a steaming cup of coffee. His stallion whinnied at him, dancing in the dirt. Chuckling, he walked over and gave all three horses some love. Then he glanced back across the river and met gazes with Gabrielle. He smiled and raised his cup in a good morning gesture. She smiled and raised her cup in response.

***

Gabrielle's heart raced. He was bare-chested with long dark hair hanging past his shoulders. Handsome. Sexy. Mercy, she thought, and shook her head, shocked at herself. What was wrong with her? Then hearing voices downstairs, she walked back inside. It sounded like they were all up. They hollered for her, and she grinned. It was so good to have them here.

A few seconds later, she stepped off the stairs and laughed. Zoe was bent over in the refrigerator, shuffling food containers. She popped up with a look of adoration on her face and said, "You got us Cinnabon rolls, Gabrielle. You always remember!"

Jade said, "I want one! My hips are calling it."

Samantha grinned and said, "We better eat good with all the workouts she will throw at us today. Sweat till you drop is her motto. Only she never drops. Just us."

Gabrielle laughed and said, "I don't know what you're talking about."

In a minute, they sat around the table with coffee, phones, and cinnamon rolls.

Jade said, "Do we have time to run your trail today? I am up for a sultry, humid, nature sweat."

They all laughed, and Gabrielle said, "Sure! I hoped we would. And don't forget we need to do a fencing workout. And as you can see in the refrigerator, we have plenty of food, so you won't starve with all the exercise. Salad and sandwiches for lunch. Lots of fruit and drinks to cool us off. And how do BBQ steaks and veggie kebabs sound for dinner?"

Samantha said, "Delicious. The day sounds fabulous. In between sweat and screaming muscles, we can hang out with music, sarcasm, tales of men, and calories galore. My kind of day!"

Everyone laughed, and Gabrielle said, "What do y'all want to do first?"

By nine a.m. they walked downhill toward the sandbar, dressed for a workout.

Across the river, the women saw Dakota with two other guys unloading Jet Skis and a skiff. They were cutting up and having a good time.

Dakota, Sean, and Adam waved, and the girls waved back.

Dakota called out, "Hey there! Where are you headed?"

Gabrielle called, "My obstacle course – it's a trail workout!"

Dakota said, "I'm impressed!"

***

The guys watched the women run into the woods.

Sean said, "Gabrielle has gorgeous friends I see."

Dakota chuckled, and said, "Yes, she does. You interested? The blonde is your type."

"What type is that?"

"A blonde firecracker."

Sean said, "She's feisty?"

"Oh yeah. And she has your name written all over her."

Adam said, "Do any of them have my name on them?"

Sean said, "I doubt it. You need a melt-in-your-mouth superhero."

After they quit laughing, Dakota said, "Sean, I've decided to tell Gabrielle about the case today. First, because she's relaxed with her friends here – and they will leave tomorrow. She will appreciate their support. And second, I think having more time to prepare her for what's ahead - is better than protecting her from the fear of knowing."

Sean said, "I'm glad you said that. The nape of my neck is jittery, and I don't like it. Something's making me edgy."

Dakota said. "Let's invite them for dinner tonight. Then I'll tell her who I am."

"What about your personal—"

"Stop. Not up for discussion."

***

The women attempted to keep up with Gabrielle on the trail. They did pretty good along the river, then after that, Gabrielle had to slow down for them to even see her. They watched her work her routine with the climbing and targets until they reached the last big oak – their favorite. It looked like the grandfather of all the live oaks. Then they took turns climbing and shooting the dart gun.

Afterwards, Jade said, "Alright Gabrielle, throw your knives! We have waited long enough."

Gabrielle grinned as she removed four throwing knives from her pouch. She said, "Pick your target."

Each one picked a different target, and Gabrielle let the knives fly. She pierced each target dead center, and they shook their heads in amazement. She grinned and blew the tip of each knife like it was a smoking pistol.

Samantha said, "Who can do that but you? That's crazy good."

After they returned and cleaned up from their run, they went downstairs under the house to the patio. Gabrielle pressed a button and four super long rope-swings lowered straight down from the floor above. Each grabbed a swing and chilled.

A couple of minutes later, Samantha said, "We never finished our talk about the NO ZONE last night."

Zoe said, "Well, what's your definition of it since you keep bringing it up?"

Samantha lifted three fingers and said, "No sex. No nudity. No touching what you can't uncover. Because, if you keep it covered, don't touch it, you can't do it. Confirming, if you touch it, you will uncover it, and do it."

They couldn't help it. They laughed.

Jade giggled, and said, "Sounds like you have all the bases covered, counselor. I agree with that definition of the NO ZONE."

Zoe said, "What about kissing, caressing, and passion? Gabrielle, what do you think?"

Gabrielle said, "I think those are the GRAY ZONE," and everyone laughed.

Samantha said, "I'm stealing that definition. That is great! I may use it in court."

Gabrielle said, "I hope no one is recording this."

Samantha said, "So, is anyone currently dealing with the GRAY ZONE? I admit, I play with heavy kissing – but keep it hot and fast."

Gabrielle said, "Of course you do. Men pant after you. But personally, I am not in any zone at the moment."

Samantha said, "Just wait. Dakota may be setting up a zone for you."

At a quiet spot in the conversation, Zoe said softly, "I met a guy." They gasped.

She continued, "I think he's the one."

"And you are just now telling us?" Samantha said.

Zoe smiled without saying anything else.

Jade, ever the coaxer said, "Come on Zoe, tell us about him. For you to say that to us, the guy must be something super special."

Zoe said, "He is. He is handsome, a big guy, an outdoorsman, a Christian of course, and has a farm north of Alexandria. He has a degree in forestry and is responsible for monitoring state parks and federal forest ranges.

"He brought a wounded bobcat to the clinic. She got caught in a trap. I kept her at my clinic for a while and we would visit when he would check on her. He asked me to go with him when he let her loose a couple of weeks ago. We have been talking since then. Now he wants to show me his ranch and I'm going. And his kisses are better than my dreams."

All eyes were on her. No swings moved. Then Zoe grinned and they all spoke at once. They couldn't wait to meet him.

Later, Samantha asked to see Gabrielle's recent paintings, so they went back upstairs. Gabrielle showed them a few canvases still drying. And the sketch that she was working on with the alligator babies and dragonflies.

Now it was time for the surprise - and she hung a canvas on the wall. She stepped back as they looked at it. It was a painting of the four of them in fencing gear – kneeling in a line – with their sword blade against their foreheads. Powerful. Beautiful. Striking. They group-hugged without a dry eye.

Then a commotion drew them to the riverside windows. Dakota and the two other men were racing Jet Skis. Dakota waved and shouted, "Gabrielle! Y'all come down!" and they ran downstairs laughing.

Once on the sandbar, they kicked off their shoes and dangled their feet in the water *trying* not to stare at the three gorgeous men acting crazy on the skis.

Jade whistled and said, "Now that's what I call an amazing view."

Zoe laughed and said, "Gabrielle, take your pick! Take them all!"

Gabrielle said, "Stop it. I'm not shopping for a man."

Samantha said, "It doesn't matter. Dakota's shopping. For you I think."

Eventually Dakota and the other men took a break and headed toward the women. He slid his Jet Ski up on the sandbar and the other two guys followed.

Gabrielle grinned and said, "Obviously, you are related."

Dakota grinned and said, "Yes, brothers. I'm the boss."

The one with wavy black hair and dreamy eyes, smiled and said, "He's just the oldest. I'm Sean - middle brother. And you are amazingly beautiful women."

The youngest, with dark hair longer than Dakota's - and sex appeal galore, smiled and said, "Forget them, I'm Adam – the charmer."
The women laughed – but glanced at each other. These men. Wow.

Ignoring her friends, Gabrielle said, "Is anyone else allowed to ride the Jet Skis?"
Dakota said, "You mean you trust us to drive you after our exhibition?"
"Unless you want to hand us the keys."
"We would love to be your chauffeurs, come on – choose a driver!"
Zoe said, "I bow out. Go ahead. I'll just watch the fun."
Dakota said, "Gabrielle, come on, ride with me." She climbed on.
He said, "Hold my waist," and she wrapped her arms around him.
Pure lean, hard muscle under her palms. She couldn't believe she had touched him twice in only two days. What was happening to her world?

He revved the engine and glanced at the others. Samantha and Sean laughed because she tried to make him let her drive. Jade and Adam played around and revved the engine - ready to go.
The skis made a deep roar as the guys hit the throttle and the ladies hung on. It was exhilarating. Gabrielle loved the wind, water, and freedom. They wove around a few curves in the river and then headed back. They noticed a few alligators, but they just napped and paid no attention to the Jet Skis.
Dakota glanced back at Gabrielle to check on her, and she yelled, "I love it!" and he grinned.

They made it back to her house and pulled up on the sandbar. Dakota said, "Do you ladies want to take a turn and drive? We can ride behind you."
The women looked at each other with a grin and nodded. The guys got off so they could slide up to reach the handlebars. Dakota climbed on behind Gabrielle and scooted forward against her. His thighs wrapped hers. Wow she thought. Being with him was so physical. And totally distracting.
He held her hips and said, "Do you mind if I hang on?"
She said, "You better. I might be a wild driver."

The women slowly revved the engines and began to cruise the same path the guys had taken – just slower.
On the way home, Dakota said, "You drive great. Have you driven a Jet Ski before?"

"A few times. Thanks!"

As they rounded the last bend in the river, a huge alligator surfaced right in front of her. Dakota immediately put his hands over hers and swiveled a hard right around the large reptile.

After he cleared the alligator, he said, "Good job," and released the ski back to her.

Before long they pulled back on the sandbar.

Dakota asked, "Would you ladies like to take a short spin on your own?"

Samantha, Jade, and Gabrielle grinned and said, "Yes!"

Dakota said, "Be careful and stay away from the bend with the monster alligator."

Gabrielle said, "You met Dragon – our local legend. He's a beast."

Dakota said, "That's comforting. I guess you don't swim much."

"Not especially."

The women puttered the skis out a little bit, looked back at the guys, leaned low, and gunned it. They flew, spun, and headed back, and spun again. They laughed at the look on the guys faces as they slid on the sandbar.

Gabrielle said, "You were saying?"

Dakota said, "Okay I deserved it. I just assumed you weren't experienced."

Samantha drawled in perfect Scarlett O'Hara accent, "Southern girls have many skills," and they laughed.

Gabrielle climbed off the ski and said, "Let us feed you to make up for our deception. We have plenty and we're starving."

The youngest, Adam, said, "Lead me to the food!"

Dakota led the guys as they headed toward the ladies. The shepherd immediately left Gabrielle's side and headed toward the men. She motioned them to stop. The dog smelled each man – checking them out - and returned to her. As they climbed the hill, she explained that he was her guard dog. The men glanced at each other in warning. They wouldn't make any moves that alarmed him. Besides, they wanted the dog to do his job. Protect her.

They passed through the patio underneath the house and Dakota said, "What a great setup, Gabrielle. You know how to make a place comfortable."

The patio had a brick floor, rockers, loungers, a gas grill, and was decorated with local potted ferns and ivy. Plus, the swings.

"Thank you," she said. "It was important to me to blend in as much as possible with the wilderness around me. I would have loved a pool, but it wasn't a good fit with the woods so close, so this was my concession."

She walked to one of the piers that had a round wooden tub at the base of it and pulled a handle. A waterfall poured into the tub.

Sean whistled and said, "Oh, yeah, we need one of those."

Gabrielle said, "It's a quick way to clean up or cool off."

Dakota looked curiously at the large, paved area that ran the width of the patio, and said, "Is this a workout area?"

She nodded yes, and said, "The four of us have special workouts that take a lot of room when they are here. But we will tell you more about that later, come on, let's go upstairs! I need food!"

***

The ladies pulled out the salads, sandwiches, fruit, and drinks while the men looked around. Dakota liked the casual open floor space and amazing pirogue light fixture on the ceiling. Then he walked to her art nook. He glanced over at Gabrielle, and she nodded ok.

He walked closer and saw the sketch on her easel. The dragonflies literally jumped off the canvas with their fragile wings. The baby alligators were adorable, at least at this tiny size.

Dakota flipped through canvases that leaned against the wall. He was astonished with her talent to paint with reality and depth of emotion. Then he glanced at the back wall - and didn't move. He stared at the canvas that hung there. It was a portrait of all four women dressed as warriors as they knelt with swords.

Sean and Adam noticed his expression and joined him. The men stared at the power of the portrait then turned to face the women, who watched them.

Dakota said, "You are fencers. I'm awed. Tell us how it came about."

Zoe said, "The story begins with Gabrielle. She tells it best."

Chapter 6

After lunch, everyone settled on the patio. They chatted for a while, but Dakota watched Gabrielle. He knew she was waiting for the right time to begin her story about the fencing. It had to be related to the kidnapping. He was sure it was connected.

She caught his gaze, and said, "Y'all aren't from Louisiana, are you?"

He smiled and said, "I wish I had that southern accent! But no, We're from Virginia originally."

"Originally?"

"All three of us have traveled a great deal the last few years, so we don't call one place home. Till now. That's why I bought the log cabin." He looked at Sean and Adam, then said, "They are still looking for their place to call home."

Gabrielle said, "I understand that. It took a while before I landed here."

And there it was. The opening. No one said anything as she walked a few steps away and leaned against one of the piers. Appearing to look downriver, her mind traveled much further. To that place. That time.

Dakota had an excellent idea where her mind went. He had read everything in her case file. Looked at all the evidence. But he had never heard it from her. Till now.

She took a deep breath, and said, "Samantha, Jade, Zoe, and I met as roommates at LSU. We were instant friends. We loved college. The classes. Social activities. The sports. Parties. And through it all, we learned to explore adult life while remaining within the proposed boundaries of Christian relationships. Especially dating. We rebelliously rode the line at times – but never crossed it. Then LSU ended and we graduated into real life.

"Everything changed of course. Samantha moved to complete her law degree. Jade moved back to New Orleans and dove into journalism. And Zoe moved to work and continue her veterinarian studies.

"I was the free spirited one with an art and history major. I stepped into the art world of museums and art galleries, but it didn't take me long to realize I had too much personal time on my hands." She sighed, and said, "I decided to join an online Christian coffee shop to make new friends – and maybe meet a guy. You know – the one."

"Cautious, I talked to several guys online for a few weeks. One appeared more sincere than the others, and I agreed to meet him. His name was Liam. Now don't get me wrong, I knew the basics of safety: Don't meet anyone alone. Don't give them your address. Don't leave your food or drink unattended. And don't give too much personal information. Watch, watch, watch, who's near you."

She was silent for a few seconds. Then voice tense, she said, "The first time Liam and I met, we had coffee at Starbucks. It was nice to visit and be with a guy. He was nice looking, a little older than I expected, but not pushy, and was funny. It seemed a good start. The next time we met at an outside café for pizza. Again, everything was exactly what I was used to. The third time we met at a church function for singles and for the first time - I felt something odd. I was uncomfortable but I didn't know why. I look back now and wonder what it was. But anyway, it was just after dark when we left the building, so he walked me to my car. We said a friendly goodnight and I left. I thought perhaps my feelings had been wrong.

Dakota leaned forward and put his elbows on his knees. His body was rigid with…fury.

She walked around as she spoke, "I went home, locked up, watched TV for a while, and fell asleep on the sofa. I woke up a little later and headed to my bedroom. I still don't know what woke me during the night. My eyes just flew open, and I was scared. It was dark. I couldn't see anything. But my skin began to crawl, and I knew something was terribly wrong.

"Then someone whispered my name in the creepiest voice I had ever heard. I stepped off the mattress to run, but a hand grabbed my ankle from under the bed and I fell. When I woke up, it was hot, and I hung, bound, from a tree in the middle of the woods. My arms screamed from the pain of holding up my weight. But I couldn't scream. I was gagged - and in full blown panic mode.

"But the panic turned to terror as a man walked out of the shadows. Liam. My new friend. He had built a raging campfire and heated metal bars. I knew something horrendous was about to happen. It did. He branded me with the words FEAR and SHAME. Both times I passed out to the smell of my own skin on fire."

She turned to face them. The girls had tear tracks on their faces. Adam's face was in his hands. Sean looked ready to kill someone. And Dakota's eyes were on fire.

She said, "The next thing I remember was a soft touch. A man dressed in black with an FBI patch cut me loose, laid me down, and cut the ropes off me. I shook uncontrollably as he comforted me – then carried me. I struggled to talk but only cried as I clung to him. He was my hero."

Dakota swallowed. Hard.

She shrugged, and said, "When I woke again, I was in the hospital with my parents and friends. We all cried. I never saw the man who rescued me again. His boss came to the hospital and told me the FBI had been tracking Liam - and that he had been killed during my rescue.

"After I left the hospital, the FBI boss came to see me again. He told me about a secret place that I could go to for healing, for therapy on PTSD, and for guidance and training for self -defense. I was there over a year. When I left, Zeus was with me. He is a trained PTSD protection dog. He means the world to me."

Everyone glanced at Zeus who watched every move she made – highly alert to her intensity right now.

She continued, "And once I returned to Baton Rouge, I found another apartment and prayed about what was next. Before long, I got together with Samantha, Jade, and Zoe - and En-Garde the ministry was born. We had taken private fencing lessons throughout our college years for fun. So, we structured a fencing routine that could be used in conjunction with scripture teaching on the Armor of God. Now, we accept invitations to teach as an exhibit. Hence, the picture you saw. And that's the story."

It was silent for a moment. The enormity of everything she had shared still hung in the air. Dakota stood. He wanted to tell her who he was. He wanted to tell her so many things. But that would have to come later.

Instead, he walked toward her, seeing the remnants of pain lingering in her eyes. He said bluntly, "I'm glad he's dead."

She nodded with the tiniest of smiles.

He softened his tone, and said, "But more importantly, I'm proud of your strength and resilience. I know that was a horrendous experience, but En-

Garde is an amazing way to testify of what you've overcome. I'm proud to know you. I'm proud to know all of you."

She said, "Thank you, Dakota. I appreciate that more than you know." Then she looked at everyone, and said, "If you would please excuse me for a few minutes, I need to take a short run," and she sprinted into the woods with Zeus on her heels.

Dakota watched her go. He completely understood.

Samantha said, "She's burning it off. She won't be long."

A few minutes later, they heard laughter and Gabrielle jogged out of the woods behind her house. Sweating, smiling, she ran up to join her friends, and said, "Go for it, Samantha."

Samantha grinned, and said, "So guys, how do you feel about helping us with a workout?"

Dakota, glad to see a smile on Gabrielle's face, said, "I'm in."

Sean laughed, and said, "You mean us men with bare hands while all of you have swords?" Everyone laughed

Adam said, "Bring it on!"

Gabrielle smiled and glanced at Dakota. He saw the weight was gone now, and said where only she could hear, "I have something from my past I would like to share with you today."

Nodding, she said, "Sure. Just say when."

After the ladies changed for fencing, and returned, Gabrielle said, "Our sword tips are covered for safety. We are going to warm up for a bit, do a quick routine, and then one at a time, you will attack. The point is for you to be spontaneous so we won't know what your move may be. We need the challenge, so we don't lose our edge. Routine can make us lazy. Are you guys willing to be a bad guy?"

The guys made tough grunting noises and the ladies laughed. After they warmed up, Gabrielle pointed at Samantha.

Samantha, hand on hip, said, "Ok, Sean, come show me what you've got."

He grinned and walked toward her, then charged. She spun, tripping him. He caught his balance and grabbed her arm, pulling her close. She dropped, throwing him off balance, and stopped the point at his neck as he leaned down. She grinned.

He said, "Gorgeous and vicious! You rock."

Zoe said, "I'll go next. Sean, come back up here. You can't be tired already."

Sean jumped up ready to go, proving his unending energy, and they laughed. He smiled and acted like he was out for a stroll. Then he darted behind Zoe and lifted her - pinning her arms. She swiveled the sword and stabbed him in the thigh, then when he moved, she elbowed him, spun, and lunged - the sword at his belly.

He threw up his hands, and said, "I give!"

Gabrielle said, "My turn." She smiled at Dakota, and said, "Want to dance big guy?"

He smiled, eyes never leaving hers as he stood. He darted at her, left to right, attempting to pin her in by the stairs. Realizing his goal, she spun and stopped his advance with a sudden swipe of her point near his throat. He dropped low and lunged left. She darted right, and with a foot on his thigh, then shoulder, she vaulted over him. When he spun, her point was at his heart.

He smiled and said, "You've got style."

Jade said, "Come on Adam, your turn, come show me some moves."

Adam said, "You haven't seen anything yet!"

She rolled her eyes. He casually walked toward her, stumbled, and fell as his ankle turned on the bricks. They hurried to check on him.

Jade said, "Are you ok?"

Adam grabbed her arm with the sword. Surprised, she grabbed the sword with her left hand and aimed the point in his neck.

"No way," he said.

Jade laughed and said, "I'm ambidextrous."

The guys clapped, and Gabrielle said, "Thanks! Now, we know you took it easy on us, but it was still good practice for our responses. Now who's ready for air conditioning and something cold to drink?"

Upstairs, cooling off, Jade said, "My reporter curiosity is peaked, guys. It's your turn. Tell us about yourselves. Anything," and she prompted Dakota to go first.

He nodded, and said, "Ok. I do a little karate."

Gabrielle said, "I believe that. So, what's a little?"

He said, "It's no big deal."
Samantha said, "You're making it worse. What are you? A black belt?"
"Fourth degree."
Jade said, "Ouch. You can kick butt. Show us something. Come on. Gabrielle's worked us all day. We want someone else to work."
He laughed and in one fluid move, stood, leaned to the left and shot his right foot toward the ceiling. He stayed in that position and then lowered his leg and sat back down.
The girls whistled and clapped.
Zoe said, "Tell us one more thing and we'll let you off the hook."
Dakota said, "I'm an author. I semi-retired a year ago to write - and love it. Sean, your turn."

Sean said dryly, "Thanks man, I appreciate that hand off."
But he grinned and said, "I tinker with aerial technology," and Adam laughed.
Jade said, "So does that really mean, you build rocket ships or something?"
They laughed, and he said, "Not as big as that. I'm working on an invention. I'll tell you about it if I get famous."
Gabrielle said, "I won't forget. Give us something else."
He smiled at Samantha and said, "I love sassy blondes and horses. In that order."
Samantha looked him over and said, "I'm first over a horse?" and they laughed.

Zoe pointed at Adam and said, "Your go, Charmer."
He said, "My list of accomplishments is really long. Where should I begin?"
Jade laughed and said, "Obviously, being humble is one of them."
Adam smiled and said, "But actually, all kidding aside, my most honored lifetime achievement is that I'm a minister."
The ladies responded with silent round-eyed astonishment.
He laughed and said, "On my down time, I am a survivalist and hiker."
Gabrielle opened her mouth to comment, but Samantha jumped in and asked, "Wait! Guys, with all your impressive traits, I have one question. Can you cook too?" and everyone laughed.

Then Dakota's phone rang, and he excused himself and headed outside to take the call.

In two minutes, he was back and said, "I hate to break up the party, but it is mid-afternoon, and we have a few tasks to work on before it gets late. But before we leave, I wanted to ask, Gabrielle, have you ladies made dinner plans yet?"

"Just to grill steaks."

He said, "Perfect! How about coming to the cabin and we can grill our steaks together? You can meet Aunt Jaz and we can chauffeur you over on the Jet Skis."

Gabrielle asked, "Ladies?" and they happily agreed.

"Terrific," Dakota said, "How about we pick you up around six-thirty p.m.?"

As the guys left, the girls turned on music and climbed back in the swings. After two workouts today, they were ready to chill.

Zoe spoke first and said "The trip's been great Gabrielle. It is too bad Trace isn't here to meet everyone."

Gabrielle said, "Go call him! Maybe he's within easy driving distance. He can sleep on the sofa. You know Dakota and the guys won't mind an extra guest at dinner."

Zoe, visibly thrilled, said, "Thanks!" and ran upstairs to call Trace.

Samantha said, "I'm happy for her. She has a heart of gold behind that lethal sword."

***

At the log cabin, Dakota joined Sean in the surveillance office. He said bluntly, "Something's wrong. The director evaded my questions today when he called. He had a one-track mind and was concerned only about information I might have gotten from Gabrielle regarding the treasure. No update from intel. No interest in our activities. Even when I pushed the issue. I don't have a good gut feeling about that at all."

Sean frowned. He said, "A clear line of communication on the status of the Posse is critical for her safety. And ours."

"My point exactly," Dakota said. "After I tell her tonight, I will be her bodyguard twenty-four hours a day. And I, more than anyone, am aware she will not do well with this new threat. But that is the wisest choice for now."

"Dakota, I know you don't want to discuss it, but because you are personally involved with her - you have to be extra cautious. Not distracted.

Six people are dead by the hands of the Posse, and we have next to nothing to go on. The only trail the Posse leaves is corpses."

"Let it go, Sean. I get your concern, but the personal side of it makes my goal to keep her safe more intense – not distracted." He walked to the window and watched her swing with her friends. He said, "And I have something to say that you won't like." He turned back to Sean and said, "I think someone's leaking intel from the FBI. These murders have been clean for way too long. We have a traitor inside."

They looked at each other – silently acknowledging the catastrophic danger if that was true.

Sean said, "Well. That's the worst scenario possible. But unfortunately, it makes the most sense. We might have to presume that's the case and go underground on our own if we can't trust FBI communication. But eventually we'll need outside help."

Dakota said, "We'll do whatever it takes to keep her alive. And us. Starting now, kill all communication with the FBI – except for your private contact no one knows about. I'll take her off-grid away from civilization to avoid technology so they can't track her. The FBI will understand the urgency of our decision later when we have connection again. I'll get my go-bag ready and tell Gabrielle tonight. We'll hide till we get a plan in place."

A couple of hours later, after leaving his go-bag in the barn, Dakota joined Aunt Jaz in the kitchen.

She grinned and said, "I look forward to having some lovely ladies over for dinner this evening with you handsome men."

Dakota chuckled and said, "You can't get us married off in one night you know."

She gave him a quick hug and said, "It's past time for you to find someone made just for you. I want to have nieces and nephews to spoil."

"Wow," he said. "You don't want to just get us married tonight - but have kids too!" and she swatted at him with her kitchen towel.

With a laugh, he dodged the towel and said, "But you will enjoy them. They are Christian warriors, you might say. Beautiful, smart, and skilled."

***

Back across the river, Gabrielle, Samantha, and Jade climbed the stairs to check on Zoe. She had disappeared since she went inside to call Trace with the invitation to come tonight. They found her sitting on the sofa with a dreamy look on her face. Obviously, he was coming.

Zoe said, "He will be here by five-thirty p.m. Oh no, look at the time! He will be here in an hour. I need to change. I want to surprise him dressed in something sexier than what he sees me in at the clinic."

Gabrielle laughed and said, "It feels like college again. Come on, we'll help you. We all need to change anyway."

In minutes they were upstairs in front of Gabrielle's dressing mirror. Zoe went first. They pulled her wavy auburn hair into a messy bun with wispy tendrils falling around her face. Her green eyes already had stars in them, so they just added a touch of gold shadow, then mascara on her long sweeping lashes. Zoe perched her lips, applying shimmery gloss.

Gabrielle said, "How long will that gloss last?"

Zoe said, "Not long if I had to guess."

Since they would be crossing the river on Jet Skis, they dressed casual for wind and water droplets. Zoe slipped on a black spandex ruffled top and jean capris. She posed for the girls. Seriously they studied her and whistled.

Zoe said, "So, do you think he will like it?"

Samantha said, "You look like a match that's been lit. Can he handle that?"

She giggled and said, "I'll let you decide when you meet him."

Gabrielle said, "Come on girls, we need to hurry and get dressed. We only have thirty minutes before Romeo gets here. Oh, I mean Trace."

They updated their look for the night. Samantha pulled her silky blond hair into a low Latin bun. Added heavier liner. Red lips. She pulled on a short floral top and leggings. She posed for their opinion.

Gabrielle shook her head, and said, "I don't know how you're single. You are classy – and sultry. So, what do you do? Kick them out of the way?"

The others laughed – agreeing totally.

Samantha grinned, and said, "I'm impressed, Gabrielle. You're close."

Jade was exotic no matter what she did. Tonight, she decided to leave her thick black hair braided. Then she leaned over the counter and swiped on green shadow and liner. She opened her lips and covered them with purple lipstick - and stepped back to inspect herself. Makeup done, she dressed in a bronze tank and cutoffs.

She spun and posed – waiting for their comments.

Zoe said, "Ouch! You're gorgeous! What is wrong with the men in New Orleans?"

Jade said, "They think I'm a prude."

"What?"

"I haven't met anyone that I can be - what I look like."

The girls knew what she meant. She struggled with insecurity which made her reserved. She just didn't look reserved.

Gabrielle said, "You're gonna blow someone out of the water one day when you let loose."

Gabrielle remembered all the times they had done this - and smiled as she pulled her long dark hair in a ponytail. She brushed brown shimmer shadow above her amber eyes. Liner. Rich black mascara. Burgundy gloss. Then she walked in her closet and looked.

Samantha walked up and said, "Let me pick. It'll do you good."

Gabrielle said, "Go for it."

Samantha slid the hangers one at a time till she found a red, low-back fringed top. She gasped as she pulled it out and said, "I can't believe you bought this fabulously sexy shirt. It's not camo."

The girls laughed and Samantha handed it to Gabrielle, who said, "I can't believe. I forgot about that. Leave it to you to find it. I don't want to look like a hooker."

Jade said, "Well, you must have liked it – you bought it. Besides, that's not a hooker look. That's a look to catch a man who rides bareback on a stallion. Put. It. On."

"I can't wear a bra."

"Well, don't get cold or excited and you should be fine."

They screamed in laughter.

With a glance at the time, they ran downstairs. Gabrielle packed the marinated steaks and veggies to bring with them. Trace would be here any minute, so they walked out on the deck.

Gabrielle said, "Selfie time!"

They were still taking pictures when Zeus barked. A few seconds later, Trace drove up. Zoe headed down the stairs as he stepped out of his jeep with a smile. The rest of them waved in greeting but made no attempt to go inside to give them privacy. Trace didn't mind at all and with no hesitation, he lifted Zoe up in his arms, for a steamy hug and kiss.

Samantha said, "That gloss won't last long. She was right!"
They were most certainly a couple. He had staked his claim on Zoe, and she liked it. The girls grinned as they watched Trace and a very flushed Zoe climb the stairs to join them. He was a rugged outdoorsman. Tall, bold, and handsome.
Zoe introduced him.
Jade drawled, "I'm thinking you are a happy man, Trace."
"How can I help it. Look at her," he said. And kissed Zoe again. "I hope you don't mind. I brought my Jet Ski since I had it at the camp with me. Do you mind if I back down to unload it?"
"I don't mind at all," Gabrielle said. "Go right ahead. And bring your bag upstairs too. Make yourself at home."

About thirty minutes later, they heard Jet Skis start across the river.
Gabrielle said, "Come on guys, let's head down to meet them."

Dakota, Sean, and Adam coasted onto the sandbar. After the men introduced themselves to Trace, they gallantly offered to assist the women on the skis.
Dakota checked Gabrielle out, giving her a soft whistle. He said, "Wow. You are killer in red fringe. And I mean killer."
Gabrielle laughed, a bit overwhelmed, and heard the girls giggle behind her. She ignored them and said, "Actually, Samantha found it in my closet, and insisted I wear it – instead of camo."
He chuckled and looked at a smug, smiling Samantha, and gave her a thumbs up. Glancing back at Gabrielle, he said, "Why don't I…" and he scooped her up. "Sweep you off your feet."
She gasped, then laughed as he carried her toward the Jet Ski. She refused to look at the girls.
Teasing, she said, "You're not going to drop me, right?"
Looking at her laid out in his arms, he said, "Not a chance of that."

In a couple of minutes, they docked in front of the cabin, and headed inside to meet Aunt Jaz. The young women loved her immediately. She was on the petite side, with shoulder length salt-n-pepper hair, and bright blue eyes. She looked lovely dressed in jeans and a gorgeous embroidered Mexican tunic.

She greeted everyone with a hug, delighted with the beautiful women around her eligible nephews, and said, "Dakota has a wonderful place. Go look around and visit before it's time to cook. I'll call if I get hungry."

Gabrielle turned to follow the others to the patio door, and locked eyes with the most beautiful cat she had ever seen. It lay sprawled on top a buffet cabinet along the kitchen wall. This was the cat he told them about.

She glanced at Dakota and said, "Please…will he let me pet him? I know cats can be finicky. But I can't stand it. He is beautiful."

Dakota said, "He expects attention," and picked him up and laid him in her arms.

Gabrielle was totally enamored. Smoothed his fur. Talked to him. She said, "He really is like a miniature leopard and tiger. I am so in love with this cat."

Dakota rubbed under the cat's chin, and said softly, "Come on. Let's join the others. I can't wait to watch you fall in love with the horses too."

Once everyone was on the patio, the horses began to show off and the brothers led the way to the corral. Dakota ran his hands up his stallion's neck. He was a spectacular shiny black Arabian. Sean's horse was a Morgan. He had a medium brown coat with a long black mane and tail. Adam's horse was a black and white paint with a black tail and a mixed black and white mane. They were amazing horses and obviously adored the men.

Dakota motioned Gabrielle forward and she melted into Midnight's neck – holding him, rubbing him, whispering to him. It was obvious she knew how to love on someone. Dakota watched the stallion's response as he lowered his head to nudge her hip. The beauty of their affection was striking. When Gabrielle leaned back and stared eye to eye with the animal, Dakota thought, I'm jealous of my own horse.

A short time later, they returned to the patio. Adam fired up the grill and before long, everyone headed inside following the mouthwatering platter of steaks. Dinner was ribeye's. T-bone's. Grilled vegetables. Fresh cucumbers and tomatoes drizzled with a thick vinaigrette. Texas toast. And banana pudding for dessert. They laughed and talked as they fixed their plates and settled at a large picnic table in the kitchen. The food was delicious, and the social atmosphere was fun.

After dinner, they went outside again. Dakota looked at Sean and Adam, and they nodded almost imperceptibly as they steered everyone but Gabrielle away from the barn.

Gabrielle noticed the men and women seemed to pair off instead of staying in a group. Sean and Samantha headed toward the dock. Zoe and Trace headed to the front porch. And Adam and Jade stayed on the patio.

Dakota touched her arm and said, "Walk with me?"

She smiled, and said, "Sure," and they walked toward the barn.

Once inside, they leaned against the fence that faced the corral where the horses grazed.

He gently bumped shoulders with her, and said, "I like you being here."

She glanced at him with a teasing smile, and said, "Yes. Dinner was wonderful."

He said bluntly, "I'm not talking about dinner." He turned her to face him, and said, "I'm talking about us. And don't tell me you don't feel this. I won't believe you."

She felt it. Silent, she let the look in her eyes answer.

He leaned closer and kissed her neck. He let her feel his warm, soft lips. Then he breathed her in, and whispered, "I'm going to kiss you."

Feeling herself get swept up in the whirlwind of wanting this, she warned him, "I…I never do this. I haven't kissed anyone in a long, long time."

Sliding his hands up her back, he said, "But I'm not just *anyone*."

"But..."

"Kiss me, Gabrielle."

She looked at his mouth, and her lips parted. He kissed her. And she couldn't believe the feel and taste of him as their mouths met.

Dakota quickly deepened the kiss as her arms encircled his neck. He held her tighter. Groaned, feeling her response. He wanted this kiss. He wanted the attraction set in stone. Acknowledged before she knew who he was – and before the case blew open. There would be no question from this point forward about what was happening between them.

Breathless moments later, she whispered, "There is so much you don't know about me. I have… issues. I might not be worth your time or trouble."

He cupped her face, brushing her lips with his, and said, "Gabrielle, listen to me. I know you. We are not strangers. And we are much more than neighbors."

Not understanding, she said, "Wait. What do you mean?"

Chapter 7

Dakota said, "Do you remember when I asked you earlier today if I could share something with you about my past?"

A little nervous now, she said, "Yes."

He said softly, "I need to tell you who I am."

Eyes locked on his, she whispered, "Who *are* you?"

"There's no easy way to say this. I'm FBI. I was the one that helped you that night with Liam."

Her knees buckled and he caught her. She held onto him, her face against his neck as he carried her to a stack of hay bales. He sat with her on his lap. It felt like a flashback in time as she breathed against his skin as tears dripped. She felt his strength. His arms around her tight - and safe. She closed her eyes as all her inner walls fell. It had been Dakota.

He kissed the top of her head, snuggled her tighter. Felt her. Gave her everything she needed. Gave her… him.

Several moments later, she shifted. He loosened his hold, and she began to rub her hand back and forth across his chest as she laid her head against him. He knew she was ready to talk.

Softly, she said, "Your first touch…I knew it wasn't him." He listened and nodded.

She paused, clenching his shirt in one hand, and said, "I struggled to hear you through the pain." He closed his eyes and grimaced with understanding.

Sniffing, a second later, she said, "You appeared from nowhere. Saved me. Got me down." He squeezed her.

Sounding stronger, she said, "I felt safe with you." He kissed her hair.

A few breaths later, she tensed, and said harshly, "The pain was bad. But the fear was insane. Mind boggling. Like, how is it even possible this is happening when I was at home in my bed." He was visibly able to see in his mind what she said, and moaned softly, heart aching.

She wiped her wet cheeks, and said, "The branding stayed with me. It was horrible. I still see him coming in my nightmares. Every nightmare the same thing. The fear. Then the searing pain."

Above her, he clenched his jaw. He wanted to kill a man long since dead, and forced the rage to subside, and said, "I'm sorry we didn't get there earlier."

She sat back and looked at him with the weeping eyes he remembered, then said, "You saved my life. I would say your timing was wonderful. But why didn't you come to the hospital so I could meet you? Thank you."

"I did check on you before I left with the team to head back to Washington D.C. You had a room full of people. You were upset."

She looked at him and whispered, "But they weren't you. I never forgot what you did – what I felt at that time."

Kissing her forehead, he said, "Neither of us forgot."

"Did you know that I went to The Fort to train?"

"Yes, I watched you train a few times when I was in town."

She said, "Why didn't you tell me who you were when we met yesterday?"

"It's not something that comes out in a first meeting conversation. Besides…" He took a deep breath, and said, "There is more that I need to tell you."

Her heart sped up. She could tell from his tone she didn't want to know what it was.

And he didn't sugarcoat it. He just laid it out there, and said, "There is another threat on your life."

Disbelief hit her first. Then shock. Next, anger. And finally, terror. She stared at him.

He saw the changing of emotions across her face, then reassured her, "This is not the same as Liam. You aren't alone this time. I won't leave you. Do you hear me? I will not leave you."

Throat tight, she said, "What is it?"

He said, "Come, let's join the others. I'll tell you what's happened."

As they walked out of the barn, everyone watched from the patio. She realized they already knew something was wrong.

She whispered, "Jesus… help me."

In moments, her friends had her in their arms.

Dakota gave them a few minutes together, then led them to the den. Gabrielle and her friends sat near each other on the sofa. Dakota and his brothers stood.

He began, "The FBI has been involved in a case for years on six serial murders throughout Louisiana. A connection between some of the victims, was a DNA website regarding the bloodline of Jean Lafitte."

"No..." Gabrielle whispered as her face paled.

Understanding her shock, Dakota continued, "As usual those DNA sites connect relatives. The big deal with this situation, is that the bloodline trail leads back to a legend of Jean Lafitte regarding a special hidden treasure."

Gabrielle hung her head in distress at yet another online motive. Unbelievable. Another nightmare.

He said, "Let me give you all the intelligence information we have, and then we will get specific in your case. The FBI has received cyber tips through the dark web on who we will call the Treasure Posse. From here on out we will just call them Posse for short. They gather information through hacking DNA website emails that talk about the treasure. Then they stalk the victim.

"Gabrielle, when your name came up on the DNA website, a flag went off to the FBI. My boss called me a few days ago because of my connection to you. Sean is an agent with the FBI and specializes in surveillance, cyber, and technical weapons, such as drones. I profile cases as needed since I am semi-retired. Adam is not FBI but has special outdoor skills that we need in this situation.

"Unfortunately, you have become a hot target for this Posse. We need to know what information you may have regarding the treasure and who you might have told. Anyone who knows will need to take precautions."

Gabrielle, horrified, looked at her friends – scared for them.

Then Dakota said, "We know all of you carry concealed weapons. Unfortunately, we haven't identified the Posse yet. So, Samantha, Jade, and Zoe, change your routines, pay attention, get a burner phone, cash, and a go-bag ready in case you need it. Keep your weapons with you.

"Trace, I imagine your concern will be for Zoe. But we need something else from you also. Please get with Sean and Adam when we are done here."

Trace said, "Will do."

Dakota said, "You may wonder why we don't call law enforcement and other FBI agents." He stopped to hold their attention. "We can't. Because now we believe there's an FBI leak connected to the Posse. We have to break ties until we know more."

Speechless at first, then overwhelmed with anger, Gabrielle said, "How in the world do I hide from the FBI? Or the Posse?"

"Yesterday we installed perimeter surveillance on your property and mine. I put a GPS tracker in your purse and on your car - but I will remove them tonight because of the FBI issue. Only those of us in this room, for now, can know of our plans or locations. The Posse leaves no survivors so we can't take any chances."

Gabrielle closed her eyes wishing she would wake up from this new nightmare.

Dakota said, "Gabrielle, help us fill in the blanks. Other than the DNA link, has anything unusual happened?"

She struggled at first to focus, then remembered. She said, "My parents gave me the house two years ago just before they died. I moved in not long after that. Just recently I found an old deed for the house and property dated close to my adoption date, with a key, and a note. The note simply listed my first name, date of birth, and explained that it wasn't safe for me. Along with instructions to give me the key, the house, and the note when the time was right. The note was signed by someone named Serena."

"I told the girls about my Jean Lafitte DNA bloodline and the key when they arrived yesterday. Jade planned to investigate banks about the key that I think is for a safety deposit box."

Dakota said, "Jade, have you said anything to anyone or tried to research the key yet?"

"No, I was going to work on it when I returned to New Orleans."

Dakota said, "Don't do anything. We will handle it. Gabrielle, where is the key?"

"At home."

He nodded and said, "Sean, we will get you the key to investigate."

Dakota knelt before Gabrielle. He said, "You and I need to run and stay hidden – completely off-grid away from civilization and technology to avoid being tracked. The FBI, as we all know, has access to everything. We will have to rough it survival style through the woods. But with your skills, that shouldn't be a problem. We will take my stallion. And I know you won't like this, but your dog can't go with us. I need to be able to control the situation, but that will go against his instincts."

Gabrielle grimaced and nodded.

Dakota continued, "Adam, you and Trace go to the surveillance room and map out the uninhabited river and forest areas around here that would be accessible to us."

Adam nodded.

Then Dakota said, "Everyone in this room, please get a burner phone and give me your numbers. Hide those phones. Write nothing down."

He held out his hand to Gabrielle and led her to his office. He looked into her shell-shocked eyes and opened his arms. She walked into them, grateful, and terrified.

After a few moments, he said, "I know this seems unbelievable, but we can do this. I will be with you through it all, *and this time,* you have self-defense skills to help yourself. You are not helpless, and we are a team."

He stepped back to look at her, and said, "Do you trust me?"

"With my life."

***

It was almost dark as the guys rode the women home on the Jet Skis. Immediately, Dakota removed and destroyed the tracking device he had hidden on Gabrielle's car, and in her purse. After that she showed him how her security system worked. Her yard, and patio had motion lights. The stairs had motion sensors once she armed the alarm. The swings raised by pulleys to lock against the floor of the house. There were only two doors – one on each floor and they locked and barred from the inside.

Once everything had been addressed regarding safety on the first floor, Gabrielle led the way upstairs with Dakota and her dog.

Stepping into her loft, he smiled and said, "I like this. It fits you."

The cypress walls, and the floor, were painted antique white. Three of the walls were decorated with paintings and photographs of nature, people, and animals – clearly portraying warmth, depth, and love. Dakota understood. He knew these images kept her from feeling alone.

"This is my personal workout and safe place," she said. "Nights can be hard for me."

"I understand that."

She pointed to the ceiling, and said, "Motion lights are in each corner and you will find another security panel near the door."

She walked to her bed covered with a multicolored boho quilt and beautiful pillows. She lifted a large pillow to reveal a hunting knife. He raised his eyebrows, impressed, and she shrugged.

Touching the trunk at the foot of her bed, she said, "These are my weapons."

Dakota looked at the massive trunk, and then at her. He said, "You have strategy skills. Faith. You are a trained warrior, mentally and physically. You are aware that your most powerful weapons aren't in that trunk - right?"

She didn't answer the question he asked, but said, "I needed all this after the kidnapping to feel safe. Both faith and survival skills. God has helped me make a way to be strong when I was afraid and alone."

"I get that. Most certainly I get that. You are a powerful, beautiful warrior," and she smiled. He said, "I presume your dog stays in here at night."

"He's always with me. And Hunter's perch is outside my window under the eave."

"Who's Hunter?"

"My hawk."

"You have a hawk," he repeated, and she grinned. He said, "Somehow I am not surprised."

She said, "Oh, wait," and knelt on the side of her bed and pulled a briefcase out from under it. She handed him the bank key, the old deed paperwork, and the handwritten note from the woman named Serena. He took pictures of all of it and sent it to Sean.

He said, "Let's get your go-bag packed."

Gabrielle opened the trunk and Dakota whistled as he saw her weapons. He said, "What do you want to bring?"

She pulled out her survival bag, weapon's belt, Glock, her throwing knives, and the dart gun, and laid them on the bed.

He said, "Even though it's hot, I suggest jeans for long rides on the horse, and bring a couple of changes."

After she was packed, she said, "Are you going to stay up here tonight?"

"Yes. Till this is over, day and night, you're stuck with me. How about we lay on the bed, and I'll just take my boots off. And try to sleep if you can. You need the rest."

They took turns in the bathroom, then laid on top of the comforter. Dakota lay with his hands under his head on the pillow. He could see Gabrielle through the moonlight. She squirmed a bit and he figured this made her uncomfortable.

He whispered, “Come see,” and tucked her against his side. A few minutes later, she began to relax and fell asleep. All was quiet in the house.

About three o’clock in the morning, Dakota heard a moan and Gabrielle’s body tensed and jerked against him. Realizing it was a nightmare, he rolled on his side and wrapped both arms around her as the dog jumped in the bed.

“I’ve got you,” he whispered, rubbing her back. The dog laid behind her.

Gabrielle, breathless, sighed. She felt them both. She was safe. And whispered, “Thank you.”

Several hours later, just as dawn was breaking, Dakota smelled coffee. The dog yawned and Gabrielle’s eyes flew open at the noise. She stared directly into Dakota’s eyes, then felt his arms around her. She blushed and he kissed her nose.

He said, “Morning, Beautiful.”

She looked from his eyes to his mouth, back to his eyes. He watched her, feeling the awareness spark between them – but gave her the lead. She touched his lips with her finger, and he opened them. She leaned forward and kissed him. He responded and pulled her closer. After a few moments, she leaned back with pink cheeks, and smiled. He was safe to explore. That was fabulous.

He read her expression and said, “You… are so fine.”

She whispered back, “And you are a beautiful man.”

He said, “One more kiss.”

She shook her head no, rolled over, and loved on the dog. Then she jumped out of bed and winked at him. He chuckled. She had found her superpower. Now she would torture him. He smiled. That was fine with him.

Trace called out, “Coffee’s ready!”

Dakota called back, “I need it black, and lots of it!”

In a few minutes, Dakota headed downstairs to grab coffee.

Gabrielle called after him, “Would you save me a cup?”

She laughed as he mumbled, “Beautiful and bossy!”

But Dakota smiled. She was going to be just fine.

***

When Gabrielle joined everyone in the kitchen, they looked like they needed coffee. She felt guilty because she felt rested. Safe. For the first time in…what seemed like forever. She hugged her friends and checked on Trace. Then she heard Hunter and grabbed a falconer's glove and went to the deck. They watched as her large hawk landed on the glove. She rubbed his breast, and he flapped his wings.

Dakota shook his head in amazement, and said, "She's incredible."

Her friends looked at each other, and grinned, for the first time in hours. Gabrielle was going to be in the GRAY ZONE big time.

***

Just before ten a.m., Dakota parked at church and followed Gabrielle and her friends inside. She saved him a place to sit, and he subtly winked as he joined her. She smiled, then tried not to think about the mess she was in as the music began. God always reminded her that He was in control. She knew that this hadn't surprised Him even though it had knocked her off her feet.

After church, Gabrielle greeted the pastors and introduced Dakota. And in minutes, she hugged, said goodbye, and watched Samantha, Jade, Zoe, and Trace drive away. A sudden wave of insecurity washed over her, and she turned to meet Dakota's gaze.

Seeing her unease, he said with a gentle smile, "I've got you. Come with me," and she followed him to his truck without saying anything.

As he drove out of the parking lot, she looked out her window lost in thought. So much had happened overnight. It was crazy. But she knew she was in the safest hands. Very handsome safe hands at that.

Dakota glanced at her as they crossed the long bridge heading into Moss Bluff. He could tell she was still processing all of this. It was a big deal. And getting bigger all the time.

***

When they arrived home, Sean motioned them to follow him to the surveillance room. He said, "Adam and Aunt Jaz left with most of the animals a few minutes ago. He left your stallion in the barn until you need him."

Dakota got right to the point and said, "What happened?"

"The bank key Gabrielle found is for a safety deposit box that was opened the day the house was deeded to her. No one has been in the box since then."

Gabrielle said, "So the box information relates to me."

Sean said, "I am positive it does. And its treasure related. I know it is. Someone forged that signature card expecting you to come one day."

"So, it's a secret."

Dakota said, "Yes, a dangerous one. The Posse knows your DNA link – but they don't know about this box. But you can bet they want what's in it. The first thing we need to do is get you disguised - and in and out of that safety deposit box. We need to know what the Posse is after. We are running blind without it. Which bank is it, Sean?"

"Gulf Coast Savings & Loan in Lafayette."

Dakota said, "We need to take an undetected trip tomorrow. We don't want to be followed."

Gabrielle said, "What if we run my trail workout in the morning and Sean picks us up somewhere along the way? No one would expect that."

Dakota said, "Perfect."

After discussing disguises for the bank rendezvous, Dakota said, "Gabrielle, my goal now is to disappear with you by dusk tomorrow. If there is an FBI leak, and we believe there is, they will make a move to come after you soon since Sean and I have gone silent on your case.

"So, for tonight, if I stay with you at your place, nothing will alert anyone to our plans. Sean's equipment will have eyes on us through the night. When we leave for the trail workout in the morning, we'll bring everything you need and won't return there till all this is over."

Gabrielle left the guys working and went looking for Dakota's cat. She found him on the sofa, and they curled up together.

About twenty minutes later, Dakota came downstairs and sat next to Gabrielle. He said, "He is terribly spoiled."

She gave the cat a kiss and said, "He should be."

Dakota glanced at her lips and said, "I could use one of those."

She grinned and said, "A pet?"

"A kiss."

Dakota leaned over to kiss her, pressing on the cat, who complained and ran off. Dakota grinned, grabbed her hand, and called out to Sean they were leaving.

***

Back at Gabrielle's house, they ate a bite for lunch, then she gathered her disguises and brought them downstairs with her go-bag and weapons.

Dakota said, "We have a long afternoon, why don't you take me out on your trail and show me how you work out. I can get the layout of your land too."

"Sure. My dog and hawk will be thrilled. Let me change."

It didn't take her long and she jogged downstairs dressed in workout gear and climbing boots. She grabbed her weapon belt off the table. When she was ready to go, she noticed Dakota watching her with an appreciative look.

"What?" she said, although his interest was evident.

He walked close - all up in her space, then said, "Do you have any idea what you look like in that outfit? And you smell…so good."

She smiled, and said, "Wow, and thank you. But in about ten minutes, all you will smell on me is sweat."

He laughed, then said, "And that won't change a thing at all."

The dog and hawk followed as they headed downhill. She explained that she ran the trails but added different activities at the large oaks.

Wanting to see her skills, he said, "Just do your thing. I'll keep up."

Gabrielle nodded and took off down the trail. Dakota loved the way she entered in and became a part of the forest. She dodged trees and bushes, ran, jumped over small things, balanced on logs, and made all the maneuvering look easy. That was an amazing skill she had developed on her own.

He saw a huge oak up ahead and wondered what her plan was. She neared the oak and jumped, then grabbed hold of a vine and up the tree she went. She ran along the branch, hidden in the leaves. A few seconds later, she lowered herself and landed back on the trail.

He said, "You are incredibly nimble," and she grinned.

Later, on the south side of her property, she shot her dart gun at the targets by the trees before she climbed them. When they reached the east side of her property that met back up to the river, she added throwing knives to her workout. One after the other, the knives flew into the targets – never missing.

He said, "Impressive. You are clearly accurate with your weapons."

"I work hard at it."

As they walked out of the trail by the river, he said, "Why the forest, Gabrielle? Of all the ways to workout, why this?"

"Where were we when you rescued me from Liam?"

And he understood. Liam used the forest as a place to kill her. She used it with reverse psychology. It was her safe place now.

***

Later, they relaxed on the swings. A nice breeze blew, and it was peaceful. Even the shepherd was stretched out in the shade taking a nap. Gabrielle thought, how crazy it was to know that danger stalked her. She glanced at Dakota. What if there hadn't been another case for him to protect her? Was their attraction simply circumstance? He was direct about his pursuit, yet, he hadn't reached out to her before now. What did that mean?

Meeting his gaze, she said, "You're obviously pursuing me. But what if there hadn't been another case involving me?"

Ah. He had expected that and pulled her swing against his. Slipping his hand behind her neck, he drew her lips to his. Hard and hot. He said, "I knew you were here. I've always known where you were. I bought the cabin six months ago. The case came up as I was packing to move here. It's always been you. Does that answer your question?"

She pulled his lips to hers. She had her answer.

***

Close to dusk, they drove into Lake Charles for a late dinner. They bought fried shrimp and oysters, coleslaw, and hushpuppies from Steamboat Bills and headed to the Civic Center seawall. They found an unoccupied bench by the lake, and ate, as seagulls begged for scraps of food. The south breeze blowing in from the Gulf of Mexico felt wonderful, and they watched as boats bobbed and swayed on the waves.

Dakota said, "It's easy to imagine Jean Lafitte on his pirate ship sailing right in here, isn't it?"

"Absolutely. Southern Louisiana in general is filled with waterways. The Gulf. Lakes. Rivers. Bayous. Canals. Swamps. No question of why he liked it here. But the southwest Louisiana from his time - known as No Man's Land – is now a thriving port and bustling cluster of cities."

He said, "Lafitte would be impressed. No doubt about it. He saw it way back then.

After eating, they walked to the seawall.

She said, "What about your ancestors, Dakota? I'm curious since I'm finding out about my own."

"The short version is, I'm a mix of the Dakota Sioux from Minnesota, with Spanish, French, and Norwegian mixed in."

She smiled, and said, "Obviously I see the Indian in your appearance. But not just that – it's the confident way you carry yourself. The calm authority you have. The way you move with your horse. The hunter and warrior in you. It's who you are."

He said, "You profiled me. And thank you."

"You mean, like you do at work?"

"Yes. I read people and situations. That's partly what you just did."

She said, "You're impressive, you know. I wish you could tell me who I really am."

Slipping his hand over hers, he said, "I think you'll find that out when you open the safety deposit box in the morning. But just to be clear, you already are, who you are. Tomorrow won't change that."

Chapter 8

Late that night on the sofa, Dakota held Gabrielle as she slept. He knew they were ready for the bank run in the morning. As for now, his gun was within easy reach and the dog lay next to them. Everything was quiet. He texted Sean to make sure all was well with surveillance and intel. Sean messaged back. Intel was silent. Surveillance was clear.

Dakota watched her sleep in the slivers of moonlight. It didn't take his profiler skills to figure out that in less than a week, he was crazy in love with her. No surprise really. Not after four years of keeping track of her. His heart had long been ready.

But tomorrow opened the door to a whole new reality for them. He knew that being on the run twenty-four hours a day in a dangerous, intense, and protective situation would send her emotions into a whirlwind.

He smiled. They both knew she was safe with him. To be scared. To need him. To sleep safe next to him. To touch him. To desire him. And to explore what she felt about him. One day soon, Gabrielle would be wild and free – as was her real nature. He had seen that in the forest. He would be waiting.

Hours later, Gabrielle heard their alarm go off. She opened her eyes and Dakota watched her in the early dawn.

He said softly, "Are you ready for this?"

"Only because you're with me."

"Get used to it. I'm not going anywhere."

They dressed, hurriedly downed a cup of coffee, grabbed their gear, and took off down the trail. As they rounded the last curve by the bridge, Sean and Adam were already waiting for them. Gabrielle sent her unhappy dog with Adam after a hug and kiss. Then Sean, Dakota, and Gabrielle headed east on Interstate 10 to Lafayette.

***

An hour and a half later, Sean pulled over a block away from Gulf Coast Savings & Loan. Dakota got out and walked toward the bank. Sean let Gabrielle out closer to the bank and parked across the street to watch and wait for them.

***

Gabrielle, disguised as a full-term pregnant woman with a messy bun and too much makeup, walked in the bank. She asked for the safety deposit box office and the security guard steered her to the vault. She handed a beautiful silver-haired woman with glasses her driver's license and the safety deposit box key.

The woman looked Gabrielle over carefully, then verified her identification and let her sign the signature card. Then she led her into the vault where, together, they unlocked the door to the box. Gabrielle removed the container and followed the woman to a private room.

Once she was alone, she stared at the box. Excited and scared. After a deep breath, she opened it and the only thing in the box was a Bible. It was aged black leather and not titled in English. She thought perhaps it was French. She picked it up and it was heavy. She opened the cover and flipped through the pages trying to see why it was so heavy. Toward the center, she found a large cavity cut out of the pages. Lying there was a black velvet pouch and plastic bag with documents inside.

Her heart pounded. The answers she sought were surely right here. Oh, God. She picked up the velvet pouch and carefully opened the fragile material. Inside was a large jewel encrusted medallion on a thick gold chain. She picked it up with both hands, incredulous at the jewels covering the medallion. Why was this in here for her? It had to be worth a fortune.

Then she picked up the plastic bag and took out a parchment document. It appeared to be an old letter written in a beautiful script in another language to a woman named Sabrina. It was dated 1814. She glanced down to see who wrote the letter, and although some of the first name was hard to read, there was no mistaking the last name of Lafitte.

She gasped, and her hands weren't quite steady as she glanced back to the top of the letter. Who was Sabrina? Without being able to read it, the only other words she was able to decipher were above Lafitte's signature, "je t'aime," which she knew said, *I love you* in French.

She looked on the back of the letter and there was a list of names and dates all written in English.

Firstborn Descendants of Jean Lafitte & Sabrina Trosclair:

Daughter:	*Chantel*	*Dec 1814*
Granddaughter:	*Sophie*	*June 1835*
Grandson:	*Joseph*	*Oct 1855*
Granddaughter:	*Angel*	*Jan 1895*
Granddaughter:	*Nanette*	*Aug 1920*
Grandson:	*Jacque*	*Feb 1945*
Granddaughter:	*Serena*	*Mar 1971*
Granddaughter:	*Gabrielle*	*May 1994*

Stunned, Gabrielle stared at her name, and obviously her mother's. Serena. That was the name on the note her adoptive parents had. Then her phone beeped. She checked and it was Dakota. She put everything back in the Bible, hid it in her bag and headed out of the vault.

She attempted to smile at the silver-haired lady, and said, "Thank you so much," and headed straight for the restroom.

She glanced across the lobby at Dakota in his old man disguise as he appeared to fuss with someone on the phone about a ride. He nodded at her and walked out the entrance.

Gabrielle locked the stall door in the bathroom and changed into leggings and a sport top. After tying a jacket around her hips, she put her hair in a ponytail with a cap and cleaned all the makeup off her face. In minutes she walked out of the bathroom with a backpack looking like she was headed to the gym.

Once she got on the sidewalk, she faked a phone conversation and crossed the street headed to the El Paso Mexican Grill. She dropped a large bag in an outdoor trashcan as she passed by. Dakota wasn't far behind her.

She entered the grill and asked for a table for one and the restroom. Again, she went in the restroom, locked the door, and changed. This time she slipped on scrubs and put her hair in a bun. She heard Dakota in the restaurant asking for directions to the restroom.

Then she simply walked out of the bathroom, through the back exit door, and climbed into the rear seat of Sean's pickup. She slid down to hide. Shortly, the passenger door opened, and Dakota got in. Sean drove out onto the highway and took a different route home.

Once they were away from the area, Dakota said, "What was in it?"

Gabrielle sat up and pulled the Bible out of her backpack and handed it to him.

He could tell she was shaken, and said, "Are you okay?"

"Yes, just shocked. Flip through the Bible. There's a hiding place inside."

She watched their faces as they found the cavity. Dakota whistled as he opened the pouch and lifted out the medallion.

He glanced at them and said, "This is the real deal. It looks like something royalty would have worn."

She nodded and said, "Look under the pouch for the documents. I only had time to look at the parchment. I need to see the white one."

He handed her the white paper, and she said, "Go ahead and look at the parchment. I will wait."

Carefully, he opened the antique paper, and said, "It seems to be French like the Bible. A letter." Then he saw the signature, and said, "It's almost unbelievable."

"I know. It's shocking to know that Jean Lafitte himself wrote it. Now, look on the back."

He turned it over and saw the names and dates listed of their descendants. He saw Gabrielle's name, and the name Serena.

He looked at her and said, "Gabrielle—" and stopped. He motioned for Sean to pull off the road and turned to her.

Tears trickled down her face as she said, "I finally know who I am. At least on my mother's side of the family – even though I don't know what my last name is. But I certainly understand now why Serena said in the note it wasn't safe to keep me."

Dakota said, "Your Mother loved and protected you. And Lafitte obviously loved Sabrina."

Sean said, "I can run the letter through a French translation application as soon as we have a chance."

"Thank you," she said, "I sure hope this last letter will explain everything." She read the letter out loud.

Gabrielle,

My girl. I knew one day you would look for answers about your birth family. I prepared this for you. Our story is long.

Jean Lafitte and Sabrina Trosclair, our grandparents, met in Lake Charles in the early 1800s. Back then, southwest Louisiana was an ungoverned place filled with lawlessness, piracy, privateers, and people seeking a new chance at life. The land was wild, mysterious, and beautiful. Perfect to hide treasure.

Although Jean was an infamous pirate, he was handsome. Gallant. Bold. Sabrina was a seventeen-year-old auburn-haired beauty visiting her cousins to help with their children. They met and the attraction was immediate. After several secret weeks, they found out she was pregnant. They both knew her family would not welcome her home.

Jean was aware his life was far too dangerous on board a ship for a woman and child. But he knew that even if she stayed behind, she wouldn't be safe if their relationship was discovered. Dangerous men would be after them for his buried treasures. Always. She would never be safe because of him.

So, he came up with a plan. He wrote her a letter confirming their relationship. Gave her a treasure map. Included a medallion from the treasure chest as proof. Made provisions for her financially. And hid the paperwork and medallion within his mother's Bible. He was determined to prove to Sabrina that one day their descendants could claim their legacy.

The buried treasure was a valuable gift from Napoleon Bonaparte for friendship and support during his reign. Jean and a close Atakapa friend of his, named Wolf, had hidden the treasure on the Calcasieu River, far away from his usual hiding places.

Sabrina disappeared one day after Jean left on his ship, and no one in Lake Charles ever knew what became of her. She settled in Lafayette, changed her name, and gave birth to a daughter, named Chantel. The old Atakapa warrior, Wolf, stayed with her.

When Chantel came of age, she was told the secret of her birth father – and the danger if she exposed her family identity. Chantel signed the back of the letter and hid the Bible with the map, medallion, and letter.

You can see through the list of descendants that Jean and Sabrina's legacy has survived. My father, your grandfather, is Jacque. After he came of age and learned the secret, he went to Lake Charles and bought land on the Calcasieu River. He built a two-story Acadian home on piers. Once he and my mother married, and I was born, we used it as our vacation home.

When I came of age, my father told me the secret and gave me the Bible. Then I met Trent, your father. He was a native of Lake Charles and a good man, Gabrielle. He worked offshore on oil rigs. But then he fell in with a group of offshore guys fascinated with Lafitte treasure stories. Your father became obsessed with it to the exclusion of all else.

Unfortunately, this is where I made a fatal mistake. I thought if your father knew the truth of my ancestry, it would satisfy him to know he was married to Jean Lafitte's granddaughter. I told him about the letter. He promised to keep the secret so we would be safe. It never occurred to me he wouldn't heed my warning.

A few nights after I told him, he confessed that he had told his new treasure friend. They planned to work with me to figure out where to search for treasure. Devastated and afraid, like our grandmother, Sabrina, I had to disappear. Only this time, I had to hide you too. The next morning, I went to my dad's vacation house and hid the treasure map in an oak tree on the property you now own. Then I went to Gulf Coast Savings & Loan in Lafayette and put the Bible in a safety deposit box. I broke my heart and brought you to a church and left you for the Sawyers. I had learned of their recent loss of a child from my church. I changed my name and disappeared once you were with them.

A week after I was gone, I read an article from a Lake Charles paper about the shooting death of your father along the English Bayou.

I am sorry Gabrielle. I will always keep track of you.

Your house sits on five acres. There is a live oak in the center of the property with a deep crevasse under the arm of a branch. Your grandfather Jean's treasure map is inside a sealed waterproof bag. This is our legacy from him. Stay safe.

I love you.

Your mother,

Serena

The tears stopped as Gabrielle read her mother's words. Now she felt the strength of the woman who had protected her, and said, "Let's go find what she hid. This is what the Posse is after."

Dakota said, "Yes, it is. And unfortunately, Sean received a text from an FBI friend warning us of Lafitte treasure activity on the DNA website. There is no more waiting – we must find it and get you out of here."

As Sean got back on the road to Lake Charles, Gabrielle said, "Dakota, do you think I can find my mother one day?"

"I do. We'll get our researchers on it as soon as you are safe."

After thinking over all she had learned, Gabrielle said, "When I found out about my bloodline, I researched to learn more about treasure hunts in general. I always wondered why people buried it in the first place. It just seemed odd.

Then I learned that treasure hunts happen all over the world. There were no banks in those days, so people buried and hid their money and valuables. I guess I never thought of needing a safe place to put it. I also learned in the news, that after Hurricane Katrina hit New Orleans, treasure was found in an oak tree that had blown over.

"And look at Lake Charles. They keep the Pirate Jean Lafitte story alive because it is such a big part of our local history. Even the Interstate 10 bridge has Jean Lafitte pistols as part of the railing. So, what this makes me realize is that the secret needs to be over. We need to nationalize it, sensationalize it, and bring out the love story. Then, if we find the treasure there would be no reason for scavengers to come after me or my family. We can donate it to worthy causes, museums or whatever is best. Then it is over."

Dakota said, "Like I said before, you are good at strategy. That's a great idea. A smart one."

He reached back and held her hand, and said, "And you are right. This is the last time you and your family need to run and hide. This time we set a trap for the Posse."

***

Back on the river, Sean stopped the truck by Gabrielle's property line and said, "Text me when you find the map. And hurry!"

Dakota ran with Gabrielle along the trail. After reaching the first oak in the area her mother mentioned, they walked around the tree looking up at the massive branches for a crevasse. Not seeing one, Gabrielle climbed up and gave it a closer look. No crevasse. She climbed down, and they ran for the next oak tree. And high underneath one of the fern-covered branches closer to the trunk of the tree, she found an opening.

She said, "I found one!"

He climbed up to meet her. The hole wasn't wide, but it appeared deep. She grimaced and hoped there were no snakes, bees, or anything else with teeth or stingers in the hole and slipped her hand inside. She dug around in leaves and other natural debris and pushed further in. She felt a large object and pulled it out.

They climbed out of the tree and knelt on the ground and carefully opened the cowhide bundle sealed in a plastic bag. She glanced at Dakota with a smile, and he nodded. She removed the leather and rolled it open. She lovingly spread out the treasure map and looked at what her grandfather had drawn. This was the real measure of love he had proved to Sabrina, and to each one of his descendants.

Dakota pointed to a large lake at the bottom of the map with a river called Crying Eagle that traveled north before it branched west, then later branched east, but still the arrows followed the main winding river headed north. Eventually the arrows reached a straighter stretch of the river where the arrows traveled inland.

Gabrielle said, "Crying Eagle means Calcasieu. The branch to the west must be the West Fork of the Calcasieu River. The branch to the east has to be the English Bayou. And I hate to tell you, but I really don't know all the landscape along the Calcasieu River."

He said, "Ok. So, why don't we just focus on the land where the arrows end for now. Then we'll backtrack if we need to."

She looked where the arrow crossed a flat bank with a hill in the forest behind it. Once the arrow left the river, it veered left into an area where a group of large trees were drawn. Specifically, to a couple of trees with a stream of some kind going between them. The arrow led to one tree with a large heart drawn with the initials JL and ST. And that was all the arrows showed. The bottom of the map was signed, Jean Lafitte.

Concentrating on the landscape pictured, Gabrielle noticed the map also showed the land across the river from the arrows. It had hills, trees, and a high bluff. She ran her finger along the flat bank on one side, then the bluff on the other side. Then it dawned on her what she saw every day from her deck.

With a whisper, she said, "Dakota." He looked at her.

"This is a map to my house. The treasure is here."

***

Dakota texted Sean: Treasure is here. Need more time.

***

Looking at the map now with awareness of the layout of her land, Gabrielle said, "I know where those two oaks by the gully are - come on."

They were sweaty and breathless by the time they reached the area. Hurriedly they searched the first tree trunk for the carved heart and initials but didn't find anything. They crossed the gully to the other tree.

Dakota found a groove around the back of the tree, and said, "I've got it."

They followed the groove till the heart was evident. The initials were harder to find, but they found them. Gabrielle leaned her head against the carved heart and fought tears.

With quivering lips, she said, "Jean Lafitte stood here and carved their initials over two hundred years ago. It's almost unfathomable."

Dakota said, "It is. And I know it's a lot to think about, but we have to leave. Come on. Rub dirt and leaves over it. Throw branches around the base of the tree like no one was here. I've got to get you away from this river by dusk. The Posse will be coming for you."

***

Dakota texted Sean: Found treasure. Be there in twenty minutes.

***

They met Sean on the back road and jumped in his truck.

He floored it and said, "Tell me."

Gabrielle said, "The treasure is hidden in a tree on my land. Serena didn't mention that. I have no idea how my family owned this particular piece of land, but there it is."

***

Just before dark, all surveillance equipment was removed from the log cabin and loaded in Sean's vehicle. The cameras and security feed around both properties remained. Dakota and Gabrielle's go-bags and gear were packed on the stallion. Dakota was armed with his Glock, knife, and rifle. Gabrielle wore her weapon belt with dart gun, Glock, and throwing knives – with her hunting knife strapped around her calf.

Dakota cinched and checked the saddle, then boosted Gabrielle up. He mounted behind her and said, "Sean, we're out of here. The trackers are in our boots so keep an eye on us. Text with updates."

Sean said, "I'll be watching. Text or call if you need help."

Dakota led the stallion northeast into the woods and in moments they were swallowed up in the pending darkness and surrounding trees. He heard Sean start his truck and leave. They were on their own.

He put his arm around Gabrielle's waist, making sure she was snug in the saddle, then said, "Are you ok?"

"Oh, yes. I'm totally fine. Just heading into the unknown with FBI on horseback. Killers after me. A grandfather that was a pirate. And buried treasure in my yard."

Dakota chuckled, and said, "Atta girl."

He planned to travel a few hours till they were away from people and technology before they stopped for the night. Trace had told him of an old homestead that a tornado took out several years ago, but the barn was partially standing. There was a dirt road that would lead them there. Till then, it was just forest, hills, streams, moonlight, and them.

Gabrielle felt safe in the saddle with Dakota. That was it. Outside the saddle, her life had crumbled. Again. But she came from a brave bloodline as it turned out. She could do this. And she had the knives and training to prove it this time.

Chapter 9

Back in Lafayette, Serena reflected on when Gabrielle walked into the bank today. Something had obviously been wrong to bring her there in disguise. But as a bank employee, she had simply led her into the safety deposit box area. It had been such irony to lead her daughter to the box she had put there for her years ago.

After Gabrielle exited the vault, with shock still evident, Serena had watched her enter the restroom. But then she exited in a different disguise and left the bank. Serena followed her out the front door. She watched an old man trail behind her on the sidewalk. They both headed across the street to El Paso. They were together.

Serena went back in the bank to get permission to leave for the day. Only she knew that she would never return. It was time to head to the river. She knew where Gabrielle lived, worked, and went to church. Even knew of her friends. She most certainly knew of the kidnapping after she had graduated college.

In moments she headed home to pack.

***

It was close to eleven p.m. when Serena knocked on the door in Moss Bluff. She glanced around. Although this place was private, she didn't want to be seen and had parked her car behind the garage. A light came on and the door opened. A tall, handsome man with salt n pepper hair gave her a wide smile.

She said, "Hi, Daddy."

He said, "Hi, honey," and she walked into his open arms.

Then she felt her mother's sweet arms wrap around her, as she said, "Aw, Serena. Are you okay?"

"No, Gabrielle is in trouble. I am positive it is Lafitte related."

Worried, her parents exclaimed, "Oh no!"

"I think she is on the run, but someone is helping her."

They sat at the kitchen table as her mom made coffee.

Her Dad said, "Tell us about it. What can we do?"

Serena removed her glasses to rub her face, and her mom said, "Take off that awful wig."

Serena grinned and took off the silver wig. Dark brown hair fell to her shoulders, and she rubbed her head. Then getting a case out of her purse, she popped out the blue contacts she had worn in disguise.

Seeing her beautiful amber eyes again, her mom said, "Thank goodness!"

Serena jumped right into her concern, and said, "Gabrielle came to the bank today and got the Bible and letters. By now she surely has the map. Whoever is after her, will want that. I need to find out more about who is helping her. The only new person around her that I know of, is a man named Dakota Nash. He bought the log cabin from me about six months ago."

Her parents raised their eyebrows in surprise.

She said, "I know. I was surprised with his offer, but his background check revealed that he was a semi-retired FBI agent and an author. He said he wanted to locate to Louisiana and loved the cabin's secluded location. And I liked him. He was direct, polite, and intelligent. I don't like her out there all alone and I do have plans to keep an eye on them from a distance."

Her Dad said, "We met him at church yesterday with Gabrielle and her friends. It was just a brief hello, but he seemed like a nice guy."

"He is a handsome man and I feel sure he has some Native American blood in him. But back to Gabrielle, I am going to peek around at the log cabin and her house tomorrow and see what I can find out. I will be in disguise as usual. If I need my rifle or crossbow, I have them with me. If I expect trouble for her, I may find a sniper spot and wait."

"Serena…"

"Dad, they killed Trent. I must do what I can for Gabrielle. I will be careful. Mom, will you call grandpa and give him a head's up?"

"I will call him, but you need to expect that he will want to be in on this. He wants his family home and safe. He has had enough of this treasure…mess, let's say. I can't repeat what he calls it."

Chapter 10

After midnight at Sean's loft in downtown Lake Charles, an alarm went off on the surveillance equipment watching Gabrielle's property. He checked his computer. A vehicle drove down her driveway, then veered into the woods, and parked. Four men got out.

Sean turned on the thermal solar cameras hidden around the property and watched the men head through the woods toward the house. The perimeter motion lights came on as the first guy stepped out of the woods. He froze and stepped back behind a tree. In five minutes, the motion lights went out. The guys split up and shot out all the perimeter lights – without any detectible sound. They used silencers. These men weren't new at the game.

Sean watched as they walked across the yard and met at the base of the stairs. The cameras caught moonlight images. One muscular guy appeared to be the boss. He pointed and one guy headed across the patio. The motion lights activated, and he shot out the lights. He stopped at the electric box and killed the power. The house went dark.

Sean said a quick thank you that Dakota and Gabrielle were not there. He would text Dakota once he knew what these guys were up to.

They headed upstairs and broke in. The cameras in and around the house recorded the guys using flashlights to tear the place apart as they searched. He knew they looked for the treasure or the treasure map.

Unsuccessful, they went downstairs and looked around. Eventually one of the guys pointed to the log cabin across the river and they headed down the hill. Sean knew that Gabrielle kept a couple of old canoes on the ground by the cypress trees. The intruders found them and paddled across the river to Dakota's dock.

The cameras at the cabin picked up the men and activated Sean's alarm at Dakota's house. They killed the power there too and broke in the back door. They searched the cabin and made a huge mess. Dakota's office drew most of their attention, but they left his room empty-handed. After grabbing food from the kitchen, they headed to the patio.

A few minutes later, two of the men went to the barn. The other two men looked around the property. After not finding anything, they headed closer to the edge of the woods. Sean tensed as they reached the spot where Dakota and Gabrielle entered on horseback. The guys walked into the woods. Then the two men in the barn came running to join them. He could see their lights searching further back into the woods.

With a groan, he knew they suspected something. When they came out of the woods, the muscular man got on his phone.

***

Several miles away, Dakota and Gabrielle had just laid down in the tornado damaged barn for the night when Dakota's phone vibrated with a text.

Sean to Dakota: Intruders. Both houses searched. They found your trail. Leader made a call.

Dakota replied: Check FBI staff to see if anyone got that call.

Sean replied: I'm on it.

Dakota replied: We will leave for camp two – can't stay here – too close.

***

Dakota told Gabrielle what happened, and shaken, she said, "What do we do now?"

"We need to get further away. I hoped that we could rest here tonight but we need a bigger lead. They can't drive road vehicles in these woods, but they may try four-wheelers. We'll need to move faster. The next safe spot is a small deck built up in a tree with a lean-to. It is another two hours or more, due north of here. Trace uses it. You sore from riding?"

She winced and said, "Yeah, but I'm good."

"Ok. You might want to grab something to eat or drink and go to the bathroom. I want to leave in ten minutes."

About an hour later, Gabrielle tried to arch her back to loosen the strain on her muscles as the stallion moved through the forest.

Dakota said, "We can take a minute, if you want to stop and walk a bit."

"Please."

He led the stallion underneath a large canopy of trees and dismounted. He lifted her off and when her feet hit the ground, she moaned. Her muscles were not happy.

He said, "Long distance riding takes getting used to. If you work a few yoga stretches, it will help you."

"I never dreamed I would get so sore just riding."

"It's from keeping your legs stretched for long periods of time. It pulls."

She said, "I feel that. Where do you think we are?"

"Not quite halfway to camp two. I haven't heard any motors or any suspicious noises, so I think we are isolated – which is our goal."

Gabrielle jogged in place and did yoga stretches. Dakota tended to the horse and let him loose to nibble grass. He walked around a bit to loosen his muscles, then texted Sean.

***

Dakota to Sean: Updates?

Sean replied: Waiting on phone records. Dark web heavy with Lafitte treasure talk. Samantha will meet in Lake Charles with D.A. tomorrow on the case. We need help.

Dakota replied: Great. Director still hasn't called me. Not a good sign.

Sean replied: No.

***

Dakota was about fifteen feet from Gabrielle when the horse panicked, and reared. Dakota heard the growl and spun. Glowing eyes were behind Gabrielle, and he darted toward her. Gabrielle spun and pulled her gun. She shot the coyote just as Dakota yanked her back and kicked the animal in the neck.

The coyote howled from the blow and flew against a tree. Growling, it stood, then shook its head, staggered, and after a couple of weak steps, dropped to the ground.

Still holding Gabrielle with one hand, and his gun with the other, Dakota said, "I don't see blood. Did you shoot? I didn't hear it."

"I used my dart gun. It will put to sleep anything from one to three hundred pounds in about fifteen seconds – and he is smaller than that. I hate to kill an animal if I don't have to."

Dakota said, "Well, I wasn't going to give him an option. But I couldn't shoot with you in my line of fire. You had already turned to respond. You're quick. Like a cat."

She grinned and said, "I like that. Especially when I think of your cat."

He chuckled and rubbed her back. He asked, "Did I hurt you when I jerked you out of the way?"

"Nope. I'm fine. I'm a tough cat."

He smiled, and said, "Go ahead and take a quick break. We will head out soon. We have a treehouse that I look forward to sleeping in soon."

***

Just after two a.m., Dakota sighed in relief as he saw the massive tree loom ahead of them in the moonlight. It had been a long ride. Gabrielle had fallen asleep against him long ago.

He whispered in her ear, "Hey, Cat, we're here."

She sat up with a yawn to look around. Then seeing the tree outlined by the moon, she said, "Now that's a terrific place to hide."

He agreed, dismounted, and helped her down. She groaned, then stretched to loosen her cramped muscles. Dakota aimed his flashlight up through the tree until he found the wooden deck with a lean-to. He unsaddled the stallion and hid him in the trees. They grabbed their gear and began to climb.

Inside the lean-to, they lined their gear against the tree, and he said, "You lay next to the bags, and I will lay on the outside of you."

Gabrielle gratefully laid down. It felt wonderful to be flat - even on hard boards. She sighed in relief and rolled to face him, watching him in the light of his phone.

Dakota checked for messages. None. He sent one.

***

Dakota to Sean: At camp two. Down for the night.

***

After putting his phone away, he rolled to face her and slipped his arm under her head to bring her close. Barely able to see her in the filtered moonlight, he said, "You ok?"

"Yeah. And thanks…Dakota."

"For what?"

"For being amazing and keeping me safe."

He slid his hand down her back, and said, "Make no mistake, Gabrielle, you are important to me."

"Why?"

"It's who you are."

"What do you mean? Who am I?"

He lowered his head, whispering, "Made for me," and his mouth claimed hers.

***

In Moss Bluff, Serena woke early and smelled coffee. She heard her parents in the kitchen and smiled. For many years, she had lived hidden away from them, but in time they found a way to see each other.

There had been painful loneliness after Trent's murder and Gabrielle's adoption. It had been hard to live alone, hide her identity, and try to make a life. As time passed, she focused on self-defense training and learned to become an excellent markswoman. As for her job at the bank, she had made sweet friends that didn't even know who she really was. Even her Lafayette church family hadn't a clue. But having to hide to see her parents and ache longingly for Gabrielle every single day was the worst struggle.

She had worked all these years in the vault just for the day Gabrielle would walk into her life again. All this time she had dreamed of a safe life that included her daughter and grandchildren. Those were the treasures she dreamed of. Never buried treasure.

Several hours later, in disguise, Serena headed to Gabrielle's house on the river.

***

Hidden in the oak tree, Gabrielle's eyes flew open. Someone was singing. It was barely dawn and Dakota put a finger across his lips to tell her to be silent. She nodded. He looked out the lean-to into the forest below. In a few moments, he saw movement through the trees, and a man strolled through the woods alone. Singing.

Dakota watched as he drew closer to their location. The guy didn't appear threatening, but he couldn't tell yet if he had weapons. Gabrielle sat up next to him and he pointed out the man headed their way. Then he eased out of the lean-to and climbed onto a limb to have a better view.

The guy stopped under the canopy of their tree and squatted to check his boot. He was a big guy, older, but in great shape. He had long salt and pepper hair with a beard. He was dressed in short sleeves with arms covered in tattoos. A large hunting knife hung from his belt.

Dakota picked up his gun, glanced at Gabrielle, and she slipped a few throwing knives in the pouch on her waistband. Suddenly the stallion snorted and screamed in panic. The man's singing ended abruptly. He stood and walked around the back of the tree.

***

The guy said in a soothing voice to the terrified horse, "Hey there big fella. It's ok. What brought you out here?" Then he saw the riding gear on the ground.

Someone was here, so he called out, "I don't want trouble. I'm just taking a stroll. I'm no threat to you."

Dakota dropped to the ground behind him, and the man spun. Dakota held out his hand, and said, "Easy there. We are just passing through."

"We?"

Dakota pointed to Gabrielle standing nearby on a huge limb.

Surprised at the agile woman in the tree, he said, "You're like a cat up there," and Gabrielle grinned. She kept hearing that.

The horse reared again, clearly upset. Dakota and the guy neared the horse as Gabrielle climbed to a closer limb.

She said, "It's a snake," and pulled out one of her throwing knives. Dakota drew the stallion away and both men watched Gabrielle throw the small blade.

The tattooed man glanced at the dead snake and back at the woman in the tree. He said, "It doesn't get more bullseye than that. You're good." Then he turned to Dakota and said, "I'm Jimmy by-the-way. I live several miles west of here."

"I'm Dakota and you can call her Cat."

Gabrielle joined them, and said, "Hi Jimmy. And your tats are amazing. How many do you have?"

He laughed, looking at his arms, and said, "More than I can count or see. I'm a veteran and spent money on tattoos instead of liquor while I was on active duty."

She walked closer to see them and said, "The colors are terrific. And speaking of color, has anyone told you that your eyes are a fabulous shade of blue?"

He grinned and said, "As a matter of fact, I've heard that a time or two. And since you are interested in tats, do you have any?"

"Actually, I do."

Dakota grinned. She never ceased to surprise him.

She continued, "I was burned a few years ago, and a friend tattooed some of my artwork over my scars. Now my scars tell a different story."

Dakota knew immediately she referenced the branding wounds. Jimmy didn't have any idea but both men understood there was more to the story.

Jimmy nodded as he met her gaze, then looked at Dakota, and said, "Is there anything I can help you with as you pass through?"

Dakota realized Jimmy picked up on an unexplained problem, and said, "You've got good instinct, Jimmy. There are four killers after her. We aim to stay off-grid for a few days. If you run across anyone asking about us, feel free to send them in a different direction. And keep some protection on you. They aren't friendly."

"I'll keep an eye out. Do you need anything else?"

"No, but it's possible we might show up here again."

Jimmy nodded and said, "You need to know there's a bad dude that runs around these woods in a beat-up red pickup. I've heard some bad tales and your lady wouldn't fare well with him. He should have been behind bars or under the dirt long ago." Then he pointed to the horse and said, "It's hard to hide with that stallion. If you need help hiding him, call me." Dakota saved his cell number.

Jimmy continued on his way, singing again.

In less than thirty minutes, Dakota and Gabrielle were ready to go. He watched as she took her knife out of the snake, wiped it off, winked at him, then climbed back in the saddle. What a woman.

***

Back in Lake Charles, Sean reeled from shock. Only one individual from FBI personnel received the phone call from the man behind Dakota's cabin last night. Director Reynolds. Their boss. The one who personally chose them for this mission.

Sean's mind spun with the possibilities to this connection. He needed to check the boss and his family's phone records. No telling how long this had been going on, and with six people dead, it was incredulous what his participation might have been. This deception had to be personal. No way would he have risked his career or prison for less. Dakota was going to be livid at the betrayal and intentional targeting of them and Gabrielle. And livid put it mildly. Furious. Enraged. Deadly, was a better fit.

Sean messaged his private FBI contact to dive into Serena's murdered husband's history. It was unbelievable that no one put together that Gabrielle was the missing child, of the missing wife, of the last Posse victim - Trent.

Serena had done an excellent job covering their trail. But he needed her husband's history before Samantha met with the District Attorney in Lake Charles this afternoon. This situation had ballooned into a monster scenario. Treasure serial killers. Dirty FBI director. Attempted murder of a missing child and two FBI agents. They needed help.

Shoulders tense, Sean walked to the window and looked out over the beautiful lake to clear his mind for a minute. Then an alarm on the surveillance cameras at Gabrielle's house went off. He watched on his computer as a truck pulled into Gabrielle's driveway and parked at the house. Gabrielle's SUV was there, so they wouldn't know she wasn't home.

A tall slim lady got out of the truck. She had shoulder length silver hair and glasses. She walked up the stairs and knocked on the door. After a few moments, she looked through the windows and gasped. He knew the mess the men made searching the house last night would have alarmed her. She looked in all the windows, then headed downstairs and just sat quietly on the patio.

He frowned. What an unusual response. What was she waiting for? He would watch her.

About an hour later, she returned to her truck and grabbed an ice chest and headed down the hill closer to the river. She spread out a mat and made herself comfortable. Sean wondered if Gabrielle had an appointment with her today. He messaged Dakota about their boss while he kept an eye on her.

***

Sean to Dakota: Director got the call from the intruders last night.
Dakota replied: I'm going to kill him.
Sean replied: I get it. We'll trap him. Stay out of sight.

***

Gabrielle felt Dakota grab his vibrating phone. A moment later he growled, and his arm tightened around her. Something was wrong. Terribly wrong.

Silently, she said, "Jesus…"

She waited a minute to see if he would explain, then said, "Dakota?"

"We'll talk about it later. I need to think. Everything is okay."

Chapter 11

In the FBI parking lot, Director Reynolds growled into his phone, "Have you lost your mind? You have to play it smarter than that. Someone could have called the police. Don't make yourself conspicuous, use some stealth for heaven's sake. Now study your maps and make your plan. If Gabrielle is on horseback with Dakota, it is harder to hide. Learn the area and try to figure out where they might be headed.

"And calm down! I mean it. You have enough dead bodies under your belt. The treasure isn't going anywhere. Do something smart for a change. And if I hear your voice again today, I might just kill you myself."

The Director dropped the phone on the car seat and sighed. He was sick of this. Of them. This wasn't what he envisioned for his future with the FBI. He rubbed his forehead. They always gave him a headache, and now he had an ulcer. He popped another Pepcid.

He'd already made the only decision left open to him and pieces were falling into place. But some days, like today, his stomach tortured him. He hated that Gabrielle had gotten involved. Like she hadn't been through enough with Liam. Now this DNA disaster. He even hated the word treasure now.

Her situation was a worst-case scenario for him. Of course, he knew Dakota would defend her to the death. And he was one smart, tough agent. He ought to know. He mentored him – and his brother, Sean. His favorites. But to cut himself lose from this and make it believable to the FBI, he would have to sacrifice all of them, including – no, especially, his nephew, Ryan. The addicted idiot. He'd caused it all.

He sighed and watched men he respected head to their cars for lunch. He knew they would kill him on the spot if they knew what he had done. They didn't realize of course that one of the Posse - was one of the FBI.

He lowered his dark tinted window, and spit. That's what he thought of that. And that's why he had called this play. He refused to care. Let the bodies fall. Life would continue. His. After all, that's what this was all about.

Chapter 12

Ryan maneuvered the small aluminum boat down a cut off the West Fork. He was still furious about his phone call with his uncle earlier. If he hadn't needed that old man, he'd have been six feet under a long time ago.

He killed the 30-horsepower engine and coasted deeper into the cut. Without much movement, he laid his pistol on his thigh and sat still until the boat stopped moving. Surely some unfortunate critter would make itself a target. The splatter of blood always gave him relief.

A couple of minutes later, he noticed a small alligator watching him. Eyes above the water, naturally camouflaged like a log, it barely moved through a few lily pads. He wondered how close the stupid gator would come to the boat - and patiently watched and waited like the predator he was.

Birds twittered in the trees. Fish splashed as they jumped in the water behind him. Bees buzzed and darted looking for more flowers – bodies already caked with pollen. But Ryan didn't notice. He just sat still and watched the gator as his finger caressed the trigger.

A few humid minutes later, sweat dripped down Ryan's forehead. Still, he sat and watched the large eyes sticking out of the water. Then for some reason, the gator moved out of the lily pads and swam straight for the boat - rising further out of the water. Ryan figured it was a three-footer. Too bad it would never be a four – and raised the pistol. He shot it in the brain.

He smiled and wiped the sweat off his face. Yes, that was it. He felt much better already. Now, where was Gabrielle?

Chapter 13

After the message from Sean about their boss, Dakota rode quietly until the fury eased off. He glanced at Gabrielle swaying in the saddle in front of him. Besides loving her, he admired her. She was tough. They had ridden for hours last night, slept in a tree, and jumped back in the saddle after meeting Jimmy this morning. They had barely talked face-to-face since they left his cabin at dusk yesterday.

He said, "How about a quick break?"

"My hero," she said.

They neared a bend in a gully, and Dakota stopped close to a group of pine trees. He jumped down and helped her dismount. But he didn't let go of her. His hands spread across her back, and he pulled her closer.

Gabrielle looked in his eyes, thinking, we are in the middle of nowhere. On the run. And all I want is for him to kiss me. Now. His lips took hers, abrupt, and hot.

Several breathless minutes later, she said, "You still have to tell me."

He looked at her but didn't answer.

"Dakota."

Bluntly, he said, "The phone call that the intruders made last night from my house, was traced to my boss at the FBI."

"Oh, so he knows who's leaking the information?"

"No. He's the leak."

Shocked, she said, "What? No, no, that can't be right. He knows me. Helped me. What about y'all? Why would he do this to all of us?"

"I understand. I do. It wouldn't have been good for the leak to be anyone from the FBI, but to have it be him, is a vicious betrayal. That's why the Posse hasn't been caught all these years. He's passed all the intelligence and helped them hide evidence, obviously. He set us up. But he will pay, I assure you."

He heard the silence and looked at her.

Her amber eyes were fixed on him. Angry. Determined. She said, "Whatever it takes, we have to stop him."

"It's going to end. And so is he." Then he looked around, and said, "Come on, let's shake it off, we need the break."

He led the stallion to the gully, while Gabrielle stretched. Her muscles had finally adapted to the endless riding, but it still felt good to move around. She watched Dakota. Running his hands over the horse. Bending over – tight muscles showing. Walking around – strong long legs. What a body. And he moved so smooth. Fluid. She knew he had to be a good dancer. A sexy one too.

He glanced up and caught her staring. She blushed. Guilty.

With a sexy grin, he said, "Now what caused that look?"

She shrugged and looked away. She didn't answer him.

He studied her with a smile, as he strolled back toward her. He said, "Tell me what put that look on your face. Or would you rather me tell you?"

She put her hands on her hips, and with an attitude she said, "You don't know."

He ran his finger over her lips, and said, "What did my body make you think about, Cat?"

Bullseye. Her eyes widened. New pink cheeks. Flustered. She fumbled the words, "Your body…your legs…I…I just wondered if you were a good dance—"

And he interrupted by lifting her arms around his neck, then sliding his arms around her waist. He said, "Why don't we find out?"

And he danced with her. Right there in the forest, he moved smooth and sexy to a beat only their bodies knew. Her heart opened and he stepped right in. And stayed. She felt the wonder. The thrill. Love for him flooded her.

Dakota groaned softly at the way they fit together. Loved the way she made him feel alive, hungry, and wild. Their chemistry was powerful. He finally slowed the dance to a stop and lowered his lips to hers.

And the sound of engines in the distance startled them. Coming from the left, they were moving fast. Dakota pulled Gabrielle toward the horse, and they mounted in a second. He looked around, deciding on the best direction to go, then headed into the gully since it wasn't deep. The Posse wouldn't be able to track them in the water. He could tell it was several engines and voices. That wasn't good and he pushed the stallion faster.

They rode east for an hour or so, then found a rocky path to climb out of the gully near a gravel road. They didn't see anyone, crossed the road, and went into the woods again. They stayed riding in thick brush for another long while, then stopped to get their bearing.

He said, "Cat?"

"Yeah. Do you think we lost them?"

"At least for now. I need to message Sean to run the tracker and see where we are."

In seconds, Sean sent a picture of their location. Dakota noted they needed to cross Highway 190 near Reeves soon. He texted Adam.

***

Dakota to Adam: Come get the stallion near Reeves.
Adam replied: Trace and Zoe will be with me. One hour.
Dakota replied: Text when close.

***

Dakota said, "We need to cross a main highway up ahead but it's too hard to hide the horse. Adam, Trace, and Zoe will be here in an hour to get him. We need to hide till then."

He pointed toward a pond in the distance next to a large grove of trees. After they got there, and dismounted, Gabrielle was quiet.

He knew it had been a close call with the four-wheelers, and said, "Come on. Talk to me. What's on your mind."

She looked at him for a moment, then said, "Have you ever killed anyone?"

Without explanation, he said, "Yes."

"Is it difficult to get past?"

"Sometimes. There are different scenarios. Self-defense. War. Criminals. Protecting others. It's all about saving innocent people from the evil that men do. It's not easy. It's necessary. And sometimes, yes, I do have to pray more than others when it's over."

She said, "Do you think I would kill someone?"

"To protect another person, or to survive, yes. Do you think you would?"

"I would. I would rather not, but I would."

He said, "That's why you trained. To be prepared."

She nodded, then said, "The posse is getting closer. People will die right in front of us."

"Yes, they will."

He rubbed her shoulders and said, "I'm going to climb this oak and scope around. Climb with me."

"No. Go ahead. I'll walk to the pond for a moment."

He climbed the large oak till he could at least see full circle around them. There was a lot of brush, trees, and a few broken down sheds. As he turned back toward the pond, he caught a glimpse of red behind some trees. He lifted his binoculars. It was a red pickup without a driver.

He looked at Gabrielle standing in the tall grass by the pond. He saw movement. About twenty feet to her right, someone crawled toward her.

He yelled, "Run Cat, run!" and pulled his gun.

Gabrielle heard Dakota's warning, and turned to bolt, but was knocked on her back when a man slammed into her. Vicious, he straddled her hips and backhanded her across the face. He ripped her shirt down the front, then a gun roared, and two bullets tore through his chest. He flew backwards and landed half in, half out of the pond. He didn't move.

Frantic, face on fire, chest stinging, Gabrielle scrambled away from the man. She heard Dakota's thud as he jumped from the tree and ran toward her. She jumped up, but he slid to a stop as she turned to face him.

She was wide-eyed with shock. Blood spray covered her. The right side of her face was red. Right eyebrow and lip cut. Nose bleeding. Shirt ripped to her waist with fingernail scrapes down her chest – blood dripping. And she held her large bloody hunting knife in front of her.

Dakota knew she was still in the throes of shock, and said, "Cat, look at me, honey."

Breathless, she stared at him.

He said, "I need you to look at your hands," and beginning to tremble, she glanced at her hands. "I need you to drop the knife."

She dropped it. She didn't even remember grabbing it out of the sheath.

He stepped close, groaned, and cupping her face, looked at her wounds. Voice ragged, he said, "Oh Cat, honey, I'm so sorry. Please…hang on."

She trembled and stared at him, blinking, not even aware that tears rolled through the blood.

He said, "I hate it, but you have to give me a few minutes. I can't hold you yet. It's a crime scene. I'm calling Sean. Can you stand right there for me?"
She nodded over, and over, and over like a bobbing statue. Then she glanced at the dead man. Eyes open. Two large holes in his chest. A long gash in his side. A total stranger. Dead. She still struggled to comprehend how it happened so fast.

***

Sean answered the video call, "What's wrong?"
Dakota said, "Gabrielle was just attacked. I killed the man – and Gabrielle stabbed him. I'm videoing everything with you now. I need the FBI to take this case without Reynolds knowing. Make it happen. We need to go. She isn't safe here."
Sean asked the crime scene questions and Dakota filmed and answered. They recorded the victim, Gabrielle's injuries and blood spray, the gun, the bloody knife, the crime scene, the man's identification, a view of the area, and the man's truck.
They finished and Sean said, "Go. I've got it. Leave it like it is. Leave her torn shirt and knife. Leave your two bullet casings. I've got the GPS location and a helicopter on the way. Get out of there."

***

As Gabrielle dropped her torn shirt by the bloody knife on the ground, Dakota took off his shirt and gave it to her to put on. In minutes they were mounted and riding away. They heard the helicopter in the distance.

A couple of miles away, he rode the stallion into the shade and stopped. He wrapped her in his arms and held her, kissed her, soothed her. All the things he couldn't do earlier. She held on. Arms tight around his neck as tears burned her eyes.
He said, "I can't stand that he hurt you…"
At the same time, she said, "But you saved me …"

A few minutes later, still in his arms, Gabrielle said, "I don't even remember pulling my knife."

Kissing her cheek, he said, "Your preservation reflex was to fight back. That was a right move. And we'll get you another knife."

"Did you shoot him from up the tree?"

"Yes. I had to wait for a clear shot without putting you in danger."

She said, "It's so hard to believe. He came out of nowhere."

"I know, Cat. I know. So many times, that's how it happens."

They dismounted. With a bottle-water shower, he helped her wash the blood off, checking for wounds again. She felt the stings from the cuts on her face and chest. Her cheek burned and throbbed from the slap. She waited, dripping wet in his shirt. He grabbed her something to dry off with and clean clothes. She dried off, changed, and twisted her wild hair into a ponytail as he texted Adam.

***

Dakota to Adam: Pinpoint our location.
Adam replied: Got it. Head east. Meet by the road.
Dakota replied: Roger that.

***

Then Dakota called Jimmy, the tattooed veteran from this morning.

He answered, and Dakota said, "Jimmy, Cat and I've had some trouble. We ran into the guy in the red truck you warned us about. Are you free to give us a hand?"

"Where are you?"

"We are almost to Reeves. My brother is on his way to get the stallion. Can you give us a ride further up the road?"

"I'll be there in thirty minutes. I'll call when I'm close." Then Jimmy paused, and said, "Are either of you hurt?"

"Cat was injured. He's dead."

***

Still at his flat in Lake Charles, Sean ended the call with the FBI helicopter. The crime scene was recorded and by tomorrow, the case would be closed after the next of kin was notified.

He glanced at the monitor at Gabrielle's house, and the gray-haired lady was finally packing up her picnic gear to leave. He couldn't believe she had waited all that time.

Then a text came in from Adam. They were headed to pick up the stallion from Dakota. Sean knew Dakota would handle explaining Gabrielle's injuries to them, so he didn't say anything about it.

Another text arrived. Samantha was almost to Lake Charles. She was due to meet the District Attorney in an hour. He called her.

***

Samantha answered abruptly, "I didn't expect a call. What's wrong?"

He said, "What kind of greeting is that?"

Huffing, she said, "It isn't like we're on a date."

"That's next."

She said, "Maybe. I'll think about it. Now what is up with Gabrielle and Dakota?"

"Why don't you pull over and focus on the call."

"You're scaring me."

"Just be careful and pull over."

After a minute, she said, "Ok. I'm parked. Tell me now."

Sean said, "The Posse paid a visit to Gabrielle and Dakota's houses last night. They were destructive. One of the guys made a call from the cabin after they located Dakota and Gabrielle's trail in the woods. So, I checked to see if the call went to any FBI staff. You will never guess who got that call."

Samantha said, "I am going to knock you out if you make me guess."

"It was Director Reynolds, our boss at the FBI that received the call."

She was stunned. Silent.

He didn't have to explain the calamity, and continued, "I am investigating the director's family and his phone records. So, there is a very real chance Director Reynolds is involved in: One, a missing person case involving Gabrielle and her mother. Two, six murders with the Posse. And three, what is happening now with Dakota, Gabrielle, and myself because of the treasure."

"Sean…"

"I know. But we will keep them on the run until we have enough to trap the director and the Posse. Before you meet with the District Attorney in an hour, you need to call the Attorney General. Jean Lafitte is a part of Louisiana history, and his descendants, along with the FBI are in danger from the Posse.

This situation has gone from bad to worse. We need other law enforcement in on this now."

She said, "I'm calling the Attorney General now. I will get back with you. Stay safe. I mean it."

***

In the shaded woods close to the small town of Reeves, Dakota sat with Gabrielle as they waited for Adam's call. He watched her fidget a bit before catching his gaze.

He said, "After all the continuous action, it seems odd to sit and wait."

She nodded and said, "My body sits, but my brain is flying."

He ran his hand down her arm, and said, "You've been through so much in such a short time. Your mind needs to work it out, then it can file it away and move on."

She touched her lip, flinched, and said, "I need a mirror."

"Maybe not yet. We need to get ice for your face at the first store we come to. Your eye, lip, and now even your cheek is swelling. And I hate to tell you, but you're going to have a black eye tomorrow."

"Well, scrap the mirror then. You're making me feel so much better about myself."

He smiled at her sarcasm, and she winked with her good eye.

Wrapping her hand in his, he said, "I know you didn't plan for me to see your tattoo like this, but it's gorgeous. Beautiful. I was speechless when you first turned around and I saw it."

Smiling, she said, "I figure God gave me the gift of art so I might as well use it on myself."

"You're an amazing artist. And I would love to get a closer look at it sometime."

She knelt in front of him, and said, "Go ahead. We can call this your private showing."

He leaned up and slid his hands underneath her shirt hem, and gently pushed it all the way to her shoulders, completely exposing her back.

He said, "Amazing," then starting at her lower back where the tattoo began, he touched all the flowers, climbing vines, multi-colored plants, and leaves in the tropical bouquet that reached all the way to her shoulder blades.

Gabrielle closed her eyes. She could see in her memory exactly what he touched as he followed the picture that she had drawn for the tattoo artist.

Dakota's hands were large on her back. But gentle. Sliding. Personal. And oh, so sweet.

"This is beyond beautiful," he said, "It almost looks real. Alive. No one would ever know what it covers. Your vision for this was perfect."

"Thank you. Did you feel them?"

He returned his hands where he knew the two branding scars were. He rubbed his fingertips over the ripples in the skin. Then he leaned down and pressed his warm lips over them. She gasped, wanting to cry at the beauty. And continuing, he caressed and kissed her entire back. As he lifted his face, he slid his hand over it one more time and smiled. Now he was imprinted there. He hoped she never thought about those scars again. As he lowered her shirt, she turned, and threw herself into his arms.

***

Half an hour later, Adam watched for Dakota and Gabrielle. He got out of the truck with Trace and Zoe. In a couple of minutes, they came riding out of the woods. Then shocked, they saw Gabrielle's injuries.

Adam grabbed the stallion's reins, as Dakota dismounted, then helped Gabrielle down. Adam said, "Mercy, Dakota, what happened?"

"Let's load up first, ok? We have to meet someone for a ride in a few minutes."

The others tended to the horse while Dakota and Gabrielle waited in the air-conditioned truck in cool relief. They had been hot since they left yesterday afternoon on the run.

When they all climbed back in the truck, Adam said, "Tell me what happened," and a tearful Zoe hugged Gabrielle.

Dakota said, "To make a long story short, she was injured in a fight with a man a little over an hour ago. He attacked her by a pond while I was up a tree scouting. I shot and killed him. She stabbed him. Case closed. The FBI will handle it."

Shocked silence filled the truck. But he didn't offer any more information. Then they all tried to talk at once.

Dakota held up his hand to stop them, and said, "This case has blown up into a multi-agency plan. There are an unbelievable number of unforeseen variables in play. We won't go into anything now. Just please, stay alert, and safe. Cat and I, have found a friend to help us for now."

Zoe said, "Who's Cat?"

Gabrielle said, "I have earned a nickname it seems," and Dakota grinned.

***

Back in Lake Charles waiting on phone reports from his FBI source, Sean heard the surveillance alarm go off again. He stared in surprise at the monitor. The gray-haired lady that had been at Gabrielle's house most of the day was now at Dakota's cabin. What was that woman up to? Why would she be at the cabin?

He watched as she got out of her truck and appeared totally familiar with the place. She knocked on the patio door. When no one answered, she knocked on the front door. Then she looked through the windows. Her gasp let him know she saw the damage from last night. Immediately she checked the barn and walked around the yard – then sat on the patio and quietly stared into the distance. This woman was not what she seemed. He would be making a trip to the river if she stayed.

Chapter 14

Director Reynold's phone vibrated in his pocket as he sat in a meeting at the FBI. He glanced at the caller without response. After the meeting, he walked to the National Mall not far from his office in Washington D.C. and returned the call.

***

The Director said, "What do you want now?" and he listened with a clenched jaw.

A headache began to pound, and he interrupted the ranting on the other end of the call, then said, "Ryan, there are four of you. Your gang has been together for years, so you are not new to this. Why is finding Dakota and Gabrielle suddenly difficult for you?"

He tapped his finger while he listened again, and his headache worsened.

Frustrated, he said, "Shut up. Did you find trace of them in the woods at all? They had to sleep somewhere."

He frowned in annoyance at the whine of a grown man, then said, "Ryan, you can't lose a horse. The tracks don't just disappear. How far north did you track it?"

After an earful, he sighed and said, "Well then start on Highway 190 and search south of Ragley to Reeves. If they came out of the woods along there, you should find tracks. And be quick about it. I want this over and done with in less than a week. And Ryan, I warn you, if you or your gang, kill or stalk anyone else regarding this Lafitte treasure - someone will find all of you floating in the Atchafalaya swamp. Got it?"

Chapter 15

On a gravel road sitting in Adam's truck, Dakota's phone rang. He answered, and Jimmy said, "I'm in town. Where do you want me to pick you up?"

Dakota said, "Pull behind the high school. We're in a blue truck with a horse trailer. What are you driving?"

"A camo Hummer."

Dakota, not expecting that, said, "I think we both have a few secrets."

Jimmy said, "Seems so. See you in five minutes."

***

Dakota and Gabrielle didn't waste any time switching vehicles when Jimmy arrived in the Hummer.

Jimmy looked in the backseat and frowned at Cat's injuries. He sighed, and said, "I'm sorry you tangled with him, Cat. He was a guy looking to get killed. I'm glad he won't bother anyone else. We need to get you some ice though. Are you hurting?"

"A little. Dakota wanted me to get some ice on it."

Jimmy glanced at Dakota, and said, "There's obviously a lot going on with you two. Why don't you tell me what I need to know?"

Without hesitation, Dakota said, "I'm FBI. I connected with Gabrielle a few years back when we saved her from a serial killer in Baton Rouge. And as if that wasn't enough, she just found out she is the very real granddaughter of Jean Lafitte - making her a target of treasure serial killers."

Jimmy shook his head, and said, "I couldn't have made that up if I had tried. So, what's next?"

"The case got complicated with: One, a dirty FBI boss. Two, Cat's adoption secrets. Three, murder and missing persons. And four, buried treasure. My brother, who is also FBI, is working with us to stay ahead of the bad guys until they step into our crosshairs. Till then, we aim to head north towards Bundick's Lake or Kisatchie National Forest to keep her out of sight."

Jimmy nodded, then said, "My help is yours, for as long as you need it. My friendship is for life. Deal?"

Gabrielle smiled, leaned up and kissed his bearded cheek, and said, "Deal!"

He grinned, then continued, "I would like to connect with my retired General to see if their help might be available, if needed. Agreed?"

Dakota said, "Grateful. What branch of military?"

"Army. I'm retired Captain James Barlow at your service," and he winked at Gabrielle.

Dakota fist-bumped him, and said, "Glad we ran into you, Captain."

"Call me Jimmy – and as for your hideout, I have a small cabin on the outskirts of Fort Polk. There isn't much traffic around there since no one wants to mess with the Army. And it sits near Kisatchie National Forest. Will that work?"

Dakota said, "Let's go."

Gabrielle said, "Please…may I get a cheeseburger and fries when we get the ice? I'm starving. Oh, and a giant fountain Coke?"

Jimmy said, "You can have whatever you want."

***

Sean pulled into the parking spot at his loft as the phone rang. It was Samantha.

He answered, "How did the meeting go with the big dogs?"

"The plan is in motion. The Attorney General called us at the District Attorney's office. I gave them the scenario with Gabrielle. The A.G. is calling in a different FBI team and will keep Reynold's under surveillance. He also plans to notify Fort Polk for possible retired soldier assistance. The D.A. said he will work with local law enforcement to prevent danger spreading beyond Gabrielle and Dakota's homes into the community.

Sean said, "It was time to get everyone on board. We appreciate you handling that. And FYI, Dakota and Gabrielle are on their way to a new hideout location. But—"

Samantha quickly cut in, and said, "But what? What is it?"

"Gabrielle was attacked by a man in the woods. She stabbed him and Dakota shot and killed him. I've seen her on video, and she has cuts, a swollen eye, busted lip, and chest claw marks."

Groaning in anger, she said, "No! When is she going to get a break?"

"I know. I hear you. But Dakota's taking care of her. And for great news, their new friend is a retired Army captain."

"Finally – some good news."

Sean said, "Now, how about a date when all this is over?"

"With you?"

"I wasn't asking for someone else."

"Good. Just making sure. I love romantic dates, defined as music, good food, spoiling..."

Chuckling, he said, "It just so happens, I do romantic really well."

"I think you might be a fun date, Agent Man."

"Fun is not my goal. I want it to be skydiving exciting."

With her famous touch of sarcasm, she said, "And how do you know fun with me won't be exciting?" and hung up.

Laughing, he put the phone down. She needed to learn phone etiquette. But then again, with her fire, who cares.

***

Gabrielle smelled the burger and fries as Jimmy got back in the vehicle with the food and ice bag. Her stomach growled. Loud. Dakota grinned as he handed her a bag of food and a giant fountain Coke. She smiled at him - with her crooked, swollen lip. His heart ached.

Seeing the look in his eyes, she mouthed silently, "I love you."

She saw the flash in his eyes, and he told Jimmy, who was backing up, "Stop!"

In a second, he opened the back door and scooted in next to her. Holding her face, he said softly, "Say it again."

Gabrielle, still holding her Coke and food, said, "I love you."

He kissed her. Gently, because of her lip, but slow and intimate enough to sizzle. He said, "You have to know I'm in love with you." Her stomach growled before she could respond, and she gasped in embarrassment.

He laughed, and said, "We will certainly continue this discussion later when we are alone."

After he returned to the front seat, he glanced at Jimmy, who grinned, and put the Hummer in reverse.

Several miles down the road, Jimmy said, "I don't live too far from the camp. I can easily bring you supplies each day."

Looking at the Hummer, Dakota said, "Is your home an underground bunker with all the amenities?"

Chuckling, Jimmy said, "Something like that."

Curious about him and his home life, Gabrielle asked, "Do you have family?"

He glanced in the mirror at her, and said, "Not anymore."

She nodded and watched him drive. They were both alone. She said, "Have you ever wanted a daughter?"

Her question hit hard. Deep. Straight to the heart. He quickly glanced at her again, then smiled, and said, "Only if it's you."

She said softly, "So…then you do want to be a dad."

There wasn't a sound in the truck as Jimmy pulled to the side of the road. He turned to face her, and said, "Do you want a dad, Cat?"

She smiled and said, "Only if it's you."

And just like that. They were family.

As Jimmy pulled back on the road, Dakota thought that had been the most amazing thing to have witnessed. He said, "Both of you are amazing - like touched from above amazing."

Jimmy said, "She's the amazing one. But we both know that."

After traveling awhile, Jimmy said, "Hold on. This road will rattle your teeth – which means, only someone on a direct mission would choose to travel this path. But I promise you, come morning when you can see the land, it's beautiful. Rich green forests, hills, creeks, and peace. There are mostly small animals in here but occasionally a bobcat or coyote roam through. Be sure to keep food inside and you shouldn't have trouble. Hiking is good too, just watch your boundary lines since we are close to Fort Polk."

They bounced down the bumpy road awhile, before he pulled into a short driveway that ended at a small cabin with a porch. They grabbed their bags and headed inside.

Jimmy said, "I hope this works for you. There is a small air conditioner, refrigerator, and water heater. You will find can goods in the cabinet and perishables in the freezer. A few T-shirts, lounge pants, or shorts are in the chest of drawers. Sorry, Cat, just male clothes. The sofa is a foldout double bed.

"Your phones will work. Just call if you need me. Otherwise, I will see you at noon tomorrow. And a head's up, helicopters and planes fly over in the mornings. And that about covers it, so make yourselves at home and stay safe."

Dakota said, "This is perfect. Thanks, Jimmy. Last night we started in a barn and ended in a tree."

Jimmy chuckled and said, "I've been there. Text or call me with updates please. Remember, you have my daughter now," and grinned as he headed out the door.

Dakota bolted the door as Jimmy drove away, then headed straight to Gabrielle. She watched him come, stomach fluttering. She knew what was on his mind…both their minds.

He pulled her close, faces inches apart, and said, "Back to our earlier conversation. Say it now, Cat."

She said, "I'm in love with you." She touched her heart, and said, "Here. Down deep I feel you. I love you in me."

She watched her words wash over him. His eyes said all kind of things as he tightened his hold. He made sure no air; no space was between them. He said, voice deep, and sexy, "I'm burning with love for you. So wild I ache with it."

She pulled his lips to hers not caring at all about the cut. Fire flamed as he lifted her, and she wrapped arms and legs around him. In the middle of the danger. Of the hiding. Of the wounds. This. Love. Mattered more.

Several breathless moments later, he looked at her, and said, "I'm crazy about you."

She smiled like a woman who knew. Agreed. And felt it. She said, "And I am…so into you."

A few moments later, kisses paused, she slid down to stand.

Looking her over, he said with a touch of humor, "We might need pillows between us in that bed," and she smiled.

With love in the air, Gabrielle started a pot of coffee while Dakota opened the sofa and prepared the bed.

He said, "Well at least this is softer than the treehouse. Are you hurting?"

"My face and upper body mostly. It's not horrible. The ice helped."

"You shower first. Afterwards I can help you tend your wounds."

"Sure. I won't be long."

While he waited for her, he checked phone messages, and gratefully grabbed a cup of black coffee.

Just a short time later, Gabrielle came out dressed in a man's T-shirt that hit her mid-thigh. Hair wrapped in a towel.

She said, "I can't believe you wanted to kiss me looking like I do. I'm awful."

"You are not awful. You are wounded. Would you tell a soldier he looks awful?"

She said, "I hate it when you're logical," and he laughed.

He kissed her softly, and said, "Cuts and bruises don't make your eyes, lips, hands, or body less for me. You taste good anyway. Got it?"

She smiled and nodded.

He said, "I'll be quick. Please stay inside, and the coffee is ready. We need to get more ice on you when I get out."

Gabrielle was sipping coffee when he came back in the kitchen dressed only in lounge pants and long wet hair. He couldn't have looked any hotter.

She forced herself to focus, and said, "Would you mind combing this wild, wet hair of mine? My arms are sore, and I don't have anything to spray on the millions of tangles I gathered from your cabin to here."

He chuckled and pulled up a chair behind her, and said, "I don't mind at all," and with her comb, he gently untangled her hair. Then massaged her scalp and shoulders.

Afterwards, she said, "That was amazing."

He chuckled and said, "Don't move, I'll grab the first aid supplies," and was back in a second.

He packed the ice bag but knew it would only help with swelling and soreness. He couldn't stop the black eye that would be evident come morning. He gave her small bandages to put on her chest scrapes, and dabbed medicine on her cuts.

Before long, they headed for bed. It had been a long, long day.

He said, "Which side of the bed do you prefer?"

She said, "The soft side." He laughed.

They slid in bed and faced each other. He pulled her closer, slipping his arm under her head.

She caressed his bare chest, and said, "I love touching you."

Sliding his hand down her back, and tucking her feet in his, he said, "Please, touch me. And I love that you say what you think. It does things to me."

"I like knowing that I do things to you."

He tilted her face to him – kissed her softly.

She said, "Did you expect love between us? This fast?"

"I did. Not sure how I knew. But I did."

She smiled. Then she frowned. He watched her struggle with a thought. Knew she had something to say. He waited. Aware that it would be important.

She said, "Dakota…I need you to know. Liam didn't…I wasn't—"

He knew what it was, and covered her lips with his, stopping the words she struggled to say. He said, "I know Cat. I know he didn't."

She nodded, relieved that he knew she hadn't been raped. He held her and they were both asleep in minutes.

***

In Lake Charles, Sean looked at the camera feed at Dakota's cabin. The gray-haired lady was still there, and it was dusk. He had been watching her all day. It was ridiculous. He needed to get there and see what was up with her.

He dressed for surveillance, grabbed his gear, and stopped to look at the camera. She wasn't in the chair. Where did she go? Then he saw her get a bag out of her truck and walk to the barn.

He watched the camera. Ten minutes passed and a woman came out of the barn dressed in camo. She had shoulder length dark hair and no glasses. She walked to the truck and took out a rifle and crossbow. He knew it had to be the same lady – her shape was the same.

She had been disguised. Disbelieving what he was watching, she headed toward an oak tree and climbed it. In no time, she was perched high in the air with a rifle and crossbow. He grabbed his drone and rifle, then left for the cabin.

Right at nine p.m. he pulled into the driveway entrance and hid his truck in the trees. He put on night goggles and slowly made his way toward the cabin. Her truck was still parked. He walked through the trees closer to where he saw her last. She was still perched up high, relaxed and alert with her weapons.

He silenced the drone and flew it high above the trees to get near her. Then he turned on the drone spotlight.

She startled at the light but steadied herself and didn't say anything.

He called out, "Who are you?"

She didn't answer.

"Leave your crossbow and gun in the tree. Climb down."

She said, "Who are you?"

"The FBI."

She smiled and climbed down. As she reached the ground, he said, "Stop."

She didn't move.

"Raise your hands and turn to face me."

When he saw her face, he said, "You are kidding me. What is your name?"

"I'm Serena."

***

Sean texted Dakota: I have Serena. We will talk tomorrow.

***

The sun's rays were barely above the eastern sky, when helicopters roared over the small cabin by Fort Polk. Startled, Gabrielle and Dakota both jumped out of bed. Then remembering what Jimmy had warned, they laughed.

Dakota said, "I see we don't need an alarm clock here."

Heart pounding, she said, "That was crazy loud! I thought we were at war."

Laughing, he said, "Well, no sleep now – and we better not crawl back in that bed. Why don't I make coffee while you get dressed?"

She yawned, nodded, and walked to the bathroom. He wasn't surprised when he heard a bloodcurdling scream.

He joined her. She stared in the mirror. One eye was now a ferocious display of color around the black eye, but the swelling had gone down. The swelling had also decreased on her lips, but a massive bruise covered most of her right cheek and jaw. Bruises were evident pretty much everywhere.

She put her hands on her hips, and said, "I'm a mess. I look horrendous, appalling, scary."

He stepped against her back and slipped his arms around her.

They looked in the mirror at the damage the morning revealed, and he said, "Cat, those bruises will fade in a few days. What will remain is what I already see, your fabulous eyes, your delicious lips, your sexy body, your gorgeous tan, your sassy feline qualities—"

"I don't have a tan. This is the color of my skin."

"That's even better. We're both naturally tan. Look how well we look together. Look how perfectly you fit in my arms."

She smiled, then giggled, and said, "All men should be profilers. Good job, Handsome. I'm fine. You can finish the coffee now."

As he walked down the hall, he said, "It's never a dull day around you, Gabrielle."

She changed into cutoffs, a camo tank, and her climbing boots. She re-braided her hair and headed for the smell of coffee.

He smiled and said, "You look like a female Rambo."

She looked at his chest again, and he grinned, catching on. He said, "You like my chest bare. You haven't mentioned that."

"You're crazy handsome."

"Can you leave off the crazy part?"

She slid her palms across his chest and said, "I like this. And thank you."

"For what?"

"For loving me."

Dakota snuggled with her, kissed her neck, then her lips, and said, "Honey, loving you is what I'm best at. You'll see. But…please go get coffee so I can get dressed. It's getting hot in here and I have to prevent out-of-control burns with us."

She giggled as he groaned heading down the hall.

In a few minutes he was back with a shirt on. He said, "I checked messages and I have good news. Shocking. But good news."

"What is it?"

"Sean has Serena."

Chapter 16

Gabrielle blinked. Stunned. And said, "He has my mom?"
"Yes."
"How?"
"I don't know. Let's call and find out."

***

Sean answered on the first ring, "Dakota."
"Gabrielle's listening."
"Hi, Gabrielle."
"Sean, is Serena really there?"
She heard a female voice say, "I'm here Gabrielle. I've always been here."
She tried to respond, but overwhelmed, she covered her face and cried.
Dakota put an arm around her and said, "Sean, can you bring Serena to us? I have someone who can pick you up in Reeves. I think face-to-face will be better for this reunion than over the phone. We have work to cover as well."
Serena said, "Yes, I'm coming."
Sean said, "Just tell us where to meet for the ride. I will be in my black truck."
"Head to Reeves and the veteran I told you about will call and meet you. He's a terrific guy."
Sean said, "Give us an hour to get to Reeves."

***

Dakota called. Jimmy answered, "Everything alright?"

"Yes. But new information has come up. Gabrielle's mom, who has been missing for years, showed up yesterday. My brother with the FBI has her. Can you meet, and bring them out here? It looks like pieces of this puzzle are falling into place."

"Yes. Say when, and where, you want me to pick them up."

"I'll text phone numbers to both of you. See you before noon."

"You got it."

Dakota glanced at Gabrielle, still emotional, and said, "Jimmy, this is the first time she will have seen her mom since she was three-years-old."

"I hear you loud and clear."

***

Later, Dakota said, "Come on, Cat, let's go for a hike. We need to burn off some energy, and keep you occupied. Your mom won't get here for a couple of hours."

They walked on the porch and Dakota set the timer on his watch. He glanced at their gear. Gabrielle had strapped on the hunting knife she found here, her throwing knives, and holstered her dart gun. Dakota had his pistol in his waistband.

She said, "Wow. We're both Rambo."

He chuckled and said, "Yep. And… you have ten seconds to run." She screamed and ran.

They played chase for a while, then he snatched her up and kissed her. And now that he had a smile on her face, they hiked down to the creek.

After a while, Gabrielle said, "Tell me about your books. What made you want to be a writer?"

"I've always loved writing. But the idea to write a novel and publish, started because of you."

She raised her eyebrows, surprised, and said, "Me? How?"

"My life changed completely after I carried you away from Liam that night. Are you sure you want to hear this?"

"Please. I want to know."

"What you don't know about that night, is that I was the age you are now, and moving up fast in the ranks at the FBI. The team I was on got called in on Liam's case. We followed and chased every lead. We fought to formulate intel fast enough to catch him *before* the kidnappings took place. We couldn't help but grieve when we were too late. And you were victim thirteen. A very special one. You lived.

"And I never forgot you. I had been deeply affected by your experience, all that I had learned about you, and of course your gorgeous eyes. After that night, I transferred out of the serial killer team, to the training academy. Then a year ago, I semi-retired to write. One, because I love it. Two, to make income for victims. My pen name is Zeke Spencer. I'm also a partner at The Fort."

"Zeke Spencer! I've read your books!" and he laughed.

The alarm went off on his watch and he said, "Your mom will be here soon."

***

Sean and Serena turned north off Highway 190, when they reached the tiny town of Reeves. They headed toward the rendezvous spot and in a few minutes, rolled to a stop behind a camo Hummer. They all got out.

Jimmy whistled as he looked at Cat's mother, and said, "I guess you don't need to be told your daughter looks like you?"

She smiled, and said, "No. We have a strong family resemblance. I'm Serena. Thank you for picking us up."

He said, "I was more than glad to. She's already stolen my heart. And both of you are beautiful women. Who minds that?" She grinned.

Jimmy and Sean shook hands, and Sean said, "Thanks, Jimmy. Dakota and Gabrielle think a lot of you."

Jimmy said, "They have come to mean a lot to me already. And I have to say, I see the strong family resemblance between you and Dakota too. Those Sioux genes make handsome men."

Sean grinned and said, "Wait till you see Adam. You ready to go?"

Jimmy said, "Hop on in."

Headed toward the cabin, Jimmy said, "I messaged Dakota when I picked you up. I do need to stop at a convenience store to get a large fountain Coke for Cat. That's her favorite and I'm partial to putting a smile on her face."

Serena said, "Who's Cat?"

Jimmy said, "It seems Cat is Gabrielle's pet name – and fit's her to a T. I can attest to that after our surprise meeting in the woods. Not that Gabrielle is not a beautiful name of course."

She smiled and said, "No offense taken. Tell me about you, Jimmy. Do you have family around here?"

With a twinkle in his blue eyes, he said, "I do now. You'll meet them," and he winked at her.

She looked surprised and he grinned. He looked forward to more time with Cat's momma.

***

A good while later, Serena did her best to keep the large Coke from spilling on the bumpy road in the middle of nowhere. This was a perfect place for a hideout. She was so excited to see Gabrielle face-to-face. It had been an achingly long time.

Jimmy pulled up in front of a cabin, and Sean pointed in the woods. He said, "There they are," as Dakota and Gabrielle headed downhill to meet them.

Sean, Serena, and Jimmy, got out of the Hummer. But Serena and Gabrielle walked straight toward each other without a glance at anyone else. Serena gasped at Gabrielle's injuries and opened her arms. They closed around her daughter. Finally.

After several emotional minutes, they looked at each other, and Serena touched Gabrielle's bruised face. She said, "Honey, I'm going to have to shoot someone," and the men chuckled as they joined them.

"It's okay Mom. I stabbed him - Dakota shot him."

Serena said, "That's my girl."

Dakota was shocked. He said, "It's not possible. Replicas in looks and actions."

The women faced him, and he looked back and forth, and said, "You are a shockingly beautiful mother and daughter."

Gabrielle grinned and said, "Mom, this is Dakota. My hero. Isn't he beautiful?"

"Cat," Dakota choked out, "Men are not beautiful."

Sean and Jimmy enjoyed his embarrassment a great deal.

Dakota said, "Serena, in all seriousness, I am honored to meet you. I can't wait to hear how you and Sean connected."

Sean said, "It's a shocker."

Gabrielle said, “Hi, Sean!”
Sean said, “Hey, wild woman.”
Gabrielle looked around, and said, “Where’s Dad?”
Serena paled in shock. Gabrielle said, “Oh! Mom, it’s not what you—"
And Gabrielle gasped, as an older, rakishly handsome man walked around the front of the Hummer, grinning.
He said, “Hey, Cat.”
She said incredulously, “What did you do with my dad?” and he laughed.
She gave him a hug, while Serena looked confused.
Gabrielle said, “Wow. You clean up good. I can’t believe you were hidden in the woods. I mean, look at the sexy bangs, smooth shave, and I can even see your amazing blue eyes. Mom, come look at his tats.”
Serena, getting frustrated, said, “I’m confused. Does he look different than normal?”
To explain, Dakota said, “Serena, he looked like a much older, hairy, mountain man in the woods yesterday. But today, obviously, he cleaned up.”

Sean spoke up, and said, “Okay, come on everybody, let’s talk inside. No sense being sitting ducks out here.”

Once everyone settled in the cabin, Dakota said, “Ok, Serena, where did you come from?”
She said, “A couple of days ago, Gabrielle walked right up to me. I had waited years for that to happen, but I was still shocked.”
Gabrielle said, “Wait, I don’t remember seeing you at all. There’s no way I wouldn’t have noticed.”
Serena smiled and said, “Give me a few minutes and I will be right back,” and she took her bag with her.

In five minutes, they all stared in shock, except Sean. She stood there now with silver hair, blue eyes, and glasses.
Gabrielle exclaimed, “You were in the bank vault!”
Serena nodded and looked at Dakota and said, “Hello, Mr. Nash.”
Dakota smiled and said, “Everyone meet Sarah Chatagnier. She sold me the log cabin.”
Gabrielle said, “Mom!”
Serena held up her hands, and said, “Ok, ok, I will explain. Let me get this off. I will be right back.”

Dakota grinned at Gabrielle and said, "Quite a mom you have there."
Gabrielle nodded, and said, "I can't believe it. She's been all around me."

In a few minutes, Serena returned and said, "The letters in the safety deposit box told you why, and how I disappeared. But through the years, I was able to keep up with your life without you knowing. My goal was your safety, and I was not safe for you to be around. I knew about your amazing art. What happened with Liam. And I have seen what you have accomplished with self-defense and ministry. And I was thrilled when you moved to your house on the river…because, of course, I also owned the log cabin.

"My Dad had given it to me. When we all changed our names, they moved out of state for a while. We connected secretly. They live local now."

Surprised at the revelation of more family nearby, Gabrielle said, "I have grandparents? Here?"

Serena knelt by her, and said, "Yes, and a great grandfather too. No siblings though. I couldn't bring a husband or more children into this danger," and Gabrielle was dazed as all the information spilled out.

Serena sighed and said, "I hate to tell you, but we are both considered missing persons. I have so much to fix for you. I have lived a lie for twenty-four years, but your safety was worth it. You already know your grandparents though."

"What? Who are they?"

"Your pastors. Jack and Angela Bordelon."

Gabrielle gasped and said, "No. It can't be. I already love them. I introduced Dakota to them Sunday. And they know I'm their granddaughter?"

"Yes. And as soon as this nightmare is resolved, you can see them openly. It wouldn't be safe for them right now. However, your great grandfather probably won't stay out of this. General Scott Romero is a very determined man - even more since he is retired."

Astounded, Jimmy said, "Wait! What? That's my general, Dakota."

Serena interrupted, and said, "What do you mean, your general? Who are you?"

"Retired Army Captain James Barlow at your service - Beautiful."

Exasperated with his attention, Serena said, "Stop that!"

"No. That's not going to happen."

Gabrielle was shocked at everything – including her dad flirting with her mom.

Dakota said, "Jimmy, have you called him yet?"
"I did, and he is seeking permission for veteran assistance. But I didn't know all this. I certainly expect an affirmative reply since they are his granddaughters."
Gabrielle said, "Dad, I can't believe you know my great grandfather. It's unbelievable."

Serena said, "Gabrielle. Stop. Please! Why do you keep calling him dad?"
She said, "I'm sorry! I should have explained sooner. It's just that when Dakota and I met him, I felt an instant connection somehow. And later, when I realized he didn't have family, like me, I asked him if he had ever wanted a daughter."
Jimmy hugged Gabrielle, then said, "And I told her yes. What man wouldn't want her for a daughter?"
Serena's eyes flooded with tears at the obvious affection already between them. She well understood the loneliness and need for family that had drawn them together.
She joined them, emotional, softer now, and said, "Thank you, Jimmy. I mean that."
He drew her closer, including her, and smiled. These two women were rocking his world.

Sean gave them a few, personal moments, then said, "We need to move on. We have a lot to cover. Serena, tell us what made you come to Lake Charles yesterday."
"I knew Gabrielle was in trouble when she showed up at the bank in disguise. By that night I was at my parent's house. By yesterday, I checked both their houses. I noticed all the wreckage and knew they had been targeted. I waited around to see if she returned.
"When neither of them did, I changed out of my Sarah disguise and climbed a tree with my weapons and watched for her. Obviously, I didn't know the FBI had me under surveillance until Sean's drone hit me with the spotlight. When I came down, he saw my face, and here we are."
Gabrielle said, "What were you going to do up the tree?"
"I'm an excellent shot and not afraid to use it. Especially for you."
Jimmy said, "No surprise there. Not with that bloodline." Serena grinned.

Dakota said, "Ok. Our Task Force is now increased by Jimmy and Serena. Sean, what updates do you have on the case?"

"Director Reynolds has one son that is strictly above board and a professor. He teaches political science and has a family with children. I didn't find any phone connection with the number that called from your house.

"However, the director has a nephew that lives in Houston with a rap sheet but no DNA record. He also doesn't have a consistent work history – so money would be an issue. His name is Ryan and the director's brother's only son. They talk frequently and based on credit card usage Ryan has been in Lake Charles the past few weeks.

"I have a couple of my friends researching Ryan's phone and finance records around the time of all six murders. We are attempting to identify the rest of the Posse. Here is Ryan's mug shot and the director's professional head shot."

***

In Washington D.C., the Director called Ryan.

"Yeah," Ryan answered, having a hard time being civil to him.

"How did the country sweep go south of Highway 190?"

"We found horse tracks east of where we lost them by the gully. We followed and the tracks ended at the side of the road. That's it."

"Undoubtedly, someone picked them up. Check around the local towns and see if anyone has seen strange vehicles hanging around and get back to me. Are your guys staying in line?"

"Sam and Jamie are cool. Butch is driving me nuts. He needs money as usual. I am having to press him hard to keep it together."

"He's a moron," the Director said. "Feed him to the alligators if he gets out of hand. We don't have time for local cops getting curious about his temper or odd behaviors."

Hating being talked down to – again, he said sharply, "Ok."

The Director said, "And one last thing, I am sending someone down there to give you a hand to move this hunt along. You should be glad about that. She's tough, and smart. Her name is Vee. Just let your men know to leave her alone. She knows what to do. Because if they mess with her, she'll blow a hole in them."

"Well, that's just great," Ryan snapped. "A female with an attitude."

"Just deal with it. I plan to be in Louisiana in a couple of days, so get productive. I want Gabrielle found. Otherwise, I'll have to do it myself, as usual."

***

On her way back to Baton Rouge, Samantha called Sean. He answered, "Hey there, we have you on group speaker."

"Hi, Sean. And everyone else. Give me a roll call so I know who's there."

"Gabrielle said, "Hey, Samantha."

"Hey. Just so you know, your attacker got off lucky with Dakota's kill shots. I would have made him suffer first."

Gabrielle understood the love behind the rough comment, and said, "I love you too."

Dakota said, "Hey, Samantha."

"Hey, good-looking."

Sean cut in, not impressed with her comment to his brother, and said, "Hey wait a minute," and Samantha laughed.

Serena said, "Hi, Samantha, I'm Serena, Gabrielle's mother."

"Hey, Momma Bear. I heard you were in town. I look forward to seeing you for myself soon. I hear you are quite a beauty – mirror image of our Gabrielle, right?"

Smiling, she said, "You can certainly tell I'm her mother."

Gabrielle said, "Or sister!"

Jimmy said, "Hi, Samantha. Retired Captain James Barlow here. Just call me Jimmy."

"Well, talk to me Jimmy. How did you get in all this?"

He said, "I got lucky," and Samantha laughed.

"I mean it. I met Dakota and Gabrielle in the woods. We made fast friends. And I adopted Cat, so we're family."

"Cat?"

"Oh, that's Gabrielle's nickname. Don't you think it fits?"

"I like you, Captain."

"I like you too, Samantha. But I have my eye on Momma Bear," and everyone laughed. Serena hit him on the arm.

Samantha said, "Sean?"

"I'm here. Do you have good news to report?"

"Yes, there is a new FBI team in place. Yes, there will be veteran Army assistance. And yes, there will be local law enforcement assistance."

Everyone cheered.

She continued, "Tonight, retired General Romero will call Dakota at six p.m. for a conference call. He will be joined by the Calcasieu Parish District Attorney, the new FBI team, and the Calcasieu Parish Sheriff. Dakota and Sean, you will have the lead.

"And Gabrielle…I am praying for all of you. This will be over soon. And, before you know it, we will be fencing again, and most likely dating those handsome Nash brothers." Then, abruptly, she said, "Sean, be safe. You promised me an exciting first date," and hung up.

Sean held up his hands, and said, "Why does she always hang up on me?"

Gabrielle giggled and said, "She wants the last word."

Sean laughed. Samantha's secret was out.

***

Serena got a text from her grandfather and called him.

He answered on the first ring, "Serena - are you and Gabrielle safe?"

"Yes. We are with the two FBI agents and Jimmy. Gabrielle was attacked but the cuts and bruises will heal. She's beautiful and tough. Here…hold on a second."

Gabrielle got on the line, and said, "Hi, Grandpa Scott."

"I can't believe we are finally talking. Are you okay?"

"I don't look it, but I am. I can't wait to meet you."

"It better happen soon. I want my family back."

Chapter 17

Vee was on her way to Louisiana. FBI Director Reynolds made her an under-the-table offer she couldn't refuse. But she had been surprised that a bonified FBI man hired her to kill. But times were crazy, and she didn't care who paid her. Or who she killed. This job was to eliminate the director's nephew, his treasure buddies, a woman that knew about the treasure, and FBI agents protecting her.

Evidently, the nephew had a treasure hunting addiction that had turned them into inept serial killers. It seemed the director didn't care about treasure - it was the serial killing that caused him trouble. He wanted them all dead at the end of the weekend.

She knew the next few days would be busy. She had a weapon's contact to meet in Lafayette tomorrow and then the director would meet her in Lake Charles by Friday. And after this job was over, she was off to the beaches and mountains of Peru.

She put on her headphones and closed her eyes. Nap time. The plane would land in a few hours.

Chapter 18

Deep in the woods near Kisatchie National Forest, the phone rang. Dakota answered, "FBI Special Agent in Charge Dakota Nash. The conference call is in underway. Callers, introduce yourselves."

"FBI Director Stephen Washington."

"Calcasieu Parish District Attorney."

"Calcasieu Parish Sheriff."

"Retired Army General Scott Romero. I am also Serena and Gabrielle's grandfather."

Dakota said, "Task Force, introduce yourselves."

"Special Agent Sean Nash."

"Serena, widow of Trent and mother to Gabrielle.

"Gabrielle, descendant of Jean Lafitte and target of the Posse."

"Retired Army Captain James Barlow."

Dakota said, "Director Washington, your lead, Sir."

The Director said, "It's a privilege to work with all of you on this case. Dakota, Sean, and Gabrielle, please accept the FBI's deepest apology for the travesty of integrity and justice portrayed by Director Reynolds. Here on out, he will be addressed only as Reynolds, the worst of the Posse.

"Gabrielle, the FBI is determined to actively engage in surveillance, intelligence, and use all necessary force to see that the Posse is stopped. Thank you for your courage to be an active participant in the Task Force.

"As for the motive of the Posse, *buried treasure*, we are all aware that Jean Lafitte played a colorful part in Louisiana history. And history indeed bears witness that buried treasure was a legitimate part of his past. That said, we have been informed, Gabrielle, that you have ownership proof of such a treasure on your property. Please be assured, that neither the U.S. Government, nor Louisiana, have any intention to claim said treasure.

"Now to move on, this phone call is to confirm and strategize a trap for the capture of these criminals. This is an astounding opportunity for civilian, military, and federal law enforcement to work together. Dakota, as Special Agent in Charge, what is your strategy?"

"Yes, Sir. Gabrielle, obviously, is the key. The Posse needs her to find the treasure. So, we strategically use her as bait. First, to draw out the Posse to learn their identity. And once all players are identified, we set a trap for them. For now, we continue to gather intel on Reynolds, his nephew Ryan - and Ryan's contacts. He will be the link for the rest of his group. We need an FBI tail on Reynolds.

"For the trap, Gabrielle's home will be designated as Ground Zero. Reynolds knows we have surveillance on her house so this would be a logical location, and not alert him that he has been discovered. And knowing Reynolds well, I expect him to introduce an unexpected element – a side attack of some kind. He is fond of double plays.

"In the end, I see Reynolds using Ground Zero as a kill zone where he will take everyone out. He is in too deep. I think he will try to play himself as undercover, kill us, and walk away. No way would he let us go.

"I suggest Army on the ground, FBI elevated in the trees, and Sheriff's Department ready for land and water assistance. The Task Force will play the contact roles."

The Director said, "Agreed. Excellent. Keep us in the loop on all intel updates and Ground Zero timelines. The FBI, the Army, and local law enforcement will follow your instructions based on future updates. I will assign two agents to tail Reynolds. Gabrielle and Serena, I look forward to meeting you. Stay safe. Goodnight, ladies, and gentlemen."

***

After the conference call, Dakota said, "Let's take a break and meet back together in about thirty minutes. I need to take a walk."

He reached for Gabrielle's hand and led her outside. They walked in silence. She felt his tenseness, and knew his mind was busy - he needed to unwind. They followed the creek until he found a grassy nook to sit. He drew her onto his lap and wrapped his arms around her. She leaned against him and waited. Several minutes passed, then he moved her hair aside, and kissed her neck.

She said quietly, "I know it's your job, but you are amazing. Clear and precise, you laid it out there. All the angles studied and analyzed. Extraordinary perception. It was glaringly obvious to everyone on the call."

He said, "I've always had an aptitude for seeing how a scenario could play out, or how the dominoes would fall as one of my trainers used to say. The tricky part is timing and being prepared for the unexpected. You have to think like the bad guy to stay ahead of them - draw them where you want them to go.

"But I don't want to use you for bait. We need to of course, but I don't like it. And believe it or not, your attack at the pond yesterday, revealed something that was important for me to know about you."

Surprised, she turned to look at him, and asked, "What in the world did you see?"

"I saw your fighting instinct. Reflex. During the battle, you were able to think and engage. You can't teach that. You have it. It will help you save your life even without a plan."

That truth washed over her. Settled down deep…and kicked some of the fear aside.

She nodded and said, "Then let's do it. Bait your hook."

***

In Washington D.C., Reynolds checked his flight and car reservations. He would arrive in New Orleans Friday, and travel as a civilian instead of FBI. That should keep him under the radar. On his drive to Lake Charles, he would stop in Lafayette to connect with his weapon's dealer. The guy was supposed to the be best in the area and guaranteed he could provide any weapons they could pay for. He better. There were consequences if he didn't.

Reynolds leaned back in his chair and smiled. Smooth sailing so far. His goal: by Saturday afternoon, the treasure issue and all those connected would be at the bottom of the river.

***

Back at the cabin, Dakota and Gabrielle returned from their walk and the smell of fried chicken filled the air. Jimmy had heated the chicken, potato salad, and peach cobbler he brought with him, and the others were dipping their plates. Gabrielle headed to the food. Dakota motioned to Jimmy and Sean, and they stepped out on the porch.

Dakota said, "We need a larger, safer place to stay than here now."

Jimmy said, "It's time to go to my place. We'll be safe there."

Dakota glanced at Sean, who nodded. They knew Jimmy's place would be exactly what he said and agreed.

Dakota said, "Let's go."

When they went back inside, he announced, "We are going to pack up and head to Jimmy's house. His place will be our safe house till this is over. Sean, if you will get your surveillance equipment from Lake Charles, and meet us there, we can have a meeting later tonight for tomorrow's plan."

Sean said, "Got it."

They were heading out of the forest in less than thirty minutes.

Gabrielle said, "Dakota, can we connect with Jade to give her a heads up to spend the weekend in Lake Charles? New Orleans is too far away when all this goes down. I want her to handle our publicity. That's what she does."

Dakota said, "Sure. Sean?"

Sean said, "I'll connect with her."

An hour later, they dropped Sean at his truck, and got back on the road.

Remembering the love letter, Gabrielle said, "Dakota, I just thought about the parchment letter from Jean to Sabrina. Do you know if Sean translated it yet?"

"He did. He has a copy for you."

Serena offered, "If you have the letter, I can read it."

Excited, Gabrielle said, "Dakota—"

He smiled, pulled a copy of the original from his case, and handed it to Serena.

By the light of her phone, she read.

***

Louisiana, 1814

Sabrina,

My Love, I can't imagine saying goodbye to you today. These last three months have been a gift to my life. Please forgive me for encouraging your love and affections. Your feisty spirit and beauty took me captive.

With all my heart, I wish you could stay with me, but you deserve more than the dirty decks of a privateer ship. My heart will always be with you. Thank you for raising our child. I will miss the hope your love gave me of a new life. Thank you for living it for me.

I leave you with a gift hidden inside my mother's Bible. A treasure map and a jewel chain. Napoleon Bonaparte, in thankfulness to me, gave me a small chest of his most personal treasure. This gift from him is my most valuable possession. I leave it for you as a legacy for all our descendants.

The main treasure is hidden. Follow the map. Keep the secret until the time is right. My treasures are often sought by dangerous men. Beware! Do not let that danger touch your life. My trusted Indian friend, Wolf, will bring you where you want to go, and stay as long as you need. He will make sure you are cared for.

Move to a safe place, change your name, raise our child, and let me go with a heart that knows you will sing to me in the wind. I promise I will think of you wherever I go.

I love you,

Jean Lafitte

***

Gabrielle wiped the tears off her cheeks.

Serena held the letter against her chest, and said, "The world doesn't know Jean Lafitte like this, but they should."

Dakota said, "That's an extraordinary letter. Even without the jewels, that is an amazing treasure."

Jimmy said, "Sorry, don't mean to interrupt, but we're here."

He braked to turn, then rolled over a cattle guard. He drove a long way through the darkness, then turned again and headed through a thick wooded area. When they pulled out of the woods, they stopped at a security fence. He entered a code, and they passed through. They followed a curvy road and came to a tall stone wall where he stopped and entered another code.

Dakota said, "Ok, Jimmy. You got me. I'm impressed."

Jimmy chuckled, and as he rolled through the entrance, the yard lit up. The women gasped. The house in the distance fit the landscape. It was built of stone and wood, with large windows and oversized doors. There were beautiful trees, a winding stream, and animal pastures. They rode over a small bridge and neared the back of the house. Four large dogs ran out of the barn and headed straight to the Hummer.

Jimmy stepped out and the dogs surrounded him, welcoming him home.

He said, "Come on out and meet the dogs."

As they joined him, he said, "The alfa is the Doberman. The Great Pyrenees, lab, and husky follow his lead."

Already on her knees with the dogs, Gabrielle said, "What an amazing pack of dogs!"

"Thanks. I have other animals too - a couple of Arabian horses, a few cows, a bull, and pigmy goats with their own playpen. They are my comedy group – you'll see! I also accept rescue animals when they come my way."

Gabrielle said, "I can't wait to see them! You know, I don't think I've mentioned it, but I have a terrific dog - and hawk."

"Really! A hawk too? Tell me about them."

"My German shepherd is for protection and PTSD support. I got him after I was kidnapped. His name is Zeus. And the hawk is Hunter. I raised him."

Jimmy met gazes with Dakota for an instant, in unspoken communication of the issues she must deal with. Then he asked her, "Do you often have trouble with PTSD?"

"Twice this week. But then, it's been an unusual week."

He nodded and gave her a quick hug. He completely understood. Many of his buddies from the Army dealt with it. It grieved him to know she battled it too.

Glancing at the others, he said, "Come on everyone, let's head to the deck. I can't wait to show you my favorite spot."

He pointed to the shadowed backyard with trees, then flipped a switch.

Dakota whistled and the women stared.

Jimmy said, "Welcome to my garden. I love nature. Water. It soothes the beast so-to-speak."

In the center of the garden, was a stone salt-water pool and high wide waterfall. Thick grass, willow trees, vines, flowers, and various trees and trails wound as far as they could see. The stream flowed through and windchimes tinkled in the breeze.

Awed, Gabrielle said, "Words don't do this justice."

Jimmy said, "I agree. Back in the forest when we met, do you know where you were?"

"I have no idea."

"On my land."

"Jesus…" she whispered.

"Exactly."

Dakota responded, "Talk about destiny. Jimmy, are you alone here?"

"Yes. My wife died young while on a trip to see her parents in Seattle. After that, I grieved and buried myself in the Army. I traveled a great deal with special ops and was able to save money and invest. After I retired, I built this place. I'm usually alone, but from time to time, someone comes my way for help. I never pass up those opportunities.

"But enough about me. Come inside and see the house. It was built with a great deal of stone, so I call it my castle. It isn't huge, but it makes an impressive stand here in the woods. I wanted something solid for security but didn't want to do without the warmth and beauty of the nature around me."

He unlocked the big door on the deck, and they stepped into a den.

Looking around, loving it, Serena said, "Oh. Jimmy. This is…"

He grinned, and said, "Thank you, Momma Bear."

Huge glass windows looked out the front, and back of the house. A large seating area filled the center of the room. Colorful braided rug. Pillowed sofas. Easy chairs. Throws. Ottomans. Low table with books and country antiques. Overhead was a beamed ceiling and a large chandelier made from branches and hanging lanterns.

The right side of the room was a kitchen and carved snack bar with stools. The left side of the house was a painted stone fireplace with a TV over the mantle. Doors opened into rooms on either side of the fireplace and stairs led up to a big loft.

He pointed and said, "The room next to the deck is my room. The door on the other side of the fireplace is the bathroom."

He motioned them to follow him to his room. The wall facing the deck was glass as well – and the view overlooking the garden was spectacular. The bed mattress laid atop a platform on a base with stone feet. The pillows and comforter were shades of blue with leather and velvet. Two large closets were on one wall with a walkway between them that led into the bathroom. He opened one closet that housed his clothes on one side and his desk with surveillance equipment on the other.

He said, "Surveillance begins with the perimeter fence. The windows have metal panels that close if necessary. If a threat is detected, we monitor from here. If danger is imminent, I have a safe room."

Dakota said, "I knew it."

Chuckling, Jimmy said, "I didn't go the bunker route, but the safe room works well."

He opened the second large closet and exposed a metal security door with a code pad. Entering the code, he revealed a vault room. There was enough area for at least six people to sit at a table and chairs. A desk area contained the same surveillance system. A weapon's rack, small bathroom, supply area, and mounted television filled the remainder of the room.

Jimmy said, "Once this door is sealed from the inside, a 911 code is activated with the police and fire station. It is fireproof and blast proof – but cell phones do get signal in here. Of course, this is not designed for long term use, but for guaranteed protection until help arrives."

When he showed them his luxury bathroom, Gabrielle groaned. She said, "This is like going on vacation!"

It was one large room with windows inlaid in the ceiling. The walls and floor were stone. A long waterfall ledge ran the length of one whole wall. Large tropical plants lent an outdoor feel to the atmosphere. On another wall was a carved wooden sink and mirror. On the other side of the room a carved divider kept the toilet private. Gabrielle and Serena smiled. It was awesome and they had to try it out.

Once they were back in the den, he pointed upstairs to the loft, and said, "There are four side-by-side bedrooms. Bathrooms are at each end of the loft. Now please, my home is your home. Settle in and make yourselves comfortable."

***

Dakota's phone rang just as he joined Jimmy in the kitchen. Sean said, "I picked up a tail north of Moss Bluff, so I backtracked to take another route to you. I lost them but I'll be late now. I'll call when I cross the cattle guard so Jimmy can talk me through. I hope you plan to feed me. I'm starving again."

Dakota said, "Good eye, Sean. It's hard to catch a tail in the dark. And yes, I see Jimmy taking out steaks now, so we'll have a late-night dinner and feed you. Call if anything changes."

***

After the call ended, Jimmy said, "Everything ok?"

"Yes. He caught a tail and lost them, but now he has to take the long way here to avoid running into them again."

Jimmy nodded as he laid out steaks and seasoning, then pulled out a black iron skillet with ridges on the bottom. He grabbed a few handfuls of fresh potatoes and green beans.

Dakota said, "I can be handy in the kitchen."

"Jump in – you want to do meat or vegetables?"

Dakota said, "Vegetables. You look like you have a personal relationship with the steaks."

"That's a fact. I'm always grilling something." He seasoned the steaks and set them aside till it was time to fire up the skillet.

Dakota washed, then microwaved the small gold potatoes to soften them. Then laid them out on a baking sheet and smashed each one with a fork till they popped. In a bowl he whisked melted butter, garlic, parsley, salt, pepper, and a few slivers of jalapenos. Then he drizzled the seasoned butter sauce over the beans and potatoes. They could roast when the steaks were grilling later.

Done in the kitchen, the guys headed to the deck.

Dakota said, "It really works for our benefit that the Posse recognized Sean's truck tonight. So, we'll use it tomorrow to lure them out in the open with Gabrielle. We need to identify, then tail these guys. We need names and faces."

Jimmy said, "Right. How close will you let them get to her?"

"She needs to be real bait and look completely accessible. So, unfortunately touching distance. But I will be close."

"What weapons will she have on her?"

"She prefers the dart gun, throwing knives, and hunting knife. By-the-way, she borrowed the hunting knife from the cabin since she had to leave hers at the pond. But back to the weapons. Her dart gun is not ideal for close contact. It takes several seconds before the target is unconscious. I plan to work with her tonight on a few hand-to-hand Karate moves. Most people don't expect martial arts from a woman."

"That true."

"Since she will be out in the open tomorrow, would you follow us and keep a rifle scope on anyone that appears threatening. Fire if we need the assistance."

"I'll keep a bead on anyone that fits that description," and they turned as the women came outside.

Dakota slipped an arm around Gabrielle and said, "We have a little chill time, Sean will be late. Do you want to take a walk in the garden?"

"You read my mind! I would love to. Is this for exercise or?"

He whispered in her ear, "Guess." Then drew her down the trail.

***

Once they were out of sight, Gabrielle laughed and ran. He caught her and leaned her back against a tree with a kiss that made her forget she was even in the woods.

Taking a breath, she whispered, "Dakota…" and wrapped her arms around him as he smiled and captured her lips again.

After a few minutes of steamy caresses and kisses, someone cleared their throat. Dakota growled, then turned to see Jimmy and Serena.

Dakota drawled, "Surely there's more than one trail," and Jimmy burst out laughing.

Still in Dakota's arms, Gabrielle said, "Mom, are you out for a romantic walk too?"

Startled at the comment, Serena said, "No! Of course not."

Jimmy smiled, and said, "Yes, as a matter of fact."

Serena pushed him, and said, "Stop it, Jimmy."

"Cat brought it up, besides, a romantic walk would be good for you," and she rolled her eyes as he escorted her further down the trail.

***

Dakota motioned to the barn, and said, "Would you like to see the animals?"

"Of course! I'll race you," and she darted out of the garden.

He caught her quickly, then piggybacked her to the barn. They stopped at the horse corral first. Two cream-colored Arabians came to them. Stunning. Gorgeous.

Gabrielle said, "I sure hope he plans to breed them. I want one."

He smiled, and said, "I can see you mounted on one of those. They are beautiful."

Eventually they made it to the pigmy goat pen at the other end of the barn. Gabrielle was captivated as the tiny goats hopped, danced, climbed, bleated, nibbled, and played on their mini obstacle course.

She squatted to touch them, and said, "Oh Dakota…look at them. I want some."

"Of course, you do. They are super cute."

Enjoying the moment, she said, "One day, I want to have a houseful of children." She blushed at her blurted comment.

Fire hit Dakota's stomach at the thought. He squatted behind her, thighs pinning her in. Snug. Running his arms around her waist, he said, "I would love to see you with a baby in your arms."

"So then…you want children?"

"With you. And we will continue this conversation when the case is over."

***

Back in the garden, Jimmy sat on a log by the stream. Serena sat close by, smiling but reflective as she gazed in the water.

Happy for her, he said, "You've had an amazing day."

"Indescribable! Being with her has been an answer to a prayer. It has been so long."

He said, "Tell me…"

She nodded, then said, "I was young when I disappeared - only married a few years. A lot of lonely years followed. But I was able to keep up with Gabrielle, which meant everything. Personally though, I couldn't let anyone close to me, any relationship, because I couldn't tell them who I was. I almost forgot what it was like to really be me. Till today."

"And today is just the beginning," he said. "I think the choices you've had to make have been extraordinary and heroic. I think you're brave, giving, loving, and very, very beautiful. And I think - you - need me. What do you think about that, Momma Bear?"

She closed her eyes for a second, then said softly, "Jimmy…it's been a long time…for a lot of things."

"I understand that." And he watched, probably long forgotten thoughts and feelings flash across her face. He continued, "One of the hardest things to do is re-learn to trust people, especially if you've lived with fear. I am what you see, Serena. Handsome to start," and she couldn't help but smile.

He continued, "You'd be safe. Laugh again. Be adored. Argued with of course," and she grinned.

Then he quit joking, and said, "But I most certainly will flirt with you. Touch you. Kiss you. And push for more for both of us. A lot more. Everything. And I can assure you that whatever is best for you, is always what would be best for me. And I think Cat would like this idea too. So, tell me, would you consider the chance at a new life? With me?"

She felt all of what he said grab hold of her, nudging her to take a chance. Glancing at him, she said, "I've seen the man you are. I mean, my grandfather respects you. I've seen your heart for Gabrielle – and all that you do for us. You're giving, strong, and caring. And even though you flirt outrageously, you really do make me feel safe. And in all honesty, I can't remember the last time I said that to anyone. Much less, a good-looking man...like you."

He watched her and waited. He had boldly laid it out there.

She struggled for a second, then said, "And yes, I feel the spark between us."

He smiled.

She said, "And your looks don't help."

He laughed.

She sighed, and said directly, "And I know we aren't getting any younger, so time does matter. But… do you have to rush… the passion?"

"Yes."

She shook her head in exasperation, and said, "You do remember we met today?"

He smiled, then said, "Serena. God prepared us long before today."

***

Gabrielle sat on the side of the pool, grateful for this sweet break with Dakota. She said, "Isn't this magical?"

He said, "Absolutely," then, taking his shirt off, slid off the side of the pool into the water in his jeans. She smiled, and he motioned her to join him. Without hesitation, she dropped off the side and pushed toward him. He pulled her underwater for a kiss.

When they came up for a breath, he kept her against him, loving the desire that flashed in her eyes. He licked her wet lips. Tasting. She held his face and kissed him. He pulled her under the water again.

***

Both couples were in the kitchen when Sean called later. Jimmy talked him through the security gates, and they went outside to wait for him.

Sean high-fived Jimmy when he got out of his truck. He said, "This place is terrific. When I grow up, I hope to have a ranch like this. But please, for now, tell me you have food. I could eat anything – even sardines and I hate sardines."

They laughed and helped him carry the surveillance equipment inside. He set it up on one end of the snack bar while Jimmy grilled the late-night dinner. In seconds, the kitchen smelled delicious.

Dakota said, "Sean, how long did it take you to lose your tail?"

"About twenty minutes. Once I confirmed the silver SUV was tailing me, I took them on a wild goose chase, then backtracked to Interstate 10. Later, I turned north on Highway 165. No problem. And now, here I sit, waiting to eat what I smell."

Chapter 19

On the river in Moss Bluff, Ryan slammed the passenger door as he got out of the silver SUV. He growled, "I can't believe you lost him. I know it was one of the guys from the log cabin in that black truck. I bet you a hundred bucks he was headed to where the woman's hiding."

The big guy got out, and said, "Look, he thought he was at the Indy 500. You couldn't have kept up with him. We'll get her, don't worry – and now we know that truck. And as for her, with her looks, she won't be hard to spot. We'll just head the direction he was going. Like you said, they'll need gas, or supplies at some point."

"Like you know anything. Just shut up," Ryan said. "If I had been driving, I wouldn't have lost him. I want that treasure. I have worked years for it, and I don't intend to walk away empty-handed again. My uncle is tired of covering up our messes, so we better be smarter this time. And now we have this woman my uncle hired to contend with. We are four armed men, so what use is she?"

***

Ryan watched Butch head to the kitchen, as always, looking for something to shove in his mouth. Still mad about losing the black truck, Ryan went out on the miserable excuse for a deck and plopped in a faded lawn chair. He cracked his neck and watched kids partying across the river. Their laughter annoyed him. But right now, everything annoyed him. He slapped a mosquito on his arm so hard, it disintegrated. Barely a blur on the skin. He smiled. There…that helped cheer him up.

He pulled out his phone and scanned through some old pictures at his high school in Houston. A lifetime ago. Back then he had been somebody. Star athlete. Strong. Cute enough. Lots of girls. But in the end, he hadn't had the grades to go to college. That's when the downhill slide started. He hadn't been able to find the jobs he deserved. Then he hadn't been able to keep the jobs he got. Then it didn't take long to stop seeing admiration on people's faces when they looked at him.

His parents had done the tough love thing and booted him out eventually, when liquor made him feel like the guy he used to be. His dad was Navy. Smart. Mean. And disgusted with him. His mom tried…many times to steer him in appropriate directions. He had never been interested. His dad retired and they moved off to the desert in New Mexico. He hadn't seen them in several years. A few phone calls or video chats for the holidays was about it.

Looking at his pictures again, he smiled at the one of the four of them standing at the beach laughing. His buddies. Butch, Sam, and Jamie. Man, they were so young back then. Happy. Hopeful. Expectant of an amazing life. Butch hadn't even been twenty years old yet, but Sam and Jamie were his age. That day their world changed. They learned buried treasure was a real deal.

But finding it was a different matter. They found bits and pieces here and there along the waterways in Louisiana. But he still had to eat so he took to stealing other people's property to survive in between scarce jobs. Then he learned what jail was like. His dad ignored him. His momma prayed for him.

Then came the stalking and killing for buried treasure. His uncle found out, and to save the taint on his own name, he got his hands dirty.

Ryan smiled. He enjoyed that a great deal.

***

It was well after dark in New Orleans, when Vee picked up her luggage from the baggage claim area at the Louis Armstrong airport. At the same time, a text notification told her the white Nissan rental was ready. Good, she thought. She was right on schedule.

Once she picked up the car, she headed to her hotel near the Mississippi River and tourist-filled French Quarter. It would be cool to get in some sight-seeing on Bourbon Street tonight. No telling when she would make it back to the states. Then again, maybe she never would. Besides, Bourbon Street would be the perfect place for her to hang out for a few hours. She would blend in with everyone else - just another blonde in the crowd.

***

Later, Vee strolled through the wild crowds on infamous Bourbon Street. Mardi Gras was over, so she was surprised to see people still dressed in costumes. It was all a trip. The crowd was like a tidal surge of partiers going up and down the street checking out nightclubs, bars, other racy clubs, restaurants, vendors, hotels, and businesses that lined the street. And she saw that even with police presence on horseback, there was an air of dangerous darkness that hung over the place.

But the food was magnificent. Anything that walked, swam, or flew was seasoned and cooked in sauces, gumbo, grilled, or fried. It was perfection. Vee saw crabs on people's plates, whole fish, shrimp, raw oysters, crawfish, steaks, duck, and chicken. She looked forward to trying crawfish and stepped into a corner restaurant – still watching through the windows the crazy sights in the street.

They brought her a crawfish platter with fried crawfish, crawfish etouffee (rich gravy over rice), crawfish hush puppies, crawfish fried pie, and a crawfish stuffed roll called a pistolet. The platter was an amazing array of southern delicacy. Vee popped a fried crawfish in her mouth and groaned. Yum. Louisiana knew how to feed you. The sounds of Jazz from the musicians on the sidewalks and streetcorners entertained her as she ate.

After dinner, full and satisfied, she rejoined the crowd in the street. Intrigued. She was sure there were people from all over the world. All ages. All races. Groups. Tourists. And even locals. But she could also see with her mercenary eye, the sneaky wiles of predators slipping amongst the people, hidden weapons bulging under their clothes. There were dark alleys with shadows that moved - and weary faces in the crowd. Men and women, tired, and wanting to go home, but too addicted to leave.

On her way back to the hotel, Vee grabbed a cup of the acclaimed coffee and sugar-dusted beignet. It was time to focus. Her lucrative weekend began tomorrow.

Chapter 20

At Jimmy's safe house, Sean and Dakota reviewed intelligence updates on Reynolds and the Posse. After reading the first report, Dakota growled.

Sean said, "What did you read?"

"Reynold's finance report. He bought a roundtrip plane ticket and car rental. He will be arriving in New Orleans Friday. He didn't make it an FBI reservation, just personal, so he's confident no one has tied him to the Posse. And he pulled fifty-five grand out of a personal savings account in Virginia, in his name only. I bet his wife doesn't know that."

"No doubt! And FYI, I've received some interesting information in his phone records. His personal cell is connecting with a burner phone in San Diego. He's received a short call for the last three days. And he's staying in touch with Ryan. But there's an additional burner phone he's called twice in Lafayette."

Dakota said, "He's pulling it together for the grand finale. That's why Gabrielle's bait trap tomorrow is critical. We've got to find out who the players in the Posse are."

"Ryan's phone records are supposed to arrive after midnight. Regular calls to people through the years should make the guys in the Posse stand out. And you're right. We need identification quick. Like yesterday."

Dakota said, "Sean, can you get someone researching plane arrivals in Baton Rouge and New Orleans from San Diego this week? That might be the only break we get on who that person is – and if they're coming here."

"I'll get on it."

"And come on, let's take a break before we start the meeting."

"Sounds good to me. I'm going to see those Arabians I glimpsed when I drove up."

***

Dakota noticed Gabrielle, Serena, and Jimmy sitting in the grass out front with the dogs. He walked out the huge front door, and said, "Hey Jimmy, is this a real castle door?"

"Yep."

"So, tell me, where do you buy a castle door these days?"

Jimmy chuckled, and said, "I met some interesting people overseas. It's amazing what you can buy."

Dakota laughed, then called the dogs and they ran to him. He played with them, then laid in the grass next to Gabrielle. They watched the stars and talked. It almost seemed like a normal evening. Almost.

***

About a half hour later, Sean stuck his head out the door, and said, "Party's over! It's time to meet - it's getting late."

They trailed in and Dakota said, "Sean, you lead with the intelligence updates."

Sean said, "Sure. To keep it short and sweet, Reynolds will land in New Orleans Friday. He should be in Lake Charles that afternoon. Next, he has connected with two other burner phones. One in San Diego. The other in Lafayette. We are working on their identification." Then he pointed at Dakota.

Dakota looked at Gabrielle, and said, "Tomorrow we will search for the Posse as much as they will search for you. They need you. Because of that, we want them to *think* they can snatch you. You and I will be visible - going inside stores, stations, whatever we need to do to expose you in these small rural towns. You need to appear easily accessible.

"Once they show up and we know they see you, we set you up – seemingly by yourself to draw them in for the attack. But I will be near you providing instructions and protection. Just do exactly what I tell you as the scene unfolds. You will need to be prepared to fight – at least for a few seconds.

"Jimmy will be parked nearby with Serena. He will be our sniper and fire if things get hot. We will use radios and earpieces to communicate. I think they will do a fast attempt to grab you and run. When they miss, Jimmy and Serena will follow them. That's the plan."

Gabrielle said, "Ok. Are we going to practice?"

"In a few minutes. I know it's late, but I want to work with you on a specific defensive plan."

Shortly, Dakota and Jimmy watched Gabrielle workout in the garden. It was Jimmy's first time to see how nimble she was. He was impressed with her quick reflexes. She ran, jumped, and rebounded off the trees – sweating, but barely winded.

Dakota knew she would handle tomorrow's attack well. But he needed her prepared for two guys – or more. He had a few kicks and blows to teach her.

He said, "Jimmy, any thoughts?"

"She's quick. And she probably prefers to fight up high, but with two big guys she may be safer with low blows. That way they can't just pick her up and run. And any fight longer than a few seconds is too dangerous."

"Correct."

Gabrielle finished her warmup and splashed cool pool water on her face before joining them.

Dakota said, "Show us where your weapons will be."

She pulled up her pant leg to reveal her hunting knife. She pulled the throwing knives out of her thigh pockets. She lifted her shirt tail to reveal the dart gun.

He said, "You need to practice for two big assailants. You can't fight them hand to hand. Aim to wound and move. Jimmy suggested a low attack, so they have to scramble for you. Leg stabs are a good target. We may add more later, but let's give it a go and see what works for you."

Gabrielle knew her small knives could disable and distract the assailants. But if she landed on the ground, she would go for her ankle knife. If they lifted her, she would stab whatever she could reach. Face to-face she couldn't use the dart gun but if she had to run, she could. She only needed to fight a few seconds.

They practiced attacking her. Then Dakota taught her a close-up groin kick from standing or if she was on the ground. Then she was ready.

***

While Gabrielle cleaned up, Serena made coffee and heated a praline bread pudding she had found in the freezer. And before long, everyone was back in the kitchen following the aroma.

Jimmy swallowed his last bite, and said, "Do you like cooking, Serena?"

She shrugged and said, "Not especially. I'm a good cook but cooking for one was never exciting."

"Yeah. I get that."

Serena watched Gabrielle and Dakota walk away, and said, "I'm nervous about tomorrow."

Jimmy nodded, and said, "Come on, walk with me," and they stepped outside.

He said, "I don't think there's a mom alive that wouldn't feel what you feel right now. This is intense and your daughter is in the middle. Our daughter now. Serena…" and he lifted her chin.

Her eyes were filled with tears, and he opened his arms. She walked into them feeling his unbelievable strength.

Holding her, he said, "Life's been a huge challenge for you and Cat. But you have help now. You aren't doing this alone anymore. Dakota would die to save either one of you. So, would I. And Sean."

"She's tough Jimmy, yet gentle and loving. She's an amazing woman. I don't want to miss another single breath of her life. I'm weary of loving from afar."

He said, "Look at me. Look at Cat. Look at all of us. Your days of loving from afar are over. You have a new life ahead of you. That is what we are fighting for. You are tough yourself, woman. I think you inherited some of Lafitte's skills and battle strategies."

She opened her mouth to say something, and he stopped her.

He said, "I promise. Your days of running are over. You are home."

Their eyes met and held. She said, "You really know how to get to the heart of the matter. You're convincing…and romantic."

He gave her a heavy-lidded, sexy look, and whispered, "I aim to please."

She gave him a teasing side glance in response, then stepped back. She felt the attraction. Wow. How did she want to handle it?

He reached to pull her back, but she quickly danced aside. He raised his eyebrows as he acknowledged her tease. Then she darted into the garden. He watched her go, smiling. Nope. She wouldn't get far.

***

Dakota finished his conversation with Sean and looked for Gabrielle. She was sitting on the stairs overlooking the den.

He sat behind her and rubbed her shoulders. He said, "You ok?"

"Yeah. Just ready to do what has to be done so it's over."

"You are amazing," he said, and ran his hands down her arms.

She leaned back against him, and said, "I'll give you ten minutes to take my mind off all of this."

He whispered, "Show you, or tell you?"

"Both."

He whispered, breath brushing her ear softly, "I crave…who you are. You make me feel like ten times a man. I want to inhale the fragrance you bring. I want to kiss you as I watch you talk. I want to feel the breath of your laughter. I love you up close - in my space. I love you, sassy, sexy, or wrapping your arms around animals. And I love to watch you…when you want to kiss me."

She turned and knelt between his legs on the stairs. Her eyes locked with his. She whispered, "I love it when you love me…just like that," and he saw the response all over her.

Holding her face, he said, "Open for me, Cat," and as her lips parted, he kissed her.

Afterwards, he said, "You. Are. Mine."

***

Serena jogged down the garden trail, lit with lights, but filled with soft shadows. She glanced back and didn't see Jimmy. She walked off the path and made her way under a fabulous weeping willow tree. She sat a couple of branches up.

In seconds, Jimmy stepped from around the tree and looked up at her. Heart pounding, she climbed up another branch. She knew…what was coming. She was nervous.

He leaned against the trunk, watching her, and said, "Where are you going?"

"How did you find me so fast?"

He said, "Isn't that the point of chase? Come on down."

She shook her head no and reached for a higher limb.

He straightened, grabbed the lowest branch, and in two steps was in the tree with her. She looked at him. Flustered. He was sexy gorgeous. He smiled as he read her expression. Nervous, she turned to climb higher, and he grabbed the back of her waistband.

He said, "Wait. Those limbs are too small." The branch cracked and dropped out from under her.

He caught her around the waist and swung her into his chest. She slammed into him hard. Holding on, she got a foothold on the branch.

Breathless, she said, "Oh."

Faces close, he looked at her lips, bodies tight together, and whispered, "I'm going to kiss you."

Her breath brushed his face as she said, "No."

He leaned an inch closer and said, "But…you're looking at my mouth."

She tried not to, and said, "I…didn't mean to."

He brushed his lips against her face with the tiniest grin, and said, "Yes. You did."

"I'm not sure I'm ready for this."

"Oh yeah. You're ready," he said, and his mouth covered hers.

Serena felt the jolt as his lips set off a fire in her. Every inch of her felt him and she couldn't think at all. He groaned, deepened the kiss, passion lighting him up. Her response was just as wild as he thought it would be. To feel her open to him…hot. The kiss rocked them.

Both breathless a few minutes later, Jimmy looked at her very kissed lips. He said, "Your mouth is delicious."

She gasped, closed her eyes, and said, "You…that…oh wow…"

Kissing her cheek, he said, "Yeah. And that's just our first."

"But…I'm too old for this."

He chuckled, and said, "Maybe for climbing trees. Not for kissing."

A nervous, excited wreck, she avoided looking at him, and said, "Shouldn't we climb down now?"

***

Grinning, Gabrielle said, "That's what I wondered. What's going on up there?"

Serena moaned and hid her face in Jimmy's chest. She said, "I'm so embarrassed."

Jimmy held her and glanced down as Gabrielle said, "We thought we lost you."

Serena said, "We?"
Chuckling, Dakota said, "Hey there. Is the tree thing in the family?"
Jimmy said, "Ignore them, Serena. They will go away," and Dakota and Gabrielle laughed and headed back to the house.

Jimmy didn't let Serena see his smile as he helped her down. He knew she was not sure what to do now.
Serena knew Jimmy watched her. She felt exposed, embarrassed because of her passion, and totally unsure of herself. She was struggling with a way to laugh it off and move past it.
As she stepped down in front of him, he took control and pulled her back in his arms. He said, "Just quit thinking. Kiss me again. Get used to it…" and when she opened her mouth to answer, he kissed her.

***

It was well after midnight when Sean and Dakota reviewed a large report from headquarters.
Dakota motioned Jimmy over and said, "We will be working on the Posse phone records for the next few hours. Would you take guard duty over Gabrielle and Serena while they sleep? I can't leave them unattended."
"You bet. I won't leave them."

***

Once the women were in bed, Jimmy sat in the loft. His life was upside down and he loved it. He had been in the Army thirty years and was fifty-five years old now. But Serena at fifty-years-old made him realize he still had a lot of living and loving to do.
He pulled up the security system on his phone and everything was calm. No activity. No alarms. All was well. He leaned on the rail and watched Dakota and Sean work for a while, then sat on the staircase and began to hum softly to himself. He never noticed when he started to sing.
His beautiful voice carried whispered music into the night. Serena opened her door and listened to him. She leaned her head against the door frame and watched him. He was…quite a man. She grinned and gently closed the door.

About two-thirty in the morning, Jimmy heard moaning and remembered Cat's nightmares. He glanced in her room, and she thrashed her head on the pillow. He sat on the side of the bed and sang as he rubbed her arm. She began to calm.

A shadow filled the doorway as Serena walked in. She sat next to him as they both soothed her. Then Dakota stepped in the room. He walked to the other side of the bed and kissed Gabrielle's forehead. He smiled and headed back to work.

Chapter 21

In Lafayette, Jason Trasker's phone rang at six a.m. He sat up, ran his hand through his hair and answered on the second ring, "What. It's six a.m."

"Well, it's seven in D.C. This is Reynolds."

Jason said, "Right. What time is the shopping trip?"

"Vee will be there after lunch today. She's heading in from New Orleans. She will call you herself when she gets close. She has your number. Just let her shop and I will pay you when I get there tomorrow."

"Agreed. Give me a thirty-minute lead time in case I have a customer."

***

After Reynold's call, Jason made a call. After two rings, someone picked up. He said, "It's set. The chick will be here today. He will be here tomorrow. Do you want me to take care of them? He'll have lots of cash on him."

He listened for a second, laughed, and said, "You have to be kidding. Talk about a haul. I can't wait till they get here."

Chapter 22

Dakota and Sean both jumped the next morning when the phone rang. Sean grabbed his phone. Dakota checked the time. Six-thirty in the morning. After a long night they had fallen asleep on the sofas.

***

Sean answered, "You're on speaker."

"Hey, Sean. It's Toby. Y'all just caught a mega break."

"What do you have?"

"Reynolds called the Lafayette cell number again. The guy's name is Jason Trasker. Turns out, Jason is undercover with Alcohol, Tobacco, Firearms (ATF), and they called us with a head's up on the sting."

Sean and Dakota yelled, "Yes!" and glanced up as Jimmy, Gabrielle, and Serena, headed downstairs to join them. The phone woke them all.

Toby continued, "That's the good news. The bad news is that we think Reynolds hired a mercenary. A woman. All the agent knows is that her name is Vee, and she'll pick out her weapons today. Reynolds is footing the bill. She is traveling in from New Orleans. Reynolds is scheduled to get his weapons tomorrow."

Dakota and Sean glanced at each other – minds working in tandem. The mercenary was the surprise element. She undoubtedly was the San Diego contact. They would find out.

Sean said, "What weapons did they order?"

"All Reynolds told Jason was that the chick was small but likes big guns. He will get back with us after they purchase."

"Thanks, Toby. This is the break we needed."

***

After everyone had time to wake up and drink coffee, they met for updates. Dakota said, "Along with the news on the ATF agent and the female mercenary, we also have projections on the Posse members. Ryan talks to three men regularly. For years. Two brothers live in Lake Charles. The third guy lives in Moss Bluff, close to Westlake on the river. We're going with these four guys as the Posse at this point. Sean will fill you in on their details."

Sean said, "The two brothers are Jamie and Sam Frisk. They are both in their fifties, just under six feet tall, and average weight. They are employed at a shipyard. One is married with kids and the other, a widower with a teenage son. Jamie drives a blue truck and Sam drives a red one.

"The third guy is Butch Holland. He's a big guy, six foot-two inches tall and almost two-hundred fifty pounds. We figure he's the muscle for the group. He's single and forty-seven years old. He drives a silver SUV which is undoubtedly the one that tailed me last night. And Ryan drives a black truck."

When Sean finished, Dakota said, "So that provides us the four vehicles that could be hunting us. Ryan's sole goal is Gabrielle. He's been treasure hunting and murdering people for well over twenty years. Before Serena's husband even got involved with them at work. The good news is, he isn't aware of Gabrielle's connection to Trent – and they know nothing of Serena. Let's keep it that way.

"To briefly confirm our plans today, Jimmy will have rifle protection for Gabrielle. Sean will be lookout. I will be Gabrielle's contact and defense as she connects with the Posse.

"And Jimmy, no matter what, follow the Posse when they run. Don't deviate even if we have unexpected circumstances. And that's it. Everyone, get your gear and come back. Sean will fit us with earpieces and radios."

Less than an hour later, they loaded their gear in the vehicles. Dakota walked to Jimmy's car and said, "The Posse can't take Gabrielle under any circumstances."

Jimmy said, "Understood. She won't leave with them. That's a promise."

Dakota saw the concern on Serena's face, and said, "Cat can do this. She's tough and trained - like you. Stay with Jimmy and do everything he says."

***

Vee left New Orleans and cruised Interstate 10 westbound. She was eager for the job Reynolds hired her to do. Intended victims of her services initially dismissed her abilities based on her height of five foot-three inches. That cost them. Watching the fear that inevitably appeared on their faces always gave her a revengeful rush.

She crossed the Mississippi River bridge in Baton Rouge before lunch and in no time at all she rolled across the Atchafalaya basin. She was impressed. Nothing like a bridge through swampland and marsh as far as the eye could see. But she wondered how in the world you pronounced the name - much less remembered how to spell it. There were so many odd names in Louisiana.

An alarm went off on her phone which meant in thirty minutes, she would be in Lafayette shopping for weapons. One of her favorite activities. Reynolds insisted this guy had quality goods – and plenty of them.

***

She called the number Reynold's gave her, and a man answered, "Trasker here."

"This is Vee. I need the address."

"Texting it now. Then delete it."

She keyed it in her GPS and said, "Give me thirty-five minutes."

"Honk twice and I will walk out on the porch."

Vee said, "Got it."

***

The undercover agent, flipped on his hidden camera and sat to finish his shrimp po-boy. He tossed a fried shrimp to his Rottweiler, also an ATF agent, and smiled. He loved his job.

It wasn't long and the dog barked. He heard two honks and walked on the porch. As Vee walked toward him, he hid his surprise. This chick looked like a high school cheerleader with short blonde hair and thick eye liner.

She climbed the steps and said, "You like what you see?"

He shrugged and said, "Cute is great but a paying customer is better."

"Exactly. I am here for what Reynolds is paying for."

He opened the door and said, "Come on in. Don't mind the dog, he won't bite unless I tell him to."

She totally ignored the dog and said, "Show me what you've got."

He pulled a ladder down out of the ceiling and pointed upstairs. He said, "Welcome to my attic store," and for the first time, she smiled.

In thirty minutes, she was back in her car driving away. He watched to make sure she didn't return to clean up her trail by taking him out. When she didn't, he called his boss. Listening to the phone ring, he thought, one down, one to go. Reynolds would be here tomorrow.

***

Sean turned into the Dollar General in the small town of Reeves and parked where they would be visible if the Posse drove past on Highway 190. This was literally the only retail business for miles around. Dakota and Gabrielle lingered chatting in the parking lot with customers before they strolled inside. Jimmy and Serena parked nearby to observe.

After a short time with no activity from the Posse, Dakota said, "Let's go set up at the convenience store in Ragley on Highway 171. They will have more traffic because of the big intersection."

As they traveled west, the countryside was surprisingly nothing but miles of thick green forests, gullies, ponds, and pastureland. There were no large subdivisions, no billboards, and not even a single gas station.

Gabrielle said, "It's hard to believe all this land is still uninhabited. Now I know why we were able to hide out there. Other than train tracks, power line trails, and pipelines, it's just natural. But yet a few miles south of here, Lake Charles is bustling with activity on lakes, beaches, massive bridges, casinos, shopping, industry, and a port – all connected by the Calcasieu River."

Dakota said, "What is it they call southwest Louisiana?"

"Sportsman's Paradise."

Before long, they veered right at the overpass and turned north. The large store was a mile or so up the highway. They cruised around the building and checked all the cars and trucks in the lot. None looked like the Posse vehicles, so Sean stopped at the gas pumps to watch the traffic. Gabrielle and Dakota went inside.

Several minutes later over the radio, Sean said, "Heads up people. We have a silver SUV doing a U-turn down the highway. It looks like the one from last night."

Dakota steered Gabrielle outside facing the back lot where there was little to no activity.

He said, "Just walk around and act like you're talking on the phone, oblivious to anything going on around you. I will be at the corner of the building. Listen for my instructions." Then he said, "Head's up everyone, bait is set."

Gabrielle clenched a throwing knife in each hand, slipped the phone under her chin, and nodded at Dakota. He leaned against the building and gazed over the top of his phone as a silver SUV neared their area. Jimmy had parked near the tree line and disappeared into the woods with his rifle. They were all in place.

Two men were in the SUV. It drove slowly through the parking lot and parked several vehicles away from Gabrielle. Dakota knew they saw her.

Sean said, "They are about forty feet away, get ready."

Dakota shifted to get a direct view of Gabrielle. The men were out of her line of sight. She played her part like she didn't have a care in the world.

Dakota said, "Jimmy."

"I've got my eye on her."

Sean said, "Here they come. It looks like Ryan and Butch – and Butch is going to reach her first from the front of the parked cars. Ryan is following from the back of the cars."

Dakota said, "Gabrielle, shift left so you can see them coming out of the corner of your eye," and she laughed on the phone and shifted. Her heart pounded. Her hands tightened on the knives.

Butch, the big man, darted toward her, and Dakota said, "Now!"

She acted like she dropped her phone and squatted. As the guy reached for her, she spun on the ground and stabbed him in both sides of his right knee with the razor-sharp knives. He yelled and staggered back, blood dripping. She stood and braced for the next attack. The guy grabbed for her again and she nimbly stabbed his forearm and danced away.

Dakota was only two steps away when the leader, Ryan, grabbed the nape of Gabrielle's shirt and held her up like a fighting cat. She pivoted and sliced his stomach. He slung her onto the hood of a red car. Dakota ran between the men and Gabrielle. The big man charged, and Dakota spun and kicked him in the head knocking him to the ground. The leader threw a punch and Dakota blocked and hit him with an elbow and a kick.

The big guy grabbed at Gabrielle as she slid off the car. Dakota hit him – and a rifle shot rang out. The windshield of the Posse's silver SUV exploded. Startled at the gunshot, both men ran. Dakota pulled Gabrielle to him as he glanced at the fleeing men. The big man pointed a pistol at them, but a second rifle shot rang out as Dakota dove with Gabrielle behind a utility truck.

Tires squealed as Dakota helped Gabrielle up. The vehicle roared down the highway headed south. Gabrielle struggled to focus. Her head was spinning, and she was wobbly. Dakota frowned and looked her over, then they both saw the drug dart in her arm. She tried to talk, but her eyes rolled back. He caught her as she fell, then glanced back as Jimmy pulled onto the highway after the Posse. People poured out of the store to see what the commotion was, but Dakota ignored them and got in the truck with Gabrielle.

Sean said, "Is she hurt?"

"She was hit with her drug dart. I'm calling Zoe. A veterinarian will know what we need to do."

***

Zoe answered. He said, "Gabrielle got shot with a drug dart. What do we do?"

She said, "Take it easy. She'll sleep for a couple of hours and wake up with a headache. Start trying to wake her up after two hours and make her drink a lot. Do not give her anything for pain. Nothing at all, you hear me?"

***

Dakota called Jimmy and Serena and they both asked at the same time, "Is she alright?"

"She is. But she's out – she was shot with one of her darts. Zoe told us what to do. I'll take care of her. Jimmy, are you still on the Posse's tail?"

"Yes, but at some point, they will have to trade vehicles since they are without a windshield."

"That was a great shot."

"I needed something to shock them and break up the attack. But then I had to shoot again when the big guy raised the pistol. I promise you his gun hand will hurt for a while."

Dakota said, "I hope so. Now keep in touch and don't take any chances. View only. No contact."

***

Heading to Moss Bluff with a shattered windshield, Ryan hollered over the noise of the wind, "Your blood is making a mess and I am sick of eating bugs!"

Butch said, "Well, what do you expect? That crazy woman stabbed me. And who shot at us?"

"How am I supposed to know? And she gave me a slice too. Just cover it up and quit whining. They were small knives. Effective, but small, and we don't have fatal wounds. And what did you try to shoot her with? That wasn't your gun."

"I took her gun. Why? What does it matter?"

"Because if you had killed her, I would have killed you. Understand? I need her alive."

"Yeah, I got it. But give me a break – between her stabs, and his kicks—"

Ryan interrupted and said, "Who was he anyway? A boyfriend? But I guess it doesn't matter. When this is over, they'll all be dead. No witness is my motto. I have six men that learned that the hard way. Now get us off this main road!"

***

Sean maneuvered through Jimmy's security gates and drove around the back of the house. Dakota carried Gabrielle to Jimmy's room and laid her on the bed. He took off her weapons and boots. He needed to get her out of the dirty clothes. He called Sean to bring him a T-shirt, a wet rag, and a towel.

Once he had what he needed, leaving on her bra and panties, he removed the dirty clothes, put his T-shirt on her, made sure she had no wounds, and cleaned her up. He knew no woman would like to be tended to unconscious, but he did what needed to be done. She would understand and trust that. He tucked her in and set the timer for the wake-up process to start.

He walked to the door and glanced back at her.

Sean watched him from the computer, and said, "You're hooked bad, aren't you?"
"Big time."

***

Jimmy called later and Dakota said, "Where are you?"
"Where's Gabrielle?"
"Clean, safe, and tucked in your bed sound asleep. I will begin the wake-up process in about an hour."
"Ok. Our two Posse guys are in a camp on South Perkins Ferry Road in Moss Bluff. Probably Butch's place. There is a black truck here too. When they went inside, I popped a tracker under the fender. And now, we are tucked out of sight behind a large patch of bamboo at a picnic area like two lovebirds enjoying the river."

***

After the call, Jimmy glanced at Serena, then said, "You're quiet."
She nodded and said, "How's Gabrielle?"
"Safe. Dakota will take care of her."
She nodded with a frown, then said, "That makes this bearable for me."
He laid his hand over hers in understanding, and she pulled her hand away. He said, "What's wrong? I can tell you're edgy."
"I just think it's important we watch these guys and stay serious right now – without personal distractions."
He said, "We're supposed to look like a couple."
"Yes, well, couples fight too, right?"
He chuckled and said, "I wasn't planning on causing a scene. I bet you have a temper."
"Do you want to find out?"
He slipped an arm around her and said, "Just lean against me and relax."

They sat for a while.
Serena loved his cologne. He smelled so good. It felt good in his arms. Eventually she said, "I really like your cologne."
With a smile, he said, "Do you?" and pulled her closer. He said, "Have I mentioned that I catch fire really quick?"

She tried not to smile, and said, "I'm not trying to start anything. You just smell really good."

He kissed her hand. She looked at his mouth touching her skin and felt the response igniting. She tried to back it down, but he nibbled on her finger. Lips soft. Warm. Her gaze lifted to his.

He said, "Now this…is the definition of distraction."

"I see that."

He glanced at the camp they were watching then looked back at her. He said, "This thing between us, is not going to be a slow ride. You better hold on."

"How fast do you think?"

"When will you marry me?"

She gasped, "That's turbo, Jimmy!"

He said, "I bet Adam and Eve didn't wait long either," and she couldn't stop the grin.

He touched her cheek, and said, "I'll give you all the time you need. I'll just work on convincing you that you don't need to wait."

"You think you can do that?"

"Without a doubt. Kiss me. Give me a taste."

A truck started and they both looked at the camp.

Ryan was in the black truck. He yelled at Butch to hurry. Butch struggled, obviously from his wounds, to put a large box in the bed of the truck.

As the rumble of Ryan's loud pipes soon faded down the road, Jimmy and Serena followed in the car. This time the APP Sean installed on Jimmy's phone flashed the beacon they tailed. Time to stalk the killers.

***

Dakota's alarm sounded. He grabbed a Coke and a bottle of water and headed to the bedroom. Gabrielle still hadn't moved. It was time to get her out of that drug stupor. He sat next to her, talked, and rubbed on her arms. He ran his hands over her cheeks and brushed her hair back. She didn't move.

He wiped her face with a wet washcloth - but still she slept. Alarmed a bit, he pulled the covers down and rubbed her legs. He rolled her on her side to rub her back and nothing fazed her. He cranked up the music on his phone and tried to sit her up. She was a ragdoll. He hollered for Sean.

When Sean stepped in the room, Dakota said, "I can't wake her. At all. Would you turn on a soft warm shower and get me a chair?"

Wearing only his jeans, Dakota carried Gabrielle, and slowly emersed her legs and hips into the warm water. Her arms twitched. That was it. He kept talking to her and pushed further under the shower to her chest. Her legs moved some, but her head still laid back – unresponsive.

He said, "Sean, cool the water down," and as the cool water sprayed over them, Gabrielle's fingers clenched a few times.

He motioned Sean after a couple of minutes to use cold water only. Goose bumps covered them as the cold water and air conditioning made it uncomfortable. Her legs and arms flexed but still she didn't open her eyes. He pulled the chair over and draped her across his lap and began to wipe her face with the cold water. She finally rocked her head back and forth, shivered, and moaned.

He called her name and rubbed her face.

She fought to open her eyes and mumbled, "Can't…"

So, he kissed her – and though they were both cold, the kiss wasn't. She responded, slowly sliding her hands up his chest. After a few moments, he looked down at a very groggy, wet, beautiful Gabrielle, and smiled. Then he carried her out of the shower toward Sean who wrapped a large hot blanket fresh from the clothes dryer around them.

Sean pushed a dry chair behind Dakota, and said, "I have another blanket in the dryer. Be right back."

Dakota sat and snuggled them in the blessedly hot blanket as he gratefully thanked God, she was ok.

Teeth chattering, she whispered, "I…couldn't wake…up."

"That's why we're wet and cold."

She said, "Need…a hot shower…now," and he smiled.

Sean swapped out blankets and Dakota said, "Thanks Sean. Just bring one more for Gabrielle. And I'll be fine."

As Sean walked out, Gabrielle said, "Guy shot me…as we wrestled by the…car. With my gun."

"I figured that."

"I need to stab him…again."

Grinning, he said, "Besides mad, how do you feel?"

She frowned and touched her head, and said, "I have a headache."

"Zoe said a headache is normal. Don't take any pain meds though. Not one. You can't mix the drugs."

She nodded and said, "Are you ok?"

"I wasn't hurt. Just concerned about you. I am better now that I can see those gorgeous eyes of yours. But we need to get you out of these cold wet clothes. Can you stand?"

She stood. Steady on her feet – just a trifle slow.

Sean carried in a hot towel for her, and Dakota said, "I have clean clothes for you in Jimmy's room. After you get dressed, we need to start you on liquids per Dr. Zoe."

She headed into Jimmy's room. He waited a few minutes to see if she needed him.

She said, "I guess you changed me?"

"I did."

"Thank you for taking care of me. Again."

***

Dakota changed and waited in the kitchen for her. When she walked out, she was still cold, so he tucked her on the sofa with a blanket and hot coffee, Coke, and water. He kept the liquids coming until she wasn't drowsy and started going to the bathroom.

When she was more herself, he heated a bowl of enchilada soup he had found in Jimmy's freezer. She finished it quick and was still hungry. He grilled her a hot ham and cheese sandwich and sliced up a peach.

She said, "Only your lips are better than juicy peaches."

He kissed her cheek, and said, "I'm good with that comparison. I love them too."

She said, "Here, taste," and perched her lips.

He kissed her and licked his lips, then said, "We need to keep peaches on hand."

Sean interrupted and said, "Hellooooooo. Remember me, the other person in the room?" They laughed.

Gabrielle thought about the attack, and said, "Was the plan successful?"

Both brothers high-fived with a laugh, and Dakota said, "You were a wildcat! Fast, nimble, you jabbed and moved. You gave them no break and they both left bloody. Did you hear the windshield blow out?"

"Was that the explosion?"

Sean said, "Yes, Jimmy blew out their windshield to get Butch off you. Then he shot your gun out of his hand when he aimed it at both of you. Can you imagine that unpleasant ride all the way to Moss Bluff?"

She laughed and said, "I feel so much better! And Dakota, those Ninja moves—"

The guys laughed.

She said, "I mean it. All I saw was spin, kick, elbow, slap, kick. You were a blur as I stabbed them. Oh. Well. I guess that sounds terrible," and they laughed again.

***

Sean's phone rang. He said, "It's Toby with intel," and answered.

Toby said, "You ready for Vee's weapons?"

"Tell us. Dakota and Gabrielle are with me."

"She got a rocket launcher with two rockets, two Glocks with silencers and large mags, a hunting knife, a rifle, and binoculars."

Dakota said, "A rocket launcher?"

"Yep, she wants something left in flames, or Reynolds does. And get this, she is five-foot three inches tall, blonde and looks more like a cheerleader than a mercenary. But he said she had dead blue eyes. Other than that, we are still waiting on her flight identification. Oh – and she is driving a white Nissan."

***

Dakota and Sean glanced at Gabrielle after the call.

She said, "If we are at my house for Ground Zero, what does she need a rocket launcher for? What in the world warrants a threat of that magnitude?"

Dakota said, "It's a projection, but we think Reynolds is shutting this case down by walking out the hero after he kills everyone and destroys all the evidence."

"Like my house?"

"And probably mine too."

"Well, what is Vee's role?"

"She kills, Cat. She is paid to kill."

"Great. Where is she?"

"On her way to Lake Charles."

Chapter 23

Jimmy called Dakota, and said, "Serena and I are tailing the guys in Ryan's black truck. We cruised through Westlake and now we're headed to Lake Charles over the Interstate 210 bridge. The tracker is working great, so we are hanging back to keep some traffic between us.

"Oh wait - here we go. They're taking the first exit by L'auberge Casino and Prien Lake Beach. Give me a second to see where they head." He continued, "We're following Prien Lake Road south for now. I'll let you know later where we end up."

Dakota said, "Wait. I need to give you an update and listen closely. The female mercenary, Vee, purchased a rocket launcher with two rockets, a rifle, ten magazine, two Glocks with silencers, twenty rounds each, and a field knife."

Jimmy said, "What the—"

Dakota interrupted, and said, "I know. The rocket launcher was a surprise. But there's another surprise. Vee is five-foot three inches tall, blonde, and possibly mean as a snake. Do not tangle with her. Avoid her at all costs. She picked up binoculars too, so she may prowl around. Keep an eye out for her. She was last seen in a white Nissan. Be careful."

"Got it."

Dakota said, "She's not good news for the Posse, or for us. Just watch them – from a distance. And last thing, Sean has tied into your tracking feed - so we have eyes on your location."

***

Still irritated with Butch, Ryan followed the road along Prien Lake. He said, "We're going to Jamie's house to get weapons ready for when my uncle gets here tomorrow. He intends to go over the plan to nab the woman – if we don't already have her - and I want him to see us prepared and on target."

Butch complained, "I need help with these stab wounds. The slice she gave you might not be bad, but she stuck me three times. And my hand is still numb. You know I can't go to the doctor and have cops snooping around."

"Jamie has a medical kit. Just bandage yourself up and go to the doctor next week out of state. This isn't your first injury."

"Look. As the muscle of the group, I'm usually the one that leaves other people bleeding."

"Shut up, Butch."

Butch ignored him, and said, "What about the Vee chick? Isn't she coming in today?"

"Yeah. She'll call and meet up with us later. Quit worrying about her."

"Right. That's what I thought about the Lafitte woman too."

Ryan punched him in the arm, and said, "Quit thinking about the women. We have other matters to tend to. You need to tell the group your vehicle is out of commission till you get another windshield."

"Whose gonna pay for the damage?"

Ryan snarled, "I am going to dump you in the bayou. Shut. Up."

A few miles later, Ryan turned left on a small lane next to a convenience store. Several houses down, he pulled into a long driveway for a two-story house – and headed towards a boathouse and dock.

Jamie and Sam were on the dock. They motioned Ryan and Butch to join them.

As Ryan and Butch walked up in T-shirts and shorts with bandages showing, Jamie asked, "What happened?"

Ryan glared at Butch, then said, "We found the Lafitte woman at the store in Ragley. We thought she would be an easy snatch, but she turned into a raging cat with knives. She stuck Butch three times, then sliced me once."

Sam laughed and said, "Cat woman cut y'all up. That's hilarious!"

Butch punched him and snapped, "Real funny. Then a karate guy came out of nowhere and joined the fight."

Jamie hid his smile, and said, "Sounds like an action movie."

Butch continued, "And to make matters worse, someone shot out my windshield, then shot her gun out of my hand. It was crazy."

Ryan, aware the brothers were trying not to laugh, said, "I will shoot every one of you if you don't end it right now. And get whiner a first aid kit before he bleeds to death from panic."

Jamie jumped up, and said, "I'll go, Boss. No problem."

***

On the other side of the inlet, directly across from the Posse's location, Jimmy pulled down an overgrown dirt road and parked out of sight. There appeared to be a few abandoned houses with unmown yards - littered with rusted-out vehicles. They made their way to the largest house and set up surveillance in an old washroom with a window on the carport.

Using binoculars, they watched the oldest Frisk brother hand Butch a white box and he headed inside the boathouse.

***

Serena said, "I bet that was a first aid kit," and Jimmy chuckled.

***

When Butch returned to join the three men on the dock, Ryan got on his phone. He walked away.

***

Watching Ryan talk, Jimmy said, "That conversation isn't going well if his red face is any indication. He looks furious." None of the Posse spoke to him after the call.

Serena said, "Looks like you were right. They look scared to talk to him."

***

Later, Jimmy noticed a white car pull in and park behind the convenience store on the corner of the road the Posse was on. He zoomed in on the car. A petite blonde woman got out. He pointed her out to Serena.

The woman had spiky short hair and wore sunglasses, jeans, and a sleeveless shirt. She grabbed a backpack from the back seat and looked down the road toward the house. Jimmy knew who she was looking for. She walked a short distance and slipped into some heavy brush in an empty lot.

When she headed back to her car a short time later, she drove to the dock to join the Posse. When she stepped out of the car this time, it was without glasses, but she had a jacket on.

Jimmy said, "She's packing."

***

They watched most of the men in the Posse scramble to their feet to greet the beautiful woman. They brought her a chair and something to drink. She talked and they listened, until Ryan jumped up out of his chair - frustration blazingly obvious.

Things got hot between Ryan, Butch, and Vee before long. She got up and walked down the dock behind the boathouse and glanced around. She said something to the men, and they joined her. She told Butch something and he angrily threw his arms in the air.

She pulled a gun from the small of her back, and without any sound at all, shot him in the head. He flew backward off the dock and landed in a flat bottom boat behind the boathouse. The other men ducked and scattered as water splashed.

***

Jimmy grabbed Serena's mouth before she could scream, then pulled her to the side of the window. They watched Vee put the gun back under her jacket and point to the boathouse. Without question, the three men quickly responded to her.

Jimmy said, "We have to get out of here. She's on a paid killing spree and Reynolds must have made her some kind of boss."

He removed his hand, then motioned for her to stay silent. He glanced back across the water at the boathouse, aware that Butch's body would disappear after dark.

***

After the men went in the boathouse, Vee turned and looked around the area. Everything was quiet. Her silencer had made sure the kill didn't alert anyone – besides, a loud engine was running somewhere anyway. She frowned and focused across the inlet at some broken down homes and junk cars in tall weeds. She would check that area later to make sure no one had seen anything. If they had, it wouldn't be hard to add a second body to the boat with Butch.

She smiled as she walked to the boathouse. Now they knew who was boss.

***

Jimmy grabbed a cap on a shelf, knocked the dust off, and said, "Tuck your hair up under this and keep your face averted as we leave. Do not look at the boathouse under any circumstances." Then he grabbed a cap for himself.

With a quick glance out the window, he confirmed Vee wasn't looking their way. They slipped onto the carport. Once in the yard, they followed a row of overgrown hedges to where a few old cars sat covered in rust from the humid heat. Before they moved into the open, he raised the binoculars. One of the guys slung a tarp over the boat with Butch's body.

Jimmy said, "I can't take a chance they'll see us run to the car. I need a disturbance to draw their attention."

He dialed 911 on his burner phone.

***

"911. What's your emergency?"

"Help! I'm hiding behind the convenience store on Big Lake Road! I think some guys in a green truck are robbing it. Help us! There are a lot of people here. Hurry! Oh, no! I have to get off the phone – someone's coming!"

***

Serena glanced at Jimmy as he hung up. That was a brilliant. He shrugged and they ducked and waited. Sirens sounded in the distance, quickly coming closer, till the police surrounded the store. Chaos erupted.

Jimmy glanced at the boathouse. Vee stepped out to see what the commotion was at the end of the road. While she was occupied, Jimmy led Serena through the line of old vehicles – then they darted to their hidden car.

He said, "Get in, and duck." Then scooping mud out of a nearby puddle, he smeared it over his license plate.

A few seconds later, he drove to the end of the dirt road and stopped at the main highway, then glanced toward the store. Vee stood on the edge of the spectators - watching him. Obviously, she knew where they came from. But they both knew she was blocked from following him. She saluted him. He ignored her and turned the opposite direction and hit the gas.

***

Dakota answered Jimmy's call on the first ring, and said, "We're listening. What have you found out?"

Jimmy said, "You were right about the Posse members. Ryan and Butch ended up with the Frisk brothers at a home in south Lake Charles. Vee showed up. After an argument she shot Butch in the head. We were hidden across the water from them and got out quick when the killing started. But she saw me from a distance. She even saluted me."

Gabrielle gasped. Dakota, knowing this didn't bode well for her emotionally, watched her, and asked Jimmy, "How is Serena?"

"Stunned. Quiet. But hanging in there."

Gabrielle's wide, terrified eyes stared at Dakota.

Jimmy said, "I covered my license plate, so she can't know who I am. And Serena wasn't visible to Vee. But we need to be prepared in case they manage to follow me. Turn on the electric fence and shut the window barriers. We need drone surveillance. Even put the dogs in the house. And Gabrielle, I know you are listening. We knew Vee was coming and that she was bad news. Tailing and watching them just confirmed what we already expected. We are fine. We'll be home in an hour."

***

As Jimmy ended the call, he reached for Serena's hand.

Tears trickled down her face, and she said, "It's bad enough that a twenty-seven-year-old woman, through no fault of her own, has been targeted by serial killers and a bad agent – but now a mercenary too! I can't stand knowing that Gabrielle feels the fear of being hunted like that."

Jimmy said, "It's a bad hand to be dealt. But we've got her. The goal is to end it all and set her – you – and your family free. And look on the bright side."

She looked at him incredulously. "What bright side is that?"

"At least she killed one of the Posse."

***

Gabrielle's gaze was locked on Dakota. He read fear all over her. Her expression reminded him of the night Liam had taken her. He opened his arms, and she sprinted across the room and leapt through the air. He braced - and caught her.

She spoke in a ragged whisper. "She's here to kill me."

"I won't let her."

He looked at Sean, wordlessly telling him to take care of everything while he took care of her. Sean nodded, understanding. Dakota carried Gabrielle into Jimmy's room, grabbed a pillow and quilt off the bed, then sat cross-legged with her on the floor outside the safe room. He tucked the blanket around her, building a cocoon, and rubbed her back. He soothed her…praying silently. Ignoring the rage, he felt inside.

In time, Dakota felt Gabrielle's quivering ease, but she made no move to let go. She turned her face into his neck, breathing against his skin. He felt her wet cheeks and tightened his hold. Loving her.

Gabrielle gradually felt safe again. The overwhelming fear of seeing evil coming for her was fading, leaving only the wonderful feel of Dakota. The smell of him. Love was replacing the fear and she fell asleep in his arms.

Later, Dakota heard the window panels rise, then voices. Jimmy and Serena were home. Their shadow filled the doorway, and he motioned them in. Gabrielle stirred, then woke, as her parents sat next to them on the floor. Dakota kissed her softly, and she leaned into their open arms.

On his way out of the room to join Sean, Dakota glanced back. He met Jimmy's gaze for a long, hard, moment. Understood. They both knew Dakota had five killers to stop. Quick.

***

Watching Dakota leave the room, Jimmy thought about Vee. He knew she thought she was invincible in this massacre Reynolds planned. But as a military man, he knew she wouldn't leave alive. She would create her own end. Her kind always did.

Then he turned those thoughts off and looked at the women he loved wrapped in his arms. One under their heads. One over them. Safe. Thank you, God.

***

Vee called Reynolds as she stood on the dock and gazed across the water by the boathouse.

He answered, "How's your trip?"

"I'm enjoying Louisiana. Thanks for the opportunity."

"What about Ryan and his buddies?"

"They're an unprofessional mess. They tried to nab the girl and took the beating themselves. Butch was out of control and wounded. A liability, so I killed him. Problem solved."

"Glad to hear it. Do your job extra well and you might even get a bonus."

She smiled and said, "Well now, incentives always encourage me."

"What about Ryan and the other two idiots?"

"They're nervous since I killed Butch, but controllable, and that's the goal. What time are we meeting tomorrow?"

"I will call you when I know."

***

Sean glanced up from his computer when Dakota entered the den.

Dakota said, "It's time to set the trap for the Posse. Vee is vicious. Do you have any identification on her yet?"

"Just got it. Her name is Sally Verrett. She was raised in California and got mixed up with a militia group at age twenty. It seems she's learned a lot in the last ten years. She normally takes jobs only stateside - since her passport hasn't ever been used. She owns a cabin in the mountains and had two hundred-fifty thousand dollars in a savings account."

"Had?"

"She moved it to an offshore account a few days ago."

Dakota said, "She's gonna run."

"Yeah. I froze her passport and we're watching the offshore account."

Dakota said, "She plans to go out with a rocket fireball and slip off while everyone sifts through the rubble."

"I agree. She may even take out Reynolds if he pays her early. Loyalty doesn't last long after money changes hands."

Dakota said, "Yeah. Go ahead and set up a conference call with all the agencies for tonight. We know all the players and their weapons now. Today's Thursday. Reynolds arrives tomorrow. He will want to get this over and done, so let's aim for Saturday to be a go for Ground Zero. That gives us one day to prepare."

***

Still sitting on the dock in south Lake Charles, Vee thought about the white car that drove off earlier today when the cops were at the store. Without a doubt, the guy had seen her shoot Butch. And outplayed her. He had left her stuck in place with a fake robbery investigation. Point one for him. Probably just an old man digging in the abandoned junk that had read to many crime novels. He would hide out and never say a word, scared she would find him.

Glancing across the water at the abandoned houses, she figured she might as well take advantage of the same place. She could keep an eye on these imbeciles from there. She grinned at the tarp covered boat bobbing in the water as dusk disappeared into blackness. The boat and its dead passenger would sink in the ship channel later tonight. Very late. And as far as she was concerned, they better handle it right, or more of them would be in line for a watery grave.

***

Gabrielle felt movement and opened her eyes. Light from the den shone into the bedroom, and her parents were propped on elbows, on either side of her.

Her mom smiled, and said, "Are you ok?"

"Oh. Gosh. Yes. It was the PTSD. The fear makes the moment terrifying and all consuming."

Jimmy said, "That's what I've heard. I'm glad it passed."

Jimmy glanced at Serena and smiled, knowing she would be relieved.

Returning his smile, she said, "You were impressive at the lake, Jimmy. Amazing response – you knew just what to do," and he winked.

Serena glanced at Gabrielle, who watched them with a grin.

Dakota, hearing their voices, stepped in the room, and said, "Anyone hungry?"

Jimmy's stomach growled and they laughed.

Dakota gave Gabrielle a hand up, and said, "How are you, Beautiful? That was an intense attack."

"I'm fine – and you're my hero. Again."

Jimmy and Serena left the room, and Dakota slid his hand behind Gabrielle's neck and pulled her lips to his. The kiss was long, soft, and caressing. Perfect.

***

Once everyone was in the kitchen, Jimmy & Serena volunteered to cook a pancake supper.

He pulled out an iron skillet, and Serena said, "Do you want me to stir up the batter?"

With his ever-ready sexy grin, he said, "You can stir things up for me anytime."

She glanced at the others and said, "He can't control himself. Don't pay any attention to what he says," and they laughed at Jimmy's obvious attraction.

Jimmy picked her up for a quick spin, and said, "Tell them you're going to marry me."

She gasped and said, "Jimmy—"

Cutting her off, he said, "You are. I know it." Then whispered in her ear, "I need you. Bad."

She smiled and touched his cheek, then whispered, "I know," and kissed him.

The others grinned at the scene playing out in the kitchen and provided a few catcalls and whistles to show their encouragement.

Jimmy glanced at them and said, "I told you."

Not expecting to be on public display, Serena just went with it, and smiled. She said, "Actually, a very wise man told me recently that Adam and Eve wouldn't have waited long either. Fast weddings aren't uncommon."

Jimmy grinned at hearing his remark called wise.

She touched his chest, and said, "But. Waiting a few weeks will be good for you. You need to enjoy the romance for a while and give me a little time to prepare."

Dakota said casually since they were all party to the conversation, "But. While waiting you must enjoy a multitude of cold showers."

Jimmy said, "Tell it like it is, Dakota."

Smiling, Serena said, "Just cook the bacon, Jimmy. After breakfast, I'll check the calendar."

He kissed her one more time as she passed by, and said, "Did I tell you that I think sassy women are sexy?"

***

Later that evening, everyone waited for the conference call between all the agencies. Jimmy brewed a fresh pot of coffee. Serena braided Gabrielle's hair. Dakota and Sean reviewed the facts of the case.

***

At 10 o'clock sharp, Director Washington called. Dakota answered and everyone introduced themselves for the record.

The Director took lead and said, "Evening everyone. Let's move on. To catch everyone up, new intel has provided that Reynolds hired a female mercenary named Sally Verrett, a.k.a., Vee. She arrived in Lake Charles today and killed Butch, one of the Posse members. The murder was witnessed by the surveillance of Retired Captain Barlow and Serena.

"Additional intel today from undercover ATF Agent Jason Trasker, revealed Vee's weapon's purchase included a rocket launcher. Trasker also confirmed that Reynolds is set to arrive in Lafayette tomorrow to purchase weapons for himself. As of now, we have a confirmed total of five live targets with serious weaponry. You take the plan from here Dakota."

"Yes, Sir. To begin, I will arrange for the Ground Zero meeting to be at noon Saturday. But be prepared, Reynolds will get there early. Everyone needs to be in place before dawn."

Washington said, "Affirmative."

Dakota continued, "Obviously, Vee's job is to assist Reynolds with the kills. And based on the rocket, we expect she will use it to eliminate all evidence at

Ground Zero – therefore, providing him the opportunity to plant his evidence afterwards. But for him to draw me on site with Gabrielle, he will have to fake undercover FBI. That's the only way they appear legit.

"So, the plan remains with Army veterans on the ground, FBI up high, and deputies on land and water. Stay silent. Stay hidden as backup for the Task Force. Sean and Serena will remain on the other side of the river in my barn - to provide surveillance and drone assistance. Gabrielle and I will arrive from the woods behind my house and ride across the river to meet the Posse.

"I project that when Gabrielle and I arrive at Ground Zero, the Posse's pretense won't last long. I will question Reynolds, causing trouble. Ryan, his nephew, will lose control once face-to-face with Gabrielle. That alone could be the trigger that sets the whole battle in motion.

"But we have to let it play out for Reynolds to expose himself. Obviously, I'll get shot protecting Gabrielle. When I go down, Sean will get her to the trees by Jimmy. The goal of this mission is that Gabrielle lives, and the Posse is stopped. Any questions?"

Each agency responded.

"The soldiers will be in place."

"The FBI will be in place."

The Sheriff said, "We will be there."

Dakota said, "The Task Force thanks you. See you Saturday morning."

***

Silence fell in the den as the call ended. Dakota waited for the explosion. No one spoke. Gabrielle ran upstairs and slammed the door.

Chapter 24

The door slam echoed through the room. They looked at Dakota because they knew why she was upset.

Dakota said, "When I get shot, make her run. Do you hear me? Scream in her earpiece. Make her run and shoot anyone aiming for her. Her instinct will be to come to me, but that puts her within arm's reach of Reynolds and Vee." Then he sighed, and said, "I need to go upstairs."

Jimmy said, "You better make sure she doesn't have a knife handy when you walk through that door."

"You can say that again."

***

Gabrielle paced, wildly upset. Dakota had lost his mind. She screamed - and her door opened. She spun as Dakota stepped in and shut it behind him. She ran and shoved him, ready to fight.

Holding her wrists, he said calmly, "Cat."

She growled and tried to back away from him.

He held her tighter, and said, "Gabrielle. Stop it," but she pushed and pulled and even tried to bite him.

Dakota sat on the bed and pulled her on his lap, forcing her to look at him, and said, "Listen to me."

Tears dripped down her cheeks as she yelled, "No! If you get hurt, I am not leaving you. Let me go!"

He held her against him. She struggled, and snapped, "I could scratch your eyes out I'm so mad at you."

"You're not mad."

"I'm furious. Let me go!"

She arched her back and screamed again. Dakota's ears rang - but he didn't release her. He knew she just needed to release her fear.

"Calm down so I can let you go."

She began to sob, and he said, "Honey."

She said, "Don't say that!" and fought to get up again.

He pulled her back down and kissed her. Startled, she paused. Then with tears still rolling down her cheeks, she responded feverishly as she wrapped her arms around him. He caressed her. Soothed her. How he loved his wildcat.

With a sigh, she whispered, "I'm sorry I hit you."

"No, you aren't."

She snapped, "Well, I'm trying to be."

He kissed her lingeringly, then said, "You just wanted to kill me before I got shot," and she bit his lip.

With a passionate groan, he kissed her, then rolled them so she was underneath him. He said, "Do you have any idea how you drive me wild?"

She slid her hands in his hair, and said, "Don't change the subject. I'm scared for you."

"I know. But we have to trust the men in place to protect us."

She said, "Don't be logical," and he grinned.

"Wildcat, we're going to have some fabulous disagreements."

She said, "Promises, promises," and he chuckled and sat up.

He said, "Come here, we need to talk about the conference call."

"Are you going to make me mad again?"

"No. It's time to look beyond your feelings and get the big picture."

She finally stilled to listen.

He said, "You and I are the bait to pull the trap together at Ground Zero. It doesn't work without us. My role is to bring you in, set the play in motion, and protect you as Reynolds reveals his deception and the killing begins. Once I am on the ground, get to the woods - away from Reynold's kill zone. My armored vest will keep me alive, so focus on using your skills to take them down and stay alive. Your grandfather left you a legacy. Fight for it. Plan for it. Draw the killers into *your* kill zone."

She sighed, and said, "I understand. But I still hate it."

***

Well after midnight, everyone was kicked back on the sofa staring at the TV. Dakota doubted they got into the movie any more than he did. But it was a good night. Everyone was safe and he was pumped and ready to face Reynolds. He knew they would hear from him tomorrow, and if everything went as planned, Ground Zero, would be over by one p.m. Saturday. He smiled as he ran his hands through Gabrielle's gorgeous hair. She sat on the floor, head on his leg. She had fallen asleep long ago.

When the movie ended, the guys drug another mattress downstairs by the safe room. Everyone would sleep there. Dakota stayed up and took first watch. Sean and Jimmy laid on one mattress, and the women on the other. Before long, it was quiet.

***

Jimmy and Serena faced each other a few inches apart from different mattresses. He rubbed his finger across her lips, and she licked it with the tip of her tongue. His gaze said everything without a word, and he got up and walked to the door. He motioned for her to follow, but she stayed in bed, and blew him a kiss. Desperate and frustrated, he closed his eyes and leaned his forehead against the door frame. In a moment, her hand slid around his waist. With a quick kiss, he pulled her with him.

***

Dakota acted like he didn't see Jimmy and Serena pass through the den, headed toward the library nook. He understood. He was praying for a short courtship himself when this mission was over.

***

Jimmy drew Serena around the corner and with both hands, held her face and kissed her, pressing her back against the wall, wanting to feel her. Completely lost in the wonder of him, she gave as good as she got.

He whispered, "Can you love me yet?"

Opening her lips to him again, she said breathlessly, "Yes." His next kiss burned her.

Nuzzling her neck, he said, "Ask me."

"Ask you what?"

"If I love you."

"Do you—"

Answering before she got the question out, he said, "Yes." Then he held her palm on his bare chest, and said, "You feel that?"

His heart pounded under her palm, and she nodded.

"I'm all yours."

She offered her lips in response, and he took them. Hot. Eager.

He whispered, "Have you looked at the calendar yet?"

"Yes…meet me by our willow tree three weeks from today - and I'm all yours."

He gave her that sexy grin she loved, and said, "I really love that willow tree. Are we going to climb it?" He kissed her as she giggled.

***

Ryan was stuck waiting at the boathouse in Lake Charles. He couldn't go back to Butch's camp on the river in Moss Bluff since the idiot's body was rotting in the boat outside. Besides, Vee demanded they sink the boat with the body in the Calcasieu Ship Channel tonight by three a.m. Not a minute later.

He knew that chick got a thrill out of killing. And he recognized the tendency since he had murdered six men. His treasure hunting buddy, Trent, had been the last victim. He wasn't supposed to have been a victim, but he found out his wife had been kin to Jean Lafitte – and she disappeared before giving them the treasure location. Trent died for that.

But now, the treasure was closer than it ever had been. Who knew a fresh DNA link would pop up after all these years. And he couldn't wait to get his hands on that wildcat with knives. She would be glad to tell him where the treasure was, or he would cut her up one inch at a time till she did.

***

Vee watched the boathouse from the abandoned house across the water. She figured she was in the same house as the man in the white car. He had seen her kill Butch. The fresh footprints in the dust and debris made that apparent, but no matter. He would sleep with one eye open for weeks. She smiled, amused, for the first time in hours.

She only planned to hang around this house till she was sure Ryan and his buddies sank the boat with the body like she told them. She expected their complete obedience because she had made it clear they were next if they didn't.

She had learned how to kill in the militia group back in her younger days – and it had been a vicious way to learn. The guys treated women worse than animals. She still didn't like to remember. She had learned to defend herself quick to survive. These days, she didn't even blink if she left dead bodies lying around. Especially if they hadn't taken her serious because she was small – or a woman. Like Butch. He had been all around stupid.

She looked over the dark lake and wondered if she would ever be able to walk away from this line of work. Most couldn't. Even if they managed to live through it. She'd think about it one day before she was too old to have kids. She knew more about raising kids than her parents had.

Their method of sticking her in time out when she misbehaved, only gave her time to plan her next catastrophe. And she loved the look on their face, as they wondered what they had done wrong to make her the way she was. It wasn't them. It never had been. They cared too much for it to be them. She just didn't care at all. And everyone along the way that hurt her, made it worse. And made it easier for her to kill.

Then again, maybe having kids wasn't such a good idea for her after all.

***

Back at the safe house, Dakota started another pot of coffee and grabbed a fresh peach to snack on while it brewed. He grinned, remembering Gabrielle's love of peaches – and the kiss with lips dripping juice. She was something super amazing.

He understood her as a profiler of course. The inner and outer scars. How it affected so much about her. Her self-defense drive for safety. The painting helping to replace ugly thoughts with beauty. But he understood her as a man too. Her man. He loved how she was learning to explore him as their relationship bloomed. Give and take. Wild as a lioness one second. Gentle and soft, the next. Sensual. Playful. Loving overall. He knew it was an adventure of a lifetime for them.

A message popped up on the computer, interrupting his reflections. Dakota clicked a live drone video feed that watched the boathouse where Ryan's truck was. It was two-thirty in the morning. Apparently, the Posse was up to something.

***

The Frisk brothers walked to the boathouse and Ryan stepped out to meet them. Without a word, they headed behind the building and removed the tarp off the old boat. They groaned at the sound of flies and the nauseating smell.

Ryan flicked on a tiny flashlight, and said, "That's disgusting. He smells like a rotting pig. Hurry up and get him out of here. And you better do it right, or you'll look just like him."

The brothers climbed in the boat, cussing as the small boat rocked on the water, rolling the large swollen body against their legs. *The FBI drone zoomed in, documenting proof of the murder victim.* The oldest brother hurriedly cranked the trolling motor and headed toward the lake – sucking in fresh air and swatting flies.

Once the boat entered the ship channel, they headed south along a secluded stretch of the waterway. After a few minutes, they headed into the deepest area – the middle – and wrapped the body with the chain and anchor. They unplugged the boat and stood, watching as they slowly sank beneath the dark water. Once the boat disappeared underneath them, they began the long-distance swim to shore.

They hadn't made it far when a loud horn blasted through the night. Startled, they looked downriver and finally made out a barely discernable empty barge bearing down on them. Frantic, they struggled to swim in the hindering life jackets as the churning current from the engines pulled at them, eager to leave them in the deadly deep with Butch.

After a terrifying battle, they broke free and swam in a panic toward the red truck that waited for them.

***

At the abandoned house, Vee watched across the water as the red truck returned and parked at the boathouse. It was four a.m. The men got out and went inside. Ryan stuck his head out a minute later to look around, and she laughed. No doubt about it. They had obeyed.

She grabbed her bag and left for the hotel room. Reynolds would call her tomorrow. It was almost payday.

***

Reynolds landed in New Orleans as the sun rose Friday. He slung his backpack over his shoulder. Finally, this treasure disaster would disappear. Forever. On his way out of the airplane, the rental company texted that his black SUV was ready. He walked to the baggage terminal, grabbed his bags, and headed out the automatic doors.

The SUV pulled up and he tipped the driver. He tossed his bags in the back and hit the road. He wanted to reach Lafayette before noon, and after that it was a short, straight shot to Lake Charles. Sportsman's Paradise, here I come. I've got more bodies to bury there.

***

At the safe house, on the sofa where he had fallen asleep, the smell of coffee woke Dakota. He laid there quietly for a few more moments. Then the fragrance of Gabrielle's shampoo wafted past, and he knew she was close. Looking forward to her sweet good morning kiss, he was surprised with a large, wet dog tongue. He jumped up, wiping his face, and scared the dog.

Gabrielle howled in laughter from the other sofa.

He grinned and joined her. He said, "Come on…give me a good morning kiss."

Shaking her head, no, she giggled.

Dakota lowered his face to hers, and said, "Kiss it better, Beautiful," and she squealed, and tried to get away from his doggy-kissed lips.

He pulled her back and wiped his face in her shirt. She pinched him.

Dakota laughed, and said, "I hope you don't outgrow this friskiness."

She said, "Not likely," and he chuckled on the way to wash his face.

When he returned, everyone was in the kitchen and Gabrielle's back was to him. He stalked her. The others didn't warn her, and he darted across the den and slung her over his shoulder as she screamed and laughed.

Chuckling, he sat on a bench and flipped her, stomach down, across his lap, and lifting one open palm, he said, "It's time for payback. One…"

She realized what he was doing, and yelled, "Don't you dare whip me!"

"Two…"

"Stop!"

"Three…" and he tickled her.

A few minutes later, they were breathless and laughing on the floor – morning entertainment for everyone. Then with a wink, Gabrielle climbed in his lap and kissed him like no one was in the room. Dakota flared way too hot as he held her. Whistles and catcalls rang out.

Afterwards, she whispered, "Morning, Handsome," and got up and walked in the kitchen leaving him on the floor.

Dakota watched her go, still smoking from their good morning kiss. With a grin, Jimmy brought him a cup of coffee.

Dakota said, "I've got one word for you. Wildcat."

Jimmy nodded, and said, "Yep, she's a feisty one alright."

Dakota smiled. It was all about feisty.

Then Sean called out, "Dakota, we've got messages. Reynolds landed in New Orleans and has hit the road with his FBI tail. But no one has eyes on Vee."

Heading to join Sean in the kitchen, Dakota kissed Gabrielle on top of the head. She batted her lashes at him with a grin.

After reviewing messages, Dakota said, "Let's plan to work outside today for training and target practice. Sean, keep us covered by drone surveillance just to make sure no one found us out here."

"Will do."

Dakota said, "Serena, I haven't seen you shoot yet, so bring your rifle and crossbow when we shoot. Sean and Jimmy, we also need to gather all the body armor we have so we can fit everyone later."

Once breakfast was over, they went outside. Sean prepared the drones for surveillance. Jimmy headed to the barn to feed the animals, pulling Serena with him. Dakota and Gabrielle followed.

Feeding the horses, Jimmy said, "You know, at one time, I thought about breeding horses."

Serena said, "Really! I always thought it would be amazing to raise them."

"In that case, if you're still interested, let's check into it. We could be a horse ranch before you know it. I'm going to have to keep us busy for three weeks."

Gabrielle said, "What happens in three weeks?"

Jimmy smiled as Serena said, "Our wedding."

Gabrielle squealed and hugged them, then said, "Where? And what can I do to help?"
"The wedding will be in the garden. Would you be my Maid of Honor?"
"Mom! Of course, yes!"
Jimmy said, "Dakota. I'd appreciate it if you would stand as my best man."
Dakota said, "That's a yes. My honor. So where are you going for your honeymoon?"
Jimmy said, "I'm not telling her. That part's a surprise."
Gabrielle said, "Wedding plans are so much fun."
Jimmy said, "What plans? The date is set. The honeymoon is set. Plans are done," and the men walked away chuckling.
Gabrielle said, "That wasn't subtle."
Serena grinned, and said, "Not even a little."

***

Before long, Sean confirmed from drone surveillance that the surrounding area was safe, so the women changed into workout gear, and warmed up.
Dakota said, "Jimmy, let's take them for a run."
"You got it. You want front or back?"
"You take the front since you know these woods."

A short time later, Gabrielle wiped sweat off her face from the warmup.
Dakota walked over, and said, "You ready to run?"
"Are you coming?"
"As if you don't know that answer."
She wiggled her knife and said, "Don't crowd me. I'm armed."
Dakota said, "Funny and sassy. But yes. Jimmy will take the lead and I'll bring up the rear."

They took off. Gabrielle focused on her speed, agility, and climbing. She pushed hard. Serena had her own routine but did the climbing too. Dakota grinned. It was like following two cats.

When the run was over, they were covered in sweat. Gabrielle pulled her boots and weapons off and jumped in the pool – clothes and all. Laughing, the others followed.

Once they cooled down, Jimmy said, "Dakota, I have an area that I use as a shooting range. Let me know when you're ready for target practice. We'll take the four-wheelers since it's two miles east of here."

"Sounds good. Let's leave in about an hour."

Jimmy advised the women to dress in pants, long socks, or boots since the trail was on the rough side, and insects were abundant. In less than an hour, they headed into the woods. Sean followed them by drone.

Dakota liked the natural path Jimmy followed. He took care to leave the forest as unblemished as possible. They followed alongside a gully and before long it opened into a ravine. Jimmy stopped and pointed to his target area against a bluff.

They challenged the women with distractions, but they stayed confident, accurate, and focused on the target. They were well trained.

Suddenly, Sean yelled over Dakota's radio earpiece, "There's a large animal bearing down on you. Get out! Now! It's less than one hundred yards and closing. Go!"

Dakota said, "Hurry Jimmy! Go! Take the women."

Without question, Jimmy hopped on his bike with both women and took off at a fast pace. Dakota followed.

Sean yelled in his ear again, "Look back Dakota!"

Dakota glanced back and a big cougar was almost on him. He couldn't outrun it. He let go of the handlebars and pivoted, pulling his pistol. As the engine slowed, the cat snarled and leapt. Dakota fired three quick shots. The last thing he heard was Gabrielle's scream.

Chapter 25

Dakota growled, covered his face at the blood spray, and the big cat landed on top of him. Hard. His back slammed into the gas tank and handlebars. It knocked the breath out of him – and hurt. His lungs burned from lack of air. He shoved and pushed the dead animal to get it off. Hot blood poured over his chest as the animal's sour odor surrounded him.

Sean screamed in his ear.

Jimmy and Gabrielle yelled as they reached him. And as Dakota pushed, Jimmy pulled, and with a thud the cougar dropped to the ground. Dakota gasped for air as they stared at the animal. Huge. Bloody. Mouth forever frozen in a snarl.

Sean yelled in his ear again, and Dakota handed the earpiece to Jimmy. Then groaning, he grimaced as he sat up, meeting Gabrielle's terrified gaze as she frantically tried to find where the blood came from.

Dakota rasped, "It's not…my blood."

Relieved, she helped him remove the bloody shirt. He got off the bike and leaned over just enough so she could check his back. He was stiff and his muscles screamed in agony.

Her hands still shaky from the scare, lightly touched his back. She said, "Oh. Dakota. Ugh. You have a few cuts and scrapes – but they're not deep. Your back though. Oh mercy. It's already bruising. All over."

"Yeah. I feel that."

Jimmy returned after assuring Sean that Dakota was ok. He said, "Do you need medical treatment?"

"No. He just smashed me. That was one heavy cougar."

"He's big. I didn't even know he was on my land. Thank God for Sean's warning, or there would have been human and animal blood on the ground."

***

Back at the house, Sean looked at Dakota's back and clenched his jaw, not even trying to hide the stress.

Dakota said, "Sean, you did it. You are incredible with those drones. Did you pick him up by thermal imaging?"

"Yeah. Out of nowhere he popped up on the screen. I aged with that scare. I'm the older brother now."

***

After a shower, Dakota laid face down on a mattress.

Gabrielle wrapped Jimmy's large gel ice pad in a towel and knelt on the mattress. She said, "Here we go," and laid it across his bare back expecting…something.

He didn't flinch or say a word. They swapped it out a few times.

After following the same routine for a while, he glanced at Gabrielle, and said, "I'm ready to get in the pool for a while. Come in with me."

After changing, she followed him into the pool. His back was…scary ugly…painful to look at. Her heart hurt. But he seemed more fluid – much less stiff.

She asked, "Did the ice help?"

Stretching, he winced a little, but said, "It did help. It's not as painful – or tight."

Turning to face her, he half drew, half floated her into his arms. Avoiding his back, Gabrielle lightly held his waist.

He kissed her softly, and said, "You alright? I know it scared you."

"It was like a horrible nightmare. All I could see were teeth and claws as that monster cat went airborne - and you raised your gun. The sound of the snarl and your shots was the last thing I heard."

"I know. It was fast. All I had time to do was shoot – knowing I had to kill it. The three of you were right in front of me. Way too close to him."

"She kissed his chest, then stepped back and praying softly, she began to circle around him in the water barely trailing her fingers over his skin. He closed his eyes and listened to her heaven-sent words.

"Thank you, Jesus, for protecting Dakota from worse injuries today. For giving Sean the eyes to see danger. And for giving Dakota the skill and strength to fight. Touch this man you created Lord. Ease the strain of his injured body. Let your peace rinse it all away."

She held up water and drizzled it over his back and shoulders, and continued, "Hear my prayer for this warrior Lord and thank you for his rest and healing tonight. In Jesus name I pray."

Dakota, silent for a moment, said, "It felt like He was in the pool with us."

She whispered, "I love it when He does that."

A short time later, Jimmy opened the patio door and called, "Serena cooked fried pork chops, mashed potatoes, and corn on the cob. She said southern women love to cook comfort food. It will be ready in thirty minutes."

Gabrielle frowned and glanced at Dakota.

He said, "What's wrong?"

"I never cook comfort food."

Dakota grinned, and said, "Honey…you *are* comfort food."

They had just stepped out of the pool when Dakota's phone rang. It was Reynolds. He looked at Gabrielle and held his finger to his lips for silence - and walked into the garden.

***

"Yes Sir. This is Dakota."

Reynolds said, "How is Gabrielle? You haven't checked in for days."

"We're staying in remote places and rarely have phone signal. Are there any updates on the Posse we need to know?"

"Yes. I've been working with a new agent that has provided intel that really kicked this case into action. In fact, I'm in Louisiana now, undercover on the case. I will be in Lake Charles tonight. I need you, Sean, and Gabrielle to meet up with me so we can finish this."

"Just tell us when and where. We're ready. The Posse deserves everything they're going to get."

"Exactly."

Dakota said, "What's your plan, Sir?"

"My intel said the Posse got word about treasure on Gabrielle's property. They're preparing a dig tomorrow morning. Let's ambush them at noon."

"We'll be there."

Reynolds said, "Call me when you are thirty minutes out so we can go in together."

***

Dakota ended the call and stood silent, fighting the rage. The betrayal. A man he trusted with his life. With his brother's life. And with Gabrielle's life. Reynolds set them up to die – maybe even would be the one who pulled the trigger. That betrayal would cost him. He would make sure of that.

Waiting, but then concerned when he never moved, Gabrielle said, "Dakota?"

He turned and walked toward her. Pulling her into his arms, he said, "They'll pay for what they've done to you and your family. All of them. But know this, Reynold's killed himself. He's just called into play his own death."

Sean looked up as Gabrielle and Dakota came back inside. He saw the look on Dakota's face. He knew he had spoken with Reynolds.

Dakota said, "The trap is set. Ground Zero is good to go for noon tomorrow."

***

Reynolds arrived in Lafayette and called the weapon's dealer.

The ATF agent answered, "I just sent you the address."

Reynolds said, "See you in thirty."

The agent smiled as he turned on the cameras and gave the ATF a head's up. This is what he called a good day's work. He walked out and sat on the porch and waited with his dog. A black SUV drove up and a tall man got out. He recognized Reynolds from intel.

He said, "Come on in. Don't mind the dog."

Reynold's said, "I don't."

The agent pointed upstairs, and said, "My shops in the attic."

"Get to it."

Reynolds picked out a Glock with large mags, two flash grenades, binoculars, and a knife. Then said, "Total it."

The agent slid the bill to him. Reynolds glanced at it, counted out the cash, with a tip, and tossed it on the counter. He picked up his box of weapons and headed downstairs. The agent was impressed at the guy's confidence and calm assurance that everything was smooth sailing.

Reynolds walked out onto the porch, glanced back at the agent, and said, "We've never met, right?"

"Nope. Never."

***

Toby called and Sean answered, "Go ahead. We're listening."

"Reynolds bought two Glocks like Vee with two, thirty round mags, two stun grenades, binoculars, and a knife. He's driving a black SUV. The ATF agent was really impressed with his confidence. Said he even gave him a tip. He acted like he didn't have a care in the world."

Sean said, "Yeah, well, that confidence will kill him tomorrow."

***

After the call, Dakota faced the others and said, "The stun grenades are a fight pretense for our benefit. I'm not much concerned with that - now that I know it's coming. Nothing else was a surprise. It looks like they plan to kill with the guns – and we will have our body armor on. As for the rocket launcher, we need to stop it. No other option.

"Jimmy, you will leave first in the morning to meet up with the soldiers and FBI. Be safe. We know where you will be stationed and have Gabrielle's back. As for the rest of us, I will have coffee made at three a.m. and we will leave at four.

"Cat and I will be in one vehicle, and Sean and Serena in the other. We will park in the rear forest line behind my cabin and walk in through the woods. We need to get in place by five a.m. while it's still dark.

"Sean and Serena will work from the barn loft. If things go bad Sean, get Serena out. If things go as planned, use those drones for anything and everything. I need you to verify the five targets – and find the placement of the good guys. Call the radio plays as you see things play out. Direct Serena. I will call Reynolds at eleven-thirty a.m., and then it begins.

"Sean, one more thing, give Adam, En-Garde, and Mom and Dad a head's up that it will be over by one p.m. tomorrow.

"Got it."

Dakota said, "Serena and Gabrielle, call your family. Jimmy, do you have anyone you want to call?"

"My family will be at Ground Zero."

"I hear that, Jimmy. Loud and clear. My thoughts exactly."

***

At a hotel in south Lake Charles, Vee answered the phone.

"Where are you?" Reynolds said.

"Tru by Hilton, not far from the casinos."

"I will meet you there in an hour. Be out front. I'm in a black SUV. I'll pick you up."

"I'll be there."

***

Late afternoon, Reynolds pulled into the hotel parking lot and stopped. He saw Vee step through the automatic doors with her bag. He drove up and without hesitation, she got in.

He said, "Do you have everything you need for the job?"

"Yes. Do you have my fee?"

Reynolds handed it to her.

She checked it and asked, "What's next?"

"We ride. Just sit back and enjoy the scenery."

Reynolds followed West Prien Lake Road till it met up with the lake. He liked this part of town. The concrete bridge arched high over the lake and the Calcasieu Ship Channel, then gracefully reached for the towns on the other side. The bridge was massive – built for ships traveling in from the Gulf of Mexico to the industries and docks along the waterway.

Majestic casinos were snugged up to the lake, jutting into the skyline on the north side of the bridge. Impressive homes lined the south banks. A large park with walkways and event centers was filled with people. On the side of the park was a busy boat launch with marine craft of all types. Picnics, pets, fishing, and fun was the point. Water was everywhere.

***

Vee was surprised when Reynolds kept going and left the lake far behind. She noticed when he passed the road where the Posse undoubtedly were at the boathouse waiting for them. He continued out of the city limits for several miles, then slowed as he neared an old draw bridge. He turned right and followed a bumpy dirt road to the bank. They were close to the base of the bridge. She thought it was a creepy place and had no intention of ending up floating in that dark water.

***

Reynolds pulled over and stopped. He reached in the backseat and grabbed a couple of Cokes. He handed her one and she relaxed – a little. She was no fool.

He said, "We need to call the guys and have them meet us for dinner in downtown Lake Charles around seven p.m. I need them to unwind and chill – and not think about the boat ride with Butch last night. Regardless, they will end up dead, but they don't need to be distracted and on edge. I plan for all of us to have a nice dinner, a few drinks, and a lot of laughs.

"Then I'll let them know about a new lead I received on Lafitte's treasure. That is the beginning. Then I will tell them the Lafitte woman will be delivered to me at noon. They won't even remember Butch after that. I want tonight to end on a good note. A lie, but a good one."

He continued, "But it will be a different story by nine a.m. tomorrow. You can follow me to Gabrielle's place, hide your car, and ride with me up to her house. The guys will meet us there and they won't be leaving. Not alive, anyway.

"I will let them dig for hours while we wait for Dakota to call me. When he calls, I will tell him that we have the Posse cornered and need him. Then they die. Just follow my lead and that's it."

Vee shrugged pleasantly, and said, "A few dead bodies and my job is done. Works for me," and Reynolds smiled.

She thought he looked as evil, as she felt.

***

Then Reynolds called Ryan. He said, "I'm in town. You and the guys come meet Vee and I for dinner tonight at Pujo Street Café. Seven sharp. We need a night to relax. My treat. Bring your appetite."

***

Chapter 26
Ground Zero

Gabrielle woke, instantly aware of what today was. She looked around but Dakota wasn't in the room. Quietly she tip-toed around the others and went to look for him. He was at the snack bar with a cup of coffee. He turned when he heard her and opened his arm for her to join him. She hugged him, and he lifted her onto the bar in front of him.

She cupped his face, and said, "Hi, Handsome."

He kissed her, and said, "Hi, Beautiful."

"Obviously, your back is better."

He smiled, and said, "All I can say is, you can pray for me anytime."

They heard more footsteps as Sean and Serena came out of the bedroom.

Voice not quite steady, Serena said, "Jimmy's gone," and Gabrielle motioned her to join them.

Dakota hugged them both – meeting Sean's eyes across the kitchen. It was one of those moments before the battle that warriors knew well. And his alarm went off.

Confident. Prepared. In charge. He said, "Here we go, Task Force. It's time for Ground Zero."

***

Less than an hour later, their vehicles pulled into the tree line of Dakota's rear property. Dakota and Gabrielle grabbed their bags. Sean and Serena did the same. They turned on flashlights and began the half mile trek through the woods.

Dakota halted them about ten yards before the edge of the tree line where the pasture began. Gabrielle and Serena hugged. The brothers did a quick fist bump. It was time for business.

Sean led Serena toward the barn, staying within the cover of the trees. Everyone knew he had a lot to do quick. There would be radio silence till he set up the drones, cameras, and radios in the barn.

Dakota and Gabrielle sat to wait in the dark.

***

In about thirty minutes, Sean said through the earpiece, "Set." Everyone on the Task Force replied the same, including Jimmy. Now they were all connected; and Sean could talk to them as a group or individually.

Dakota waited. The drone mission was next. It would fly above the whole area to get a thermal count of concealed soldiers, agents, or anything else large and alive at Ground Zero.

A few minutes later, Sean said, "Count twenty-three," which meant the good guys. Now they waited for the bad guys.

***

Just after dawn, Gabrielle heard her hawk call an alarm. She couldn't see him, but she knew he didn't like the people hidden on her property. He was warning her.

She told Dakota, "Watch," and gave a loud hawk call.

Gabrielle pointed when she saw Hunter coming. She held up her arm and he glided silently to land on her forearm. The body armor protected her from his talons. She soothed him and ran her hand up his breast. He flapped his wings and fluffed up.

She said, "Hey big guy."

Dakota said, "He's impressive," and eyed the huge talons that gripped Gabrielle's arm.

She grinned and gave the hawk a boost, and off he flew.

***

About eight-thirty a.m., the good guys watched as a blue pickup parked at Gabrielle's house. Three guys got out – Ryan, Sam, and Jamie. They pulled shovels out then stood around smoking. After a while, a black SUV pulled up next to them. Reynolds stepped out and grabbed a bag. Then the passenger door opened, and a petite blonde climbed out with a large duffle bag. Vee.

***

Dakota knew she was TNT and could blow at any second, with barely any provocation. And she had two rockets in the duffle bag. She was danger with a capital D. The smallest volcano in history.

Dakota said, "Blonde with duffle bag. Mercenary. Rocket launcher, two rockets in bag. Prevent launch. Repeat, prevent launch."

Then he looked Reynolds over. The flash grenades he had were nothing to worry about. They all knew about them. But this play was his baby. He wanted dead people on the ground. Which meant he would die.

***

All five of the Posse talked on the patio. Reynolds showed them a piece of paper, and Ryan and his guys were pumped and cheering about something. Reynolds pointed to the left side of Gabrielle's property and the three men took off with shovels.

***

Gabrielle whispered, "What are they doing?"

"Probably killing time digging for treasure."

Disgusted, she said, "Now I have to fill in all those holes."

***

Right at ten o'clock the three men trudged back to Reynolds. They were hot, sweaty, and frustrated. Reynolds shrugged, looked at the paper again, and held up two fingers. Then pointed in the woods behind the house. The men grabbed their shovels and took off again.

***

Gabrielle said, "Why do they believe him?"
Dakota said, "He's Ryan's uncle. He's helped them for years. Anyway, obsession obliterates wisdom and common sense."
"They are digging up my trails. Can I hurt them for that?"
Sean chuckled over the radio, and said, "Open mic."
Gabrielle covered her mouth – she had forgotten.
Dakota said, "Roger that," with a laugh.

***

At eleven-fifteen a.m., the guys came dragging back with their shovels again. Ryan shouted in Reynold's face. Reynolds talked to him and then shoved him and held up three fingers. Then he pointed to the woods where they had no way to know the real treasure was hidden. They grabbed their shovels and took off again.

***

Gabrielle gasped. "No!"
Dakota said, "They won't find it. It's almost eleven-thirty a.m. They'll run out of time."
Then Dakota said one word, "Drone." She understood.
Sean said, "Done."

***

Good guys and bad guys watched the clock.

At eleven-thirty a.m. Reynolds and Vee grabbed their bags and headed up the stairs into Gabrielle's house.

***

Watching Reynolds, Dakota called him, and said, "We're thirty minutes out. On our way."
Reynolds said, "Good news! We've cornered the Posse in Gabrielle's house. We need you. Double-time it here!"

Dakota said, "Ten-four," and they continued watching Gabrielle's place.
Two lies in play.

***

In a couple of minutes, Reynolds and Vee walked out on the deck upstairs. He hollered for Ryan. Ryan didn't answer. He hollered again. Ryan still didn't answer. Vee turned to walk downstairs to get the men and Reynolds stopped her. He picked up his phone.

A few minutes later, the Posse stormed out of the woods without shovels. Ryan was furious and Reynolds motioned them upstairs.

***

It was time. Dakota and Gabrielle stood, tucked their pistols in their front waistband. Dakota put an FBI patch on his chest.
He touched her face and said, "We've got this."
As they walked out of the woods, Dakota said, "Ground Zero is a go."

They crossed the pasture, went around the house, and headed down to the boat dock. Two loud explosions sounded from Gabrielle's house, and she screamed as Dakota pulled her behind a tree. But there was only smoke – no fire.
Dakota said, "Flash grenades."
He called Reynolds.

***

"Director! What happened?"
"We've overpowered them! They're under arrest. Get over here! Backup is on the way."
Dakota said, "I can't see anything with the smoke. You know I can't expose Gabrielle without visual. We'll meet in the yard."
Reynolds snapped, "Done. We're heading downstairs, get over here, Nash. Now."

***

Vee led the way down the stairs, gun in hand, with an FBI patch on her chest. The Posse followed, hands behind their heads. Reynolds brought up the rear, with a pistol in Ryan's back, and an FBI patch on his shirt.

All five walked into the backyard between the house and the river. Vee yelled and the three men that had been digging, knelt. Reynolds pointed at Dakota and Gabrielle across the river and motioned them over.

***

Dakota said, "Come on, Cat. Let's finish this."

They rode a Jet Ski across the river and slid to a stop on the sandbar. Dakota pulled his gun - protocol - and held it by his side as they walked toward the Posse.

Dakota paused thirty feet away, halting Gabrielle, and said, "Where's backup? I don't even hear them. I'll call 911 for ETA." He took out his phone.

Reynold's said, "Don't worry about it. They're on their way."

Dakota looked at the men kneeling on the ground. Then looked at Reynolds, and said, "Why aren't you following protocol? They aren't even cuffed. And where's the rest of your team?"

"Nash! Get over here and cuff them yourself."

Dakota and Reynolds stared at each other, then Dakota said, "Who's the blonde?"

Reynolds shook his head, and said, "Dakota, Dakota. You always were a pain with the details. Always thinking. You just couldn't make this easy for me."

Dakota aimed his gun at Reynolds.

Reynolds turned his gun on Gabrielle, and said, "Checkmate Nash, and you know it."

Dakota lowered his gun, and said, "What do you want - before I kill you for this."

"Stifle your indignation. Nobody cares. I need you and Gabrielle, to very gently, lay your guns on the ground in front of you. And don't make any sudden moves unless you want to see her splattered on the ground because of you."

Dakota and Gabrielle glanced at each other. This was it.
Reynolds yelled, "Do it now!"
Dakota glanced at Gabrielle again, this time indicating how she needed to pick up her gun with two fingers and lay it on the ground in front of her.

Once their guns were down, Vee laughed, and ripped the FBI patch off her chest.
Reynolds said, "Vee, get the guns. Dakota, don't you even twitch. I mean it. I have an itchy trigger finger already."
The mercenary walked toward Gabrielle first. Even though Gabrielle knew the description of Vee, seeing the tiny, beautiful blonde with dead eyes was spine-chilling.
Vee sneered, "Stupid victim. I hate weakness," then she grabbed the gun off the ground and walked to Dakota.
She smiled seductively, and said, "Nash. Well now. You're something else. I would have enjoyed a little time with you one-on-one. You missed out."
Dakota said dryly, "Hardly. I hate snakes."
The three guys on their knees howled in laughter. Vee growled and raised her gun at Dakota.
Irritated, Reynolds said, "Stop. Vee, get over it. We don't have time for games. Bring me the guns and stay on mission."

Dakota had seen the desire to kill flash in Vee's eyes. She was filled with venom. Someone had messed her up good. He glanced at the men on the ground and Ryan looked ready to explode. He was tired of playing games too.

Gabrielle looked at the men that killed her father, wishing she could retaliate, but decided to stir the pot instead. She said, "What's happening Dakota? Do they want my treasure?"
Ryan blew. He jumped up and yelled, "Give me my treasure!"
Ready for him, Gabrielle growled, "No."
Ryan snarled, "Don't be stupid. Tell me where it is, or I'll kill you slow."
Furious, she spat at him. Dakota moved close to Gabrielle as Ryan stepped toward her.

Reynolds grabbed the back of Ryan's shirt and said, "Later! Control yourself! It's not time for that yet."

Snarling, Ryan jerked away, and screamed, "No! I'm tired of waiting!" and went for Gabrielle.

Dakota spun and slammed Ryan upside the head with a roundhouse kick. He landed on the ground with a bloody cheek, and Dakota stepped in front of Gabrielle. Blind with rage, Ryan clambered to his feet and tried to dart around Dakota - who nailed him with a side kick in the stomach. He doubled over, gagging.

Disgusted with his nephew, Reynolds said, "Alright, alright. Enough of that. Get up Ryan and stop looking like an idiot. That is getting you nowhere."

Ignoring his uncle, Ryan stood, and yelled to his buddies, "Come on, let's get her!"

As the two men stood, Vee quickly stepped forward and shot them in the back of the head, one after the other – barely a pause in between. Dakota flung Gabrielle to the ground and covered her before she could even scream.

Enraged at the kills, Ryan pulled his knife and spun to Reynolds. Obviously, lethal now, he charged him. Without a blink, Reynolds shot him between the eyes. His head flew back, and he dropped to the ground.

Dakota stood and faced Reynolds and Vee. It was quiet for a moment. All he heard was Gabrielle's fast breathing as she got to her feet behind him.

Reynolds shrugged, and said, "Dakota, this only has one way to play out. My nephew led this Posse of idiots. I never thought covering for him would involve either of you. Gabrielle's DNA issue was a fluke I never considered. This treasure obsession ends now. Unfortunately, so do both of you, and Sean, when I find him."

Dakota said, "What insanity drove you to get involved in the first place? You know this never works."

"He was my brother's son. That said, what difference does it make? You won't remember anything in a second."

Dakota kept his eyes on Reynolds and Vee, then stepped back. Gabrielle started backing up.

Reynolds shook his head and said, "There is nowhere to go," and shot Dakota twice in the FBI patch.

With two thuds and a groan, Dakota flew back, and landed on the ground in front of Gabrielle. She screamed.

Sean yelled in the radio, "Run!"

Gabrielle sprinted for the woods. Fast. Vee, struggling with her duffle bag, followed, but quickly fell behind.

Reynolds glanced at Dakota. No blood. He glanced at Gabrielle. She was too fast and would lose Vee any minute.

He yelled, "Stop Gabrielle or I'll shoot him in the head."

Gabrielle nimbly pivoted to see Reynolds look down at Dakota – whose leg moved.

She yelled, "Wait! Don't!"

Gabrielle's mind spun as she headed back toward Dakota and Reynolds with a panting Vee. Dakota needed help. A head shot was out of the question. She would just have to change the game. Reynolds had her man. On her land. Because of her treasure. It was time to up the ante and play it her way.

Reynolds kicked Dakota in the ribs, hitting the plate he figured was there, and Dakota gasped in pain and passed out. Reynolds said, "I should have known you would have a vest on. Now I get to kill you twice."

Gabrielle stopped once they reached Reynolds, and said, "You're missing the best part. I'll give you the treasure if you let us go, or at least give us a head start."

Reynolds grabbed her by the hair and yanked her close. He said, "I'm insulted you think I'm anything like Ryan. There is no treasure." And shoved her back toward Vee.

Gabrielle said, "You're wrong. It's worth millions and I know where it is. But if you shoot Dakota, it's location will die with us."

Vee's eyes flickered with interest.

Reynold's tapped the barrel against his leg and said, "Vee, go check. If she lied, kill her. If it's there, call me. I want to see it myself."

Vee stepped aside and motioned for Gabrielle to go. She adjusted the heavy duffle bag on her shoulder, and said, "Show and tell time, treasure girl, move it."

Gabrielle glanced at Dakota. He was breathing. She led the way into the woods.

Reynolds stood over Dakota and hummed as he contemplated the turn of events. What if the treasure had been real after all?

***

Sean radioed, "Jimmy, you on Gabrielle?"
"Yes. Just get Dakota."

Sean inserted the second of Serena's crossbow arrows into the ammo chutes of the drone. He set the target path and let it fly. The drone rose high and headed across the river to hover in the trees near Dakota. It waited for instructions.
Sean said loudly in the radio, "Dakota! Wake up!"

Sean's yell woke Dakota on the ground, but he stayed still and silent. He didn't know where Reynolds was, or what was going on around him now. His chest pounded with pain, but he gritted his teeth not making a sound. Reynold's kick had been brutal on top of getting shot. Twice.

Sean said, "Serena, watch his right hand – little finger." Then he said, "Dakota, if you are alert, move you right hand little finger."
It moved. Sean and Serena cheered. Sean said, "Reynolds is standing behind your head, his back to the river, pointing his gun at your head. Gabrielle is leading Vee to the treasure. Smart girl. The team will cover her. Reynolds is waiting to hear about the treasure. Hang tight a second. He won't be breathing much longer."
Based on Sean's description, Dakota could picture everything. Ok. This was just a pause. The final play was still ahead.

***

Vee shoved Gabrielle with the end of the barrel and said, "Hurry up. I have places to go and money to spend. And you better not be lying, or I will be amazingly creative when I kill you. Painfully so."
"It's just over the hill by the gully. I'm not lying."
"Shut up and walk."
Gabrielle reached the treasure tree and was shocked. The Posse had actually dug around the tree. They hadn't finished and left their shovels on the ground.

Vee said, "Well it doesn't look like they found anything here."
"Because they didn't know where to look."
Vee slapped her in the mouth. Gabrielle flinched at the blow, then stared at Vee as blood dribbled down her chin.
Vee said, "Well, what are you waiting for? Another slap?"
"I need my knife to cut the treasure out of the tree."
Vee followed her behind the tree and watched as Gabrielle brushed the leaves and dirt off to reveal a carved heart.
Sneering, she said, "Isn't that sweet. You got a knife?"
Gabrielle nodded yes.

Vee backed to the front of the tree, gun aimed at Gabrielle, and said, "Pull it out nice and slow."
Gabrielle leaned down and pulled her pant leg up and grabbed the knife. She stood.
Vee motioned toward the tree and said, "Hurry up. This is kind of exciting." Then Vee touched her bag and said, "I even have fireworks for later."
Gabrielle carved around the heart. Deep. Then ran the blade underneath the heart to loosen it all the way around. She paused and looked at Vee, aware of the battle coming next.
Vee said sarcastically, "What's the hold up now?"
Gabrielle hit the hilt of the knife hard, shoving it through. The heart cracked and fell to the ground. Two large leather bags sat in a deep cavity. Jeweled sword hilts stuck out of the big bag. The other bag was barely closed it was so full. She untied it. It was filled with jewels and gold coins.

Vee snapped, "Well, where's the treasure?"
Gabrielle threw a handful of treasure at her feet.
Vee's eyes widened as she looked at the coins and jewels. She said, "You just made my day." Then smiled and began to raise her gun.

Jimmy stepped from behind the nearest tree, gun aimed at Vee's temple, and said sharply, "You are one very dead woman if you move. I have a bullet with your name engraved on it."
Vee was livid – but stilled. Gabrielle swore the flames of hell flashed in her eyes. Then without warning, Gabrielle's hawk swooped through the trees,

talons extended, and grabbed ahold of Vee's scalp. He flapped his wings, screeched, and tried to pick her up.

Chapter 27

Vee screamed. Crazy screams. The kind that gives you goose bumps and makes your hair stand on end.

She dropped her gun and duffle bag to fight whatever huge bird was on her head. It gripped and yanked her skin. Pain exploded beyond description. Its savage beak pecked her hands as she fought to free herself.

Gabrielle was shocked at the grisly scene before her. Blood poured down Vee's head and body. Hunter had attacked!

Jimmy grabbed Vee's gun and bag with the rockets and handed it to another soldier, who vanished in the trees. He looked at Gabrielle and waited – giving her the call as warrior in charge.

***

Back at the kill zone, Sean called in the radio to Dakota, "Now!"

***

Reynolds heard the bloodcurdling screams coming from the woods and laughed.

He looked down at Dakota, who still appeared unconscious, and said, "Time's up Nash. I hope you're awake to appreciate it. It's your turn. I think Gabrielle's already gone ahead of you by the sound of those screams."

Dakota opened his eyes, fury visible now – and stared at a surprised Reynolds. He said, "We knew. And you're dead."

One bolt arrow went through Reynold's arm holding the gun. At the same time, the second one pierced his heart. Dakota rolled out of the way as the gun and body dropped. Then he was up and running toward Gabrielle, one arm holding his chest.

When he neared the treasure tree area surrounded by agents and soldiers, the screams were piercing. It was Vee. The hawk had her head in his claws. Jimmy stood close – gun on her. Gabrielle was a few feet in front of her. Everyone stared at the unbelievable scene between mercenary and hawk. Then it turned loose and flew away.

Jimmy looked at Gabrielle and she held up a hand. She pulled a gold sword with a hilt of diamonds out of the treasure bag. Jimmy nodded and stepped back.

Dakota smiled. Go get her wildcat.

Vee wiped blood out of her eyes. The ragged pain was something she had never experienced. She struggled to focus. To get a grip. To survive. She glanced up and saw Gabrielle standing there with a fancy sword.

Spitting blood, she snarled, "What are you gonna do with that?" and pulled a large hunting knife. She brandished it at Gabrielle.

Gabrielle glanced at all the agents and soldiers around them and walked to a clearing near the river. She dropped into her fencing stance, and said, "Allez!" and motioned Vee to come on.

Vee growled, "I'm going to cut you into pieces and feed you to the fish."

Gabrielle laughed, then saw Dakota just beyond Vee's shoulder, and smiled at him. He was here. Safe. He smiled.

Glancing back at Vee, she said, "Come on short stuff, show me what you've got."

Enraged at the insult, Vee charged. Gabrielle lunged and slashed her across the torso just hard enough to rip open her clothes – thereby disgracing her and drawing first blood. Vee hissed.

Gabrielle circled her, and said, "You've lost. And you're bleeding to death. Yield."

Vee yelled and ran, then slid along the ground to get under Gabrielle. Gabrielle leapt high and sent the sword point through Vee's thigh. Vee screamed.

Gabrielle landed and nimbly moved aside. She watched Vee grimace as she struggled to stand.

Vee said, "You haven't won yet," and tossed the bloody knife back and forth between her hands.

Then she darted to stab Gabrielle - who easily deflected the knife, spun, and slammed the hilt of her sword on Vee's breastbone. The force knocked the air from her lungs and her knife hit the ground as she grabbed her chest.

Gabrielle watched the deadly mercenary just a few feet away. She gasped to breathe. Was blocked by the river. Covered in blood. This was over.

Gabrielle glanced at Dakota who had followed with the other agents. She said, "Take her. There is no reason for me to kill an unarmed, dying woman."

Hearing Gabrielle, Vee turned to run, not realizing the river was so close behind her, and fell down the bank into the water. Blood turned the water burgundy. It was a horror show.

Several agents slid down the bank and stepped into the water to get her. She tried to swim away, but through a gush of water a massive alligator lurched up and clamped teeth-riddled jaws over her head and chest.

Dakota yanked Gabrielle away from the bank and the other agents scrambled to safety. Shocked, they all stared at the water. Vee was gone. Swallowed by the gator and the river. The only reminder she had even been there were the bloody waves that lapped the shore.

Appalled at the horrible death, Gabrielle whispered, "It was Dragon."

Dakota said, "Vee made her choices, and ended up with a hawk, a dragon, and a warrior with a sword. I know she never saw any of that coming."

Gabrielle said, "What about Reynolds?"

"Dead. Literally on the spot where he shot me. A drone killed him with your mother's crossbow arrows."

She nodded, and said, "Fitting."

He caressed her cheek, and said, "You did it. It's over."

Then he turned her to face all the agents and soldiers who waited. He pushed her forward – to a place of honor. This was her win. She lifted the antique sword, saluted the men, and bowed. The cheer sounded like a roar.

Then he kissed her.

***

Before long, Dakota and Gabrielle exited the woods to the wail of sirens and emergency vehicles drawing closer. Flashing lights filled the yard and Dakota didn't hesitate as she led him to the nearest ambulance. When the paramedics realized his injuries, they sat him on the stretcher and removed his shirt and vest. His chest was fire engine red with two purple impact circles. Blood lines ran down his stomach from one of them.

Alarmed, Gabrielle quickly met his gaze.

He reassured her and said, "One barely penetrated the vest. Just enough to break the skin. The vest held," and she leaned her head against his shoulder, breathing again as her panic subsided.

A paramedic said, "What are these injuries to your back?"

"A cougar jumped me yesterday."

The paramedics looked at each other with raised eyebrows, and the oldest one said, "You need a new job."

Dakota laughed, groaned from the pain, and said, "I've heard that before."

They verified his vitals were normal, cleaned him, bandaged the bullet wound, then wrapped him in thick white gauze from his chest to his waist. They insisted he head to the emergency room for an EKG once he was done at the crime scene. He assured them his boss required a doctor's release.

A loud screech interrupted as Hunter circled above, calling Gabrielle. She stepped away from the others and held up her arm. He swooped down to land – flapping as she touched him assuring him that she was ok. Every pair of eyes watched the woman hold the hawk that had just protected her. Several took pictures. And off he went.

Dakota received a text from the director, and they headed downhill to the kill zone. At the same time, Sean and Serena ran uphill to meet them, and Jimmy jogged out of the woods. The Task Force met in the middle of the yard for a relieved reunion. They had survived. And the Posse was gone.

Dakota high-fived Sean, and said, "You are the man! The bolt arrows were an amazing choice of weapon for the drone. As usual, your timing was perfect. I bow to the drone master. You are my superhero!" and Sean flexed his muscles with a smile.

Dakota said, "Were you able to watch Gabrielle and Vee fight?"

Sean fist-bumped Gabrielle, and said, "Yeah, through a drone. Never in a million years would a fight with a sword have occurred to me for this battle."

Serena and Jimmy wrapped Gabrielle in their arms, beyond grateful. Gabrielle said, "Dad, you appeared out of nowhere when you threatened Vee – which was great by-the-way. And I appreciate you giving me the lead to fight her. It was personal."

He kissed her on both cheeks and said, "I know. We all knew. The warrior in you deserved the right to fight her."

Gabrielle looked around her yard. Agents gathered evidence. From the bodies on the ground. From up in her house. From around the treasure tree. From along the riverbank where Vee went in. They were everywhere.

The Sheriffs' Department guarded the perimeter of the crime scene and surrounding area. The marine vessel still patrolled the river looking for Vee's body. Everyone knew they wouldn't find it.

Jimmy pointed toward the Army veterans standing in a group and called, "General!"

An older man turned - with familiar amber eyes. He headed toward them with a smile and grabbed Gabrielle and Serena in a bear hug.

He said to Gabrielle, "What's this I hear we have a wildcat swordswoman in the family?" and she grinned.

Dakota held out his hand to introduce himself. The General man-hugged him instead.

He said, "You're quite a man, Agent Nash. Thank you for what you did for our girl. Not just once in her life, but twice. We are forever in your debt."

"No debt. She's all the reward I'll ever want," and the General smiled.

Serena slipped her arm around Jimmy and smiled at her family – truly, a dream come true. Jimmy whispered something in her ear, and she blushed crimson, and elbowed him. He picked her off the ground in a kiss.

Gabrielle whispered to her grandpa, "They're getting married in three weeks."

He chuckled, and said, "I'm surprised he put it off that long."

***

Dakota and Gabrielle walked toward the kill zone where four dead men still lay on the ground. Forensic teams worked. Stretchers and body bags waited on the side. Gabrielle saw a dark, distinguished man in a navy pinstripe suit with an FBI badge.

He joined them and offered his hand to Gabrielle. He said, "It is an honor to meet you. Please know that you have my greatest respect. You are quite a warrior, Ms. Sawyer."

She shook his hand and said, "Thank you, Director Washington. And I want you to know that Dakota and Sean both worked above and beyond in every way to keep all of us safe.

The Director looked at the old, and new, wounds and bruises that covered almost half her face. Anger flashed in his eyes, and he gave a sidelong glance at Reynolds body on the ground. Dakota knew that look. Justice was served.

When he looked back at them, he shook Dakota's hand, and said, "It's a pleasure to work with you Agent Nash. Today was no small endeavor. I look forward to working with you and Sean many times. Oh. Gabrielle, we called in a museum curator to collect, confirm, clean and value all the treasure in the tree. They of course, will need to speak to you in the days ahead. You will need to make plans for the treasure. It is yours."

The Director's phone rang. He answered, listened, then responded, "Set it up. We will broadcast in an hour."

After the call, the Director explained, "Because of the national interest in catching this serial killer gang, as well as the connection to Jean Lafitte, the FBI will broadcast a breaking news bulletin. The team at the podium will be both of you, myself, the General, the Sheriff and the D.A. – and of course, the rest of the Task Force. There may be questions from the media. Are you prepared for that, Gabrielle?"

"Yes. However, I prefer, Jade Lavergne, an investigative reporter from New Orleans to handle any questions for me." He nodded.

She glanced down at herself, and said, "I'm a mess."

Dakota said, "You just fought a battle. You're a warrior. No shame in looking like it."

The Director handed Dakota a new FBI patch and said, I'll call when it's time."

They gave the Task Force notice of the news broadcast.

Serena said, "I need to tell my parents before they hear it on the news."
Jimmy handed her his phone, and said, "As soon as we are free, I know they prefer to see you in person. Besides, I'd like to meet my soon-to-be in-laws."

Gabrielle called Jade about the news broadcast.
Jade said, "Is everyone ok?"
Gabrielle looked up as news helicopters flew overhead, and said, "We're alive. The Posse's dead. But you better hurry and get here. The news copters are hovering."
She said, "I'm coming!" and the line went dead.

Dakota watched Gabrielle glance up at her house as she joined them.
He said, "Do you want to check it?"
"No. It's been enough for one day. Well, enough for many days, actually. But I would like to take a few pictures of the treasure to show my grandparents. The family will have to decide what to do with it."
"Sure. Come on, let's head back to the tree."

Deputies stood guard at the treasure tree. They stepped aside as Gabrielle took pictures and looked in the bags. Then she knelt on the ground to gather the treasure she had thrown at Vee and returned it to the bag. The sword she fought Vee with still hung on her belt loop.
Dakota picked up the broken heart.
Gabrielle touched it and said, "It's unbelievable that their heart covered the treasure for over two hundred years. But how do you think he got the treasure in the tree?"
"I think he cut the heart and cavity out, then put the heart back, hiding it. It grew back into the tree over time."

***

Dakota's phone rang and he said, "Hey Adam!"
Gabrielle listened to the brothers talk a few minutes then tapped Dakota's arm and pointed to the phone.
"Hang on Adam, Gabrielle wants to talk to you."
Gabrielle said, "Hey there!"
Adam said, "Hey, sweetie."

Dakota said, "She's not your sweetie," and Adam laughed.
Gabrielle asked, "When are you coming back?"
"Why, are you missing a very powerful, hairy, four-footed protective male?"
She giggled and said, "I am."
"I will bring your very lonesome German shepherd home in the morning. How's that?"
"Perfect."
"Are both of your homes, ok?"
Dakota answered, "Well, they're damaged but we haven't been in them yet."
Adam said, "Why don't Aunt Jaz and I bring the animals home tomorrow and help get the houses back in shape. I have some free time and I know you and Sean have to leave for Washington D.C. for a few weeks."
Dakota glanced at Gabrielle, as she nodded, and said, "Thanks. That's perfect in fact. I will be leaving for D.C. later tonight, so your help is appreciated."

***

After the call, Gabrielle said, "I forgot you have to go to D.C."
Dakota hugged her and said, "It usually takes about two weeks to close out a case, but I'll push it. Maybe we can finish earlier," and his phone rang again.
It was time for the news broadcast.

***

FBI Director Washington approached the news podium set up in Gabrielle's driveway. He stood with the Sheriff, the District Attorney, and the General – with the Task Force nearby.
Reporters were roped off six feet from the podium. Cameras and microphones were shoved in the air ready to record every morsel of news. Word had spread like wildfire and even spectators and locals joined the commotion.

The Director said, "This breaking news bulletin is to inform the community of Lake Charles and southwest Louisiana, that the Treasure Posse has been killed today in a joint Task Force operation here at the home of Gabrielle Sawyer. The Task Force was led by FBI Agent in Charge, Dakota Nash, and included FBI Special Agent Sean Nash, retired Army Captain James Barlow and civilians Gabrielle Sawyer and Serena Palermo."

Reporters shouted questions but the Director raised his hand for silence, and said, "We'll get to the questions later. Task Force - line up front and center," and Dakota, Gabrielle, Serena, Jimmy, and Sean stepped in front of the podium.

The Director continued, "While loss of life is never good news, the removal of serial killers from society is a victory. The FBI commends the assistance of the Calcasieu Parish Sheriff's Department, Army veterans, and the Calcasieu Parish District Attorney's office. It has been an honor to work with each of you.

"And the rest of the story is not mine to tell. May I introduce to you, Agent Dakota Nash and Gabrielle Sawyer." Excitement spread through the crowd as the couple approached the microphone.

Dakota spoke first, and said, "Jean Lafitte is a well-known historical figure - captain, pirate, and privateer. What you don't know is that Gabrielle is his 8th generation granddaughter." The crowd went wild asking questions.

Silencing them, he continued, "Unfortunately, the Treasure Posse found out about her connection to Lafitte and targeted her for buried treasure. The FBI stepped in to protect her. However, Gabrielle - skilled in self-defense, survival, and fencing, agreed to be the Task Force bait to trap the Posse – resulting in today's battle."

"All locals and historians are knowledgeable of Louisiana's previous history as *No Man's Land territory* back in the 1800s – part of which is the very land where we now stand. And most people have heard the tale of Lafitte's buried treasure gifted to him from Napoleon Bonaparte. That said, today, on Gabrielle behalf, I proclaim that the legend is no longer a tale – but truth. She has found the treasure."

Screams and cheers rang through the crowd.

Dakota motioned Gabrielle to stand before the podium. Tall, bruised, battered, proud, and still very beautiful – the crowd stared in awe at the granddaughter of a famous pirate they had heard tales of all their life. Thrilled, they watched the historical drama unfold to the world.

Dakota said, "Gabrielle! En-Garde!" She pulled the jeweled sword from behind her and brandished it in fighting stance.

The crowd went wild.

Dakota waited a few moments, then said, "I introduce to you, Gabrielle Sawyer!"

As she stepped to the podium, Jade neared the reporters.

Gabrielle said, "I'm thrilled to be here with you today because that means I survived. My loved ones survived. And evil did not win. Our freedom – all freedom - is precious, with value worth far more than gold, jewels, or treasure.

"My family and I, look forward to sharing the story of our ancestors in time. But for now, I want you to know that Jean and my grandmother, Sabrina loved each other. And they loved Lake Charles - the place they met. Where I too call home."

She pointed to Jade and said, "Jade is the publicity agent and investigative reporter for my family, and a best friend. I would appreciate your kindness to her as she asks questions for this news report. Jade…"

***

Jade asked, "How did you find out you were a descendant of Jean Lafitte?

"I sent in my DNA to an online website. Being adopted, I was shocked to find out I was related to him with many distant relatives. We shared emails, and of course there was talk of treasure. That is how the Treasure Posse found me. I only recently discovered that my birth father had been their sixth victim."

Jade asked, "Do you have any other immediate family members that have the Lafitte bloodline?"

"Yes, my mother, Serena (she motioned to her), and my maternal grandfather. He is a local pastor here in Lake Charles, Pastor Jacque Bordelon."

Jade asked, "Can you describe the treasure you found?"

Gabrielle held up the gold sword with a diamond hilt and said, "There are five more swords made of gold with various jewels, jeweled knives and goblets, and other weapons, gold coins, and a tremendous amount of jewelry."

Jade asked, "What will you do with the treasure?"

"Our family will determine that once the museum curator completes an analysis of the treasure. We will publicly announce our decision in the days ahead. There will certainly be historical displays."

Jade grinned, and asked, "Is there anything you would like to tell Agent Dakota Nash, who has protected you?"

Chapter 28

Gabrielle turned and faced Dakota. Smiling, she pulled him closer, and said, "Hi, Handsome."
He smiled, looking into her sparkling amber eyes and slid his arms around her. He said, "Hi, Beautiful." Then dipped her in hot, public kiss.
Gabrielle dropped the antique sword and wrapped her arms around him.

Jade laughed as the crowd cheered, and said, "I think that's enough questions for today."

***

An hour later only a few reporters remained, but two news helicopters still hovered above watching the activity. The EMTs and the Coroner's office were gone. The Sheriff's Department and the FBI agents would be busy for hours longer. The Task Force visited on the patio with the General.

Dakota's phone rang. He listened and said, "Let them in."
He said, "Gabrielle, Samantha and Zoe are here," and she went to meet the car as it pulled up.

After the emotional reunion, Gabrielle introduced them to her mother first. They stared, shocked at the resemblance between her and Gabrielle.
Serena laughed, and Jade said, "I told you; they look just alike."
Samantha said, "Wow, Momma Bear, I'm glad to finally meet you."
Zoe said, "We love your daughter, I know we'll love you!"

Gabrielle said, "And this is my new dad, Jimmy."
Jimmy smiled, that sexy smile, and Samantha whistled. She said, "You are one fine dad, Captain," and he winked.
Gabrielle laughed and said, "Right!"
Jade said, "You sure don't look like my dad."
Jimmy drawled, "I guess genes have a sense of humor sometimes. Ask Gabrielle about genes," and they laughed.

Gabrielle said, "Now, meet my grandfather. You can just call him General. He will love you."
The General grinned at the beautiful blonde and redhead, and said, "So, you are the rest of En-Garde?"
"Yes Sir."
He said, "Beauty with a blade. Works every time," and they group-hugged - loving him already.

Then they group-hugged Dakota and Sean.
Samantha wiped tears off her face, and said, "I love you, Dakota. Thank you for protecting Gabrielle. You're awesome."
Sean held his hands up, exasperated, and said, "Really? He's all that? What am I?"
Samantha closed the gap between them and grabbing his shirt, pulled his mouth to hers. His arms kept her there.
After a moment, Samantha stepped back, and said, "When's our first date, Agent Man?"
Sean said, "What's wrong with now?" as the others laughed.

Once introductions were over, Gabrielle noticed Dakota seemed a little pale. She glanced at Sean and motioned to Dakota. He nodded.
Gabrielle said, "Dakota, don't you think it's time we get you to the emergency room?"
"Yeah, let's get it over with."
Jimmy tossed his truck keys to Sean. Gabrielle left the sword with her mom.
Serena asked, "Do you think you can meet us at Mom and Dad's when you are through at the hospital? They would love to see you."
"Yes! I can't wait to see them. Then she looked at her friends and said, "Text me. I need to go. I love you."

***

Sean stopped the truck at the Memorial Hospital Emergency Room doors. As they walked through the automatic doors, the sound of applause broke out. Surprised, they stopped, then saw themselves on the evening news in the waiting room.

Dakota smiled but groaned under his breath.

Gratefully, he smiled as the nurse met him before he got to the registration counter, and said, "Your boss called. Come right this way, Agent Nash. The doctor is waiting."

Dakota sat on the bed and the nurse removed his shirt. Sean and Gabrielle watched her peel away the gauze wrapped around his chest. Bruises were already forming under the red angry skin, purple impact marks, and dripping blood. The nurse cleaned his chest then walked around to his back. She frowned at the bruises there.

She asked, "Agent Nash, are you taking anything for pain?"

"No."

She cleaned his back and checked the two cuts on his shoulders and said, "The doctor will be in shortly."

Dakota glanced at Sean and Gabrielle's pained looks at his chest, and said, "Stop it. You look - like I feel. I'll be fine once they finish."

Sean leaned toward Gabrielle, and said in a purposeful loud whisper, "He doesn't like the doctor's office. It makes him cranky."

Gabrielle said, "I see that," but Dakota grinned.

The doctor knocked and walked in, looking at the two obvious bullet blows in Dakota's chest, and said, "Well, they didn't show that on the evening news," and Dakota laughed, then winced.

The doctor checked the impact locations and asked questions. He called the nurse for an EKG. Then he walked around to his back and whistled.

He said, "Agent Nash, you need a vacation."

"I agree. A long one."

The doctor ran his hand over Dakota's back from shoulder to waist, asking questions. He said, "I want x-rays of your chest and back to make sure no bones are cracked. I don't think we will find any. And I don't think a cat scan is necessary – you're in good shape considering what you've been through. I'll return when radiology is done."

Before long, a nurse rolled in an EKG cart. She shaved circular spots on his chest as he raised an eyebrow in annoyance. Gabrielle and Sean looked away to keep from laughing. Once he was attached to her sticky patches and wires, she ran the EKG.

As she left, an elderly nurse came in with a wheelchair to bring him to radiology.

Bluntly, he said, "No."

Sean coughed to cover his laugh, and Gabrielle bit her lip to hold the giggle in. The nurse straightened her five-foot two-inch frame and pointed to the chair, and said, "Get in."

Dakota grinned at her spunk, and after obeying, she wheeled him down the hall.

Gabrielle and Sean sat on his bed and waited for him to return.

She said, "Sean, what's happening with you and Samantha?"

He said, "That's what I want to know. She's a fabulous mystery that I intend to solve."

"Beware, there are trails of men behind her, all shocked at how fast she dumped them."

"Good for her. It keeps her available for me. Tell me something that I need to know about her."

"No."

"Just something small about her personality."

She thought about it and said, "She's as gentle as a kitten on the inside."

He rubbed his face in contemplation of that meaning, and said, "I think our first date needs to be the zoo."

"Sean, the kitten is only a metaphor."

"So is the zoo."

Gabrielle laughed and said, "You will be good for her."

A good while later, the door opened, and the nurse wheeled Dakota back in the room.

He said, "You're in my bed," and they laughed and jumped up.

The doctor walked in with a nurse and asked Dakota, "How are you feeling now?"

"Hungry and annoyed."

The doctor chuckled and said, "Give him a pain shot," and she left to get it. He continued, "Agent Nash, your test results indicate only muscle and skin injury. Nothing permanent. You are a very lucky man.

"And I understand that you are getting on a plane. This pain shot will relax your muscles so that you can sleep on your trip. Make sure that you do. Your body needs it to heal. Take these," and he handed him a filled prescription. "It's an anti-inflammatory that will make your next week much less annoying."

Then the Doctor pointed to Gabrielle and called her over. He checked her face wounds and asked her about pain.

He said, "You'll be fine. Get back with me if you notice anything not healing. And I hope the one who did this to you looks worse."

She glanced at Dakota, deciding not to tell the doctor they were dead, and just said, "They paid for it."

He shook their hands and said, "I am proud of what your team accomplished. Enjoy the freedom you fought for. Agent Nash, you're already checked out. You are free to leave," and he saluted and left.

***

When they walked out of the hospital, Director Washington was waiting, and said, "I hear you are cleared to go."

"Yes Sir."

The Director said, "I'll give you ten minutes." Then Sean and the Director walked to the waiting SUV.

Dakota put his arm around Gabrielle's waist, and said, "Walk with me."

She tried not to cry as they walked down the sidewalk. She understood why, but still couldn't believe he was leaving. They had just spent almost two hundred intense, intimate, desperate hours together. Saying goodbye hurt…even for two weeks.

Finding a spot for privacy, he stopped and turned to face her. A tear dropped from her lashes and rolled down her cheek. He kissed it.

He said, "Although my schedule will be crazy, we'll find time to connect. Call. Text me. Video. Even dinosaur email." She smiled, a little.

Wiggling his phone, he said, "That means you need to start carrying your phone again. Do you even know where it is?" She blinked. She would have to think on that.

He chuckled, winced, and drew her in his arms. He whispered, "Kiss me, Cat. A taste before I go."

She softly kissed his left cheek, then his right, then moved her warm lips over his.

After their kiss, he handed her Jimmy's truck keys, and said, "You'll be staying with your parents, right?" She nodded and gazed at him with those eyes that changed his world.

He whispered, "Wait till you see what comes next with us." Then she watched as he walked to the waiting SUV.

He turned, winked, and was gone.

***

Next to Dakota in the SUV, Sean started a text:

Sean to Samantha: I am headed to D.C.
Be at the Zoo seventeen days from today
I will meet you there at 10 a.m.
Samantha replied: If you're lucky, Agent Man.

Sean laughed. She was crazy sexy.

***

Jimmy smiled as Serena laughed and visited at her parent's kitchen table. She had bloomed in the last few hours since the removal of danger from their life. He could only imagine what freedom felt like after so many years. He felt a rush of love and rubbed his leg against hers. He saw her brief smile, then she responded with pressure against his. Public love-talk since forever. At least in their generation.

He noticed Jacque watching him. Her dad had the wisdom of the ages in his green eyes. He was a tall, good looking, athletic man. Serena and Gabrielle had his long lean build. But neither of her parents had the amber eyes. Undoubtedly, they came from the General.

Her mother, Angela, was lovely, graceful, and had a spunky wit that exposed itself from time to time. And she felt compelled to feed them. He knew that was normal for older generations – especially here in Louisiana –

and accepted everything she offered. One, because she was grateful to finally feed her family openly. In her home. At her kitchen table. And two, because it was mouthwateringly delicious, and he was starving.

Serena glanced at him with a smile, then said, "Jimmy and I have news for you."

Her dad said, "Three weeks, I heard."

She laughed and said, "Grandpa told you."

"As fast as he possibly could," her mom said. And glancing at Jimmy she continued, "But we are thrilled to get a son."

Jimmy scooted his chair back from the table and walked around to her chair. He kissed her hand and said, "I'm a lucky man to get a beautiful mother like you."

Her mom smiled, and said, "Thank you, Jimmy. And Serena. This is what you call a romantic man."

Serena met Jimmy's eyes. She said, "Mom. That's putting it mildly."

***

Gabrielle headed north on Highway 171 to her grandparent's home. She knew where they lived. They had been her pastors for years. She had been to their home for several women's events and meetings regarding En-Garde. They lived deep in Magnolia Forest on a private road. Their home was warm and welcoming - and today it was her home too.

She crossed the first bridge over English Bayou. It was a large winding waterway that forked east off the Calcasieu River. It was a scenic bayou with trees draped in moss alongside dark mysterious water.

The next bridge rose higher and crossed over the large Calcasieu River for boat traffic, then sloped down and rode over a large swamp to connect Lake Charles to Moss Bluff. Moss Bluff was unincorporated but had grown to be a large suburb of Lake Charles. It was also the home of Sam Houston State Park on the West Fork of the river, near another bridge that connected the suburb to Westlake.

Gabrielle took a right turn off Highway 171 and knew she was only about ten minutes away from her dream. She felt a mixture of thrills and tears. Her journey to family was almost complete.

A few minutes later, she noticed an unusual amount of traffic through the trees lining the road ahead, so she slowed. Then she saw it. People parked and stood along the roadway near her grandparents' place, waving and cheering at her. Gabrielle lowered the windows as she neared, and recognized faces from church. She cried as she waved back.

She turned down the driveway and the love parade continued almost to the house. Her grandparents waited for her with open arms, and she ran right into them. After a moment, Jimmy and Serena joined them.

After tears, laughter, and waving goodbye to the crowd, Serena said, "Come in and eat, honey. Your grandma cooked. You must be starved."

"Yes, but I really need a Coke."

Jimmy said, "Ready and waiting, Cat."

With a quizzical look, her grandfather said, "Who's Cat?"

They laughed and explained as they headed inside.

Gabrielle inhaled. The whole room smelled like Cajun heaven. They ushered her to the table and served her a steaming bowl of shrimp and crab gumbo (even though it was normally a cold-weather dish) with rice, and a side of potato salad. They knew it was her favorite. With her fingers, she picked up the largest shrimp in the bowl and closed her lips around it. Scrumptious flavors filled her mouth.

After dinner, Gabrielle rocked with her grandparents on the back porch. They watched the moon rise over the magnolia, pine, and oak trees for a few minutes, then Gabrielle said, "I was shocked, you know, but thrilled to find out who you were. I had been around you all this time, totally unaware. Unbelievable."

Her grandmother touched her hand, and said, "I can't imagine what this revelation has been like for you. But for us, to see you, be around you, hug you, love you, touch you, and watch you blossom into the powerful young woman you are today…has been…indescribable."

Her grandfather said, "I second that. But you also have something else going on in your life. Why don't you tell us about Dakota?"

Gabrielle smiled, and her grandparents glanced at each other with a grin. They knew that look.

She said, "He's gorgeous. Brave. Protective. Brilliant. A believer. Has Sioux heritage. Loves horses. Has a black belt in Karate and is a published author.

But most of all, I'm in love with him - and he is one fabulous kisser." They laughed softly.

Her grandfather said, "We are grateful God has provided a man like that for you. We look forward to getting to know him. We figured he had to be an amazing man."

Her grandmother said, "And let me tell you, being a good kisser is critical. Your grandfather knocked my socks off when we met."

"What do you mean - when we met?" he said. "What about now?"

"Well, I'm barefooted." They laughed.

Jimmy and Serena joined them outside. Serena said, "I love hearing laughter out here."

Her Mom said, "We were talking about smooching."

Jimmy said, "Great conversation."

Gabrielle watched them with a full heart. Overflowing. Grateful. First, a wonderful adoptive family, and now, her birth family. A new dad. And especially Dakota.

She borrowed her dad's phone and messaged En-Garde. They made plans for breakfast at Jimmy's in the morning. It was late and she was exhausted.

As she joined her family again, Serena said, "Gabrielle, we need to get you home, it has been a long day. You look so tired."

Everyone hugged goodnight and her grandparents followed them to the truck for the second goodbye hug. There was never just one. And they headed home.

Gabrielle said, "Oh, wait Dad, can we stop by my house and get my very, very, dead phone out of my car?"

"Sure. But please don't go upstairs tonight. Your day has been long enough."

Before long, Jimmy glanced at the sleeping women as he drove home. They had been sound asleep before he even stopped at Gabrielle's house to pick up her phone. It was charging now.

As for tomorrow, he knew that a lot of people would be at Gabrielle's house at noon. They had a lot of cleaning up to do, but eventually all evidence from Ground Zero would be gone. Ready for new memories.

***

Dakota slept on the plane enroute to D.C. for a while, then woke and saw Sean still asleep. The Director and the rest of the team were discussing the case. He appreciated the break. They needed it. He straightened and winced. But the pain was much less. He wasn't one that cared for pain meds but thank God, the doctor insisted on the pain shot.

He looked out the window into the night sky, forty thousand feet above the ground. He missed Gabrielle already. He had it bad…and smiled.

***

Jade and Zoe eyeballed Samantha in the Lake Charles hotel room.

Jade said, "Samantha, you look like you are up to something. Who texted you?"

Zoe said, "I bet that something starts with an 'S' and ends with fine," and Samantha rolled her eyes at the obvious reference to Sean.

Jade poked Samantha. Zoe hit her with a hotel pillow. They tried to force her to talk.

Samantha said, "You know it's assault to attack someone."

Jade said, "Shut up and tell us."

Samantha said, "Sean and I planned a date. That's all."

"When?" They both said at the same time.

"In seventeen days."

"Where?"

"None of your business," but then Samantha grinned and said, "The Baton Rouge Zoo."

The girls were speechless. That was unexpected for a first date.

Samantha rolled her eyes, and said, "You have no sense of adventure."

"But the zoo?" Jade said.

Samantha crawled on the bed like she was stalking prey.

Jade wide-eyed, looked at Zoe, and said, "She will eat Sean alive. We need to warn him."

Zoe said, "No way. Sean is an alpha and he's on the hunt. I'm the veterinarian, I know these things."

***

At the Ranch, Gabrielle and Serena took showers as Jimmy played catch-up with tasks. He prepared his bedroom for them. Started a pot of coffee. Texted Dakota the video of the parade celebration at Gabrielle's grandparents. And even called the Louisiana Department of Wildlife & Fisheries about the dead cougar. They would come by early in the morning.

He had just taken a sip of coffee when they came downstairs. He could tell they were glad to wash the day away.

He smiled, and said, "New rule. No arguments. Both of you will sleep in my bedroom until our ceremony under the willow tree in three weeks. I'll crash on the sofa."

Then he handed Gabrielle her phone, and like a teenager, she smiled and called goodnight as she ran for the bedroom.

***

Snuggled in bed, Gabrielle checked her phone. She was shocked at all the missed calls, messages, texts, and emails since her birthday. Was that only seven days ago? Seemed like forever. Regardless, it would take a while to go through them. But she scrolled looking for one name in particular. And smiled. Dakota had sent an audio text.

She hit play and listened as his deep, sexy voice said, "I love you. Dream of me. All night."

She responded by audio, "I already do. I'll tell you about them sometime. I love you."

Chapter 29

Gabrielle opened her eyes to sunlight. Remembered. And rolled over to look at her mom.

Serena said, "Welcome to your new life, honey."

Gabrielle laughed and hugged her, then said, "You're getting married in just three weeks!"

She said, "I know. Amazing, isn't it?"

Jimmy drawled from the doorway, "Ask me. I'm counting the hours. And speaking of hours, you only have one before your poor fiancé is surrounded by three more gorgeous women for breakfast."

***

Samantha, Jade, and Zoe arrived right on time. The platter of waffles and sausage, with various syrups and butter was ready. Rarely allowing themselves that type of feast, the ladies raved as they ate. And glad to forget yesterday, the wedding was the thrill of the morning. Laughter, squeals of delight, teasing, and honeymoon suggestions had Jimmy laughing as he headed outside.

Gabrielle said, "Mom, tell us what you have in mind for the wedding."

Serena said, "Other than decorating the weeping willow tree, we really prefer simple. And simple to me is defined as hydrangeas and a few tables and chairs on the deck. Inside, a small wedding cake, champagne, and only hors d'oeuvres. Music is already piped outside. Close family and friends – which includes all of you, and your dates of course."

They divided tasks. They would shop for the wedding dress in New Orleans with Jade as chauffeur. The church would handle hors d'oeuvres. Serena's parents would officiate. Gabrielle and Dakota would be the maid of honor and best man. And twenty days from now, the willow tree was the place to be.

About an hour later, Jimmy came in and said, "I see smiles. I bet the wedding is planned to the last detail."

Serena said, "Absolutely! These women know how to make things happen."

Gabrielle said, "Dad, do you plan to take a honeymoon trip?"

Jimmy grinned at Serena, then answered Gabrielle, "Yes, but it's a secret. We'll leave the morning after the wedding. That's all I can say."

Serena said, "No hint at all?"

"Not that I can tell you in front of these women."

She laughed, then slid her arms around his waist. She said, "Girls, he did tell me: One, I can pick out any horse I want. And two, we will add some female decor to this already fabulous house."

Jimmy kissed her cheek, and said, "I want to see you in every room, even when you aren't in it."

The girls groaned at his charm. Samantha said, "You're killing me. You're so romantic I can't stand it."

Seconds later, Jimmy's phone rang. Adam and Aunt Jaz were on their way to Dakota's cabin with the animals.

Zoe's phone rang. Trace was following Adam to the cabin.

Serena's phone rang. Her dad was on the way to Gabrielle's house with a bunch of men from the church.

Concerned, Jimmy said, "Cat, are you sure that you're ready for this? I know you expect repairs will be needed; but seeing your home damaged won't be easy."

"I don't like knowing that they tore it up, but I'm ok. Maybe redoing it will remove the memories of them in it. And Dakota will be gone a couple of weeks – hopefully repairs will be completed by then. But all that aside, I'm ready to walk on my land. Safe. Free. And finally celebrate where it all started generations ago.

***

In D.C., Dakota took a quick break to grab a cup of coffee and sandwich before the next round of meetings. He thought of Gabrielle's message last night. Her voice made him want these two weeks in D.C. to fly by. Especially when he had decided Paris would be the perfect place for their honeymoon. It was time to marry his wildcat.

***

When Gabrielle stepped out of her dad's truck at her house, she heard Zeus' frenzied barking across the river. Adam, Trace, and Aunt Jaz waved at her as they climbed into a boat. He barked the whole trip across the river. Her hawk screeched flying circles in the air. She laughed. Grateful. Oh, so grateful. No secrets. No danger. Not alone anymore.

Everyone smiled as she ran downhill to meet the boat. Zeus jumped out when it hit the sandbar and Gabrielle knelt to wait for him. He knocked her down and laid on top of her. Everyone laughed till they cried.

They had just finished introductions when Grandpa Jacque and half the church showed up blowing their horns. Once the new greetings were over, the men divided into task groups. Some went to Dakota's cabin with Trace, Zoe, Adam, and Aunt Jaz. Most stayed on Gabrielle's side of the river and worked with Jimmy to wash away the blood. Then they filled a tremendous amount of holes from the treasure digging.

A few contractors and carpenters went upstairs with them to inspect Gabrielle's house. Once they were sure it was safe to enter, she went inside. Speechless at the enormity of the destruction, she viewed both floors before she made any decisions.

They had broken or damaged her furnishings downstairs – even the boat chandelier on the ceiling. And flash burns and soot marks took care of the rest. Fifteen of her paintings, and twenty of her photographs survived that were wrapped and hidden behind her paint counter.

Upstairs was terrible. The trunk was broken. Her swords damaged. Weapons taken. Many of her personal items, and all the bedding were destroyed.

Gabrielle said, "I think I'll just grab my art and a few other things that are salvageable, but the rest can be thrown out as trash. Grandpa, would your contractors let me know if there is any structure damage, or is it surface only?"

Then she turned and saw the compassionate tears in her mom, Samantha, and Jade's eyes.

She hugged them, and said, "It's ok. I promise. I saved the majority of my art. The rest is a can of paint, new furniture, and a few shopping trips."

Then she made stacks of what to keep. The others made trips down to her car with salvaged items until both floors had been searched. The contractors confirmed there wasn't any structure damage. They also agreed with her suggestion to clear it out and remodel. A contractor from the church took the job so the guys began to haul out trash.

After Jimmy's crew finished in the yard, he called Trace to come pick them up in the boat. Gabrielle was ready to see Dakota's cabin.

***

Midway across the river, Gabrielle's phone rang. It was Dakota. She answered with a smile, "Hey there."

"Tell me about your place. Are you upset?"

"I'm fine. Really. My house was a mess, so I trashed most of it. I was able to save all the hidden art and a few other things. The rest of the house just needs paint, new floors, and new decorating. That works perfect for a new life, right?"

"I'm so sorry I can't be there to help right now."

"Dakota, what you've done for me through all of this has meant everything. And what you do loving me is priceless. I understand, but don't feel bad. Half the church is here for heaven's sake. This is what they do. It is their way to make it better for all of us.

"And by-the-way, we are crossing the river to check your house and see what the crews are doing there. Have you heard from Adam?"

"Yes. There was little to no actual damage, just mess. Aunt Jaz will have it ship shape in no time with those guys to help."

"I'm really glad for you."

He said, "Whatever you need…whatever I have is yours. If I don't have it, we will get it for you." He groaned and said, "Sorry, I have to run. We'll talk later."

***

Serena helped Jimmy in Dakota's barn. They were both sweaty from tending to the horses. She glanced at him. Summer heat aside, he was her kind of hot from head to toe. A mixture of gallantry, sensuality, and faith. That combination was irresistible to her. But she wasn't twenty years old anymore. She was fifty. But she still wanted to be all that - and more to him.

He turned, muscles bulging as he carried a saddle, and caught her look. He smiled, and said, "I know what you're thinking about."

She whispered, "Then come show me," and without a word, he dropped the saddle and reached for her.

A few sweaty moments later, he said, "Come swimming with me when we get home to cool off."

"Do you really think less clothes in a pool is going to cool us off?"

***

Twelve days later, Gabrielle stood on her new snack bar, lost in thought. With her arms high in the air and her bare feet spread apart for balance, she worked on her salvaged pirogue chandelier – daydreaming about Dakota.

Since he had been gone, she had treasured the romantic moments they had snatched out of every day. Calls. Texts. Videos. Many hot and sexy. Some gentle, sweet, and caressing. Even funny and embarrassing ones. Like when she leaned out of the shower to answer – not realizing it was a video call until he whistled – and she screamed. Like when she texted him a kiss and his boss saw the text. And the time that he video-called her while he was shaving - bare-chested, with a towel around him – and she couldn't focus on what he said. They ate in front of eat other. Both fell asleep sometimes on the late-night video chats. At times one might be cranky – or busy – or tired. But all the time, they were missing each other desperately.

She knew when he came home, they would know so much more about each other. But even more, their love and passion were even hotter. Tomorrow couldn't get here soon enough.

She startled when a husky voice said, "Gabrielle," and she spun, long hair fanning, to face Dakota.

Tall, dark, and handsome, he leaned against the doorframe watching her. Hunger in his eyes. Long hair loose. Tight jeans. He was gorgeous.

She whispered, "Dakota…"

He headed across the room – not missing one thing about her. Sizzling amber eyes. Sexy athletic body in cutoffs. Long firm legs. She was fabulous. His. She ran a couple of steps along the top of the snack bar and jumped. He caught her. Lips and bodies connected for a wild kiss. A long, breath-stealing one.

When they parted, she said, "I've waited for this."

He tasted her lips again, and said, "So have I… sweet Cat. So have I."

***

Later, passion paused, they sat outside on the hill. Relaxed. Flirted. Talked. Teased, and joked. No fear. No urgency. Just them. And it was wonderful.

She said, "So, are you semi-retired again with the FBI?"

He glanced at her, then said, "They asked me to go full time again. They offered me a position in Miami."

She sat up on her knees, trying to hide her dismay, and still show how sincerely proud she was of him.

She said, "I would never be surprised at that. You are amazingly gifted at what you do." She forced a smile, and said, "You have more than earned it. I should know, you've saved me twice. So, does that mean you plan to sell the log cabin?"

He touched her cheek, and said, "I turned them down."

Her eyes narrowed, and she jumped on him. They tumbled and wrestled on the ground, and he couldn't stop laughing.

She hit his arm, and said, "You set me up."

"Just to get a rise out of you. I'm not going anywhere – I told you that. Though, I may take a Louisiana case if I am free to do so."

Straddling him, she leaned down and said, "Kiss me and make up for that." He made it a whole lot better.

Many kisses later, she said, "Will you go back to writing?"

"Yes. I love it. The stories just come together in my head like mini movies. I get to enjoy them before anyone else."

"You are an amazing storyteller, Dakota. Why don't you write my family's story with Jean Lafitte? You wouldn't even have to research it."

He smiled. What an amazing idea. He said, "I might just do that."

***

Later, back at his log cabin, Dakota's phone rang. He answered, "Hey Jimmy!"

"Hey Dakota! It's good to have you back. I know you're glad to have that case behind you."

"You know it. The FBI is still reeling from one of their own being a traitor. But enough about that, how about the wedding? You only have a few days left."

Jimmy said, "I'm counting down now."

"No doubt. I get it. What about the Hawaii trip? All planned?"

"Yes. Tomorrow, I head to Houston to pick up her ring."

"Can I help with anything?"

"Can you make the guests leave five minutes after we say the vows?"

Dakota laughed so hard he couldn't answer.

***

Gabrielle hung up her phone and screamed as she danced around her new kitchen. John Alexander, the museum curator, and appraiser for the treasure, said it was cleaned, catalogued, and verified. It was authentic antique treasure. There were three hundred Napoleon French gold coins, thirty jeweled necklace sets, six jeweled daggers, eight gold goblets with jewel designs and seven gold swords with jeweled hilts. It all dated back to the Napoleon era. And the love letter and map from Jean Lafitte were authentic as well.

It wasn't like they didn't believe it was real, but to have it confirmed was thrilling. Now the curator wanted to meet with the family tomorrow at First Federal Bank in downtown Lake Charles. Too excited to contain herself, she ran down the hill, to cross the river to tell Dakota personally. He insisted on leaving a Jet Ski for her now.

***

Sean parked at the Baton Rouge Zoo and walked toward the gate. He knew he was a few minutes early but couldn't take a chance Samantha might try to throw him off by being early herself. He found a bench and kicked back to wait. He intended to make a different impression on her today, so he dressed in tan linen pants, a white shirt, and sandals. His black hair was growing longer and blowing in the breeze. He adjusted his sunglasses and smiled. She would appreciate his effort to play the game.

A few minutes later, he watched her park and step out of her car. Her long blonde hair was loose, and she had on a black and white pinstripe sundress. But when she turned, the front of the dress was split up the middle from the hem to the waist like a tuxedo shirt and matching shorts. In black sunglasses, sandals, and red lipstick, she was smokin' hot and ready to play.

He met her at the gate, and said, "You look gorgeous."

Samantha pulled her sunglasses down to look over the top of them, and said, "This old thing?" and he laughed.

She looked him over, and said, "You look so fine, Sean. Tell me, are you looking for a special attraction at the zoo today?"

He said, "I'm passionate about rare, magnificent animals. Kind of like the white tiger. The ones you want to touch even though they are dangerous. What about you?"

"The gorillas always amaze me with their intelligence, intensity, strength, and hidden fire. Almost like a man, wouldn't you say?"

Sean said, "I would say," and offered her his arm as they strolled into the zoo.

***

The next day, Dakota and Gabrielle met her family at the bank. Mr. Alexander was already there. The bank manager and security guard escorted them into the vault and led through a security door to reveal the treasure.

It was breathtakingly impressive. The map and letter were framed. The swords were mounted. Jewelry sets were mounted on jeweler stands. The daggers were in a rack. The goblets were beautiful. And the gold coins were separated in black velvet bags.

They took pictures and inspected all of it. It was exciting to know this was a gift from an emperor to Jean Lafitte. On top of the fact, that Lafitte traveled a long mysterious river, to hide it in a tree instead of burying it.

Gabrielle lifted the sword she fought Vee with and saluted her ancestor. The beginning of her bloodline.

At the end, Mr. Alexander gave historical and financial value on all of it. It was worth millions if sold but advised them there were multiple options for them to choose from. A personal family collection. A traveling historical exhibit. Selling some at auction for charity. And a Smithsonian exhibit.

He recommended the family meet with an attorney to finalize those decisions and the treasure could be held in the vault till then.

***

The three weeks of engagement had passed. Jimmy walked Serena up the garden path toward the house. The decor was beautiful for their wedding tomorrow evening. The willow tree where they first kissed. The garden. The deck, pool, and inside of the house were tasteful and romantic.

He met her gaze. She saw his desire. Impatience. And he slipped his hands into the back pocket of her jeans and pulled her against him with a groan.

She slid her arms around his neck, and said, "I know. Just a few more hours."

After one more heated caress and kiss, they went inside where Dakota and Gabrielle waited. Dakota took one glance at Jimmy and knew tomorrow night couldn't get here fast enough.

He said, "Ladies, everything is loaded. It's time to go," and he and Gabrielle headed outside to give them privacy.

Serena said, "I'll miss not seeing you tonight."

Jimmy said, "Me too, honey. And I bet you a million dollars that a man didn't come up with this tradition of not seeing each other till the wedding." She giggled and gave him one more kiss.

With eyes full of promise, he said, "I'll make you a happy woman tomorrow."

"I already am."

With a sexy grin, he whispered, "Just wait till tomorrow."

***

At Dakota's house, it was late when Gabrielle finally headed upstairs with Zeus to what would be her bedroom for a while. Dakota led the way. They snuggled on the bed for a few minutes. She had missed not being in his protective arms at night, like when they were on the run.

She said, "I can't wait to see you in a tux tomorrow."

He grinned and said, "What about you? Are you wearing a short little dress as maid of honor to show off your gorgeous legs?"

She slid his hand to her thigh, and said, "It stops about right here."

He rubbed her thigh, then pulled her into a tight caress…then groaned and left for his room before he needed a cold shower.

Chapter 30

The next morning at the ranch, Jimmy watched the men assemble the surprise chalet bedroom suite he had ordered. Serena never noticed he saw her looking at it online. The new linen had been hidden upstairs for a week. He smiled. Today was the day. She would be his tonight and every second after that. They would finally enjoy the promises their eyes made.

The doorbell rang, interrupting his thoughts. A few minutes later, he grinned at the perplexed look on the delivery man's face as he unloaded two more dozen potted hydrangeas to decorate a bedroom. Jimmy was determined to have a private garden inside.

Then the contractor called. The surprise archway sign for the driveway was installed. J&S Ranch was now a reality.

***

At the log cabin, Serena and Gabrielle walked in from the porch at the same time Dakota rounded the corner. He smiled. Gabrielle completely forgot what she had been about to say and stared at him. Already a gorgeous man, today he wore a black tux and a thin black tie. Long hair down. Dark eyes. Sexy body. She had known he would look amazing. But this…

He chuckled as Gabrielle checked him out and spread her hands across his chest.

Serena laughed softly as she passed them to go upstairs, and said, "I see smoke," and he laughed.

Gabrielle said, "You are the sexiest man I have ever seen."

His hot kiss quickly followed, then he said, "You are good for my ego, Cat."
She watched him walk to the door to go meet her dad. He said, "I will see you at six p.m. at the ranch. I can't wait to see that short number you're going to be in."
She smiled. He had a shock coming too.

***

Dakota thought the J&S Ranch sign looked great as he turned in the driveway. Serena would love it. And Jimmy would be terrific at breeding horses - on top of being the perfect husband for Serena.

A few hours later, Sean, Adam, Trace, and En-Garde arrived to help Jimmy and Dakota. Everyone greeted, excited about the wedding. Time was ticking. It wouldn't be long.

Sean made sure he got Samantha alone for a minute, and gave her a tight, warm, I'm-thinking-about-you hug. She smiled with a teasing look under her lashes. He glanced appreciatively at her beauty in a short turquoise dress, and she returned the favor, looking his body over in black slacks and shirt.
He said, "You look delicious."
She said, "And you look hungry," then walked away.
Sean chuckled at her sass as he watched her. It had been intriguing at the zoo as they played their game. But he knew they could be so much more than a game. He looked forward to some one-on-one repartee' with her tonight.

A sudden flurry of activity took center stage as the food and wedding flowers arrived. Samantha easily directed the setup. At one point, she turned and caught Sean's gaze on her. She liked his clever moves. And he was one handsome man. Much like Dakota and Adam, but his personality was a unique mix of intellectual and sexy charm that made her stomach tighten. She could tell he liked the dance of romance. But…she would wait and see.

***

Gabrielle helped her mom finish dressing. Serena's dark shoulder length hair was striking. Her amber eyes were dreamy accented with smoky shadows and liner. And her cherry-colored lips were like icing on the cake.

"Mom. You are so beautiful. But hurry - I can't stand it – it's time for the dress!"

Serena laughed, and stepped into the rich gold material, and pulled it all the way up. The silky wedding dress was a one shouldered sheath that hugged her curves. Not tight at all. But like liquid. Her left leg and gold heels peeked through a long slit in the skirt. She looked in the mirror and smiled.

Gabrielle said, "Dad's going to remember the way you look today for the rest of his life."

"That's the point, honey. Now come on, you get dressed. Mom and Dad will be here in less than an hour."

Gabrielle finished and stood in front of the dressing mirror. Her long dark hair was in a single braid that hung down her back. Her amber eyes were enhanced by sheens of burgundy, chocolate, and gold shadows with red matte lipstick. She smiled as she pulled on the little black dress. There was nothing simple about it. Strapless and fitted to the hips, the short skirt flared with a sassy flurry of black net. It was sexy feminine. And her long shapely legs ended in black patent stiletto pumps.

Gabrielle said, "I feel like a pop star."

Serena said, "You look like one too," and the doorbell rang.

Gabrielle excitedly opened the door to her grandparents, and they hugged and exclaimed over her appearance.

She said, "Wait till you see Mom!"

They walked into the den and watched as Serena descended the stairs. She was breathtaking, and they wiped away quick, but happy tears and took a few pictures. In minutes, they left for the ranch. Gabrielle texted Dakota and Jimmy that they were on their way.

***

Jimmy knew the limo would be here any minute. He looked around and everything was in place. The food was ready. The hydrangeas were warm and rich smelling throughout the walkway and deck. Garden lights flickered. Saxophone music played in the background. Candles floated in the pool. The guests visited at round tables.

The wedding ceremony setup was gorgeous under the willow tree. A two-deck platform sat under a curtain of willow branches floating with hundreds of fairy lights. It was magical.

Several minutes later, Dakota met Jimmy by the window overlooking the deck, and said, "They're almost here. I'll let you know when it's time for you to come out."

They fist-bumped, and Jimmy entered the bedroom. Fairy lights and flowers surrounded the bed. It was perfect. Like her.

***

The limousine arrived in front of the house. Dakota stepped outside to greet them. The driver opened the limo door and offered his arm. Serena stepped out and stood. Beautiful. Dramatic. Stunning in a gold dress that matched her amber eyes.

Behind Serena, Gabrielle stepped out of the car. Dakota groaned as her exotic eyes met his. She smiled. She was wildly gorgeous. Make-his-blood-boil gorgeous. He looked at her lips. At the sexy black dress. At her long bare legs to die for.

Aware of her successful impact, Gabrielle touched his chest, and whispered, "Hi, Handsome."

Dakota said, "Cat, you're killing me," and she smiled.

He escorted both women inside, then Gabrielle followed her mom upstairs. She knew Dakota watched her. Yes indeed, her man liked what he saw.

Gabrielle prepared her mom for the procession, then walked to the top of the stairs and nodded at Dakota. It was time. Sean opened the drapes across the back of the house so the guests could see inside. Dakota knocked on the bedroom door.

Jimmy stepped out. Sexy. Debonair. Oozing charm as he strolled across the room in a black tux jacket, black slacks, and an open neck white silk shirt. His gaze rose to the top of the stairs. He whistled at Gabrielle as he stopped next to Dakota.

She laughed, then started down the stairs. Dakota met, and escorted her to the deck door, where they turned to watch. Everyone stood. Jimmy watched for Serena.

The song changed. Serena glided to the center of the loft and paused. Jimmy's eyes flamed as their gazes met. She smiled. Sexy. Promising. This was their time. She began to descend the stairs and he lowered his gaze slowly, to see every inch of her body move under the silky dress on her way to him. When he glanced back at her, she slid her gaze to his chest, stomach, hips, and legs – then back up. She reached the bottom.

He drew her close, and whispered, "This better be the fastest wedding in history," and both smiling, they faced their guests.

Dakota escorted Gabrielle down the garden path to the willow tree platform. Then every eye was on Jimmy and Serena as he escorted his bride up the aisle. The unspoken communication between them was beautiful.

They entered the tree canopy and stepped on the platform and faced each other. Love spoke with each glance and every touch. The wedding message spoken over them declared God's purpose in the joining of a man and a woman. The prayer was next. Then vows. Then rings. And finally, the kiss. Jimmy took his time in a very heated kiss and caress as everyone cheered.

Then they walked back down the path to join their guests.

***

Dakota and Gabrielle stayed under the willow tree lost in each other. He pulled her close. Smelled the perfume on her neck. Slid his hands down her back to her hips – loving the feel of her against him. He wanted to taste her.

She watched as his soft warm lips kissed her palm. Then he lightly licked the inside of her wrist. He smiled at her immediate response. The blink. The tiny gasp. The yield as she leaned into him. With knees not quite steady, she clutched his lapel. His arms tightened as his lips took hers. Hungry. The twinkling lights around them long forgotten.

***

On the deck, Samantha watched the bride and groom visit with their guests. It was such a romantic wedding, and she was thrilled for them. They were an amazing couple.

People began to dance, and in a moment, warm breath whispered in her ear, "Dance with me."

Teasing Sean, she said, "What kind of dance do you have in mind?"

He stepped in front of her and drew her close till their bodies brushed, teasingly, against each other.

He said, "A slow dance will do," and held a hand on her lower back to move her with him.

She stayed there - surprising herself. There was something about him that drew her in.

After a few moments, Sean said, "What happens if I won't let you go?"

She laughed and said, "Did you forget I have a sword?"

He laughed. She was the coolest woman on earth.

Adam laughed with Aunt Jaz by the pool. She had endless tales of Dakota, Sean, and his antics, growing up practicing Indian skills in a city environment. But then, he caught a second glance between the General and Aunt Jaz and realized something was going on. So, he casually strolled with her in the General's direction.

The General was quick to intercept them and enter the conversation. Adam smiled. Aunt Jaz was still a beautiful woman with her feminine flair, petite frame, and quick wit. Obviously, the General was enchanted already.

Adam excused himself to visit with Jade and smiled as he walked away. Thank God romance doesn't have an age limit.

Jade had just finished a conversation with Serena and Jimmy, when Adam said, "Hey, wild woman."

Grinning, she said, "Who me?"

"You and three other women here. You all have super long knives. That's wild."

She laughed, knowing he referenced the swords, and said, "Funny man."

As their laughter faded away, he said, "I do have a serious side you know."

"Prove it."

"I signed up yesterday for a medical mission trip to the mountains of Brazil."

Shocked, she said, "Adam! For how long?"

"I leave next month for almost a year."

Frowning, she said, "You don't mess around. Where did that come from?"

"I feel the calling and don't want to miss God by dragging my feet. Besides, I hate to think of people in need when I could help them."

Jade hugged him, and said, "Bless you, Adam. Be safe," then as she stepped back, she said, "I bet you come back with a Brazilian wife with your sexy looks."

He laughed and said, "A sexy minister. Now who's funny! And as for THE woman for me - I'll find her. Now what about you, Jade? What's next for you?"

"I'm thinking hard about opening a private investigator business. I already do the reporting."

Adam sighed, and said, "While I think that is perfect for you - I wish you would think about getting a male partner. And I don't care if it seems sexist. Maybe some extra self-defense training too. You can't be too prepared these days, and two heads are better than one in that line of work. Men and women both bring different strengths to the table."

"Wise advice. Thanks, Adam. I'll add that to my thinking pile."

A short time later, Dakota danced with Gabrielle. He said, "How am I supposed to focus with you looking like that?"

"It was my mission to see that look in your eyes."

He groaned and said, "Gabrielle…"

She said, "Just kiss me." He did.

A moment later Dakota saw Jimmy's wave. Jimmy held up his watch with a non-subtle hint, and Dakota laughed.

Gabrielle said, "What's funny?"

"I think your dad's ready for the party to end. Can you help me?" and they began to thank the guests for coming and lead them out.

Samantha got the group in gear, and the food was put away in record time. Clean up could wait till tomorrow after the honeymooners had left on their trip. In short order, the guests were gone, and Dakota and Gabrielle's taillights faded in the distance.

***

Jimmy locked the door and turned around. His flaming eyes found Serena's. She licked her lips as she slid her hands down her thighs and slowly began to pull the hem higher and higher. He headed across the room dropping first his jacket, then the shirt.

Both were breathless when he reached her, and in one motion, he pulled her hips and lips against him. Hot and urgent, their bodies collided - and they groaned at the contact. Burning, he scooped her up and carried her toward the bedroom.

Serena squirmed in his arms, reaching for him, needing him, and said, "Jimmy…I…"

Their blazing gazes met, and he kicked the bedroom door open. He said, "I know baby…I'm coming."

***

Samantha and Sean met at the Civic Center seawall in Lake Charles after they left the wedding. Watching the lake, they leaned against the rail and enjoyed the salty breeze. It blew just enough to take the edge of heat out of the night air.

Sean caught a long piece of her blonde hair in the breeze and wrapped it around his finger. He said, "I like what I see."

Meeting his gaze, she said, "And what's that?"

"A fabulous woman that I want to know."

"So, you're into long distance relationships since you live here?"

"That's the thing, Samantha. It looks like I'll be working in your neck of the woods."

Sassy as always, she said, "I don't live in the woods."

He smiled and said, "No. But I might," and she waited, recognizing his teaser.

"The FBI offered me a position in Baton Rouge. I accepted effective in two weeks. I'd like to buy a ranch out by St. Francisville. So, I thought in your free time, you might help me look. And I'll just live in Baton Rouge till I find the right property."

Trying to hide her eager response to that news, she glanced away, and said, "Really? That sounds interesting."

But he had already noticed the double blink of interest and impact, parted lips showing attraction, and knew what that could mean.

His eyes met hers and he said, "I think it's getting more interesting all the time."

***

Dakota watched his stallion run along the fence as they drove up to the cabin. He killed the engine and looked at Gabrielle. They were aware the night was far from over.

He slid his hand up the back of her neck, and said, "How about a late-night ride with me?"

She wet her lips, and said, "That sounds perfect. I've missed our rides."

He pulled her lips toward his, saying, "So have I," and kissed her.

***

Aunt Jaz waved at them as they walked in. She rocked the cat on her lap, her heels kicked off haphazardly on the floor.

She said, "My feet are killing me, but I had a wonderful time."

Dakota asked, "Can we do anything? Just name it."

With twinkling eyes, she said, "The night is beautiful, go enjoy yourselves. I am fine and who knows, perhaps my prince charming will find me out here in the woods."

Dakota kissed her cheek, and said, "You deserve a prince charming."

She laughed and said, "Enough about me. Hand me your phone and let me take some pictures of both of you before you change."

***

A short while later, dressed in jeans they headed to the barn. Gabrielle knew Dakota appreciated her tight jeans and black laced-up crop top. Teasing him, she gave a sexy runway model walk ahead of him. He growled, loving the show, then ran and slung her screaming over his shoulder.

Laughing, he carried her the rest of the way to the barn. Captured. His. And before he lowered her, he kissed, then bit, her thigh. Gabrielle gasped at the hot caress. His touch was driving her crazy.

He whistled for the stallion. Once saddled, Dakota gave Gabrielle a leg up and he mounted behind her. He said, "I want to show you one of my favorite places. It's a terrific ride there at night with a full moon."

Gabrielle loved the feel of being snug in the saddle with Dakota again. His firm thighs around her. His hand around her waist, thumb hooked inside her waistband, and his cologne teasing her.

It took her a minute to even pay attention to the smells around them. Earthy. Moss, trees, the river, the rich mud on the riverbank, and magnolia flowers. And the sounds. Owls. Crickets. Hawks. Frogs. Alligators. The breeze rustled through the trees. The water lapped the bank. It was still breathtaking in the dark.

Dakota tightened his hold on her. He had missed being with her like this. Loving her made him hungry and he knew they were in their mating dance. The want they felt. The touch and smell season that opened the door for more…later. Much more. He drew her back against him. Tighter.

As the stallion climbed a hill, Gabrielle asked, "Have you ever tried to locate any Sioux relatives?"

"We have. Sean, Adam, and I commit to head north every year or so and spend time with a few distant relatives. We don't have much in common with them in lifestyle, but we recognize and honor the bond and blood we share.

"And not just that, but the three of us strive to continue to experience what it must have been like for our ancestors. To live riding with the wind in your face, hair blowing, bare-chested, on the back of a horse with no saddle. The joy. And the survival. Personally, I don't ever want to lose that feeling, that depth, that nature connection. It is a part of who I always want to be."

Laying her cheek against his chest in a caress, she said, "I love to watch you race with the wind. It is a look I would love to capture in a painting – as well as experience with you. It exposes what's inside you. I hope to ride with you bareback one day."

"You will, Cat. Many times. That's a promise."

When they reached the bluff, it was mysterious and beautiful to sit there overlooking the river and forests through the flickering moonlight and shadows. Gabrielle pointed out a few alligators that looked like logs, a few racoons washing their hands, and animals trying to grab a sip of water before they became a predator's late-night dinner.

Then Dakota began to tune everything out but her. He moved her hair aside. Kissed her ear, her neck, and ran his hands firmly down her thighs and back up. Desire evident. She arched back against his chest in response, and he groaned. She turned toward him. He repositioned her on his lap, her legs locked around his hips, and they faced each other.

He kissed her. Devoured her. Deeper than ever - searching her hidden places. She opened her lips to him. Held on. She loved the man he was. The protector. The agent. The author. All of him. She knew she would love him for a lifetime.

Minutes later, he held her face, and said, “I love you. I need you. Every inch of you. Marry me, Cat. Marry me.”

Her smile was instant. She said, “Yes! I’ve always been yours. I love you. And there isn’t an inch of me that isn’t yours – that won’t always need you.”

“How soon?”

With a quick pause to think, she said, “Six weeks.”

He nodded and said, “Not a day longer, or we’re eloping.”

***

While back at the honeymoon, Serena smiled as Jimmy walked through the twinkling fairy lights and hydrangeas toward the bed with two glasses of champagne.

He took her hand and said, “Come with me.”

“Where are we going?”

“To the garden – then the pool – for starters anyway.”

She kissed him, running her hands down his thighs, and whispered, “Will we sleep?”

“In a couple of weeks.”

Chapter 31

Gabrielle smiled as she walked downstairs the next morning, remembering last night with Dakota. She was marrying him in six weeks. Six weeks. Forty-two days. She would walk down the aisle, into his arms, his bed, and his life forever. She was breathless thinking about the reality of it.

She heard him joking with Sean, Adam, and Aunt Jaz as she stepped into the kitchen – out of his line of sight. She held her finger to her lips and tiptoed toward him. But he spun, facing her.

He gave her a sexy grin that flipped her stomach, then pulled her close and said, "I would know your scent anywhere." Then lifted her off her feet and kissed her, completely unconcerned with the catcalls from his brothers, and cheers from his aunt.

Sean said, "Looks like you should have gotten married under the willow tree last night too."

Dakota hugged Gabrielle, and said, "She promised to marry me in six weeks. Six long, long, long weeks. But not one day longer," and she winked at him as the others congratulated them.

Gabrielle said, "Two weddings in six weeks – love is definitely in the air guys. You could be next."

Adam said, "No. Not yet. If there's something in the air, I'm wearing a mask."

Sean appeared deep in thought.

Gabrielle said, "I think it's too late for Sean to get a mask."

***

After breakfast they headed to clean up at J&S Ranch and tend to the stock. They were feeding the animals when a truck drove up. The General got out.

Surprised, Gabrielle gave him a hug, and said, "Hi, Grandpa Scott!"

"Hey, sweetie. Do you happen to know where Jimmy took your mom for their surprise honeymoon?"

Gabrielle shook her head no.

Dakota grinned, and said, "Hawaii," as Gabrielle gasped in delight.

Aunt Jaz walked up to join them, and said, "Morning Scott."

Dakota, Sean, Adam, and Gabrielle blinked in surprise. Scott?

The General said, "Good morning, Jaz."

She said, "Are you ready for your coffee?"

"You bet I am," and he followed her inside where she had been cleaning.

Gabrielle laughed, and said, "I think it's too late for grandpa's mask too!"

***

Back on the river that afternoon, Gabrielle was up a ladder hanging paintings at her house when her phone rang. She checked the caller and gasped, then climbing down the ladder, answered professionally, "This is Gabrielle Sawyer."

A woman said, "Ms. Sawyer, this is Dorinda with the Gallery by the Lake. I am calling to invite you to schedule an exhibition in the Historic City Hall Arts & Cultural Center with us. After your exposure with your family lineage, we've had several requests from patrons and guests asking to see your artwork. We would love to extend a hand of support to you as one of our local artists. Is this something you would be interested in scheduling with us?"

Gabrielle wanted to scream she was so excited - but didn't of course.

Dakota walked in about that time. He smiled as Gabrielle danced silently around the empty room shushing him while she was on the phone.

Then she paused, and with utter control, said, "I would love to schedule an art exhibit with you. I have several paintings, photographs, and possibly a live exhibit I would love to show."

"Wonderful. Perhaps we could arrange an appointment. We have an exhibit opening in four and a half weeks. Is that too soon for you?"

"Not at all. It's perfect in fact."

"Are you available to meet with me this week to fill out the contract? Perhaps, Wednesday, at two p.m.?"

"Yes, thank you. I have it on my calendar."

***

After the call, Gabrielle screamed, ran, and jumped in Dakota's arms. Thrilled for her, he said, "Congratulations Cat! That is terrific news! You're a fabulous artist. I am so proud of you."

Then her eyes widened, and she said, "Oh no! It is in four and a half weeks. I will have to hurry and finish the pieces I've already started! And our wedding! Oh Dakota, I'm so happy I could just scream!"

Dakota laughed, and said, "You did, honey. You did."

A few minutes later, they toured her newly renovated house. He said, "Now that we are getting married, what are your thoughts about your place?"

"Just fleeting thoughts so far. I realize your cabin is a much larger home."

He said, "I have a few thoughts to run by you. We both work from home. My house already has a study. But you need an art studio. The best light for that is here. Upstairs, right?"

"Yes. It is. And I think I get where you're headed."

He chuckled and said, "My suggestions are to have your studio upstairs. Make the main floor a treehouse style cottage for our kids in the years ahead. We could even add more garden activities to your trail."

She walked her fingers up his shirt, and said, "Yet again, you confirm the brilliant man I'm in love with."

After a kiss, he stepped back, and said, "I also have a surprise for you. Close your eyes."

He turned his back to her and lifted his shirt, and said, "Ok. Look at the waistband of my jeans."

Intrigued, Gabrielle opened her eyes, and his back faced her. She slid her hand to his waistband and screamed. He laughed.

She said, "It's a cat! You tattooed me on your hip!"

The cat was stunning. She was about two inches in diameter and posed in a very sassy manner. She was dark brown with amber eyes and a jeweled collar.

He said, "I knew you would like it."

Her eyes danced with joy, and she said, "I can't believe it! I can't wait to tell dad you got a tat."

He spun, kissed her firmly, and said, "Never, ever, tell him that I got a cat tattoo on my hip."

Gabrielle said, "But…"

"No buts."

She grinned mischievously, and said, "But she's so cute," and he moaned, knowing Jimmy would find out. And harass him forever.

***

After Dakota helped her carry all her art supplies and paintings to the loft, Gabrielle was knee deep in art. She unwrapped and inventoried her work for the exhibit. Portraits. Animals. Nature. Many were already prepared to show. Some were almost finished. But the last two sketches had been damaged by the Posse and she would have to draw them again.

***

But first, she texted Samantha, Jade, and Zoe with her news:
Wedding in six weeks.
Black bridesmaid dresses.
Any style.
All of you are maid of honor.
Can't talk now. I will call later.
I promise.
I love you.
Her notifications dinged over, and over, and over.

***

Then she called her grandparents and gave them the good news. They were not surprised and planned to officiate their wedding. She hoped her parents would call in a day or two. She didn't want to interrupt them on their honeymoon. Then she shook her head with a grin, she probably wouldn't hear from them for a week or two.

***

Dakota called a contractor when he got back to his study. His next call was to a decorator. They both promised to complete the project they wanted done in her house by the weekend. Next, he called a diamond broker. He ordered a three-carat marquise amber colored diamond surrounded by white diamonds.

He sent the broker a close-up picture of Gabrielle's eyes. It had to match perfectly.

The last call was to his parents, and they couldn't wait to meet Gabrielle. He promised to call more often and knew they were lonesome. He also knew they would love her, and that she would love them.

***

A week later, Dakota smiled as he hung up the phone. Gabrielle would love her surprise honeymoon in Paris. She would be enraptured by the City of Love. His travel agent was emailing him the confirmations now. Dakota wanted a whole month in Paris with his wife.

He had been busy as well working on the plot of his new book. His agent already harassed him for a peek at it. He knew Gabrielle would love it - but this was a surprise for a later date.

Smiling, he sat back and looked across the river. He loved their new *thing.* He'd call her on video chat, and she'd prop the phone where he could watch her paint or draw. He loved her focus and passion for creating. She made the cutest faces and got paint all over her. A lot of times they barely spoke.

She did the same with him. He might be writing, plotting, or even working with the horses and she watched him. Sketched him. Today she texted a picture of her lips puckered for a kiss. He had ridden the Jet Ski over for an energetic kissing session that left them both sweating.

He looked forward to the next time.

***

Gabrielle's phone rang. She groaned. Her hands were full of paint. She checked the phone screen, and it was her mom. Excited after not talking to them for two weeks, she looked around – no rag. Oh well, she wiped her hands on her T-shirt and answered the call, "Hello newlyweds! How is Hawaii?"

Serena and Jimmy both answered, "Amazing! Gorgeous! You would love it."

Gabrielle said, "Have you done a lot of sightseeing?"

Serena glanced at Jimmy who wiggled his eyebrows. She grinned, and said, "Not a lot. We've stayed close to the bungalow which is fabulous and on the beach. We've had lots of exciting things to do." Jimmy smiled.

Gabrielle said, "I can't wait to see pictures! But…I do have some news to tell you."

Her Mom, concerned, said, "What? Is everything okay?"

"Oh. Yes. But you might want to save the date for my wedding in four weeks."

***

A couple of days later, Gabrielle pulled up at the bridal shop for a fitting. Her wedding dress had arrived from New York City this morning. The boutique ladies were excited and waiting on her when she walked in. They led her to a dressing room, and she waited as they carried in a fabulous bundle of white lace. They pooled the dress and she stepped into it. When she turned to the mirror, she stared in amazement as the ladies clapped behind her. This was absolutely the dress. No doubt about it.

An exquisite creation, it hugged her body with fragile, almost shear lace. The princess neckline dipped low enough for sexy and romantic. The frill that set it off was a luxurious tulle train that clasped at her waist and flowed back as she walked, revealing her lace covered body. Everything about it was perfect and she couldn't wait to walk toward Dakota wearing it.

After the fitting, she headed to Luna's Bar and Grill downtown. Samantha, Jade, and Zoe had insisted on coming to Lake Charles to celebrate her dress over dinner. They found a table out of the way to catch up on everyone's news.

They asked Samantha how things were going with her and Sean. She leaned forward like she was going to tell an exciting secret, then said, "I'm not telling you."

Gabrielle said, "Come on Samantha, give. I am aware the Nash men are born with something in their genes to make women weak in the knees. Don't be shy. Tell us."

Samantha batted her lashes and remained silent.

Jade said, "Sean is reeling you in. You'll never make me believe otherwise."

Zoe asked, "How does he kiss?"

Samantha laughed and said, "Hotter than a blazing fire, and that's all I'm saying."

Jade asked Zoe, "What about you and Trace. You weren't even touching the ground the last time we saw him kiss you."

Zoe smiled and held up an engagement ring. They screamed and disturbed all the patrons.

Jade asked, "When is the wedding?"

"Valentine's Day."

"R.O.M.A.N.T.I.C.!" Gabrielle said.

Zoe said, "Mark it on your calendars. You are all in it. You will wear red dresses and be gorgeous."

Then Gabrielle asked, "Jade? What's going on with you? Anyone tall, dark, and handsome?"

"As a matter of fact, I have a partner now. We are officially entitled Southern Investigative Services, Inc."

They cried, "Tell us about him!"

Jade said, "He is an ex-marine—"

Gabrielle said, "Stop. What does he look like first?"

Laughing, she said, "Ok. He's just over six feet tall, handsome, and has Latino blood."

Samantha motioned her to keep going, and Jade said, "Christian, divorced, no kids, short black hair, green eyes, intelligent, and a body builder." She paused. "And in all honesty, he gives me that 'I've got your back' feeling. He's also the hottest salsa dancer around."

All three sat back, satisfied. Just what they hoped.

Jade shrugged, and said, "We make a good team so far. That's it. Really."

Samantha narrowed her eyes, knowing there was more, and said, "Liar."

Jade said, "Look. I don't want to mess up anything. I like working together."

Zoe said, "Come on, it's your turn - Gabrielle, Cat, soon to be Mrs. Dakota Nash."

Gabrielle laughed and said, "Take a look at this," and turned her phone to show them a picture of her wedding dress.

Samantha sighed, and said, "That is the most fabulous wedding dress I've ever seen. Dakota is going to burn up."

Gabrielle laughed, "Right! That's the point. And we take romantic night rides on his stallion. He's taking me bareback riding for the first time tonight when I get home." As the girls tried to interrupt, she stopped them, and said, "And, I have an Art Exhibit scheduled."

The girls screamed in excitement, and the manager frowned at them – while they apologized for the commotion.

Gabrielle continued, "It's week after next in Lake Charles. And I'm sorry it's short notice, but I would love to have a live En-Garde exhibit to close out the show."

Thrilled, they all quickly checked their calendars. After making a few adjustments, it was scheduled. All four of them would exhibit as En-Garde in fencing gear.

***

Dakota walked out of the barn leading the stallion when Gabrielle got home. He smiled and joined her as she stepped out of the car.

He said, "Hi, Cat," and kissed her, before adding, "Are you ready for your first bareback ride?"

She said, "I've thought about it all day," then slipped her hands under his shirt, and said, "With you shirtless."

Without a word he dropped his shirt on the ground and pulled her against his bare skin. He tugged her shirt and said, "Do you plan on taking yours off too?"

Meeting his teasing, but steamy gaze, she said, "In a few weeks, I'll walk out of the house naked and ride your stallion. How's that?"

Biting her lip, he said, "You bet you will, wildcat," and kissed her.

Then, with a groan he pushed her toward the cabin, and said, "Hurry and change. Please. I'm ready to ride with you."

"I see that…I won't be long. But would you mind if I took a few pictures tonight before we go?"

Teasing, he said, "Naked?"

She laughed, then said, "In a few weeks hot guy. In a few weeks," and headed inside.

Dakota had just fed the horse an apple when he heard the door shut. He turned to see Gabrielle walk toward him with her hair loose, wearing low rise blue jean shorts and a bikini top. Her camera hung around her neck. He whistled – and growled.

Walking into his arms, she said, "That's what I think about you too," as she touched his bare chest.

He kissed her, then said, "So direct me – tell me what you want a picture of. But know this - I get a turn with that camera afterwards," and she nodded, then pulled his ponytail loose.

She pointed to the stallion and picked up her camera. He leapt and straddled the horse. Gabrielle blew a silent whistle at the vision of him. Barefoot. Bare chest. Riding bareback. Sexy and intense. He watched her, his hair blowing in the wind. She raised the camera.

During the photo shoot, she could tell he grew impatient. Hungry. He became what he looked like. A warrior. A hunter. She leaned against his leg and slowly slid her hand up his thigh. And there was the shot – she snapped the picture. That was the look she wanted. Then she stepped back and held out the camera to him.

He swung his leg over and landed in front of her. He leaned close and breathed against her neck – then whispered in her ear. Gabrielle's face went bright pink and their gazes met. He grabbed her jean shorts on each hip and lifted her till her parted lips met his. Then he put the camera around his neck and gave her a leg up.

He watched her on his stallion. Her body was unbelievably sexy and gorgeous astride the powerful animal. Her long dark hair fluttered in the wind. Eyes steamy and fixed on him. He snapped pictures and smiled as she began to feel the freedom of the moment. Her shoulders went back. Her hand slid into Midnight's mane.

Now was the time. He stepped close to her bare leg and slowly licked up her thigh – and there she was. His wildcat. Bold. Free. Magnificent. He snapped the picture.

He walked to the patio to leave the camera and Aunt Jaz walked out. Without speaking, she held out her hand for the camera, then motioned for him to mount.

She took several pictures of them. Touching. Looking at each other. Sexy. Loving. Longing. Then she disappeared back inside.

Without question, Dakota and Gabrielle headed to the bluff. Their place now. With the energy and passion still hot from the photo shoot - it was a passionate journey. Kisses. Caresses. Groans.

When they reached the top of the bluff, Gabrielle whispered, "Would you bring me here for our first time? I want to be with you here. Ride with you."

He kissed her and it was impossible to kiss her deep enough. Voice ragged with love and laced with passion, he said, "We will come straight here. I just hope we can make it the whole way."

***

A few days later at J&S Ranch, Dakota laughed as he killed the engine. Gabrielle had jumped out of his truck and was already running to hug her parents. Still grinning, he joined them on the deck as the women tried to catch up in one quick conversation. Jimmy caught his eye. Dakota saw the satisfied look on his face - well aware of why – and waited for what he knew was coming.

Jimmy slapped Dakota on the shoulder, buddy style, and said, "God sure gives amazing gifts to old men like me."

Dryly, Dakota said, "I don't think old describes you accurately."

Jimmy grinned, and said, "No, me either. So, Dakota, three weeks before your honeymoon, right?"

Dakota said, "Five-hundred-four hours." Jimmy laughed.

***

Two weeks later, Dakota walked out on the porch to take a writing break. He had been working hard on his new manuscript. He glanced across the river and Gabrielle was taking a painting break on her upper deck. He smiled and waved. She smiled and turned some music on and danced for him. He laughed – loving it. Then his heart stopped as she perched on top of the second-floor railing and posed for him.

No! He thought. And yelled, "Get off there!"

But she continued to playfully balance on the rail. Before he knew it, he was on the Jet Ski traveling full throttle across the river.

Gabrielle hadn't heard what he said over the sound of the music, but the expression on his face as he got closer confused her. She watched him from the rail as he slid the machine on the sandbar, ran uphill, up the stairs, and through the house. She had just climbed off the rail and turned off her playlist when he walked out of her studio.

His face was a myriad of expressions. Fierce. Serious. His body tight. Intense. But not understanding and feeling threatened, she stepped back. And for a millisecond she was scared.

Dakota winced, reading her alarm. Moaning, he crushed her in his arms, fear finally fading that he might never be able to hold her again. Catching a grip, he said, "Don't ever do that. Ever."

"But…what did I do?"

With a sigh, he drew her to sit with him. He looked out into the woods, silently for a few moments as he gathered his thoughts.

He looked at her solemn face, and said, "All agents have witnessed tragedies. On one case, a man in Oklahoma kidnapped a fourteen-year-old girl. As leverage against us, he dangled her off a three-story balcony to prevent us from breaking in. His move had been effective because of the shear danger to the victim. We had almost come to an agreement when he stumbled. He dropped her.

Heartsick for his memory, Gabrielle wrapped her arms around him.

He said, "When you climbed on that rail, the memory jolted me. I didn't mean to scare you. I just wanted you off that rail. I need you safe."

"I know. I'm so sorry. So, so, sorry."

Chapter 32

Ten days before their wedding, Gabrielle contemplated the art groups set up in her studio. Paintings in one group. Photographs in another. Fencing art in the third. The art show was tomorrow night, and it was time to go set up.

The gallery had several showrooms. She wanted her oil paintings in the twin rooms with arched doorways. The rectangular room would be perfect for her photographs, some of which were large. The biggest room would be for the fencing photographs as well as the En-Garde fencing exhibit to close out the night.

Dakota watched Cat bite her lip as she studied her work. He stepped behind her for a warm hug.

She relaxed into him and said, "I can't believe it's here. I'm excited, but I hope everyone else enjoys the exhibits. What if they don't like it? I'm trying not to be nervous, but the jitters won't leave me alone."

"I understand – but you're going to amaze everyone. You'll see. The nerves will fade quickly when it starts. I've been there with book tours and speaking engagements. I promise they will be mesmerized by your work – as well as with you. Now tell me, what are you wearing tomorrow night?"

"I have a green silk gown that's actually part of my show."

"What do you mean?"

"My dress was custom made to show my back tattoo. I also have an oil painting of the tattoo with me wearing the dress. It's for display only."

He caressed her back, and said, "Your tattoo is extraordinary." He kissed her shoulder, sliding his hands to her hips, and said, "But then, all of you is extraordinary."

She turned to him, smiling, and slipped her arms around him. She said, "You're prejudiced."

"Of course, I am – but it's still true."

***

Late the next afternoon, Gabrielle finished the last stroke of black mascara. Smiling, she stood to check out her handiwork. She was an artist after all. Her cat eyes were enhanced by a mixture of green, bronze, and gold shadows and liner which made her eyes pop even more than they already did. Her lips were her favorite shade of fuchsia. Her hair hung in one long braid down the right side of her chest. Her only jewelry was a pair of shiny gold loops. It was drama night.

She turned to the floor length emerald-green gown. Wearing only panties because of the completely open, low-draped back, she held it up and let the silky material slide all the way down. She slipped her arms through the delicate spaghetti straps and stepped into ankle-tied black heels. She posed in the mirror – and smiled. She was ready.

Dakota's blood pressure shot up as Gabrielle came down the stairs. She was easily the most beautiful woman he had ever seen. Her face exquisite but alive with mysterious fire. Her body flawless and simmering in green silk. Especially the long leg the slit revealed. Their eyes met.

She gave him a slow smile, then looked him over as he walked toward her. Sexy from head to toe, he was dressed in black pinstripe slacks and a green silk shirt. Long hair. Sculptured cheekbones and lips. Dark eyes. He was crazy hot. He winked, knowing what she thought, and offered his arm.

As she joined him, he whispered, "I see a midnight ride in our future with you in that dress."

***

A short time later, Dakota and Gabrielle entered the Historic City Hall Art & Cultural Center in downtown Lake Charles. Dakota expected a large showing of patrons, visitors, and locals for this event since Gabrielle was now an active part of Louisiana history in this area. And Jade had recently given a great interview for Gabrielle on KPLC that went national.

An hour later, the place was packed as Dakota walked around. He passed the doorway to the En-Garde live exhibit and Samantha saw him. She whistled and fanned herself like she was burning up and pointed at him. He grinned.

But Gabrielle was the shining light of the night. He looked around at her exhibits and guests. Her art was titled with story cards underneath to explain each exhibit. Some were for sale, and some were not. Customers could request commission work.

He stood looking her largest photograph. He was bareback on Midnight from a few weeks ago. She had caught exactly what he had felt at that moment.

She walked up and slid an arm around his waist, then said, "I see you found the man of my dreams."

He said, "They just don't know I was looking at you."

She said, "You're just too beautiful for words, Dakota."

"Cat…"

"And hot too."

He chuckled, and said, "I get it. You must have talked to Samantha. She fans herself every time I walk past."

Gabrielle laughed and said, "She swears smoke follows you tonight."

"Well, in that case…" he knelt on one knee, pulling a ring out of his pocket – and she gasped.

The crowd around them cheered and cameras started recording.

Seeing only him, Gabrielle whispered, "Dakota…" as he drew her to his knee.

Touching her cheek, he said, "I wanted you to have your engagement ring tonight. So, in front of the world, will you marry me?"

Lowering her lips to his, she said, "Always, yes," and kissed him.

Afterwards, he put the ring on her finger and stood, pulling her into his arms for another kiss.

***

Toward the end of the evening, it was time for the En-Garde fencing exhibit. Gabrielle changed into her fencing gear and stepped to the podium, pulling Dakota with her, as guests poured into the area.

She said, "Before we begin the live exhibit, I want to share some background. Some of you may not know, but Dakota Nash, my fiancé, is the FBI agent that saved me from not just one - but two different serial killers," Gasps and whispers echoed through the room.

She continued, "But he is also Zeke Spencer the nationally acclaimed author of FBI thrillers." Applause and whispers.

She said, "And now I want to thank you for sharing this wonderful evening with us. Louisiana has much to offer the country and the world. While most of my art is locally focused, an important component of my art is focused on Christ – which is explained on my story card with my tattoo painting.

"En-Garde was created because not all Christians have an easy journey. It isn't always a sit in the pew, go to Sunday school, gentleness, and smiles, kind of experience. Some people have to learn to step from victim shoes to overcomer shoes, and fight to take hold of His promises."

She motioned the team to join her and said, "We stand as Christian warriors to teach others to fight the good fight visibly. The swords we brandish are a reference to the Word of God. Sharp. Active. Penetrating. We are all warriors. And tonight, we give you an image of faith in motion."

The four women paired off in the exhibit room and put on their face guards. They leapt. Jabbed. Spun. Lunged. They swapped partners. It was exciting, but it also revealed the effort and power it takes to face the enemy spiritually and physically. Then they finished in a battle line where they performed synchronized moves in perfect precision – and bowed.

Dakota was as amazed as the crowd, and everyone applauded. The women removed their face guards – winded, sweating, and smiling.

***

Later with all guests gone, En-Garde neared the exit of the building. Dakota saw a few groups of guests lingering on the sidewalk outside. He opened the door and the women walked out still dressed in their fencing gear. Sean followed with the sword scabbards looped over his shoulder. Adam, Trace, and Jade's new partner, Angel, brought up the rear.

Once they reached the parking area, motion in the shadows by nearby vans caught Dakota and Sean's attention. They darted in front of the women and stopped them. A tall, angry young man rounded the end of a vehicle and headed straight for them.

Dakota held out his hand to halt him, and said firmly, "Hold on, fella. What can we do for you?"

The soon-to-be man had his hands in his hoodie pockets. Dakota and Sean watched his body language while they waited for him to speak. The young man tensed up and Dakota prepared to move.

Loud and angry, the kid yelled, "You killed my dad!"

Hearing the gasp from En-Garde behind him, Dakota allowed the guy some leeway, and asked, "Who are you?"

"I am Blaze, Sam Frisk's son."

They all knew that Vee had killed his father. Dakota softened his tone with compassion, and said, "Blaze, you know that it wasn't us that killed him. But yes, we were there."

Blaze's lip trembled as he struggled with his emotions. He lowered clinched fists and Dakota and Sean relaxed now that they knew he didn't have a weapon.

Tears slipped down his face as he said, "But it was your fault over that stupid treasure. Now I don't have a family. I don't have anything. I was forced into foster care, and I ran away to come here tonight to confront you. Why does the world think I don't matter anymore?"

Dakota felt a hand on his arm and turned to see Gabrielle.

She said, "Let me…" and stepped through Dakota and Sean to face Blaze. She saw the pain in his eyes – not just anger.

His tears broke her heart, and she said softly, "I care, Blaze. I care very much about what happened to you. I understand even. The men in that group killed my dad too."

Surprised, he stared at her.

She said, "Because of them I lost my family and had to be put up for adoption. So yes. I know what it's like. But Blaze, I want you to know that you aren't alone. There is someone waiting for you. He has something more priceless and valuable than that stupid treasure." She touched his arm and asked, "Do you know Jesus, Blaze?"

"I thought I did. But I guess I was wrong since my whole life just fell apart."

Gabrielle said, "I think you do know him. And I think he brought you here tonight. To us."

At that, Blaze began to break, and his gut-wrenching sobs moved all of them. Gabrielle wrapped her arms around him, and the rest of En-Garde passed through Dakota and Sean to join Gabrielle.

After a few moments, the women gave the young man some room to breathe. He looked drained, but no longer angry.

Adam walked up and said, "Hi Blaze, I'm Adam. I'm a minister and a part of these terrific people. You are welcome to come home with us tonight, to a safe place, with good food, a warm bed, and even some great animals that would love your attention."

Blaze's eyes brightened at the word animals, but he remained silent.

Adam continued, "I think you will like it there. And tomorrow we can look for answers. How does that sound?"

Blaze nodded.

Adam looked at Dakota, and said, "I'll bring him home. Aunt Jaz and I will take care of him."

Dakota called the authorities and let them know. The rest could be handled tomorrow.

***

After saying goodnight to everyone, Dakota drove to the north beach and backed his truck to the sand. He helped Gabrielle out of her hot fencing gear and in a flash, she took off barefoot across the sand in her workout shorts and top. He smiled as she spun in the breeze, cooling off. He kicked off his shoes and joined her in his slacks and shirt. They walked along the shore.

He said, "You were extraordinary tonight. I'm impressed. Proud. In awe even."

She smiled and leaned into him, then said, "Thank you. It was a special night for me. Looking back over my life, I can finally see the pieces that fell into place after my experiences. I still have scars, but they don't mean the same thing anymore. I still have memories that I don't want, but I have new ones now that mean so much more. But mostly, I have you."

He stopped and turned to face her, his green shirt fluttering in the breeze. He said, "And I have you." He lifted her and she wrapped arms and legs around him.

A bit later, they sat on the tailgate of his truck. They listened and watched the seagulls, the stars, the city lights flickering in the lake, and even the traffic that rode the tall Interstate 10 bridge high into the night.

She admired her new engagement ring, and said, "You shocked me with a formal proposal. That was totally romantic! And where did you find this diamond? It's spectacular."

"I ordered it from Israel. It's a fancy diamond. And if you didn't realize it, the diamond matches your eyes…exactly." He stepped in front of where she sat on the tailgate, pressed between her legs as he laid her back. Looking down at her, he said, "Because…I wanted you to see…what I see…every time I look at you."

And to the sound of the waves, talking was over.

Chapter 33

A few days later, Dakota glanced at his phone with a live feed of Gabrielle in her art studio. She had been working earnestly on a secret project for days and he was ready for some time with her.

He said, "Gabrielle."

Without looking at her phone, she stayed on task and said," Hmmmm?"

He chuckled and said, "Look at me."

Glancing at the phone, she smiled at him.

She had paint on her neck and cheek, and he thought she looked adorable. He said, "Want some company?"

Gabrielle picked up the phone and kissed the screen. When she put the phone back down, he wasn't there. She looked out the window and he was running to the dock. She smiled. Nothing like watching your man come to you.

She went to the first floor to wait for him. Glancing out the window as he raced across the river, she had a thought. Then with a smile she walked behind the snack bar. She heard the Jet Ski slide to a stop on the sandbar. In a minute, he ran up the stairs. She shifted her weight, moving side to side. Ready.

He came through the door smiling and headed toward her. She let him get closer, then darted around the other side of the large bar, keeping it between them.

Instantly he caught on to her game. His eyes narrowed in heated anticipation, and said, "So… Cat wants to play," and pulled his shirt off.

Running his hand along the counter he hunted her. Her heart pounded at the look on his face. Forget that. The look was all over him. She blew him a kiss and he ran. They chased back and forth around the bar. She was fast, but he was faster. She was nimble, but he was hungry. Finally, he went for the capture and dove across the top, scooping her up, and fell on the sofa with her.

Pumped from the chase, he laid on top of her, loving the feel of her underneath him. He teasingly licked her lips, and she opened her mouth, pulling his lips hard against hers. The shepherd, excited from all the running, still wanted to play, and licked them both.

Dakota growled and wiped his face, not pleased with the interruption. He said, "I love Zeus but I'm your alpha protector now. He needs to go play somewhere when I am with you."

She touched his lips and whispered, "You don't seem to mind when I lick you."

He smiled, "Not hardly…" and kissed her.

On the coffee table, her phone rang. He ignored it. It rang again. Groaning, he checked the phone as she giggled. It was Jimmy, so he handed her the phone, then sat up. He was determined that both the dog and the phones would go outside next time they played.

***

Gabrielle answered, "Hi, Dad."

"Cat, I'm just letting you know that I found your mom passed out in the garden. She cut her arm and has a big knot on her head."

Alarmed, Gabrielle said, "No! What happened?"

"I don't know. She seems fine but I am on the way to get her checked at the emergency room. She seems light-headed and nauseous too. I need to make sure she doesn't have a concussion."

"Okay, we'll meet you at the hospital."

"She'll be fine. We'll see you there."

***

Dakota, back in his shirt, was waiting with her keys as she hung up.

He said, "Let's go in your car. I'll drive."

She told him about the conversation with her dad, and said, "Maybe she tripped or something. The doctor is bound to run tests - it will take a while to get answers. It is never fast at the hospital."

"True, but you'll feel better once you can see her. She's tough. She'll be just fine."

***

They arrived at the hospital and her parents were already there. Led to her room, they found her in bed with a large knot on her forehead. The doctor was checking it. Her arm was cut, and it looked like they were about to do stitches.

Jimmy joined them, and whispered, "They've collected for lab work and are about to stitch her up. He thinks the head knot is just a bruise, but he may keep her overnight for observation."

Once they stitched her arm, the doctor said, "I'm going to wait for the preliminary lab work results before we begin the admission process. Try to relax, Serena. The nurse will bring some ice for your head."

Jimmy joined her on the bed, and she said, "I want to go home." Then she looked at her stitches and burst into tears.

Surprised, Gabrielle looked at her dad.

"It's ok," Jimmy said. "She's been really emotional the last few days."

After a long wait, the doctor returned and said, "Mrs. Barlow? We've received some test results. Can I speak with you privately?" Dakota and Gabrielle stepped out of the room.

He asked, "Are you on birth control?"

"No. I haven't taken birth control in over twenty years. I just got married a few weeks ago but I went through menopause last year."

The Doctor said, "No, you didn't."

She frowned, and said, "How do you know that?"

"Because you're pregnant."

The Doctor chuckled as the couple looked at each other in shock.

He said, "You're healthy and just need to schedule an OB/GYN appointment. I know you are surprised, but it happens all the time at menopause age. So, I don't think you'll need that hospital room tonight after all. Congratulations," and he shook their hands and walked out.

Jimmy looked at Serena, then pulled the covers back, and her gown up. He gently laid both palms over the baby – then kissed her.

After a knock on the door, Jimmy covered her, and said, "Come on in."

Gabrielle entered first and Dakota followed. She said, "Mom? Is everything ok? The doctor was shaking his head but wouldn't tell us anything."

Then she noticed her parents seemed a little flushed as they glanced at each other.

Her Mom said, “How do you feel about being a big sister?”

Gabrielle screamed.

***

Two days later, Gabrielle finished the last touchup on the oil painting for Dakota’s gift. She stretched her back and lifted the painting up to the light. It was a 16x20 oil painting of her and Dakota sitting bareback on the stallion. She remembered that special night and knew he would love the memory too. Aunt Jaz had taken the picture, but she had wanted to paint the scene. It would have to dry for at least another day before she could wrap it and bring it to the cabin.

Then she smiled and put on her cat ear headband she bought yesterday. She felt sure it would provide a playful touch at some point during the honeymoon. Very sure. Dakota liked his cats.

***

At the same time, Dakota walked into the jewelry store in Lake Charles and picked up the gold link charm anklet he had special ordered for Gabrielle. One charm was a heart engraved with *D loves G*, like the heart in the treasure tree. Another charm was a cat to match his tattoo. Another charm was a black stallion for their honeymoon ride. Another charm was a sword to match the one she used to fight Vee. And the last six charms were for the babies to come.

He had already picked up another special order from the lingerie shop. The women there had a great deal of fun with his purchase. He hadn’t minded since he looked forward to seeing Gabrielle in the leather catsuit. She would love it. And so would he.

After hiding his packages in the truck, he left to meet her at the bank.

Chapter 34

A short time later, Gabrielle, Dakota, her parents, and grandparents met with the new family attorney to complete the treasure arrangements. The attorney was from Baton Rouge and the bank allowed them to use a conference room.

In moments, the door opened, and Samantha walked in smiling. She said, "Hello beautiful people! Are you excited about today?"

They laughed at her exuberance and chimed in with yes. After greetings, they settled back for her legal guidance.

Samantha said, "Alright then, let's get started. I'm going to pass around the contract. Please review, and initial with your approval, the following foundation positions you have created:

Jimmy Barlow for the Lafitte family Executor

General Scott Romero for the Exhibit Director (Including John Alexander as the independent curator handling the treasure.)

Jade Louviere for the Publicity Director

Samantha Rutledge for the Lafitte Family Counsel."

The family passed around the contract, approved it, and returned it to Samantha. After her review, she said, "The Jean & Sabrina Foundation is now formed."

Then she opened a packet and pulled out a stack of 8x10 color photographs. She said, "These are the pictures of each piece, or set, of treasure recovered from Gabrielle's property. Jacque, Serena, and Gabrielle have

reviewed and indicated on the back of each photograph the placement of these items within the following categories:
Auction donation for charity
Smithsonian exhibit
Traveling Jean Lafitte exhibit
Personal Family Collection
And the remainder of the treasure will remain in the bank vault under the control of the foundation."

Samantha smiled, seeing the reality finally settle on them. She laughed, and said, "All that's left to do is come back this afternoon to pick up the Personal Family Collection. And that's it – we're done. Let's celebrate! Lunch is on me!"

***

Mid-afternoon, the family, the attorney, and curator gathered at the bank vault. The bank manager led them into the room where the treasure trove was laid out. Samantha handed the curator the photographs with the instructions for each piece.

He worked on the items for the family collection. There were eleven items and fifty gold coins. They were placed in one long box and handed to Samantha, who handed it to Jimmy, the Executor.

The curator put additional pieces of treasure into boxes labeled Smithsonian, Charity Auction, and Jean Lafitte Traveling Exhibit. The substantial remainder of the treasure would remain here.

***

Leaving the bank, the family went to Gabrielle's grandparent's house. The last piece of the past was in place.

Gabrielle said, "We honored Jean Lafitte's wishes. The inheritance and legacy continue." Then she looked at her grandfather and said, "You had to know the treasure was there to buy that land. There is no other explanation. How did you know?"

He smiled and said, "My grandmother was from Lake Charles. She used to sing me songs of God, of family, and always of hidden treasure. When I was given the Bible, letter, and map, I remembered the words of her songs. And I knew the river from spending time with her during the summers. So, for me it was easy to follow where Jean led. I found the tree and knew the treasure was there. So, I bought the land and built a vacation home. Eventually I passed the property, documents, and secret to Serena. But I never told anyone about the tree."

Chapter 35

The day before the wedding, Gabrielle woke excited. Only one more day before she would wake up with Dakota. She smiled and rolled over coming face-to-face with Zeus. He licked her. She wiped her wet face but smiled at his adoration.

She said, "I love you too."

A knock sounded on her door, and Dakota stuck his head in, and said, "Did I just hear you tell someone you love them?"

Giggling, she said, "Zeus."

Dakota came in and ruffled the dog's fur, and said, "In that case, I don't have to kill anyone this morning."

She grinned at his threat, and he leaned down and kissed her. She laughed.

"What's funny?"

"Zeus just licked my mouth," and he frowned, eyeing the dog, who happily wagged his whole body with his long tongue hanging out.

Gabrielle couldn't help but grin. In response, he tickled her, and she screamed and fought to get away.

Sean hollered from downstairs, "Go play outside."

Liking Sean's idea, Dakota said, "Let's go run your obstacle course. I have some new ideas to tell you."

"Let's do it! First one to the Jet Ski gets to drive." Everything was a competition with her, and the race was on.

***

Dakota beat her to the Jet Ski.

Frowning, Gabrielle stood, hands on hips, and said, "You cheated."
"How did I possibly cheat?"
"Your legs are longer." He laughed.
Sean called from the porch where he sat drinking coffee, and said, "Don't fight. It's just pent-up passion."
Dakota said, "Go to work! Or call Samantha! Otherwise, I'm going to throw you in the river."
But Gabrielle did not laugh at the brothers' usual antics. She crossed her arms. Insistent.
Dakota loved her feisty spirit - and thought of a different reward for him winning. He said, "I fold."
Surprised, she said, "Really?"
"Yes, I fold. You win."
She laughed and said, "Ok, I'll take the win," and jumped in front of him on the Jet Ski. But then she turned in appreciation and kissed him long and sweet as a reward.
Afterwards, he smiled. He still won. Then hung on as she hit the throttle.

***

Later, after running the trails, they paused to catch their breath. She said, "This is going to make a fantastic garden and playground for our kids."
"It's perfect. And on that note, I wondered if you would like to add tree houses and decks throughout the trails."
She screamed and jumped in his arms.
Laughing, he said, "That idea's a yes obviously. But I have to be honest. You love to climb, and I need you able to get in the tree safely. Especially when our babies start coming."
She said earnestly, "Lots of them."
He tilted her chin to look in her eyes, and said with a sexy growl, "We are going to work…*hard*…making those babies."
She felt his meaning wash over her, and bit her lip. She whispered, "How hard?"
Her feet left the ground as his lips met hers. Only one more day.

***

When they returned to the cabin, Aunt Jaz was packed to leave. She said, "The house is clean and prepared for tomorrow's new husband and wife."

They hugged her, and she said, "Sean will be at his flat in town. Adam will stay at Jimmy and Serena's with Blaze. And I am staying in a cottage at a friend's house."

Dakota said, "Who's the friend?"

"Scott."

Gabrielle said, "Grandpa has a cottage?"

Jaz winked, and said, "He does now," and Dakota laughed.

***

It was late afternoon when Dakota and Gabrielle pulled back up to the cabin. They had been busy all day getting ready for tomorrow.

Dakota said, "Come on! I want to do something," and he pulled her across the yard to the back tree line.

Gabrielle followed Dakota into the woods. He stepped close to a huge oak tree and pulled his knife. She knew what he was going to do. She smiled and watched as he carved a large heart with their initials.

In awe, she ran her hands over it and said, "This is beautiful. Thank you. Too hundred years from now our descendants will see this."

He stepped up behind her. Lips on her neck. She turned in his embrace. He slowly backed her against the tree. Against the carved heart. And wedged his knee tight between her legs. Less than eighteen hours now. They were ready.

Several hot kisses later, he groaned and looked at her.

She said, "I'm going to love being married to you."

Touching her lips with his tongue, he said, "Oh yes, we both will."

Later, they carried Gabrielle's bags to the truck so she could stay the night with her parents. But before leaving, they walked down to the dock and looked across the river just as the pink tinges of dusk painted the sky.

Gabrielle said, "It's almost here."

Dakota said, "Less than fourteen hours, Beautiful. And counting."

***

Hours later, Gabrielle prowled downstairs at the ranch. She couldn't sleep. Standing by the window, she looked out over the garden and pool. She saw

Dakota everywhere in her mind. Then she heard footsteps and turned. Her mother joined her.

Gabrielle said, "I'm sorry. I'm restless."

"I know, come see."

Serena led her to the sofa and sat. She motioned her on the floor between her knees. Then she slowly finger-combed Gabrielle's long hair. Massaged her shoulders. And eventually Gabrielle relaxed, then swayed with the motion.

Jimmy entered the room. Serena glanced at him with a smile. Returning her smile, he sat on the steps overlooking the den. He watched them, humming softly. It didn't take long after that and Serena noticed Gabrielle's eyelids getting heavy. She coaxed her on the sofa, and she was sound asleep in minutes.

Serena stood, and Jimmy came up behind her. He whispered, "That was beautiful."

She nodded, and whispered, "A momma knows."

Chapter 36

The next morning, Dakota unrolled a massive white fur rug on the grass at the bluff. It laid amidst an outdoor bedroom he had created for their honeymoon ride in a few hours. He straightened and stepped back to make sure everything was in place. Solar lanterns framed an invisible room in case they stayed into the night. A large trunk sat to the side and contained anything they may want or need.

Gabrielle wanted their first time to make love to be outside. He thought that was wild - and hotter than hot. How he loved her. Every glance. Every laugh. Every touch. Every promise her body made. The way she talked. The way she tasted. He knew it would be a miracle if they made it all the way here on horseback in time.

Wiping sweat off his brow, shirtless and sexy, he walked to the edge of the bluff and glanced down the Calcasieu River. She loved it here. They both did. It was the perfect place to do life. And it began in – he glanced at his watch – less than three hours.

Climbing back on his four-wheeler, he headed home for a shower. He had a bride to get ready for.

***

Gabrielle sat at the side of the pool, hanging her feet in the water. Thinking. Dakota consumed her mind. They were going to make love in a few hours. How could she think of anything else? Finally, husband and wife, skin to skin, nothing but them. Freedom to love with abandon. Then babies to come. Life to share.

When she had seen him across the river ten weeks ago, she never dreamed she would be able to trust a man. But Dakota changed everything. He *was* everything.

The door opened, and she glanced back.

Her mom smiled, and said, "Come eat a little breakfast with us. Your dad cooked your favorite. What time will the limousine be here to pick us up?"

"Eleven. We need to be at the church by noon to prepare since service ends at twelve-thirty. Grandpa will surprise the congregation with our wedding. We will be in and out."

"Then come eat. You need to get something on your stomach before you dress. You will have butterflies, believe me. Love and passion will make them swarm."

After breakfast and a shower, Gabrielle sat at the mirror. Her mother braided her dark hair into a long fancy braid - entwined with the tiniest floral ribbon. After that, Gabrielle began her face artwork. She chose a rich lavender shadow, a touch of deep purple, then highlighted with shades of pink and white. Next was the liner and mascara. And lastly, she painted on a velour liquid lavender lipstick that would last for hours. Very kissable hours.

She glanced at her mom, who whispered, "You are perfect. Dakota will be a happy man."

Smiling, she headed to her dress. Her mom held it ready, and she stepped into the exquisite sheath. The feeling was like stepping into a princess bodysuit. The reflection in the mirror seemed unreal. A dream. She gently slid her hands down the body-hugging, floral lace. It was so fragile - so shear that a lot of her body was revealed. Which made it sexy. Romantic. Feminine. Absolutely perfect for Dakota.

After putting on the white glitter heels (that would kill her feet but be worth it), she clasped the tulle train – that was sort of a long fluffy fly-a-way skirt - around her waist. And she was ready.

Her mom said, "You look like a Victoria Secret wedding model. Mercy, but you are a gorgeous woman, Gabrielle. And I refuse to cry this soon." Hugging her, she continued, "Embrace every second of your life with Dakota, sweetie. Your man is crazy in love with you."

Jimmy knocked on the door. He said, "It's time, beautiful women. The limousine is here."

***

Dakota dressed in a black-on-black tux with a thin black tie. His black hair was loose of course – Gabrielle insisted. He thought he looked like a panther – and knew she would like that image. He moved his hair to see his new, tiny diamond loop earring. She would certainly like that. After putting on cologne, he checked the time.

The limousine would be picking up Gabrielle and her parents now. With a grin, he picked up the wedding bands, the license, his phone, keys, and was gone in a flash.

***

By eleven forty-five a.m., Dakota, his brothers, and Trace waited in the preacher's office as Sunday church finished.

Sean said, "You look good, Dakota. And I have no doubt that Gabrielle is blindingly fabulous. So, let me go ahead and tell you now, I'm expecting some gorgeous nieces and nephews. Spunky and tough too."

Dakota fist-bumped him, and said, "Thanks, Sean. You're undoubtedly next in line for a wife. And you know it." Sean smiled.

Adam hugged Dakota, and said, "You have the real deal with Gabrielle, Dakota. God's been good to you. Take it and run with it. Don't stop."

Dakota said, "Yes, He has. Thanks, Adam. But like Sean, I have a feeling you will be heading up the aisle when you return from your mission trip to Brazil. With your looks, you can't possibly stay single much longer."

After a knock on the door. Dakota's Dad came in, hugged all his sons with tears in his eyes, and headed back to join their mother. Dakota glanced at his watch. Gabrielle would be here soon.

***

In ten minutes, the limousine arrived.

Jimmy walked in. Recognizing Dakota's impatience, he grinned and said, "I know a gorgeous bride that is just as eager as you."

Dakota smiled - and glanced at his watch again.

***

Gabrielle met up with the bridesmaids in the bridal suite. They looked beautiful in their different styled black dresses. Very chic. Very beautiful. They stared at her.

Samantha whistled, and said, "Goodness gracious, Gabrielle, you're…a vision. Dakota is going to all but roar when he sees you."

Jade said, "Samantha, obviously, you and Sean spent way too much time around the animals at the zoo," and everyone laughed.

Gabrielle handed them a black velvet pouch with a magnolia flower to carry. She said, "Open the bags at the reception – and don't lose it. You will want what's inside. I promise."

The door opened, and Serena entered with a woman who had to be Dakota's mother, Laurie.

Gabrielle smiled and hugged her. She said, "Hi, Mama Laurie. I'm Gabrielle. But Dakota also calls me Cat."

Laurie looked at the warm, gorgeous woman in front of her, and fought the tears. She said, "You, my dear, are going to make my Dakota a very happy man. Thank you. I love you already."

Gabrielle said, "I love you too. Because of you, I have Dakota."

The door opened again, and Aunt Jaz said, "Line up beauties. You have five minutes."

The procession was ready. In the back of the line with her dad, Gabrielle listened to her grandpa explain the surprise wedding to the church congregation. When the clapping stopped, the music began and both mothers stepped to the main auditorium doors. And less than ten minutes later, the bridesmaids and groomsmen waited on the platform for the bride and groom.

Dakota walked across the platform and joined the wedding party. Shockingly handsome in his tuxedo, female whispers carried through the pews. But his eyes were locked on the entrance doors. A love song began to play, and everyone stood and turned to face the bride.

Gabrielle appeared at the entryway and paused. An enchanting vision to all, she barely noticed the gasps in the room. Looking only at Dakota, his sexy smile sent the butterflies in her stomach soaring. She began the journey down the aisle as he walked toward her.

Her unmatchable beauty dazzled him. The tight-fitting lace dress hugged her curves. She was sensational. Gorgeous. And the material that flowed behind her made her look like a sexy angel walking through clouds. A husband's vision.

He saw the look in her eyes. She liked him in the tux. A lot. He winked. Then reaching her, he ran his finger under her chin, lifting her eyes to his. Sparks flew as he stepped close – and everyone thought he would kiss her early. But he whispered in her ear, and she touched his chest. They had a private moment for all to see, then he drew her from Jimmy, and escorted her to the platform.

Wide-eyed, breathless women in the congregation looked at each other with wonder and amazement. OMG.

Dakota and Gabrielle stood before her grandfather, and before long, the two became one. A celebration of love. Vows of commitment. Rings that sealed the promise. And prayers to cover their union and future.

When they were proclaimed husband and wife, and it was time to kiss his bride, Dakota dipped her, kissing her all the way down – and back up, as everyone clapped. Then he scooped her up, and carried her down the aisle, through the church, out the door, to the waiting limousine.

Dakota sat beside her, then lifted her onto his lap – tulle cloud, lace, and all. Holding her face, he said, "My wife," and kissed her like he would never get enough.

A few, very passionate minutes later, Gabrielle said, "Dakota, you look like a panther in that black tux without a touch of white. I could barely focus. Do you realize you just made a room full of church women gasp and swoon?"

Smiling, he said, "Ah, but they didn't see this," and showed her the diamond loop earring. "This is for your wild side."

She groaned as she played with it, "You are so…so...incredibly sexy."

Groaning himself, he said, "Says the one dressed to kill in almost shear lace. Do you have any idea how mouthwatering you are? What is this material anyway?"

"French leavers lace. Isn't it delicious?"

He whispered, "Perfect word," and found a way under the massive cloud of net to run his hands up her gorgeous legs.

In minutes they arrived at the River Palace glass pavilion. Surrounded by massive oaks covered in moss, gardens, and the mysterious winding river - the event center was romantic, private, and beautiful.

Music drifted on the air as Dakota stepped out of the limousine to assist Gabrielle. Then the second limousine carrying the remainder of the wedding party pulled up. Once inside, they formed a receiving line for the guests already arriving.

After pictures and cutting the cake, Dakota led Gabrielle to the floor for their dance. She gave him a teasing smile and unhooked the tulle train around her waist, and let it flutter to the floor. Dakota whistled and gave her a slow spin as he checked out every inch of the tight, sultry, lace gown. *Michael Buble'* began to sing their song.

***

Sean leaned over and whispered in Samantha's ear, "Next song can be ours if you're brave enough."

Giving him a sidelong glance, she grinned and said, "All this passion and romance revving your engine?"

He pulled her chair between his legs, and said, "You do that all by yourself."

"Excellent answer, Agent Man. The next dance is all yours. Maybe more…if you're lucky."

***

After Dakota and Gabrielle's dance, Jimmy slid his arm around Serena's waist and said, "Come rub on me to all this love music."

Laughing softly, knowing he really meant it, she said, "I better not rub too much. We can't leave for a while."

They stood and he drawled in her ear, "But we can take a walk in the woods."

Kissing him, she laughed as he drew her to the dance floor. He liked making love outside.

***

Angel, Jade's new business partner, friend, and salsa enthusiast, pulled her to her feet and said, "It's time to shock some guests with our salsa moves. Let me show them how it's done."

Jade laughed and said, "Not an ounce of humility in all those muscles and hot moves, right?"

"I'm humble. I just know what I'm good at. Dancing with you, making you laugh, and being the perfect business partner in our investigation business are just a few. I'm handsome too, don't you think?"

She shook her head with a grin, and said, "You don't need me to tell you that. Besides, that's not part of our business partnership. Friends. Partners. Dancers. Right?"

He spun and danced with her through a few intricate sexy, dance moves, then smiled at the gorgeous woman in his arms. He winked – and thought, for now, Jade. But not for long.

***

Zoe and Trace kissed on the dance floor. He said, "Are you sure you want to wait till Valentine's Day to have the honeymoon?"

She laughed and said, "Did you forget the wedding?"

He chuckled, and said, "That too."

She stuck her finger between the buttons on his shirt to reach his bare stomach.

He said, "Keep going. I dare you. Please," and kissed her again.

***

Later, the bridesmaids, taking a break from dancing because of killer heels, kicked their shoes off and talked.

Samantha said, "We forgot our pouches from Gabrielle! Did anyone open theirs?" and all three pulled the black bags out of their purses.

They opened them and looked at each other in shock. At least a dozen large diamonds and gemstones lay at the bottom. She gifted them some of the treasure! They stood and looked around the room for Gabrielle. She watched them with a smile and cupped her hand in a heart gesture. They burst into tears.

***

It was almost four when Dakota glanced at his watch again. Jimmy caught his eye and they grinned.

Dakota whispered in Gabrielle's ear, "It's time. Come home with me."
She smiled, heart fluttering. His blood pumped.

After their goodbyes, the limousine headed to the log cabin. Home. It was time for their honeymoon ride. And without the cloud of tulle around her, Dakota slipped his hand under her gown and ran it up first one leg, then the other. Kneading. Caressing. Wanting so much more. Soon. He loved the way she laid her head back, against him, lips parted, just feeling his touch, and watching him. She grabbed his jacket and pulled his lips to hers.

Before long, they stood in the yard and ignored the limousine as it drove away.
Dark eyes hungry for her, Dakota drew Gabrielle into his arms, and said, "The stallion is ready. Do you want to change?"
She whispered, "No…" and meeting his gaze she pushed his jacket off.
Heat ran up his spine. He knew what she wanted. She saw awareness reflected in his eyes – his body. He stepped out of his shoes and reached for his tie. Impatient now. She unbuttoned his shirt, trailing her lips on his skin as it was exposed. He tossed the shirt aside and pulled her close again. Kisses deeper. Hotter.
Then he stepped behind her. Reaching around her, he ran his hands over her breasts, stomach, thighs, and pulled her tight back against him. Caressing her through the lace. Then he unzipped her dress and his lips following the zipper. When he turned her to face him, the lace dress landed in a puddle at their feet - leaving her all but naked in glitter heels and tiny lace panties.
Bare-chested, but still in his slacks, he groaned, scooped her up, and kissed her. The heels and panties dropped as he carried her to the stallion. Gabrielle clutched him. Kissed him. Drove him wild as he tried to focus on making it to the stallion. He draped a white fur over the horse's back and sat her on it. In a half second, he was behind her leading the stallion out of the barn.
Turning, she said, "Wait," and spun to face him. In his lap, she wrapped arms and legs around him. Tight. He groaned deep. Kissed her. Holding bare skin. She reached for his zipper.
He groaned, "Cat…" as his hand covered hers. Voice ragged, kissing her, he said, "We'll never make it out of the yard…just hold on to me. We'll run," and holding her tight, he leaned low, and the stallion flew across the field.

But it wasn't fast enough. Long before they reached the bluff, Dakota pulled back on the reigns, spun the stallion, and stopped as they reached for each other.

Groaning, he said, "I can't…"

Kissing him, she thought…I never intended to.

The End

Epilogue
Early May

Heat rose with the dawn, as the mist swirled around the sails of the ship that slipped unseen into the lake. The ship's captain caught glimpses of the city peeking through the fog, so he aimed the ship west of the city dock. He scanned the area and motioned his men forward. Their shapes silently appeared from behind him.

Barely audible, they whispered, "Aye, Cap'n."

"Lower the boat and head to the north side of the dock. Get me the mayor."

"Aye Aye, Cap'n," and they climbed down the net to the rowboat and disappeared into the fog.

Vigilant, the captain watched and waited for the signal he knew would come. His men knew better than to fail. A half hour later, he heard sounds of a fight and the sting of gunfire as it carried across the water. The deep boom of cannons followed but the captain didn't blink an eye. He knew they shot wild, trying to guess the ship's location. He smiled. This wasn't the first time he had captured a city.

Before long, the sound of rowing paddles neared the ship, and the rowboat with his men and three captives broke through the thinning fog. Excellent. As expected, the city was now his. His men drug the captives across the deck and dropped them there. Bloody. Wet. Terrified.

One of his men shoved a bald man forward, and said, "This one's the mayor."

Captain Jean Lafitte said, "Surrender and you live."

The man screamed, "Never to a pirate!"

Lafitte said, "Fool! You die for nothing. You've already lost." Then he told his Quartermaster, "Steer close to the dock. The city is ours!"

A cheer erupted from the crew as the ship sliced through the water – visible now to the city as the glare of the sun burned off the fog. The ship dropped anchor as it neared the dock and Captain Lafitte climbed into the small boat.

The Quartermaster called from the ship, "Cap'n! What about the captives?"

Lafitte yelled, "Lower the plank," and turned his attention back to the land ahead. He never acknowledged the cries of the captives, or the splash as their bodies sank into the deep.

In moments, handsome and bold, Pirate Jean Lafitte stepped on the dock. Victorious. Dominant. Proud. Scanning the townspeople that gathered along the bank, he smiled, aware they knew who he was.

He proclaimed, "Lake Charles is mine! Is there anyone to challenge me?"

The city surrendered in silence. Now that the battle was over, he looked for her. He walked along the bank looking into the faces of the crowd, until finally, he caught a glimpse of her. Behind everyone.

He was tired of their secret and strode through the crowd – parting them - until he stopped before a beautiful young woman. She covered her mouth in shock at the public proclamation. He smiled, loving her. Long beautiful hair. Eyes that saw into his soul. And a passion that matched his.

He said, "Sabrina. It's time."

She whispered, "Jean…but…"

Pulling her into his arms, he said, "No more secrets, Sabrina. This city will accept us. They will respect you or die."

Then he kissed her, claiming her, completely disregarding propriety in entirety.

***

A few seconds later, Dakota looked at Gabrielle in his arms, and said, "You are mine!" and Lake Charles went berserk with more gunshots, cannon booms, music, and screaming.

The announcer said, "Welcome to the Lake Charles Louisiana Pirate Festival!

Gabrielle laughed as Dakota carried her through the people toward their tent.

She said, "So how did it feel to be a pirate, my handsome rogue?"

"The ship was wonderful. I need one of those. I could do without the bloodshed though," and she laughed.

Reaching their tent, he said, "The best part is you of course. I know Lafitte must have felt the same way about Sabrina. Your grandparents weren't perfect Gabrielle, and he didn't actually take the city and stay with her, but the love and legacy they left behind was amazing."

"Thank you, Dakota."

He said, "I have a gift for you. I saved it for today."

"I love surprises!"

He chuckled and pulled something out of his back pocket and handed it to her.

She screamed in excitement and held it to her chest. She said, "You wrote it, Dakota. You wrote our story. Bloodline is a book!"

"It's your story, Cat. How could I not?"

She smiled and said, "I have a gift that I saved for today too."

"Tell me."

Pulling him down for a kiss, she whispered, "Hi Daddy."

He yelled like a pirate - snatched her up and swung her around as he kissed, smiling at the same time.

The mayor hollered for them and strode up with the camera crew.

Taking pictures, Dakota saw something sparkle on Gabrielle's side. She didn't! He pulled her close and whispered in her ear, "Really Cat? I can't believe you wore that priceless sword with thousands of people within bumping distance of us."

"Who cares. I should have been Lafitte."

He laughed and said, "I agree, but unfortunately they needed a man." Then he said, "But come on, I need to tell everyone about the baby!"

They headed to Jimmy and Serena's tent. They were enjoying every minute with their six-week-old twin girls.

Hugging on her new sisters, Gabrielle glanced at Dakota, and he nodded, so she said, "Mom, Dad, are you ready to be grandparents too?"

Her mother screamed, then grabbed her in a hug, while her dad group-hugged them. Then the twins began to scream.

While each of them tried to calm one of the babies, her mom said, "When are you due?"

"Around Christmas," and her mom burst into tears.

Her dad, not quite prepared for his wife and daughters to be in tears at the same time, with a bit of panic, glanced at them for help. Dakota picked up Isabella. Gabrielle picked up Sophia. And Jimmy held Serena.

Blaze, now an adopted, loved member of the family, ran up and said, "What's wrong?"

Jimmy said, "Your mom's overwhelmed because we found out your sister is going to make you an uncle around Christmas."

Surprised, he said, "I get to be an uncle! Cool! But…that's a lot of babies," and they laughed.

***

The mayor interrupted them again, still wet and smiling ear-to-ear, and said, "Dakota that was the best Jean Lafitte act that we have seen yet. You made a realistic pirate!"

Dakota laughed and said, "Thank you. I think. But I assure you Gabrielle was all the inspiration I needed."

The mayor said, "Gabrielle, your family's story, and the part you played, was wonderful. Thank you for agreeing to be a part in this year's festival."

***

Shortly, they returned to Jimmy and Serena. And all the rest of their family and friends were there.

Gabrielle handed Dakota the book, and said, "Show them."

He smiled, and said, "Bloodline has been published. I have copies for everyone!"

Excited, everyone passed it around.

Samantha inspected Gabrielle and frowned. She said, "What else is going on with you? I can tell you are hiding something."

Dakota drew Gabrielle in front of him and wrapped his arms around her. His hands settled on her stomach. Gabrielle smiled and waited. Ever the agent, Sean checked them out. He noticed the placement of Dakota's hands and laughed.

Samantha elbowed him, and said, "You guessed. What is it?"

Gabrielle said, "We are having a Christmas baby," and more tears and celebration followed.

When Gabrielle had a moment to herself, she looked around at everyone. Her life was wonderful. Amazing parents and in-laws. A new brother. Twin sisters. Her pastor grandparents. And Grandpa Scott married to Aunt Jaz.

Then she smiled as she watched Sean and Samantha getting singed by the flame growing between them. And Jade and her P.I. partner, Angel were here. They worked well together. But Gabrielle knew she detected a twinkle in Angel's eye when he watched Jade. And Zoe and Trace's Valentine's Day wedding a few months ago had been gorgeous.

As for En-Garde, they would have an Armor of God exhibit tomorrow at the festival for Christian Family Day. And the Lafitte Treasure Exhibit opened today in Lake Charles. The only one missing was Adam. He was still in Brazil on a mission trip. She knew that the Latin women were certainly enjoying his good looks and charm.

But mostly it was Dakota. He was everything she had been scared to dream of. Off the chart, he was the hottest gift she had. Especially when she wore the catsuit he bought her.

Dakota caught her steamy gaze on him and smiled. Joining her, he said, "I have another surprise for you. While I can stay in Lafitte costume, I need you to change into the clothes I brought for you. You have fifteen minutes to meet me at the dock," and she grabbed the bag he pointed at and ran to change out of her costume.

He headed to the dock. Smiling. Loving her more than he could even express – and he was a writer.

Less than fifteen minutes later, sparkling-eyed, breathless Gabrielle joined him on the dock. Spinning around in leggings, boots, a sash, her sword, and silky shirt, she said, "I'm a pirate!"

He kissed her and said, "Aye, Captain."

She said, "No! You mean I get to tour a real pirate ship?"

"You do. Come on, climb in the boat, the crew will bring us over."

He watched the wonder in her eyes as they neared a replica of a wooden brigantine with square and triangular sails. The boat pulled alongside the net, and they climbed aboard. The three-man crew followed them to the deck of the ship.

Gabrielle spun, looking up, down, and everywhere.

The helmsman said, “Captain. Where do you want to go?”

Gabrielle ignoring the question, looked at Dakota and danced a jig. He laughed and pointed at the crew.

The helmsman said, “Captain. It’s time to get underway. Where do you want to go?”

Gabrielle realized he was talking to her and gasped, as she looked at Dakota.

Dakota said, “On behalf of Captain Gabrielle, real granddaughter of Jean Lafitte, head to the Gulf of Mexico,” and she screamed.

He led her where an actual ancient helm (wooden wheel) hung. Smiling, he said, “I leased the ship which is outfitted with an engine. We will be passengers on it for a few days as we head to New Orleans. Our room is the captain’s quarters. The crew run the ship from below.”

Mesmerized, she ran her hands over the old wood of the helm and closed her eyes. Imagining another place, another time, with her grandfather.

Dakota walked in front of her with his camera. He backed up until he found the perfect view. Ah. There it was. Long dark hair blowing in the wind as she held the wheel. Treasure sword at her side. Shirt billowing in the breeze. Amber eyes sparkling as she smiled at him. He captured the image.

As he lowered the camera, Gabrielle motioned for him to come to her. He walked around the wheel and stepped up behind her. Sliding his hands down her hips, he pulled her tight against him. She reached back and held him there.

Breathless, she said, “Can we…”

Dakota bit her ear, and said huskily, “Aye, Captain…”

Romantic Suspense Books by Patti Corbello Archer

Novel
Double Target

Louisiana Secrets: Series
Bloodline - Book One
Book Two Pending January 2023

About The Author

Patti was born and raised in Lake Charles, Louisiana, surrounded by lakes, rivers, and bayous. She loves the Cajun culture and cuisine and is always ready for a road trip to the Gulf of Mexico or other scenic areas. Family, faith, reading, writing, and research fill most of her days. She loves the holidays, movies, and dreams of living in the mountains.

She published her first novel in June 2022. Her next novel is pending publication in January 2023 – Book Two of the Louisiana Secrets series.

You can follow her blog at PattiArcher.com or at Amazon.com/author/patticorbelloarcher.cajunlady.

♥ If you enjoyed the story and characters of Bloodline, no matter how you received the book, you can still leave a review on Amazon. Simply go on Amazon – search Patti Corbello Archer – and all her published books will populate. If you click on the book you have read, then scroll to the bottom, there is a place for you to enter your review.

She would love to know! Thank you!